SAVING THE
DODO

A Major Revision of Second Chance Bird

Garrett W. Vance

1632, Inc. & Eric Flint's Ring of Fire Press handle **D**igital **R**ights **M**anagement simply: We trust the *honor* of our readers.

Cover designed by Laura Givens

This book is a work of fiction. Names, characters, places, and incidents either are products of the author's imagination or are used fictitiously. Any resemblance to actual persons, living or dead, events, or locales is entirely coincidental.

Garrett W. Vance
learn more about him at https://ringoffirepress.com/authors/vance-garrett/

Printed in the United States of America

First Printing: July 2021
1632, Inc.

eBook ISBN-13 978-1-953034-97-7
Trade paperback ISBN-13 978-1-953034-98-4

CONTENTS

I was fortunate growing up to have two grandmothers who were both avid *birdwatchers,* and am forever grateful to them for instilling their love of nature in me. I realize the term *birdwatcher* is outdated, and that modern enthusiasts prefer to be called *birders,* but in honor of my dear old grans (and a certain amount of stubbornness) I personally retain the old title—I am a birdwatcher. **Birdwatcher** is also the title of my first story sale to the Grantville Gazette, and where all this started.

In the back of most printed collections depicting bird life, there is usually a sad little chapter titled something along the lines of *Those We Have Lost,* or more succinctly, *Extinct Species.* Here we find the sad tales of the great auk, the passenger pigeon, the Carolina parakeet, and without fail, the veritable poster child of extinction, the dodo, among far too many others!

As a child seeing this made me inconsolably sad. I would never get to see, for example, an ivory-billed woodpecker. That beautiful creature, and so many other that shared its fate, had been removed from existence, permanently. Thier song had ended, or rather, someone had ended their song for them. It was plain that the common cause of a species' demise was mankind, it was always people destroying their habitats, hunting them into extinction, or even eating them all to death. I always wished that somehow I could go back in time and put a stop to those tragedies. Obviously I couldn't, but I could at least write about a world where there was a chance such a wonderful thing might happen!

Having already established my character, the doughty Pam Miller in earlier stories as the celebrated *Bird Lady of Grantville* due to her determined conservation and education efforts, I came to realize that due to the fortunate timing of the Ring of Fire she was placed perfectly in history to attempt to prevent the extinction of the dodo. This novel tells that tale. I like to think my grandmothers would be proud.

Garrett W. Vance
Baan Mawa, Thailand
2021

SAVING THE DODO

CHAPTER 1: DODO STORY

Cair Paravel, Grantville, Early Spring 1635

They were on holiday, enjoying the warmest day of the year yet, sitting on the broad back porch of the rambling old house named after a castle in Narnia. Princess Kristina's Swedish guards were invited to have a glass or two of lemonade, for which they thanked her profusely before becoming part of the backyard scenery again.

It was now story time; the young girl sat in rapt attention as her tutor and sometimes guardian Caroline Platzer read aloud in the comfortable twang of up-time English. Caroline was a social worker, and once it was found she could weave a kind of spell over the headstrong young princess, she was often called upon to give Kristina's beleaguered ladies-in-waiting a much needed break. The book today was Lewis Carroll's *Alice's Adventures in Wonderland*. The princess, at a most precocious nine years old, could certainly have read it for herself, but it was much more fun to listen to Caroline, especially since she used funny voices for many of the characters.

The denizens of Wonderland had just run a "caucus race" (in which everyone runs but no one wins), and Alice had finished awarding prizes to all the participants, when the Mouse pointed out that Alice herself had not received one.

"*'Of course,' the Dodo-',*"whom Caroline chose to characterize with a Foghorn Leghorn old-time southern drawl, "-*replied very gravely. 'What else have you got in your pocket?' he went on, turning to Alice.*

1

"'*Only a thimble,' said Alice sadly.*'" Caroline wondered if Kristina was aware that she always tried to read the part of Alice in her best imitation of the princess herself.

"'*Hand it over here,' said the Dodo.*

"'*Then they all crowded round her once more, while the Dodo solemnly presented the thimble, saying 'We beg your acceptance of this elegant thimble'; and, when it had finished this short speech, they all cheered.*'"

Kristina laughed. "But her prize was something that already belonged to her, Caroline!"

"I think it was the spirit of the thing that mattered, finishing the ceremony correctly, whether it made any sense or not."

Kristina nodded, being well aware of the importance of ceremonies, as well as their tendency to be illogical. She was required to attend many in her capacity as princess, and usually found them to be a dreadful bore. Kristina was also aware that although Alice's adventures were written as a children's story, they often contained satires of adult activities, even if she wasn't always quite sure which they referred to. Getting a prize that already belonged to you seemed quite in keeping with the general silliness she had witnessed in royal doings. Before Caroline could begin reading again, Kristina asked, "Caroline, just what *is* a dodo?"

"It was a kind of bird. Here, in the illustration." Caroline turned the book around, a hardcover that had come through the Ring of Fire, to show Kristina the original John Tenniel illustration from the now never-to-be Victorian Age.

"What a strange looking bird! Are dodos a real animal or a make believe one?"

"Actually, dodos were real, although they did look pretty weird." Caroline saw something flash in Kristina's large and liquid brown eyes.

"What do you mean '*were*'?" Kristina handed the book back to Caroline with a serious look on her young face.

The princess was very sensitive and Caroline knew the sad story of the dodo's demise would not go over well. It was much better to level with Kristina, than face the consequences of getting caught in a lie, even a white one, later. The girl was truly a prodigy, *scary* smart just like her father, the Emperor.

"Well, there aren't any more dodos, Kristina. They're all extinct."

"Like the dinosaurs?"

"Yes, well, kind of. No one is completely sure how the dinosaurs died out, but we do know what happened to the dodos . . ." Caroline saw a shadow cross those great, dark eyes, so much more aware than other children her age.

Kristina pursed her lips and blew out a thin puff of disgust. "I suppose it was *people* then."

Caroline nodded solemnly. "I'm afraid so. From what I recall they lived on a small island with no dangerous animals to eat them. They had never seen humans before and didn't know that they should run away. I think hungry sailors ate them all. By my time, the dodo had become a symbol for endangered species, a reminder of our responsibility to protect animals."

"That's just not fair, they didn't even know they were in danger! Why didn't anyone try to stop those sailors from eating them all?"

"I don't know, Kristina, it was a very long time ago."

Kristina's eyebrow's arched. "*How* long ago did the last dodos die, Caroline?"

Caroline felt a brief shiver; the small town normalcy of quiet backyards and shady porches during this springtime visit to Grantville tended to make her almost forget. *How long ago indeed?* She sat frozen there, with her mouth partially open while the princess's eyes narrowed, lightning-quick thought working behind them.

"The library," Kristina announced. She jumped up and ran into the house so fast she left behind a breezy wake to gently riffle the pages of *Wonderland*.

Caroline closed the book. She looked up unto the crystal clear blue of the seventeenth-century sky.

"How long ago?" Caroline whispered, caught up in the princess' excitement herself now, goose bumps forming on her arms. "Or, *when*?"

She followed Kristina into the converted sitting room that served as Cair Paravel's library, where Kristina stood on a step stool with her nose deep in an up-time encyclopedia, eyes focused in careful study. At last, she looked up at Caroline, her cheeks flushed with excitement, her voice tense.

"We still have time."

Pam Miller's House, Grantville

Thorsten Engler surveyed the wide, sloping front yard from the street, wondering if there was indeed a house somewhere up there behind all the gigantic, yellow flowers; either some strange, early-blooming up-time variety, or the product of magic. He found the narrow concrete walk, almost a tunnel, and started up it. A breeze rustled the bright green stalks that stood nearly as tall himself, the dinner-plate-sized flower heads, with their still unripe seed pod faces and bright yellow petals, seemed to nod at him in greeting. He had never seen anything like them before and mused that he had perhaps really wandered into one of the princess's fairy tales.

At last, he reached a funny-looking little pink house, a rectangular box with a door, a curtained picture window, and a concrete front porch. The sight of a porcelain garden gnome lurking under a bush below the window actually made him jump. Thorsten wouldn't have been surprised if it had doffed his hat to him in such odd surrounds. He pushed the tiny doorbell button and heard electric chimes sound within.

Shortly, the door opened to reveal a middle-aged woman wearing a green sweatshirt blotched with a rainbow splatter of paint, faded blue jeans, and muddy boots. Her age might have been anywhere between mid-thirties to mid-forties. It was always so hard to tell with up-timer women. In any case, she appeared to be very physically fit. She wasn't exactly pretty, but she wasn't unattractive, either. She had a broad, serious face colored in the ruddy tan of someone who spends a lot of time outdoors. Her unruly, dishwater-blonde hair was pulled back in a no-nonsense ponytail, the hairstyle showing off her steel gray eyes with flecks of a winter sky's blue. They were the eyes of a keen observer, like a soldier's eyes, and as a soldier himself Thorsten recognized their power.

"Yes?" she asked. Her alto voice was polite, but by no means filled with patience.

"Pardon me for bothering you, ma'am," Thorsten replied in the West Virginia style English he had been practicing. "Are you Miss Pam Miller?"

"That's *Ms.* Miller, and, if you're here because your church, school, barn, or castle has a bat infestation, you are out of luck. I am *not* in the bat removal business, never was!" She began to close the door, so Thorsten had to talk fast.

"Please, wait! I am not here about bats, ma'am, er, Ms. Miller. I am here about birds."

"Even worse!" the door began to close again.

Thorsten quickly stuck a heavy riding boot in its path and tried again. "That is to say, *one* bird in particular! Please, let me introduce myself, I am Thorsten Engler, the, uh, Count of Narnia." How he had gone from being a simple soldier to a count was a chain of events that still amazed Thorsten, and he wasn't sure he would ever be comfortable with the title. This was made worse by the suspicious look Pam Miller gave him.

"The count of *what?*" Those eyes could freeze a pond in summer, if they chose to.

"The *Count of Narnia*, ma'am. The district used to be called Nutschall, but Princess Kristina had it renamed to honor her favorite children's stories. I'm here at the princess' request, as her representative." Thorsten found himself feeling flustered, this was a most formidable woman.

"Here at the princess' request, huh? Well, these days who knows what the hell might happen next? Come on in then, *Count of Narnia*, but if you brought any satyrs or talking hedgehogs with you, they are going to have to wait outside." She motioned for him to follow her into the house, stomping ahead of him in her muddy boots.

Thorsten entered a space that might have once been a twentieth century living room. All that could be seen of that former role was a lumpy old sofa along one wall. The rest of the space was filled with art supplies and a hodgepodge of canvases featuring works in various stages of completion. The floor was completely covered in paint-stained drop cloths. Apparently, the artist was going through a "birds" period. Thorsten thought the drawings and paintings of avian life were quite realistic. He noticed a large, hand-painted poster of a black-and-orange songbird he had never seen before. Its uneven lettering proclaimed, "Don't Shoot, I'm an American!" It was plain to see it was the work of a child rather than the house's artist, but still quite well done. On an incredibly cluttered desk he saw a hand-printed manuscript titled *Birds of the USE.*

"So, it appears I have come to the right place. You must indeed be the celebrated 'Bird Lady' of Grantville!'

At this Pam Miller gave him a murderous look and took a step back toward the door.

"I beg your pardon, ma'am, but you *are* the Pam Miller who is working with the school system to promote the protection of wildlife, in particular, birds . . . are you not?"

The fierce looking woman softened her gaze somewhat. "Yeah, that's me. Is the princess interested in joining our summer birdwatching and nature program?"

"Well, perhaps she would be, the princess is interested in just about everything. She is an exceptionally bright young person. She has sent me here to invite you to visit her at her Grantville residence, Cair Paravel. She has a project related to the protection of a certain bird species that she wishes to consult with you."

"What species?"

"I am sorry, but the princess prefers to tell you herself and has instructed me rather strongly not to 'spill the beans.'"

Pam Miller's eyebrows rose. "Well, I do love a mystery. All right then, I'm game. Never thought I'd be consulted by a princess." A hint of a smile appeared on her stony face.

"I know the feeling," Thorsten confided with a cautious grin.

"Well," Pam declared, "no time like the present. Wait out on the porch for a minute while I get ready." She didn't need to ask Thorsten twice, as he retreated to the relative safety the outdoors might provide and closed the door behind him.

Pam ran a hand through escaped strands of her unruly dishwater blonde hair, then gave up on it.

"Meet the princess, huh?" she muttered to herself as she changed her top. "Sometimes down-time is like living in a magical kingdom that reeks of manure."

She emerged onto the porch with a sturdy-looking oak walking stick in hand and a battered canvas knapsack over one shoulder. She was still wearing the same well-worn jeans and mud-caked boots, but she now had on a clean sweatshirt and denim jacket, Grantvillers being just as casual about a royal audience as they were everything else.

Thorsten, as a professional soldier, was impressed with the woman's pace as they walked quickly across town. He was pretty sure she could last all day in a forced march. They arrived at an ornate old mansion, one of the town's "painted ladies," occupying a spacious, fenced garden that took up at least half a block. It had been repainted in bright blue with yellow trim, the Swedish colors, and the front gate boasted an arch with a sign proclaiming *Cair Paravel* in a fanciful, gold-inlaid script.

Pam rolled her eyes at this bit of princessy excess, but thought it was kind of charming, too. *Gawd, I'm going to meet a princess in Narnia, wonder if they have a talking lion?* Pam made her face straight as they neared the gate.

There were several USE soldiers bearing shotguns standing guard, they nodded politely at her and one of them, a high school friend of her son Walt, greeted her with a hearty "Howdy, Ms. Miller! Welcome to the castle!" She couldn't recall his name so she just said "Hi!" and gave him a friendly smile in lieu of any small talk as he unlocked the gate for her.

At the top of the stairs a rather attractive woman dressed in casual, but obviously high quality up-time clothes met them. Thorsten introduced her as his fiancé, Caroline Platzer, Countess of Oz, which almost made Pam snort aloud, but she managed to keep her mirth to herself.

Caroline shook Pam's hand. "Thank you for coming, Ms. Miller. Please call me Caroline. I am a social worker by trade and have been assigned as a tutor to Princess Kristina, in order to help her learn about our up-time ways." Pam could tell that there was a lot more to that than what was being said and filed it away. *Very interesting...*

"Hi, Caroline. Call me Pam. I am a birdwatcher, a conservationist, Queen of the May and a stubborn old pain-in-the-butt. Nice to meet you."

That made Caroline laugh. "That last part is very much in your favor, just wait until you meet the princess!"

Pam turned to her escort, Thorsten, who she realized had edged his way three feet closer to the door while wearing an expression that said he would much rather be somewhere else. Pam raised a questioning eyebrow at him.

Knowing he had been caught, he gave her a guilty smile, and said, "She's a lovely child. You will see."

That made Caroline laugh again. "Thorsten has never quite forgiven Kristina for making him a count and is frightened of what honors she might embarrass him with next!"

This made Thorsten blush, but also laugh a little, too.

Pam smiled along and thought to herself *Good Lord, I hope this kid isn't a royal spoiled monster!*

Caroline, who was quite adept at reading expressions, recomposed herself and gave Pam a reassuring smile.

"Well, like all children, Kristina can be quite stubborn, but she very much means well. She is excited about meeting you, Pam, as she's recently developed a keen interest in birds."

"Well, that's good to hear. I've been promoting youth birding with the school district, perhaps she would like to join us sometime?" *THAT would be some good PR for the summer nature program* . . . Pam knew from the news that the princess had achieved great popularity in Grantville as well as throughout the odd, patchwork version of Germany they had become a part of, an impressive feat.

"I'll bet she would!" Caroline kept Pam's hand a moment longer to catch Pam's eye. "Ms. Miller, I should say that the princess has a *very* keen interest, *intense* actually. Kristina is an extremely intelligent and kindhearted girl. She is also a princess, and so can be a bit demanding at times, although we are working on that. I do hope that you will be understanding."

"I'll keep that in mind. I've worked with kids quite a bit lately and raised one, too. So, you are the princess' teacher, is that a challenge?"

"Well, at times, but it's also very rewarding. I'm mainly Kristina's cultural adviser, but I'm also her friend, and temporary governess on this visit. Her regular governess, Lady Ulrike, is on vacation." Pam could infer from the weight placed on that last word that said vacation might have been well earned, and much needed.

Pam blew back a wisp of hair that had come loose from her ponytail. She followed Caroline through the house to its library. She had met some royal types over the last couple of years and generally couldn't stand them. Despite Caroline's praise, it was also plain that the princess was a girl who knew where she was going, and used to getting her way.

"Kristina, Pam Miller is here." Caroline announced as they entered a large, book cluttered room that featured an impressive variety of Brillo the Ram memorabilia. Pam was something of a Brillo fan herself. *At least the princess has good taste!*

"You're here! Thanks for coming! I'm Kristina!" The princess marched enthusiastically over to Pam and stuck out her hand to shake.

Pam had fully expected to be confronted by a pretty little spoiled brat dressed in fluffy pink princess gowns, and a diamond-studded tiara. Instead, she found herself looking at . . . a kid. A rather gawky one, at that. The princess wore white jeans, a Power Puff Girls T-shirt, and a West Virginia Mountaineers baseball cap that strained to hold back a cascade of flyaway brown hair. Despite being a bit on the gaunt side, she looked more like a playground tomboy than a prissy princess, and her hawkish nose and huge brown eyes were several sizes too large for a thin face that hadn't yet grown into them.

Pam smiled and took the princesses' hand. The girl had a strong grip for being a bit frail looking, and there were even some calluses on that palm, softball perhaps?

"Nice to meet you, Princess. I'm Pam Miller."

"Please call me Kristina! May I call you Pam?" There was a slight accent, but the princess was obviously comfortable with English.

"Uh, sure. So, I hear you are interested in birds, Princess."

"I am! I have heard about you from some of the kids I met at the school. I also fully support your motion to move the American redbird as the USE's symbolic bird from unofficial status to official. I am quite tired of eagles. I think the new American birds are wonderful!"

"Apparently you do your homework. At least now the *Amerikanische rotvogel* has been declared as the official state bird of Thuringea-Franconia, as it once was for West Virginia, so that's something, anyway. The Germans love the color red, after all. It's nice to hear you are interested in birds, Princess."

"Pam, you *can* call me Kristina!"

"I think Princess will do, for now." Pam's expression was politely impassive.

The princess looked a little taken aback by that, which was a good thing as far as Pam was concerned. She had been working with school children in the nature education program she had started, and although she was more comfortable than she used to be, she felt a need to keep them at a certain distance, especially those who obviously wanted to be treated as adults. *That, you have to earn, kid. I did.* Pam's sixth sense told her she was going to be pressed into service somehow, so she was wary. Although she hid it well, Pam could be more than a little shy, and she guarded her privacy fiercely.

The princess smiled a bit thinly and started again. "Please forgive me. I sometimes get a little excitable, or so I am told." That was said with a glance at Caroline, who responded by taking a close interest in the bookshelves. "Let's sit down and have a cup of tea, and I will explain why I've asked you here."

Pam nodded in what she really hoped was a gracious sort of way and followed the princess to a table in the center of the room. A servant appeared from nowhere with the tea. Pam noted that Kristina thanked the servant, which spoke well of the child. Thorsten excused himself from the proceedings, and she saw Caroline roll her eyes as he made a hasty exit.

"Once a soldier, always a soldier," she said shaking her head with a mix of exasperation and affection. "My darling Thorsten is not much for teatime. He's going to go chew the fat with the guards."

"The men do love to shoot the shit," Kristina commented, eyeing Caroline to see her reaction. Pam couldn't help but let out a small laugh.

"Just because Lady Ulrike isn't here, don't think you can get away with murder, my dear." Caroline responded, favoring the princess with a crocodile smile. The princess flushed slightly, but still grinned at Pam, whom she had seen laugh at her little flirtation with adult language. *Darn it all,* Pam thought, *maybe I'm actually going to like this oddball princess. She sure isn't acting much like Snow White so far.*

Having had a sip of tea, Kristina focused on Pam with her enormous, soulful eyes. "Please allow me to cut to the chase, Pam. I want to consult with you on a very important matter concerning an endangered species."

Pam's eyebrows rose again, she had thought she might be here to supervise the building of a bird feeder, or to tend an injured chick fallen from a nest. She was also impressed with the kid's vocabulary, the sign of an avid reader. "What species might that be?"

The princess produced her copy of *Alice's Adventures in Wonderland*, opening it to the page of the caucus race.

"The dodo," she said with the breathy drama of a nine-year-old revealing a newly discovered wonder to her friends.

Pam studied the line drawing; the odd beak that stretched all the way to the back of the head in a long, skeptical scowl above which saucer-like eyes were mounted in bony turrets, looking more like some helmeted dinosaur than a bird. She shook her head sadly. "I'm sorry, Princess, but the dodo is extinct. There aren't any left."

Caroline looked as if she was about to speak, but the princess gave her a quick glance that said *please, let me.* Caroline got the message, contenting herself with smiling encouragingly. Kristina went on. "So I have heard. And just when did that happen?"

Pam thought of her copy of *Birds of the World* and the sad little chapter in the back that detailed the loss of the passenger pigeon and the Carolina parakeet. The dodo was there, too, of course, a creature of remote islands, one that didn't have the sense to avoid hungry sailors. Pam had hated reading about such extinctions since she was a kid, the subject was sure to make her feel depressed. She started to answer, "Why, that was sometime in the seven . . . " and stopped. A bewildered expression came to her face. She looked at Caroline who was nodding knowingly, and the princess whose eyes were bright with excitement. Pam continued in a very small voice "The seventeenth century. No, you have got to be kidding me. The *dodo*? The dodo is still . . ." Her words trailed away into air as she stared at the picture.

"Alive." the princess finished for her. "At least we think so. There is not a great deal of information available in either the up-time or down-time books I've been able to find so far, but the last sighting was reported in the 1660's. That's some thirty years from now."

Pam felt the world spinning under her chair, her hands gripped the side of the table. *The dodo!* The charmingly strange bird she would never get to see because people had killed them all off in her former timeline. But now, here they were, still decades ahead of that tragedy.

"It took me a while to get used to it, too," Caroline remarked. "The world's most famous extinct animal, next to the dinosaurs, is still alive right now."

"And we must keep it that way!" Kristina announced fervently. "The dodo *must* be saved!"

Pam blew out a long sigh of air. "You know, the worst thing is, why the hell didn't *I* think of it myself? I've been so busy trying to protect the wildlife around here that I haven't even taken one minute to think globally. Or, for that matter, temporally." She looked a bit dazed by the news.

Caroline said, "Pam, everyone who came through the Ring of Fire is still, to some extent, in a state of shock. We may never be able to adjust one-hundred percent. There are so many possibilities, chances to change history, but we are just a bunch of normal people dropped into extraordinary circumstances. Don't be too hard on yourself."

Caroline was right, there were times Pam felt as if she would never really be completely comfortable here in the past. She looked at the princess, whose face was a study of earnest determination.

"Okay, Princess, how do you intend to save the dodo?"

"I want to send a rescue mission. Bring enough for a breeding population back to Europe where we can keep them in a sanctuary. I've been studying up-time zoos and I am sure it can be done."

"Wow, that sounds really great, but it's a massive undertaking. How will you finance it?"

The princess smiled cheerfully. "Well, I *am* a princess. I have access to certain funds, even at my current age, and I know *a lot* of people. And, of course, I intend to ask my papa for his support."

Pam looked at Caroline.

"You can't get much more connected." the woman answered.

Pam studied the princess from across the table for a moment. This was the daughter of the man who ruled a huge swath of Europe, including their little circle of America, and who seemed bent on increasing that real estate. From what she had seen of Gustav, he was probably a pretty good guy, the 'Captain-General' who had saved a bunch of schoolkids, including her own son from the Croat raiders, a real hero. Even so, it seemed unlikely that he would put much backing into something as outlandish as what the princess proposed, especially with the situation on the continent still so volatile. On the other hand, grown men often go to amazing lengths to please their darling daughters. So far, the princess had demonstrated that while she might not be a spoiled brat, she *was* adept at getting her way.

"Say you can get your father, The *Emperor*, to agree to this. What do you want from me?"

"Why, to lead the expedition of course!" Those giant brown eyes were not blinking.

"What? Me? Why me?"

"Because you are a bird expert. As far as I know, you are the *only* bird expert Grantville has."

"I'm no expert. I'm just a birdwatcher."

"You have identified, studied, and cataloged every species of bird that survived the trip through the Ring of Fire that has established breeding populations here. You have done the same for every native bird species in a fifty-mile radius. You have led a successful nature education program with an emphasis on conservation. You are an experienced hiker and outdoors-person, trained by a retired *jäger,* from what I understand. You are currently writing a book called *Birds of the USE* that you intend as both a field guide and behavioral study of every species in the country. In addition, you are working as a scientist in the Grantville Research Institute sponsored laboratory testing program and have extensive up-time training in the scientific method. I have no doubt there is no one more qualified than you."

It was obvious the princess had been practicing that little speech. The kid was one smart cookie, and scarily organized. Pam rubbed her temples, her mind racing. Lead an expedition? Impossible! She had too much work to do, she couldn't possibly! She looked down at the open book on the table to see the dodo handing Alice a thimble. For most of her life she had felt sad when looking at any portrayal of the dodo, a pathetic creature that was obliterated by human carelessness. It always made her sad and angry. But now . . .

"Damn it all," she muttered beneath her breath. The princess and Caroline waited expectantly. "Damn it all! She said louder, frustration in her voice. "Just what island does the dodo live on? Is it near Europe?"

Caroline fielded this one. "No, I'm afraid not, Pam. It's Mauritius, the largest in a group of islands called the Mascarenes, lying some distance off the coast of Eastern Africa, in the Indian Ocean. It also seems that there is another dodo species on Rodriguez, but this is a bit unclear."

"Africa!" Pam's voice held a note of laughing hysteria. "All the way around the horn of Africa? Of course! It couldn't be the Canary Islands or in the Mediterranean, could it?" *The dodo is still alive, I could see one, I could save them . . .* Pam's mind whirled, trying to grasp this new reality.

Kristina and Caroline were beginning to look worried. Pam's hands had developed a slight quiver. A tremble entered her voice when she spoke again. "Look, this is all just too much to swallow in one gulp. I've got to be honest with you two, I am still getting used to the idea that Germany is just a few hills over from my American house, and not the nice, clean, modern Germany that produces fine machinery and has an autobahn, either. I feel like I'm in some old movie half the time! Asking me to leave Grantville to sail around Africa in a ship of the day, which has got to be damn dangerous, is an awful lot."

The princess looked down at her tea, crestfallen. "I'm sorry, Pam, it's just that you are the only person we thought of who might . . . *care* about this."

Pam touched a hand to her forehead, her fingers kneading out the stress building there. "Well, you were right. I *do* care. And now I have to figure out if I can even say *no* to this crazy plan of yours. Saving the dodo, yeah, that's something important. Look, I have to think about it, give me a little time, okay?" This made the princess look hopeful again.

Pam stood up. "Thanks for the tea, Princess. I'll give you a call when I've made my decision, maybe in a couple of days." Caroline and Kristina both stood up as well.

Kristina went around the table to look up at Pam's rather pale face. "You're right, Pam, it will be dangerous, although I promise we'll do whatever we can to make it safe for you. I will send my very best men with you, they will protect you through any danger. I assure you, I am serious about this, and can make it happen. I am confident in this."

Pam managed a small smile. "I believe that you are, Princess. I just don't know if I'm up to it. I will let you know as soon as I make a decision. Caroline.

Princess." She made a small bow to the two of them, then hurried out of the room.

* * *

That night Pam sat in her favorite spot at her writing desk looking out the window at her backyard's big birdfeeder. It was evening so there wasn't much action, just a couple of blue jays having an argument while gobbling sunflower seeds. This was one of the species that had come through the Ring of Fire with Grantville that was proving highly successful in Europe. The gray-and-orange Eurasian jays were still around, but the blue jays were more aggressive and tended to bully them at the feeder. Pam was barely paying attention to their noisy antics.

There was only one bird on her mind tonight and it was thousands of miles away on an obscure island in the Indian Ocean. It was a bird she never thought she would see in her lifetime, unless some genius managed to clone it back from the dead. But, *that* was a different lifetime. In this here and now, the dodo was still alive, and she could prevent the catastrophe that had made it the poster child of modern extinction. Pam poured a healthy splash of *kirschwasser* into a shot glass. The cherry-flavored liquor would help calm her scattered nerves.

Up-time, the farthest she had ever been from home was Vancouver, Canada, out on the west coast, and a brief holiday in the Bahamas. Those were also the only foreign countries she'd ever visited, and hardly exotic. Now she was contemplating a long sea voyage from Europe to the far side of Africa, and not in a modern luxury liner, but a sailing ship of the seventeenth century! A dangerous journey that would give her the chance to do something wonderful, something she dreamed of in her youth: The chance to save the dodo. If she survived it.

A small voice in her head chided her; *what makes you think you can pull it off? You're just a frumpy small town divorcée. You're no Charles Darwin!* Pam scowled into her glass, sloshing the deep-red liquid around. That was the old Pam Miller talking. The Pam Miller of that other life where she had pretty much been a nobody. Her marriage had failed, and her adult son was only now just beginning to talk to her again, the result of his new bride's insistence more than any desire on his part.

Still, that was something. In some ways, things really were better here, living in the past. The one thing she had been good at in her former life was her job. She was a damn good lab tech as well as an accomplished researcher, and was highly regarded for her skills, although never very popular socially. That was better now, too. Here, her abilities mattered a lot more. The projects she was working on for the Research Institute were helping keep Grantville alive in this new time. She was well respected by her peers and had even tentatively made a few friends there. At least they didn't forget to invite her to the office parties anymore.

Pam looked up to see herself reflected in the window as darkness fell. She was a bit older, thinner, and most definitely tougher. She realized, with some pleasure, that she had never looked so good! God, how had she been such a marshmallow? Was this woman in the glass really her? Pam smiled as she brought the shot glass to her lips. This was a new life. There were new chances available. She had changed, going through that Ring of Fire, it had tempered her into something harder. She had crushed a man's jaw with her grandmother's walking stick to save her dear friend Gerbald's life, who was himself a fighting man, a dangerous man, but needed her desperately in that critical moment, and she had come through. She had found the courage. The old Pam of the year 2000 would have melted into a blubbering mass of goo in the face of such peril. Not *this* Pam, not anymore. Well, she hoped not, anyway. She was feeling confident now, but would it last? That whiny, chocolate bon-bon devouring, feel-sorry-for-herself divorcee was still inside her. Dismissing her doubts and fears wasn't always easy.

She got up from her chair to stalk around the living room, no, her *art studio and office*, looking at the evidence of her accomplishments. Thanks in part to her efforts, blue jays, Baltimore orioles, hummingbirds, and many other up-time North American bird species were establishing themselves in Europe. Her favorite of them all, the bright-red eastern cardinal, now went by the colloquial moniker 'redbird' that her grandmother had used when Pam was a little girl. *Redbird* translated well into German as *rotvogel* and didn't have any religious connotations. It had been the official bird of the state of West Virginia back up-time and was now in use again as the official state bird of Thuringia-Franconia, United States of Europe. They were strikingly handsome creatures and the down-timers adored them.

The redbird's survival here had given Pam hope and helped her to adjust to her new life more than anything else, except, of course, Gerbald Leitz, and his wife Dore Baum, the very close German friends she had made who had taught her much about the ways of the seventeenth century. Dore had started out as her washer woman/cook and Gerbald as her bodyguard/nature guide when she decided to take up her beloved hobby of birdwatching again. Over time they had grown into much more, becoming a kind of family. They were both a good ten years older than she was, and they called her "Our Pam!", treating her like their little sister, or perhaps even the daughter they had never had. She smiled at the thought of them, then frowned. *What would they say if I told them I'm thinking of sailing away around Africa?*

She pushed that uncomfortable thought aside for the moment and focused once again on her garden. Seeing the up-time birds that had come through the event with them thriving here had inspired Pam to go to work raising public awareness about protecting native European species along with the up-time immigrants. Through her school programs she was fostering a love of nature in the youth of Grantville that she hoped would spread throughout this new country as time went on.

But, would it spread fast enough? The fires of industry were burning bright, and she feared they would scorch this new version of planet Earth into an ugly cinder, just as they had the forests and plains of the up-time world. And that process was starting earlier. If nothing were done about *that*, saving the dodo would be meaningless. She sat back down.

You need to be smart. Think this through. This morning when she woke up, she was a woman who had become well known, and fairly well regarded in the local community: "The Bird Lady of Grantville". That goofy nickname still occasionally flooded her with embarrassment, but now she had come to realize she was beginning to *like it*. People actually *liked her,* and her 'Save the Birds' campaign was succeeding in over a hundred-mile radius and spreading. So, she knew people now and they listened to her, but when she wrote letters to the *national government* regarding conservation initiatives, all she got in return were official form letters thanking her for her input. Some things were very much the same in this time as they had been back in the twentieth century.

She had even considered taking the train up to Magdeburg, and giving that cock of the rock "President" Mike Stearns a good old-fashioned talking to in person regarding his new country's complete lack of an environmental protection policy. He might even listen to her. . . Pam gripped the arms of her chair. The thought that had been forming in the back of her mind ever since her visit to Cair Paravel this morning pushed its way to the front and took shape.

Who does Mike Stearns listen to? That would be King Gustavus II Adolphus, the high king of the Union of Kalmar, the emperor of the United States of Europe, as well as the Captain-General who had earned his place as a folk hero in their little circle of misplaced West Virginia. Mister fast-talking union man listened to *that* guy, the truth being, all their lives depended on it. And, *who* did Gustavus Adolphus listen to? Who had the emperor's ear? A small smile came to Pam's face. She knew one person who would have that ear, and that person wanted something from Pam Miller, wanted it badly. Pam tossed down the rest of the *kirschwasser*. She was exhausted and decided it would be best just to sleep on it.

Pam knew it was a dream because she was wearing a little girl's dress she wouldn't have been caught dead in even at age seven, a frilly blue-and-white thing of a century that both had and had not happened. She stood in Wonderland with The Dodo beside the shore, the other participants of the caucus race having all wandered away. The Dodo regarded her with sad, heavy lidded eyes.

"Are you quite sure you've nothing else in your pocket?" it asked in a wistful voice.

Pam found her pocket and reached in. With some surprise her hand closed on something round and heavy. She pulled out what could only be the White Rabbit's pocket watch and held it up to The Dodo.

"Ah, that's something I don't have." said the Dodo. Nodding sadly, it turned away and walked into the lake until its odd-shaped head passed beneath the still, black waters. Pam cried out and started to wade in after it, but instead woke up thrashing in the sheets like a feverish child.

After regaining her senses she lay her head back on the pillow, sighed at the bright morning light creeping in around her curtains, and mumbled, "I'm so screwed." It was eight 'o' clock in the morning, she was on flextime at work so she hadn't set the alarm. Sighing resignedly at her fate she reached over to the nightstand to pick up the phone.

* * *

"Cair Paravel."

"This is Pam Miller. I'd like to speak to Caroline Platzer, please."

"A moment, please."

"This is Caroline. Pam?"

"Yeah, it's me. Listen, I want to ask you something. In your opinion, is this 'save the dodo' expedition something the princess could really pull off? Would these people she knows, and her father, really listen to her, and help make it happen?"

There was a brief pause.

16

"Well, I can't make any promises, but I believe it's *very* possible. Gustav is at heart a pretty nice guy who loves his daughter very much. He dotes on her, as do her many admirers and friends. And, as I think you saw for yourself, the princess is one smart kid, and a bit of a zealot when she has chosen a cause—just like her father. He knows that and is definitely grooming her to one day take her place in the affairs of state. In any event, he will at least listen to her ideas, and give them serious thought."

"Okay, that's good enough for now. Can I talk to the princess, please?"

"Why, sure. Just a sec." Her voice could be heard turned away from the receiver. "Kristina, Pam Miller is on the phone! She wants to talk to you!" Next came the sound of swiftly running feet on hardwood floors. "Here she is." Pam could hear the smile coming through the phone. Caroline liked her, that was good. A young voice, out of breath came across the line.

"This is Kristina! Hi, Pam, thanks for calling!"

"You're welcome, Princess. Listen, I've thought hard about your project, and I'm interested. If you can really make it happen, I'll lead the expedition." Pam heard a shrill shriek of excitement blast from the receiver and held the phone away from her ear until the cheering subsided.

"That's wonderful, Pam, that's really wonderful! I'm so glad you will do it, you are the best person in the world for it!"

"Well, thanks for the vote of confidence. That said, we need to be clear that most of the work needed for this project is going to fall on your young shoulders. I have a pretty important job with the Research Institute, some serious responsibilities, and it's going to take a lot of work on my part to get to a place where I can even think of asking for time off . . . sheesh, it's probably going to take a whole year just to make this trip, isn't it? Anyway, it's going to be *you* and your people are who are going to have to do all the expedition organizing, okay?"

"Okay! I'll take care of all that. I've already talked about it with Ulrik, and some other people I know, and they have promised to help!"

Pam crossed her eyes a bit at the mention of the princess's youthful betrothal, that was an issue she decided it was best not to think on too much.

"That's great, whatever it takes. Now for my part, I'm going to do all the necessary research. I need to know everything I possibly can about those islands, and I'm not too confident that Grantville's libraries will have much, so I'll probably have to use down-time sources as well. I'm also going to have to study up on how to transport live animals on a long ship journey, hopefully that's something up-time science can help improve the odds on. I'm going to be honest with you, Princess, getting from here to there and back again is going to be very complicated, a lot could go wrong, and there is a chance we will fail. Can you handle that?"

"I can handle it. All we can do is our best. I have great confidence that we can save the dodo, Pam, but I do understand the difficulties. I can only promise that I and my people will do our utmost to make it succeed on our end." The princess' nine-year-old excitement had been replaced with the calm voice of a girl much older. That made Pam feel a bit better. Heavy negotiations had been breakfast conversation all of Kristina's young life, and she already knew how to play the game. There was a shrill inner voice in the back of Pam's head telling her she was crazy, but she would have to deal with that later. For now, she focused on the princess.

"That reassures me . Now listen, saving the dodo is important, but it's just one corner of a very big picture. I want you to understand how and why tragedies like the dodo extinction happen in the first place. Are you willing to do some reading?"

"Of course! I enjoy reading anyway. I'll read whatever you ask me to."

"That's good to hear. Have you got a pen handy? Yes? Okay, write down these keywords: *Extinction, pollution, deforestation,* and *habitat destruction.*" Pam only had to spell out a couple of those terms, Kristina's skills in her second language were nothing short of amazing for one so young. "Go to the library and see what you can find. You don't have to read everything in detail, just try to get the main ideas. When you have, call me back and we'll go from there. All right?"

"Gotcha. Will do, Pam," Kristina agreed readily.

Pam mused that she was on the phone with a new kind of person, a child of the most powerful European royalty in the current century influenced and educated by Americans from the future. What might this eager young girl accomplish as she matured? For just a moment, Pam felt a little guilty at the rather unpleasant educational course she was sending the kid on, but it was for the best. Pam had never believed in hiding the truth from children, better they find distressing things out in their youth so they can be better prepared to face them as adults. Kristina would have to see that big picture, the sooner she did, the sooner she could use her influence to prevent the worst from happening in this time. If they were going to save the dodo, they had to start in their own backyard.

"Okay, Princess, do your homework and I'll look forward to hearing what you have to say about it. Bye-bye."

"Bye, Pam. And thanks, I really appreciate your getting involved! Thank you!" The line clicked off.

Pam put the phone down. "I hope you still feel that way tomorrow, Princess." she whispered.

CHAPTER 2: OF CABBAGES AND KINGS

The Princess looked awful. The more she read, the worse she looked. Her assortment of ladies-in-waiting clucked their concern and disapproval in the quiet of the library, but stayed in their seats, cowed by Caroline's cool gaze. Caroline was concerned, too, but she knew the princess had to see through this course of study that Pam Miller had laid out for her, however bitter it may be. She, herself, was somewhat irritated at the woman for opening Kristina's eyes to the darker side of the up-time industrial revolution so soon, but it would have happened eventually. At last, the princess closed the final book of the sizable stack. She looked like she might cry.

"Pretty sad stuff, huh?" Caroline asked, taking Kristina's slender hand.

"It was so terrible! I didn't know how bad it was! I knew that life up-time wasn't perfect, and that there were horrible wars, but the things they did to the land, to the animals! It was cruel . . ." She sniffed loudly and wiped at her prominent nose with the sleeve of her cotton sweatshirt, causing another round of clucking disapproval from the ladies in waiting, which she ignored, as usual.

Caroline nodded sympathetically. "Are you okay?"

"Yes, I suppose so. Anyway, I think I understand what Pam Miller wants from me now. I've seen her 'big picture' and I don't like it either. Something needs to be done soon, or all that awful stuff will happen in this time, too. This isn't just about saving the dodo, it's about saving *everything*."

"Well, no one can do that, Kristina, but there are things we can do to help. I'm quite sure Pam hopes you will use the advantages of your position to do so. But remember, these are adult problems and adults are responsible for them. You're still only nine-years-old, so let's take it slowly."

"Yes, adults are responsible all right, look what a mess they make everywhere! I may just be a kid now, but I'm also the king's daughter, and what has he, and you, been trying to teach me if not responsibility?" Her large brown eyes were sad, but there was also a certain hardness there, a determination. *She's so like her father,* Caroline thought, not for the first time.

Kristina took a deep breath and let it out. She spoke again, the quaver of near tears gone now. "The Lord tests us, Caroline, my father says. I believe this is my first test, at least the first adult kind of one. Let's find a phone. I'm going to call Pam right now and tell her thank you for educating me. Then we'll discuss our next steps." She stood and walked confidently out of the room, and down the hall to the library offices with her bevy of ladies following, looking every bit the royal princess of all the realm.

*   *   *

Pam cradled the phone on her shoulder while she started a new pot of coffee.

"Yeah, it sucks, doesn't it? Look, Princess, I really am sorry I didn't warn you first, but nobody understands things like that unless they see it for themselves. Now that I have your attention, I have some more subjects for you to study up on: *National parks, conservation,* and *environmental protection.* A smart kid like you is going to be able to see where I'm headed with that. There were a lot of *good* people up-time, too, people who worked hard to protect nature. I think there may be people who will do the same here and now, don't you?" Over the line Kristina assured Pam that there were such people here and now, and that she was one of them. Pam smiled as she hung up the phone. The seed she had planted was sprouting nicely, hopefully it would take root and really grow.

Later, Pam walked among her rows of sunflowers in the sweet light of the afternoon, thinking of cabbages and kings. She had admitted to herself it had been wrong of her to want the up-time animals to survive here, as she had always known deep down. Transplanted critters were so often destructive. She had already begun her own research, and had learned that pigs, rats, and other invasive species had also played a part in the dodo's demise, creatures nature had not intended to have on those islands, brought there by humans. Now, the Ring of Fire had unleashed a whole raft of North American animals into the European ecology, and she had personally helped them get established instead of eradicating them as a sensible modern conservationist would have. *Oh well,* she sighed to herself, *there's no undoing it now.*

For around the ten-thousandth time, Pam wondered if the Ring of Fire was something nature had intended, a so-called 'Act of God', like a hurricane or an earthquake? Pam's gut told her that it wasn't, that it had been some strange cosmic accident, or a secret government experiment gone terribly wrong— the circle was just too perfect. That debate would likely go on until they reached this universe's twentieth century. Whatever the cause, she and a six-mile round piece of rural West Virginia, full of people and wildlife, had ended up here, and their numbers were growing. The bird species she was so fond of didn't really seem to be doing any harm to Europe's ecology, just a little extra competition for similar birds in the available niches. The seventeenth century ecology of Europe seemed capable of absorbing them all. Apparently.there was room.

On the other hand, raccoons were spreading rapidly, and earning notoriety as a real pest. The down-timers called them *maskierte teufelchen*, the masked devils. The coons could be amazingly destructive with their hand-like paws and the down-timers had never seen anything like them. No garbage was safe, and you had better stand guard on the orchards and chicken coops! Yet another destructive invader. Pam expected the coon-skin cap would be making a big comeback soon.

So, there were definite negative effects on nature thanks to their arrival here. Pam tried not to think too much about the early industrial revolution they had ignited, and the environmental disasters it was sure to cause. She hoped the up-timers involved would at least consider what a mess they had left of their former world, but it was a faint hope. Money ruled the day, and there was a lot to be made. A bunch of hillbilly coal miners found themselves richer than Croesus because they had discovered a way to reproduce a flashlight battery or a hundred other such examples of up-time ingenuity— they weren't going to care if entire ecosystems were slaughtered wholesale in order to make their profits. Measures to protect their natural resources needed to be taken, and soon.

Pam had long wanted to do something positive, something *big* that would wake more people up to what they could lose. Saving the dodo, despite all the difficulties involved, still seemed like the best bet. It was such a perfect poster child; cutely ugly, pathetically incapable of defending itself, already gone extinct once in human reckoning, but still here *now*, at least for a little longer. They would all die in this world, too, if something weren't done.

Another thought kept niggling at her and she finally had to face it. Bringing dodos back to Europe was great, a step in the right direction, but it might not be enough to guarantee their survival as a species.

Even if they were able to transport a breeding population of dodos to the USE, there were still too many things that could go wrong. Diseases, diet—Pam knew very little about the bird she wanted to save. Of course, she would take the time to study them in their natural habitat, *if* she could get there, but the dodos she brought back to Europe would be the equivalent of a few eggs in a very small and fragile basket. The real way to be sure would be to protect the dodos in their own natural habitat. But how? She couldn't very well erect impenetrable glass domes over the islands.

Pam managed a cynical laugh at the thought of a couple of lonely guardsmen patrolling miles of empty beaches in order to ward off potential threats to the dodos. If nothing were done, the humans would eventually settle there, according to the up-time history books, along with the pigs and cats and rats they would bring with them. It was all going to happen again unless there were controls in place. So, who was going to do the controlling?

Pam didn't like to think it, but there would have to be people there, and they would need to be people she had influence over, who would agree that the dodo, and the natural environment of the island should and would be protected. That meant colonists. Pam shuddered a little. Colonists had historically never been good for *any* environment. She couldn't do anything to keep people from eventually coming to the island, but if they were *her* people... If dodos were going to be saved in their native Mauritius, there would have to be a reason for people to be there to see to it.

She laughed bitterly again to herself. It was pretty risky. Save the dodo by colonizing their island with people who might, with a lot of education and coaxing, agree that protecting the dodo was their civic duty. Pam visualized herself with a coonskin cap and a sawed-off shotgun, holding off an angry mob of settlers bent on cutting down the dodo's forest to build log cabins.

Still, she had found an angle she would have to think about. Pam Miller, leading the Mayflower to the Mascarenes. There were going to have to be some really good reasons to found a colony that far way. What would make such a venture profitable? An undertaking of that scope would also need money up front and she suspected that the amount the princess could offer without her father's support wouldn't be enough. What could she do to sell a colony on Mauritius to Emperor Gustav? What was of value down there? She thought about what she had learned about the islands so far.

The Mascarenes were three paradisaical islands at just about the halfway point on the sea route from Europe to India, and then on to the Orient. Currently, the islands had no indigenous peoples, no permanent residents, and no firm claims by foreign powers. The Dutch had a tentative claim, but Pam read the papers, and knew that they were a bit too preoccupied now to be focused on things like future colonies. Besides, possession was nine-tenths of the law. In the long run, Mauritius would become a strategic military port, as well as a handy trading post. The Dutch had thought that, and later the French. It held true now, as well, since there wasn't going to be a Suez Canal any time soon.

The region was a fruit ripe for the picking. The Swedish and their allies had a chance to get there first, but would Gustav see that? In her research, Pam had learned the Swedes had completely missed the Asian money boat in the other timeline, forming a Swedish East India Company far too late to be a competitive player in the region. Maybe they would have if Gustav hadn't died in battle in that reality, an event the Ring of Fire had prevented. Colonizing the Mascarenes would pave the way for the Swede's empire to become an Asian power, another of many second chances for a man spared an untimely death.

It was time to do more research, so Pam decided to head to the library for a few hours. Besides learning as much as she could about farming the various tropical cash crops, she would re-read *Alice in Wonderland* and its companion *Through the Looking Glass*. She had first read them as a child, so it would be interesting to take them in as an adult. Wonderland would provide a nice break from her studies, a distraction from the lunacy she was embarking on.

As she walked down the slowly disintegrating pavement of Grantville, it occurred to her she hadn't bothered to tell anyone else about her planned adventure yet. It was something she wasn't quite ready to deal with. She needed more time to let the reality of her choice sink in. She decided she would start with her best friends, Dore and Gerbald at dinner tonight. They weren't going to like it, not one bit, but they would just have to understand. Pam tried not to think about what her son and daughter-in-law would say.

＊　＊　＊

That evening when she got home from her studies, Pam found Dore finishing up the weekly house cleaning and Gerbald lounging on the sofa watching *Gilligan's Island.* There was so much wonderful entertainment that sadly had not come through the Ring of Fire with them. It was painful to think of it, but someone in town had owned the complete series on DVD, insuring the castaway's goofy antics would continue to rerun in perpetuity across all space-time. After the round of greetings, Pam flopped on the sofa next to Gerbald. The show was almost over. She knew how much he enjoyed it so she kept quiet until the credits rolled. They both sang along with the rather catchy theme song, and laughed like kids.

"Pam, today I learned there was a special episode of *Gilligan's Island* that didn't come through the Ring of Fire. The castaways were rescued! Have you ever seen it? Oh, how I wish I could!" Gerbald's voice was full of excitement, he had become a diehard fan of TV and movies. They brought out the overgrown kid in him.

"Yeah, I saw it, Gerbald. The truth is, you didn't miss much. It pretty much sucked, and then in the end, Gilligan screwed up as usual, and they all ended up back on the island again." Pam had had watched the show growing up, and was rather fond of it herself, a guilty pleasure.

"Ah, such a shame. Still, I wish I could see it. Perhaps one day when Grantville starts making new TV shows here, we could do a remake! I think I would make an excellent Skipper, although I would have to put on some weight." Pam looked at her enthusiastic friend and found it hard to believe that he had once been a very dangerous professional soldier. Pam smiled to herself. There were a multitude of up-time shows that deserved a remake and *Rescue from Gilligan's Island* was not on that list. Dore came in and shook her head at her husband, a look of disgust on her red-cheeked face.

"Buffoon. Imbecile. Wasting your time staring at that picture box, it's almost as bad as the drink." Pam decided to decline to comment that having the TV on in the background had been an important factor in improving Dore's once broken English and it had certainly added to her impressive list of put-downs. She jumped in before the usual banter could get started.

"Hey, you two, I have something I need to talk to you about. Maybe you better sit down, Dore." Dore eyed her curiously as she took the desk chair, the only other piece of furniture in the room that was not covered with Pam's work. Gerbald, also curious, straightened his lanky frame up a bit and turned to Pam. It was unusual for their friend to look this serious during their weekly get together.

"Why, what's on your mind, Pam?" he asked in his much practiced West Virginia drawl.

"Well, it's kind of a long story. A few days ago, I got a call from Princess Kristina."

That made Dore's eyes widen. The woman was quietly a fan of the Vasa royalty and doted on news of their young princess. "*The* princess?" Dore asked, trying not to sound excited.

"Yes, *the* princess. She's really a nice kid, very, very smart. Anyway, she has asked me to help her save a bird."

"Then she has asked the right person!" Gerbald said smiling, ever proud of his American friend.

"Well, yeah, I guess I'm the 'Bird Lady' after all. The thing is, it's not a bird from around here . . ." Pam paused to engage in a careful study of her shoes, suddenly not sure she wanted to be having this discussion right now after all.

After a while, Dore grew impatient and asked "Well, tell us, dear Pam, where is this bird from?"

"Um. From an island." Another pause.

"An island,.In the Chiemsee? Or perhaps one of those in Switzerland?"

"No, it's one near Africa," Pam answered in a rather small voice.

"Africa!" Dore exclaimed, then went silent, trying to parse that distance out.

Gerbald frowned, a serious look coming to his face.

"That's a long way to bring a bird." He said, "It must be a very special one. When it gets here you will help save it, yes? Another protected species?"

"Yes, that's part of the idea. The thing is, getting it here." Pam still wasn't able to meet her friend's eyes.

Gerbald's eyebrows had begun to rise. "Pam, who will bring the bird from Africa?"

"I will." Pam looked up at them and managed a bit of a silly smile. Gerbald returned it, but Dore was definitely *not* smiling.

"Africa! *You* plan to *go* to Africa? Yourself? *Africa!*" Dore's voice was rising to the incredulous pitch she sometimes used when grilling Gerbald about his adventures at the tavern.

Pam gave her a helpless look. "Yeah, that's it. Actually, all the way around Africa, then over to some islands called the Mascarenes in the Indian Ocean. That's where the dodo lives, and if I don't go get some now, they will all be killed over the next few years. The princess has asked me to do this." Even that last bit didn't budge the incredulous expression on Dore's face, an expression that was quickly turning to a righteous disgust.

"Madness!" Her voice sounded half-strangled. "All the way to Africa, even to save some bird for the princess, it's madness!" Dore's arms, powerful from years of difficult labors, were crossed now in front of her impressive chest, the picture of a woman who had long suffered foolishness and would brook no more. "You must not go, Pam, it is far too dangerous. There are savages and pirates there, and wild beasts that can chew you up, I have seen it on the TV. You simply must not!"

"Now, Dore. " Gerbald switched into German. "Pam is a grown woman and must make her own decisions, you cannot mother her so! You know how strongly she cares for the birds and other living things, and besides, one cannot take a request from the royal princess of the land lightly! Please see reason." Dore answered only with a dismissive caw, unable to find her voice, she was so appalled at the events turning before her. Pam spoke up again, also in German.; She was nearly fluent, having decided it was a big advantage in her new here and now.

"Dore, please, my dear friend, I don't really want to go, really I don't, but I feel I must! Doing this will get the princess on my side when it comes to stopping an environmental disaster here. If I help her, she will help me, I have her word on this and believe it. I must go."

Dore shook her head, her initial outrage changing to sincere concern for her dearest friend. "Oh my, Pam, I can't bear to think of you making such an awful journey. When is this to happen?"

Dore's red-cheeked, guileless face was now so mournful that Pam walked across the room and gave her a hug. "I don't know yet, we've just started. It will probably be a few months, things don't usually happen very fast in this era. I need to go talk to the princess again tomorrow before she leaves town. From there most of it will depend on her. Whatever happens, I assure you I will be very careful, I intend to come back to you alive!"

"Well, of course you will! And that is why we are going with you!" Dore announced in a suddenly confident tone.

"You are?" It wasn't really a question. Deep down Pam had already known this was the likely outcome of the conversation.

"We are?" Gerbald turned to his wife, his face alive with anticipation.

"Of course, we are! We can't let Pam go off around the world alone! She will need our help on such a long journey! We *must* go!"

Gerbald studied his wife as if she had suddenly transformed into something miraculous like a talking horse. This was too good to be true! "Why, of course we must!" he bellowed heartily. "I've always wanted to experience a sea voyage! Africa, the Dark Continent, land of adventure! How wonderful!"

"Actually, we are just sailing *around* Africa as far as I know, but maybe we could stop and take a look around a bit . . ." Pam was starting to feel a bit giddy now. Her hesitation at breaking the bizarre news to her best friends had passed. *They are going with me. Now I really know I can do this.* She grabbed Dore once more in a bear hug. "You two are the best, thank you!"

Dore patted her friend gently on her back, her upset finished, her eyes smiling now. "You can't be rid of us, dear Pam. We will follow you everywhere. In any case, it can't be any worse than following this lout through all those wars."

Later, Dore was cooking the evening meal while Gerbald napped on the sofa. Pam sat at her desk, staring out her garden window, tired from too much reading, and way too much thinking. *God, how I miss the Internet.*

"I need to come up with a plan," she mumbled into the fist that supported her chin. "I need a reason for people to want to go live on those islands. Something that will sweeten the deal up for that fat king to insure his support."

"Dinner is almost ready!" Dore called from the kitchen, giving Gerbald a chance to wake up, and Pam a chance to reach a good stopping place in her work.

"Dinner . . . fat . . . sweeten . . ." Pam's eyes widened. Quickly, she pushed her chair back, startling Gerbald out of his nap, and rushed into the kitchen.

"Dore! Do you know much about the emperor? About Gustav?"

"Well, certainly I know some things, who doesn't? I read the newspapers and listen to the talk down at the shops."

"What does he like to eat?"

"I believe he is very fond of meat, as most men are, and also of cheese."

"What about desserts?"

"Why yes, I have heard he loves chocolate and sweets. One must be a king to be able to afford such! Why are you smiling in this funny way, Pam?"

"How much does chocolate go for these days at Johnson's?"

"Oh, it is much too dear, even if it is available at all. I do not understand what the fuss is about, it's so bitter tasting unless you mix it with cream and sugar."

"Sugar! How much is that?"

"Well, sugar has gone down somewhat thanks to sorghum, but it is still quite expensive. We are lucky none of us here have that 'sweet tooth' so many Americans suffer from."

"Yes, that wonderful sweet tooth that King Gustav has acquired. And where there's sugar you will surely find spices." *Spices, where do they come from? Why, from Spice islands! Islands like... the Mascarenes!* Pam began to look around her kitchen.

Since Dore had come into her life Pam didn't cook much anymore. The leftovers from their Friday night dinners always lasted several days, after which she enjoyed simple meals of seasonal fruit, bread with cheese, and sometimes sausages. Her chocolate bon-bon munching days were long over!

Pam went to the cabinet where she kept her humble supply of cooking supplies and peered in. In the front, small bottles of herbs lined the shelf, their original contents long since replaced with plants grown down-time. Dore, by nature a wonderful cook, had developed a taste for herbs such as rosemary and thyme and used them to delicious effect. Pam slid the herbs aside to reach farther into the back. After some groping about, she produced a motley collection of tins and bottles with achingly familiar labels from up-time brands like Schillings and Lawry's. She began arranging them on the counter while Dore looked on with great curiosity.

"We want spices that are used in cakes and cookies. Cinnamon, cardamom, allspice, mace, oh- nutmeg! I'd almost forgotten about that stuff, we'll have to make eggnog sometime!"

Gerbald was now watching from his usual spot leaning against the door to the living room, which provided him with a ready escape route for when Dore inevitably passed her tolerance point for his 'nonsense' and shooed him out.

"Eggnog? Ain't never *heared* of that." he said in his long-practiced hillbilly drawl, which was good enough to fool most up-timers.

"It's a traditional Christmas drink, made of raw eggs and milk."

Gerbald grimaced. "That sounds plum awful."

"We put rum or brandy in it, too." Pam told him with a knowing smile.

"Well, that's different! Maybe I should give it a try then!" he replied with a grin while sneaking an impish look at his wife.

"You two are a couple of those 'booze-hounds', oh, the shame of it!" Dore growled. Dore was a teetotaler except for the few occasions in which her husband and friend had managed to get her to try a little wine or kirschwasser in the name of celebration, the consumption of which made her cheeks go from rosy pink to fire engine red. A few more sips later she would really loosen up, laugh loudly, and tell slightly ribald jokes she had heard from the women she worked with, things she would never consider doing while sober. This had proven to be highly entertaining and only encouraged Pam and Gerbald to try to get her tipsy again.

Pam and Gerbald shared a quick wink, a little 'let's get Dore drunk' fun was long over-due, but after all the drama she would be on her guard, so it was probably out of the question tonight.

Pam went back to her spice collection. "What's missing... oh, vanilla!" she added a bottle of dark brown liquid to the line-up, soon followed by a jar of molasses and a very small bottle of almond extract. She had to climb up on the kitchen stool to reach to the very back of the cupboard to see if she had missed anything and was rewarded with a tin of powdered cocoa and a rock-hard bar of baking chocolate. Pam wiped her brow and took a moment to muse over her collection. *Mmmm, chocolate. Where the hell does that stuff come from originally, anyway? Somewhere warm I think, much warmer than Europe or it wouldn't be so dear. Even up-time most spices came from far away places, usually tropical. I have a lot of research to do, but I think I'm on to something big here.* Gears were turning in her head.

"Dore, can dinner wait a bit? If you don't mind, I'd like you to help me make some cookies."

"Of course, I don't mind! Dinner can wait and it would be my pleasure to help!" Pam rarely joined in the cooking and Dore relished the chance to have some company in the kitchen. *Female* company that is, Dore gave Gerbald the 'Stay out of our way' look as they went to work so he returned to the safety of the couch, a tall glass of Küchelstorf's American Style beer tiding him over until dinner eventually materialized.

"Okay, great! We're going to start with something simple like cinnamon snicker doodles. My bake sale mom career ended quite a while ago and I'm a bit rusty." Pam began moving about the kitchen like a whirlwind, locating mixing bowls and pans and spatulas while Dore washed the dust off them.

Dore paused to study her suddenly inspired friend. "Pam, may I ask just what has gotten you so excited about making cookies? There is always a reason when you become like this. Has it to do with this African journey?"

Pam grinned merrily. "Yes, it does, we're making these for the princess. Upon her recommendation, I hope we will be able to use them to bait a bear. . . or maybe a lion."

Dore gave her an askance look, but declined further comment, busying herself with washing Pam's long-neglected and dust-coated rolling pin.

✳ ✳ ✳

The next morning, Pam paid Cair Paravel a visit.

Not long after, the princess and her ecstatic guards were well on the way to demolishing all four-dozen cookies she had brought, in one sitting. Pam chewed on one herself, silently patting herself on the back. They were delicious! She looked on with a beatific expression while Caroline, who had declined the offer to dig in, just shook her head, not having the strength to try to slow down the feeding frenzy.

"You like?" Pam asked Kristina, who held half a snicker-doodle in each hand while eagerly working on a huge, greedy mouthful, making her somewhat resemble an underfed chipmunk.

"Urummph!" came the enthusiastic response.

"Do you think your father would like them?" Pam asked casually. Caroline's eyebrows rose, seeing that Pam had an angle to bringing them this unexpected treat.

The princess nodded, taking a moment to swallow, with the help of a glass of milk, before replying. "Yes, he would, he has acquired quite a sweet tooth! He loves to stop at those coffee shops that are springing up all over, the ones that serve sweets and cakes, although he always complains about the price."

Pam nodded, her suspicions had been dead on.

"Do you know why these desserts are so expensive?" she asked the princess.

"I think it's because the weather here is too cold to grow the things that go in them. The ingredients come from far way places making them cost a lot."

29

"Exactly. Have you talked to your father yet about your plan to save the dodo?"

Kristina's expression became a bit self-conscious. "Well, no, not yet. Maybe I don't need to! I have money of my own you know, enough to get a ship for you to use on the mission, and guards, and supplies . . . I think." Suddenly she didn't look so sure. The cookies were nearly gone, so she sent her guards away with one-for-the-road each and turned to Pam, doubt and concern in her large, dark, yet luminous eyes. Caroline sat beside her, lending the support of her presence, but allowing Kristina to handle this on her own, at least for now.

Pam just smiled, exuding confidence in what she considered to be her rather cunning plan.

"Yes, well, Princess, I've been doing a lot of research on all this and I need to get you caught up. I'm afraid it's going to take more than one ship to *really* save the dodo and here's why."

The princess listened quietly as Pam explained.

"The problem is, the dodos might not survive outside of their native habitat. Even if we bring a whole bunch of them to Europe, they might die anyway, and if they do live, they might not breed. Instead of the other Europeans and Africans who will eventually come to the Mascarenes and cause the dodo's extinction, we need to get there first with *our* people, people whose *duty* would be to conserve the dodo and its habitat, farming sensibly alongside the nature preserves. We need to found a colony."

Pam gave the princess a moment to absorb the knowledge dump before continuing.

"So, you see, I'm not sure you can afford all that on your resources alone."

The princess nodded soberly. "No, I probably can't do all that on my own, but with father's blessing and some of his money to help I could pull it off. But how can we convince him its worthwhile? I already know what he will say if I just tell him its all to save a bird. I would be scolded for such foolishness. He's spending a lot of money on his wars right now so we have to come up with some other really good reasons for him to support this." The child sitting across the table looked much older than her tender age of nine right now, her brow furrowed in thought.

Dang this kid is smart! Pam gave her a warm smile, knowing that she had the answers at the ready.

"Right. Okay, I've come up with some other really good reasons!. There's not as much info in Grantville's library on those islands as I might like, but I have learned that they have a mild, tropical climate. Up-time they raised warm weather plants like vanilla and sugar cane. If they could grow those, then why not chocolate, or coffee, or cinnamon?

If Sweden had a colony down there, producing all that good stuff, it would be a lot cheaper than we can get it trading with foreigners. Even with the long distance involved I think it would be profitable, ships are just going to get faster, and then someday airplanes. TEA airways already flies to Venice regularly. Looking at the maps it's really not that much farther if we could get some other stops laid out on the way. I know for sure people are going to want to buy those goods. We might eventually be able to produce extra to sell to other countries. It has the potential to be a real moneymaker for the empire. We could make the Mascarenes into our very own spice basket!"

Caroline, who had listened silently so far, leaned forward, her interest now thoroughly piqued. "Pam, that's a wonderful idea! It would be good for everybody in the USE and up in the Kalmar Union as well! God, I'd love to be able to afford to buy more spices, I miss them so much!" The woman's mouth was nearly watering. Pam passed her the cookie plate and with a guilty grin, Caroline helped herself to the few that remained.

"Exactly. All of us up-timers miss them. Now coffee shops selling pastries and sweets are cropping up everywhere, it's the Starbucks virus all over again. If this plan works then we can get our hands on a lot more of the flavors we miss, and a lot cheaper to boot! That will mean better prices and availability, bringing in more customers and making more profit. I'm no expert, but the specialty food industry would really boom, definitely good for our economy."

They nodded, taking a moment to let it all sink in. After a while Pam turned to the princess.

"I have a tin of cookies here we baked for your father. Mail them to him and then ask how he likes them. That's the bait. Once you have him hooked by the sweet tooth, run this plan by him. Can you explain it to him as I have explained it to you?"

"Yes, I can, I think he will see the wisdom in it, he is always looking for new ways to make more money. He says you always have to spend some to get some!" They all laughed. Kristine continued "Even if Father says no there are many important people who wish to be in my favor that I can call upon as well if need be, powerful people who will gladly work on my projects if asked, especially if there is a profit to be made." Kristina paused. "I hope that doesn't sound conceited. That's just how it is being a princess."

"Must be an interesting job. The truth is you're not what I expected. Other than being freaky smart, you're almost like a normal kid."

Kristina rolled her eyes and added sarcastically, in a nearly perfect West Virginian accent, "Golly, thanks!"

"I said *almost.*" They all laughed and continued plotting. This went on until nearly noon at which point their sugar highs had burned out and they were finally running low on energy.

"Okay, Princess, we need to wrap this up for now. I know you need to get back to Magdeburg soon. Will you stay in touch?"

"Of course, Pam! Here is a list of the numbers and addresses you can contact me at. I will inform the staff to give you priority. I will get to work right away. Hopefully it will just be a few months until you can go. Meanwhile, is there anything else you need from me?"

Pam cocked her head for a moment as gears turned inside there. "Actually, yes. Please get a piece of paper and a pen, preferably royal stationary if you have it. I'd like a little something from you, just in case I should ever need it."

CHAPTER 3: PERSONAL AFFAIRS

O ver the next few weeks, the reality of Pam's looming journey began to sink in. Favorable reports were coming from the princess and her staff, the big box of baked goodies she had mailed to Kristina to ply her father with had worked! It sounded like the mission was definitely going to be a go, and they would be able to leave a lot sooner than expected, maybe even the end of May. The initial giddiness of such a grand adventure was harder to feel now. More and more Pam found herself fretting over it. This was big, this was scary. She had taken the day off from it all to have some time to think. She sat in her comfy lawn chair in the backyard most of the morning, watching the birds visiting the bath and feeder while she savored a pot of coffee. It was pricey, but now that the wonderful bean was available again, she spared no expense. It was too hard to start her day without its hot cheer. After a while she began feeling hemmed in by her garden's cool confines, so she decided a long walk might help clear her head. It was a bright, sunny day. The great outdoors would be just the thing to help keep her worries at bay.

Soon she was climbing up a familiar West Virginia hillside, feeling the comfortable warmth of sunlight on her back. She came to the hill's abrupt edge, marveling as always at the glass-sheened cliff left by whatever event had caused their journey through space-time, presumably slicing the strata on a molecular level. A Thuringian stream, blocked by the new heights placed in its path, had created a sizable lake below, its cool waters lapping against the smooth walls of the transplanted hills.

Pam sat near the edge with her back against a sycamore tree. She forced herself to relax, to go into what she thought of as "birdwatcher mode," a state of calm awareness, quietly paying attention only to the world around her, ignoring the incessant, worried whispers coming from the back of her mind. This odd place was where she felt most at home anymore, along this edge where two realities fused to make something new. She gazed contentedly at the lake and the comings and goings of its small inhabitants--birds, fish, frogs, insects. Having found her comfortable space, Pam allowed herself to drift inward, looking at herself dispassionately, as if examining some new species of life, not judging, just observing.

She had been changed by the Ring of Fire as much as sleepy old Grantville had been, the totally unexpected revitalization of a declining small town. The experience of time travel had awakened something in her as well, she had seen it in other up-timers, too. *Second chances.* The old Pam, who had lived in a dull gray state of self pity in that other life and time, had metamorphosed into something different, something *better*, a being of energy and convictions. A small smile came to her lips as she realized she *liked* herself better now, at least most of the time. Maybe this new Pam really was a person who could take on something as big as the wide world, do something as Quixotic as save a doomed species halfway across the globe.

She thought of the time she had passed by this spot on her way to save Gerbald from murderous bandits, knowing she was heading into danger, but ignoring the fear, conquering it, finding the strength to fight and win against the evil men who threatened her friend. She clutched the solid weight of her grandmother's walking stick, her body remembering how she had used it to devastating effect on their attacker, used it to survive, to win, the seasoned oak wood channeling an inner strength she hadn't known she had. Despite her increasing unease at what lay before her, that power was still within her, the power to fight for what she held dear.

The mission to Mauritius would surely be dangerous. It would be frightening. It would be uncomfortable. But most of all she knew it would be worthwhile. In Pam's mind's eye she saw herself, saw the sensitive girl she had been as a child, who had wept when reading the sad story of the dodo in those dreary back pages of the bird guides, that terrible rollcall of the victims of extinction. She felt that little girl somehow looking at her grown-up self with her own steel-gray eyes, the message clear: "*Change this.*"

Pam stood up, shaking her head to clear her reverie. She had seen enough. She took a big, deep breath of the fresh breeze coming across the lake and smiled.

"All right, you dodos, hang in there, I'm a-comin'!" she shouted merrily across the lake.

A noisy thought suddenly crashed into her mind: She had yet to tell her employers at the Research Institute of her plans, not to mention her family, starting with her father. The world spun a little too fast beneath her feet for a moment. *Deep breaths, deep breaths!*

* * *

Surprisingly, her father took it well. He had aged a bit since the Ring of Fire, but there was a sparkle in Walter Miller's eyes, becoming the high school chemistry teacher had revitalized him. Being around kids could do that, in those cases when it doesn't age one even faster. In Pam's experience, things always went better with other people's kids. Not to say her father hadn't done a good job of raising her, she had never wanted for anything, and even if he was not one for a lot of overt affection, she always knew she was loved. Most importantly, he had always been encouraging when it came to Pam's choices growing up.

This time, considering the dangers involved, Pam had expected, and maybe deep down, *wanted* him to be upset by the news, but he took it all in stride. He looked at her with eyes that closely resembled her own and told her "Pammie, I'm real proud of you. Always have been, but now more than ever. I like what you are doing with the school kids, I see it making a difference with them, and I like that you are taking a leadership role in environmental protection. I dabbled in it myself in my youth, and I'm glad to see I raised a daughter who is going to really do something to help this new old world. I know you can. When Pam Miller puts her mind to it, she can do anything!"

This unexpectedly stirring praise managed to make Pam cry, so her father held her and gently stroked her ever-unruly hair for a long, quiet time.

Unfortunately, it did not go so well with her mother, who wept for over an hour. Pam did her best to provide comfort, but eventually had to leave her to her husband's tender care, deciding that was enough drama for one day. It was Friday night, so she went home to get a bit drunk with Gerbald in front of the TV set while Dore prepared a heaping helping of comfort food. Thank God, they were coming with her, they had become the family she needed, and she tried not to feel guilty that she would be putting them in danger, too. Well, they had insisted and she was damn glad to have them. They were her rock.

The next morning Pam went to see her daughter-in-law Crystal, who was bound to be today's designated crier. When the weeping began, Pam was by no means surprised, and felt simply awful as a just-got-pregnant Crystal cried and cried while Pam looked on helplessly.

"Oh, Momma Pam, you just can't be gone for a whole year! What about the ba-ba-baby-y-y-y!" Her voice broke up into incoherent sobbing.

Pam grimaced, she had known Crystal was going to take it hard, but *yeesh!* So, she overrode her embarrassment at the outburst, and hugged Crystal tightly. Crystal Blocker had come through the Ring of Fire with only a single aunt for family and was whole-heartedly invested in changing that. Now that she had married Pam's son Walt and become Crystal Dormann, she had a mom again, and Pam, being very fond of the sweet, good-natured girl, had encouraged the relationship, wondering what it would have been like to have had a daughter to balance her often stubborn and difficult only child. She buried a rueful grin that her grown boy, Walt, was Crystals' problem now instead of hers, and patted Crystal firmly on the back, then took her by the shoulders to very gently shake her out of her sorrow.

"Hey, hey, honey, listen! It's not as awful as you're making it out to be! It's just for a year, and that's a blink of the eye, trust me. Come on, what's a regular old *year* to a bunch of time travelers like us, huh? I'll be back before you know it!"

"But you're going all the way to *A-a-a-africa!* It's so *far*, it will be so *dangerous*!" More tears poured from Crystal's bright green eyes down her pretty-as-a-penny, freckled face.

"It won't be that bad. Besides, Gerbald and Dore will be with me, and you know they won't let anything bad happen to me, right?" Pam knew that Crystal regarded her new German 'Uncle and Auntie' very highly. This served to calm her down a bit. "And, when we get back, we'll all have a big birthday party for my new grandchild, I promise. I'm so proud of you, honey! You are the daughter I always wanted. Now, I need you to be strong for me, this is something I just gotta do." They hugged again, and Crystal allowed as how she understood. Eventually, Pam got her settled down enough to where she could leave her, still sniffly, but coming to grips with her mother-in-law's decision. As she left the house, Pam found Walt standing in the driveway, with a very dark look on his youthful face.

Uh-oh, Pam thought, *this isn't going to go well.* Walt had listened silently to his mother explain about her dodo rescue mission. He had walked out without saying a word when Crystal's tears came. Pam's stomach clenched. No doubt her son was ready to have his say now. *Here it comes..*

"Way to go, *Mom.* Nice." he told her in well-practiced sarcastic tones. Pam was pretty sure he had been dipping into some moonshine out in his garage. She suspected he kept a stash there.

"Crystal will be fine, Walt. I've got her calmed down. She's a strong girl." Pam stood up straight, meeting her son's eyes, so like her own.

"Yeah, right. Crystal lost everything coming through that fucking ring and now she's losing you, too, *Momma Pam.* Obviously, you don't give a shit." Walt glared at her, his flushed face full of disgust.

Pam took a deep breath. "I'm sorry you think that, Walt. You are wrong, of course. I care about Crystal and you, and your babytobe, very much. Even so,

I am an adult and there are things I have to do. This is one of them. I'm sorry it doesn't fit into your plans for me."

"Oh yeah, sail halfway around the world to save some freaky-looking bird that's too stupid to run away from hunters. And that is going to what? Somehow save the world from a new industrial revolution? Good fucking luck! What the hell does it matter anyway? This world is going to end up just as screwed up as the last one and there's nothing you can do about it!"

"I'm very disappointed to hear you talk that way, Walt. I didn't think I'd raised such a negative person. I thought I'd taught you better than that."

"Yeah, like you were a ray of sunshine while I was growing up. What I remember is you were usually depressed, and only took a break from that, to bitch at me about doing my homework. Now, there was a great waste of time, all that 'getting ready for college' is doing me a lot of good now, isn't it? They don't even have colleges back here in the dark ages. You made my life miserable for *nothing!*" Pam blinked at him for a moment and accepted the fact that she was about to get really pissed off.

"Well, I am *so* sorry I wasn't some perfect *Leave it to Beaver* mom for you, Walt." The sarcasm in her tone dripped and sizzled like acid. "God knows, your father wasn't exactly helping me any, nitpicking my every move! And actually, they *do* have colleges here, not that you would know since you decided to make the 250 Club the extent of your down-time travels. Yeah, I wonder if Crystal knows about that? *'You're going to be home late from work again? Okay, I'll keep supper warm for you!'"* she said, very accurately imitating his wife's sweet-as-honey twang. That actually got under his skin, he had started to say something and stopped. Apparently, what she had heard about Walt's less than savory social life was indeed true, which made Pam start to get *really* mad.

Pam continued, the heat rising in her. "Ya know, sometimes I don't love our new reality much either, but I've come to accept it. It's whatever *you* decide to make of it, and it most certainly is not the 'Dark Ages', which you would know if you had ever actually bothered to give one tiny shit about your education. As for wasting time, I can see now that is exactly what I was doing when I made you do your homework, nothing in my power could possibly stop you from your chosen path of becoming an ignorant, moonshine-swilling, cud-chewing redneck, destined to go nowhere while you man your bar stool until the booze finally knocks you off it and into an early grave! Well, don't let me stop you now, you're a real hillbilly, I can see that. Go kick some cow pies for me, I've got better things to do."

"You self-righteous bitch! You've never loved anybody but yourself! It was always all about *you.*"

Pam took a long look at her son and then in a lightning quick motion stepped in close to him while landing a swift, hard slap across his face. It was the first time she had ever applied a hand to him in his life.

"That's for thinking I don't love you, son." While Walt was stunned from the first blow, she slapped him again even harder. "And that's for not living up to your potential, for not even *trying* to. Crystal deserves better than what you have become. God, I hope you see it in time and get yourself straightened up before it's too late!" Pam held him frozen in a long, soul-piercing glare until he looked down at his shoes, his face red-hot with shame and pain, the fight all knocked out of him. Then she turned and walked away.

Well, that could have gone better. God's own truth is I should have done that a long time ago! She ignored the tears that streamed down her face as she marched back to her little pink house in the sunflowers. She was ready to go now.

CHAPTER 4: OUT THE DOOR

Grantville, near the end of May, 1635

How does one go about leaving on a year-long journey? A journey around Africa on a ship about as technologically advanced as the Mayflower?! Pam stood in her bedroom scowling at the things she had arranged on the bed, feeling very put out with the whole exercise. The clothes she had chosen were the most sensible and weather resistant she owned, she knew she would be facing extreme conditions, so she had selected items for both hot and cold weather. She had gone through her medicine cabinet and put anything that might be remotely useful in one of her carefully hoarded Ziplock bags. There were other things that she should bring; the flashlight from the bedstead drawer and some of her precious batteries, needle and thread for repairs... the list got longer and longer. She found herself gazing numbly into her closet, feeling confused and overwhelmed by the scope of the journey she faced. Shaking her head, she blew out a long, plaintive whistle.

Well, I'd better bring along my best little black dress, so they'll have something decent to bury me in when I'm shot dead by savages with poison blow guns or succumb to some rare tropical disease.

Enough was enough. This could wait. She swept the closet door shut with a bang and stalked off to the kitchen to make coffee. Would there be coffee on the ship? There damn well had better be! She would mention it to the Princess' clerks.

Pam set her cup on her desk to let it cool off a bit, her mind still busy going over things. She had hired friends of Dore's as caretakers, a young couple who were new to Grantville and needed the work. She had written careful instructions in German (with a little help from Gerbald) telling them how to harvest the sunflower crop, and how to keep the birdfeeder stocked. Pam's daughter-in-law, Crystal, would be their paymaster and check on things once in a while, which made her more comfortable with the situation. Once Crystal had come to terms with Pam's looming absence, she had proven to be a rock, helping Pam to get ready . Meanwhile, Pam and her son, Walt, avoided each other, which was sadly the usual state of their relationship.

Things had gone amazingly well when she broke the news at work, much better than she had expected. She had managed to nearly finish her latest round of research and smoothly pass what little was left to do on to her colleagues. Pam had expected to resign, but the director had insisted she remain an employee Moreover, an employee on official leave of absence, drawing a reduced salary, which was quite generous to her mind. They asked her to document anything she found along the way that may be useful to their mission in Grantville and she vowed she would. In a flash of inspiration, Pam asked them to look into the subject of artificially pollinating the vanilla orchid, if they could find some live specimens. Apparently it was a lost art and she wanted to revive it for use in her spice colony. They even threw a farewell party for her! That had really helped her mood. She had been lonely since Gerbald and Dore had left a week earlier to supervise the loading of their ship, especially the stowing of the many pounds of coffee she had made it very clear were an absolute necessity. Well, she would see them soon enough. Meanwhile she would try to enjoy the time remaining in her cozy little home as best she could.

Now that it really was getting close to time to go, Pam had to once again face the fact that deep down she was a homebody. Sitting at her window watching the birdfeeder was her idea of paradise. Chasing around Africa in a seventeenth-century sailing ship had never been something she would have considered in her old life. She blew softly into her steaming cup of coffee to cool it, making this peaceful moment last as long as she could.

The princess herself had called the other day to say the issue of the colonists was finalized. "They aren't annoying religious nuts, are they?" Pam had asked, and was assured they were nice, quiet Lutherans who were looking for a better life, and willing to take a chance. They would travel in a fleet of four ships; one for Pam and her expedition materials, two for the colonists, and one military escort. Once the business discussion was done, there was a long pause from Kristina.

"You still there, Princess?" Pam asked. She could hear a deep, child-sized breath being taken.

"Pam, I want to thank you from the bottom of my heart for doing this. I know it's not easy for you and I feel a little bad now that I talked you into it." Kristina's voice was freighted with emotion, as if she might cry, enough so that it made Pam wonder if things were all right at home for her. It had only recently occurred to Pam that being a princess might not be all parties and favors and could very well be stressful for a young girl.

"It's okay, Princess. I wouldn't do it unless I wanted to. You see, I was once a little girl who cried when I read the story of what happened to the dodo. This is something I need to do and in no way do I hold you responsible. In fact, I'm glad you came along to help me out the door. I needed a shove. You are a real good kid, and your heart is in the right place. I hope you will continue to work to preserve nature. It's going to need your help in the years to come. I've seen what a bunch of Americans can do to the land and it ain't pretty. You keep at it!"

She heard Kristina sniffle away from the receiver. "Thank you, Pam, I will try my best. Please come back to us safely!"

"You can count on it, kid."

"May God be with you!"

"He's welcome to come along, I could use the extra help." This made Kristina laugh, which somewhat assuaged Pam's concern for the girl's emotional state. Pam laughed too, injecting as much good cheer into it as she could, then said good-bye, and put the phone down.

* * *

The day had come. Pam took one last look at her beloved birdfeeder, full of sunflower seeds and currently hosting a pair of young, up-time descended Eastern bluebirds, fellow immigrants through the Ring of Fire. She wondered where the transplanted bird species wintered now, in their former homeland, it had been Central and South America. Here in Europe, she wondered if they found the balmy southern reaches of Italy or Greece to their liking or if they ranged farther, across the Mediterranean to Africa? Well, now that she was becoming a globe-trotting adventurer maybe she would find out. On a whim, she took a handful of the sunflower seeds and put them in her pocket. Who knows, maybe they would grow on Mauritius, too?

As she collected her last few things, Pam became aware of a noise coming from up the road, growing louder as it drew nearer. She peered out the front window to see just what the ruckus was. She could hear...cheering? And music. A bit irritated at the disturbance, she went out on the front porch to gaze over the nodding heads of her hillside full of sunflowers, to the road below. There was a parade coming.

"Oh, that's just great!" she grumbled to herself, "Now the road into town is going to be all jammed up and I'll be late for the train." She was about to return to saying her final farewell to her little pink house when an odd thing caught her eye. There was something large coming into view, what must certainly be a parade float. Today wasn't any kind of holiday that she could think of, but with all the different kinds of people living in Grantville these days it certainly could be somebody's special day. It looked like it might be a chicken, or a turkey, or maybe a... Pam gave it a good study with her sharp eyes, her hand cupped over her brow, then grimaced.

No. It's a dodo.

Pam rolled her eyes. She had already said all her good-byes to family and friends, not wanting a scene at the train station. Now she considered quietly slipping the door closed, then sneaking off over the wooded hill behind her house. She could make her way cross-country to the station with nary another soul knowing. As a dedicated birder, she knew every secret path and hidden hollow in Grantville, and figured she could go most of the way without using a road, or even being seen at all, for that matter. *Yeah, no problem, I could do that, the baggage has been sent ahead, just my rucksack left...* She looked back at the road to see that the parade mostly consisted of a large group of children led by Stacey Antoni Vannorman, a teacher who often helped Pam with the summer nature program, and who had kindly offered to take it over during Pam's absence. The parade came to a halt at the bottom of her steep walk, the kids bearing painted signs that said 'Our Hero, Pam Miller the Bird Lady of Grantville!' and 'Save the dodo, Pam!'

Oh. Dear. God. Pam nearly swooned from embarrassment. *I swear I'd rather be lost in the Congo than be the leader of a damned parade.*

"We're here to escort you to the station, Ms. Miller!" one of her favorite girls from nature program outings cried out between giggles, beating her teacher to the punch. Stacey, knowing Pam's fluctuating moods pretty well after several seasons of working with her, grinned merrily at her current discomfiture without regret and said, "I'm sorry Pam, but they insisted!" She definitely didn't *look* sorry. Pam did her best to maintain the deadly expression of disdain she favored disruptive students with during her planned activities, but it broke into a really silly, grinning girl, giggle of her own.

"Gawd, you guys! I'm simply mortified! Okay, I can't possibly get more embarrassed than this, so let's have a parade! Maybe no one else will notice if we move fast enough, I have a train to catch! Just give me a minute to grab my pack!" With one last look back, she took in her living room and her desk by the window, beyond which her lay her beloved garden. She felt a sharp pang of regret, blended with a murmur of fear, at leaving this island of reason in a turbulent world, a world that all too often struck her as violent and incoherent. With an effort of willpower, she pushed the uncomfortable feelings aside. It was time to go. She was ready .

Pam turned toward the door, slipped her trusty rucksack over her shoulder. She spied her grandmother's sturdy walking stick leaning in its usual place beneath the coat hooks. It had saved her and Gerbald's life once. She had nearly killed a man with it in their defense. *Might as well take it with me!* She gripped it firmly in her hand, the solid oak weight of it reassuring, lending its strength to her. If you could just see me now, Grandma! Pam stepped out her door, closed it tight with a twist of the lock, and took her place at the head of her parade, gamely raising her walking stick up and down like a grand marshal's baton as she led them forward.

Pam hadn't expected anyone to attend her departure. She had warned her relatives away, being as how it was going to be hard enough as it was. But now, to her great discomfiture, Pam found a host of noble types and local muckety-mucks waiting on the station platform, and it looked like half of Grantville had turned up! Her cheeks achieved a rosy red they hadn't known since high school. A stunned and thoroughly embarrassed Pam Miller was escorted by gentle hands up the stairs onto the platform.

Stacey climbed up with her, clearly the master of ceremonies. She spoke up in the far-carrying voice of an experienced teacher. "Ladies and gentlemen, I am very proud to present Pam Miller, champion of nature, and soon to be rescuer of the poor, helpless dodo!" Cheers and clapping erupted, some of the town's original hillbillies shouting out "Way to go, Pammie!" Pam inwardly cringed, but resolved to make the best of it. *This is all part of it, too. Smile, Pammie!* and she did, waving back at the ebullient crowd.

Mercifully, before she could be asked to make a speech, the train conductor blew a loud whistle and hollered "Alllll abooooooarrrrd!" with old-time American gusto, albeit with a slight German accent. Pam was ushered to the open door of the converted school bus that someone had repainted a day-glo lime-green popular in the 1970's, a hue still found on several brands of construction equipment, apparently in a misguided attempt to make the thing look less like a school bus. It certainly didn't make it look like a train, either. It more closely resembled a giant caterpillar.

Pam waved at the crowd one last time, then stepped onto the ersatz 'train'. She made her way to the very back, even though it turned out that this was a 'special non-stop express' just for her. *Thank you, Kristina!,* she thought, grateful not to have any company but her own for the ride north.

She collapsed onto a dull-green, vinyl school bus seat as the converted vehicle rumbled out of the station, the festivities' noise diminishing behind her as they picked up speed. She didn't look back. Instead, she studied the bright red-and-white up-time safety stickers. These urgent messages from another universe, combined with the familiar smell of up-time plastics, metals, and artificial fibers, suddenly made Pam painfully nostalgic for her childhood. This quickly grew into a longing for up-time life in general, filling her with an intense feeling of loss she hadn't felt since her very first years here in the 1630's. She watched as the landscape made its abrupt, unnatural change from West Virginia to Thuringia when they crossed the rim of the Ring of Fire, a round peg thrust into the wrong hole by forces beyond comprehension.

She began to weep silently while the now familiar German countryside, with its thatch-roofed barns and half-timbered farmhouses sped by, beyond the fingerprint smeared windows. She had spent many hours wandering this quaint, pastoral landscape in search of elusive birds. This, too, had become her home, and it wasn't until now that she was leaving it behind, she had come to realize it.

She belonged to both worlds. This Germany, this time and place, was a part of her as much as that lost USA had been. Once a soft, twentieth-century woman, she had been forged in seventeenth-century iron. Pam found a handkerchief in her pocket and wiped away her tears, then blew her nose so loudly it made the conductor in the front of the bus-train jump. With professional courtesy, he refrained from looking back to check on his only passenger, giving her all the privacy she might need. Pam smiled at his good manners. She opened the satchel containing her many notes, maps and copied pages of useful books, studying the long journey ahead, as they chugged their way toward the distant sea, on the ever spreading rails of industry.

CHAPTER 5: OUT TO SEA

Port of Bremen, The North Sea

A fter the train ran out of track, Pam enjoyed a variety of uncomfortable conveyances, including horse-drawn carriage, and river barge. She sometimes felt as if she were in a never-ending historical reenactment, sure that she would turn the next corner to find a visitor parking lot full of cars and tired tourists, but the bumpy roads of the seventeenth century just stretched on and on as did the days. She eventually arrived in Bremen on a windy, overcast morning, travel worn and weary. Dore clucked worriedly over her and sent her directly to a hot bath. The princess' agents had made arrangements for them to stay in a decent inn, not too fancy, but clean and well maintained. Pam slept most of that afternoon away, then joined her friends for a hearty dinner of baked salmon from the North Sea, which Pam declared to be divine manna from the gods. The next day they would meet the colonists. Tonight was for good beer, a round or two of schnapps, and an early bed.

Time flew by like a whirlwind for Pam. She met so many people that their names and purposes became a hopeless blur. She put on her brightest smile, and tried to look heroic, but inside she felt old familiar fears beginning to creep around. That evening, she met with the colonists at an outdoor picnic-style gathering in a wide meadow on the riverside. Everyone was very polite and deferential to her. The princess's agents had made it clear to the colonists Pam would be the leader of the venture and should be treated with all due respect. They were mostly young couples, only a few children or people over forty in the group, which she estimated to be around two-hundred souls. Their pleasant demeanor put Pam at ease, and when it was finally time for her to deliver her speech, she was feeling pretty confident, aided perhaps by numerous toasts during the party.

She spoke in her nearing fluent Thuringian-style German and kept it short, hoping that her translator, (his name had already escaped her), a multilingual merchant from Stockholm, would at least get close to her desired meaning. She reminded them that their sponsor, the young and much adored princess, was concerned for the future of the dodo bird, as well as the many other unusual animals found on the islands, and that it would be everyone's duty to act as stewards of the land, living in harmony with nature while enjoying its bounty. They would be growing many new crops and would have to learn different ways of farming. It would be difficult at first, but ultimately very profitable.

The Swedes listened with eager expressions on their faces. Pam hoped this was because they were tired of the old ways, and were ready to try something better, something she could definitely deliver. When she finished, she gave them all a polite bow. Everyone cheered, which caused her to blush and almost trip on her way down from the makeshift platform. Gerbald caught her with one strong arm, handing her a tankard of beer with the other.

"You have missed your calling, I think," he told her with a grin, "You should be running for Prime Minister!"

"I'd sooner chew my leg off. Leaving on a creaky wooden ship for a long and dangerous journey tomorrow is far preferable to a career in politics." She tipped her tankard back, taking a long swig. There were merry cries of "skål!" around her, and she stood swaying happily as they all joined in yet another round of toasts.

*　*　*

Pam walked slowly down the Bremen docks, flanked by Gerbald and Dore, escorted by a retinue of Swedish soldiers. Her head felt twice as large and three times as heavy as it should, thanks to their frolics the night before. After crawling out of bed with a moan, she had taken quite a bit more than the recommended dosage of that crumby Gribbleflotz aspirin, which was better than nothing, and probably why she could manage at all. A sharp, salty wind whipped across the harbor, capping the waves in white. Pam shivered even under her best wool sweater. A bit of winter was still hanging around Bremen this morning, even this late in the spring. She felt as if she were trooping toward the gallows rather than leaving on the adventure of a lifetime and she longed for her little pink house in Grantville with a surprisingly deep ache. Wrinkling her nose, she pushed such thoughts aside. She had wanted this, she had gotten it, and by God she was going to go through with it.

"There she is, Pam!" she heard Gerbald proclaim, his voice excited.

She looked ahead to see a red-painted sailing ship tied to the dock, with a group of sailors standing by the gang plank. One of them, a tall fellow with a confident demeanor wearing a very captain-ish burgundy long-coat, stepped forward to offer his hand to Pam.

"Frau Miller, it is such a pleasure to meet you. I am Torbjörn Nilsson, your captain for the voyage. Please just call me Torbjörn. Allow me to present your ship, a Dutch fluyt, which has been refurbished to help make you more comfortable. We have renamed her the *Redbird*, in your honor. We are at your service."

The captain was indeed quite tall, around 6'3", and had a very fit, wide-shouldered frame. His angular, windburned face sported a broad smile that beamed out of a full, but very neatly trimmed, red beard. Long, red-blonde hair, with a touch of gray at the temples, was tied back in a pony tail, blowing about his wide shoulders in the wind. He was pretty much what Pam had expected a Swedish sea captain of the era might look like, but a lot more handsome! She guessed he was somewhere near her own age, but it was often hard to tell with down-timers. He reminded her quite a bit of Kris Kristofferson, who had been something of a movie star crush of hers. She stared at him for a few moments, then realized everyone was waiting for her to say something. With an inner groan, she mentally shoved her old schoolgirl self out of the way, this was business! She took his proffered hand and pumped it firmly, American style.

"Pleased to meet you Captain Torbjörn. I am most honored by the renaming and modification of your ship. That was all very thoughtful and no doubt a great inconvenience."

"It is our pleasure, *Frau* Miller, merely a gesture to honor you and our beloved Princess Kristina. We hope to make you and your staff as comfortable as possible during *Redbird's* long voyage." Captain Torbjörn spoke an understandable, but slightly odd-sounding German, touched by northern dialects, and spiced with the music of the Scandinavian tongues. Even so, he had pronounced *Redbird* in crystal clear English. Pam suspected he had practiced that.

Pam looked up to see the name painted across the aft in an elegantly curved font, bright scarlet with gold trim. She paused to take the whole thing in. There was a lethal-looking, big gun mounted on her deck. The sight of its polished metal gave her a chill and she hoped fervently its presence would prove unnecessary. Her gaze continued around the vessel. It was not quite what she had imagined; shorter, stouter, and despite the fresh coat of paint, a bit more used looking than the great old ships of days of yore she had seen in the movies. It didn't quite manage to be ugly, but it was by no means a graceful schooner. Was it really seaworthy? She hid her concerns and smiled back at the captain.

"She looks great, I love the red! Thanks again, Captain Torbjörn."

This pleased the captain, who obviously saw something beautiful in his vessel that she didn't, as he regarded the lumpy-looking thing with pride. He then turned and beckoned for another of his party to step forward.

"My usual small crew has been augmented by a group of soldier-sailors from the princess's own guard. You might call them *marines* in your American English. Please allow me to introduce their leader, *Löjtnant* Einar Lundkvist."

The *Löjtnant* was a very earnest fellow in his late twenties, close-cropped sandy-brown hair, thoughtful hazel eyes, and what looked like a perpetual knit of concern on his still youthful brow, the kind of man who took his responsibilities very seriously indeed. He wore a brand new, Swedish-blue uniform with gold trim, modeled after that of an up-time US Marine's dress blues, a very smart touch that had 'Kristina' written all over it.

With an unexpectedly radiant smile *Löjtnant* Lundkvist told Pam, in charmingly accented English, "I promise you, Frau Miller, you and your staff will be well protected during your voyage. The men in my platoon are volunteers, most were hand-picked from the very best of Princess Kristina's royal guard, and the rest from the king's top bombardiers. All of us have sworn an oath of fealty to our dear Princess Kristina, we are committed to serving her cause with all our heart. As is her wish, please consider us at your service. We are yours to command." He ended his welcome with a charming bow, which Pam returned with a radiant smile, more than a bit pleased at the idea of having her own royal guard, albeit a borrowed one.

There was another pause while Pam processed all of this. She felt slightly overwhelmed by all the pomp and circumstance, but suddenly remembered that she had not come alone.

"Oh, how rude of me! Please allow me to introduce my staff! Well, my dearest friends, actually, but they are very much like having two right hands, I don't know how I would get along without them! This is Herr Gerbald Leitz, and his wife, Frau Dore Baum. Gerbald, who spent his youth training as a jäger and served as an infantry sergeant in the wars, is my field guide and bodyguard. Dore is my major-domo and head chef."

Gerbald grinned widely and snapped a salute at the captain and *Löjtnant*, who returned it with the mutual respect military men afford each other, no matter which nation they serve. Dore rolled her eyes at the fancy titles Pam had given her, but smiled cordially at their hosts.

With the initial greetings finished, the captain motioned toward the *Redbird*. "Now, please allow me to welcome you all aboard! This way please!" he said as he and his men cleared the way to the gangplank for them.

Dore sidled next to Pam to give her a disapproving frown and muttered in her ear, "'Major-domo and head chef', HA! What uppity nonsense is that? A simple 'Housekeeper and cook' is what I am, and proud of it!"

Pam laughed and took Dore's sturdy, wash-worn, but soft and warm hand in hers. "And my very dear friend first and foremost, Dore, I'd be lost without you and Gerbald!"

"Hmph! Lost at sea no less!" but she was mollified, and squeezed Pam's hand with her usual fierce affection.

The captain beckoned them to follow him up the steep gang plank, leading the way with a spry and well practiced step. Pam followed slowly, holding tightly to the rope handrails she was pretty sure were not standard issue. They were secure, but looked to be hastily rigged, very likely installed recently, for the passenger's comfort. Making a point not to look down at the icy, gray water an uncomfortable distance below, she stepped onto the deck of the *Redbird* with a quiet sigh of relief. Mercifully, her hangover was mostly gone, dissipated by the salt air and excitement.

Once assembled in an area of the deck relatively clear of casks, coiled ropes, and sundry other nautical apparatus, the captain asked them to wait for a moment while he made sure their cabins were indeed ready.

As they waited, Dore's face had grown paler than usual, giving her bright red cheeks the appearance of two poppies on a field of snow. Pam smiled, took Dore by the hand once again, to comfort her while hiding her own grumbling fear as best as she could.

"Don't worry, Dore," she said softly to her older-by-a-decade friend, "I think I like this captain, and the *Löjtnant*, too. In any case, I am sure we are in very capable hands."

"Of course, of course!" Dore agreed in her usual confident tones, but there was no mistaking the tremble in the nearly painful grip she held Pam's hand .

Gerbald, for his part, was grinning like a lunatic, looking around the ship as if it were the most wonderful thing to ever happen to him.

"Ah, the life of a seaman, braving the waves and winds in search of adventure!" he exclaimed, his exuberance earning a dour scowl from his wife.

"Now he fancies himself a sailorman, does he?" she said in a quiet tone, so as not to be heard by the busy crew going about their duties around them, "Well, from what I know of the breed, a scoundrel like my brute of a husband here will fit in well, although a pirate's life would suit him better!" Gerbald merely grinned all the wider, cheerfully taking Dore's disparaging remarks as compliments.

"Do you think so? How fun that would be, the yo-ho-ho and bottles of rum! With luck, I'll have the opportunity!"

"We'll just see about that, you black-hearted fool!" Dore rolled her eyes and blew her usual puff of disgust-filled air his way, while the unrepentant Gerbald continued his happy inspection of their new home for the months to come.

The captain returned soon after, along with a stout fellow with a harried-expression on his rather chubby face. "This is my first mate, *Herr* Janvik, he will escort you to your cabins. We shall be setting sail in an hour's time. I hope you will join us on deck as we bid farewell to Bremen."

The first mate was a bit dour looking. He had squinting gray eyes, pudgy cheeks, and thinning hair over what might be a permanent scowl.

"This way, please." the First Mate told them, his tone all business, speaking in rudimentary-sounding German. Pam vowed to herself that she would take the opportunity to add Swedish to her growing collection of languages during the long trip. Gerbald was falling behind, still gawking at the sailors and their sails, as they entered the dimness below-decks. Pam gave him a quick whistle.

"Come along, Smee," she called to him in wry tone, "before you get in the way and they decide to make you walk the plank before we've even left the harbor."

"Ah, another pirate tradition! How grand! It wouldn't do much good though, I am quite unsinkable." Gerbald exclaimed, then chuckled, pleased with himself until Pam heard a dull thud and looked back to see him rubbing his forehead at the spot that had bounced off a low beam, knocking his misshapen, mustard-colored felt hat even more askew than it usually was.

"I wouldn't be so sure my friend, all those rocks in your head might take you right to the bottom." Pam retorted. Once they had ascertained only his pride had been injured, the women shared a laugh at Gerbald's expense. He gave them a sheepish smile, then made sure to bend low as he followed them to the waiting cabins. Pam and Dore exchanged a guilty grin. Annoyance or not, Gerbald's boyish antics had served to alleviate the fear they shared. At least they were all together in this mad endeavor.

*   *   *

Pam looked at her bed, a rectangular opening in the wall, surrounded by storage cabinets and drawers. It was narrow, and a touch claustrophobic, but the mattress and bedding had been shipped from Grantville, so it would be clean and comfortable. There was a foot-and-a-half-tall wooden rail along the outer bedside that must be there to keep her from rolling onto the floor in heavy seas, with a gap in the middle just wide enough to allow for easy exiting and entering. Suddenly tired, she sat down to try it out. She lay her walking stick down between the edge of her heavy wool blanket and the thick timbers of the outer hull, a good place to keep it safely out of the way until needed again.

Looking about at her rather a-bit-too-cozy cabin, she saw there was a thick glass porthole letting the day's bleak, northern light fall on a fold-away desk. She had specifically requested these features and was glad to see them. She could live without a lot of things, such as a private bath, but a desk she simply had to have, plus a bit of natural light was always a good thing. The heavy wooden chair was ornately carved in a floral motif, boasted a soft, velvet cushioned seat, and looked fairly comfortable. She moved to the desk and sat . *Not too bad! Time to get settled in.*

Pam unpacked her books and writing supplies, which she had insisted on carrying herself in her rucksack along with other precious and irreplaceable items such as her field glasses and birding scope. After a moment's thought, she stopped. Considering the inherent dangers of the sea voyage to come, she decided to adopt a policy of keeping her most important things in the rucksack at all times. She would only fish them out when necessary, then put them back as soon as she was done with them. If things went wrong, she could grab that bag and be gone quickly, well worth any inconvenience in the meantime.

During the voyage she intended to work on the text for her book, *Birds of the USE*, and upon arriving in the Mascarenes, begin writing about the species she would find there. The thought sent a wave of happiness through her. Yes, it was likely to be a hard journey, but the prospect of seeing the unusual birds of far-off lands held a current of electric joy. And then there would be the dodo, a creature out of legend, the bird that she was coming to save. The very thought of it made her feel pleasantly dizzy.

As she put her books and papers back into the rucksack, she noticed the stiff corner of a photograph protruding from a dog-eared notebook. She pulled out the up-time style publicity shot the princess had given her on their last meeting, a black and white glossy of a bright-eyed Kristina, smiling shyly at her subjects. On a whim, Pam stuck it firmly into the crack between the wall and the low ceiling, a bit of decoration in the otherwise featureless cabin. She was well aware the princess had secretly yearned to join the expedition herself. At least now she was along with them in spirit. Pam found t she liked this strange little ship better now there was an echo of home in it. Her things were here, she was here, this was her place. She was brought out of her reverie by Dore's knock. Time to go up on deck.

The trip up the Weser River toward the sea was pleasant, as they watched Bremen harbor's stolid buildings recede, replaced by farms and villages painted in vibrant spring colors. It was a cheerful-looking scene, despite the brooding skies. The rest of their small fleet followed . There were two more *fluyts* holding the colonists, *Annalise* and *Ide*, and their military escort, the modest sized, but well-armed *Muskijl* brought up the rear. The *Muskijl* had been a captured Imperial warship. It was now close to retirement and was apparently the best the princess could do. When the Bosun, a cheerful, rather pudgy fellow who had some English, told her the name literally meant 'muscle,' Pam smiled at the odd name.

"That's good, we might need a little muscle before we're through."

As they came to the end of the bay, the ever-unsmiling first mate, Janvik, came to ask them to the wheel, as the surf would be rough, and it would be somewhat drier there. Standing behind the pilot, while chatting with the captain, they got their first look at The North Sea, a dark, brooding mass topped with white spray. The wind picked up quickly, and was reaching what felt to Pam like gale force, as *Redbird* bounded over the rollers.

"Refreshing, isn't it!" the captain shouted cheerfully over the blusterous wind to his guests, who were beginning to turn alarming shades of green.

Pam, not sharing the man's cheer at all, managed to shout back, "Maybe we should go back to our cabins?" She had never been in high seas before. It felt like her internal organs were all jumping into the air, then landing again in new and uncomfortable configurations.

"No, my friends, it is better if you stay here for now, keep your eyes on the horizon and breathe deeply. You will get used to the movement soon enough." he told them, smiling sympathetically, but with a crinkle of amusement visible around the corners of his eyes at the landlubber's plight. He shared a quick, subtle look and a grin with the pilot and Mr. Janvik, that said *"They're going to spew, any minute now!"* The men all grinned back, sharing the captain's impish sense of humor.

Pam caught the exchange and felt resentment rise in her. It seemed the seamen were having some fun at the greenhorn's expense. *We'll see about that Cap'n Crunch!* she thought darkly, turning away so he wouldn't see her scowl. She vowed even if she did get sick, she would take it in stride and deny them any pleasure in her suffering.

"I hadn't expected to be tossed around like a doll in the hands of an angry child." Gerbald muttered, trying to keep his balance as the deck moved beneath his feet. He was struggling mightily to maintain composure, but his complexion nearly matched the sage-green of his many-pocketed wool longcoat. Pam looked at him, his green-tinged face a comically cartoonish depiction of seasickness. Despite her annoyance at the crew for finding their plight entertaining, she couldn't help but start to laugh, which turned out to be a mistake as her breakfast rushed up to join her mirth. The captain nodded knowingly, his prophecy realized. He motioned for a nearby youthful sailor to gently escort Pam to the back rail where she was shortly joined by Dore and then Gerbald in a chorus of retching and spitting.

"Speaking of 'tossing'" Pam said nonchalantly to her friends before another round of vomiting began.

The captain, who was still enough of a gentleman to politely decline observing their suffering directly, called over his shoulder, "There, now you have it out of the way! There's no shame to be had, it happens to us all the first time we feel rough seas. Before you get your *sealegs*, you must get your *seastomachs*! Fear not, you will begin to feel better soon. Pers, kindly escort our esteemed guests belowdecks, and get them cleaned up."

The young sailor, who looked to be still in his teens, tugged gently on Pam's coat sleeve. She was grateful for look of sincere commiseration in his bright-blue eyes. She pushed Dore and Gerbald into his care ahead of her. They meekly followed Pers down the stairs, nodding at the captain on their way, but too ill and embarrassed to manage eye contact.

Pam, still feeling (perhaps a bit irrationally) out of sorts that the captain and his crew had found their discomfort at all humorous, meant to leave them with a lasting impression. She wiped her mouth on her sleeve in a show of indifference as she stalked regally past the crew, her chin held high. Pam met the captain's gaze for a moment, and he seemed taken aback—the North Sea had nothing that could match the storm in *those* gray eyes! With a dismissive toss of her head, Pam went down the ladder after her friends.

"Loving life at sea now, Greenbeard?" Pam managed to croak at Gerbald as they made their bleary way to their cabins.

"Having sacrificed our breakfasts, perhaps the sea gods will be appeased enough to provide us with gentler waters."

"May merciful God help us, he has been out here less than an hour and is already becoming a heathen." Dore muttered irritably.

CHAPTER 6: GETTING TO KNOW YOU

The North Sea

After a miserable night of suffering through each stomach-churning roll of the waves, the North Sea had calmed somewhat by dawn. Pam, her seasickness in remission at least for the time being, spent the morning wandering around the decks, trying to stay out of the way of the sailors while working on her sealegs. The sailors were all very polite . Several of them could speak a form of German she could mostly understand, and Pers could speak fairly decent English, albeit with a potent accent which Pam found rather charming.

The young fellow was handsome in a classically Scandinavian way, with pale-blonde locks and bright-blue eyes. He explained he had lived some of his youth in the Faeroe Isles. The Faeroes were owned by Norway, but lay much closer to the British Isles, with which they shared many ties. Pers had often done odd jobs for Scots and English merchants in the port and had picked English up quickly as a useful tool. He was a bright and friendly kid, not much older than her son Walt. Pam soon determined he would make an excellent Swedish language coach for the voyage. During what seemed a relatively idle hour for the crew, she went about the ship with Pers in tow, asking how to say things in Swedish, or *Svenske* as she must now think of it.

"What is the sky called?"

"*Himmel*" Pers happily told her, proudly enjoying the attention of the 'foreign lady from the future'.

"And the sea?"

"*Hav*"

Pam jotted the words down in one of her notebooks. *A lot of it is pretty close to German,* she thought, *that might make this go even quicker.* Soon, other sailors became interested, fairly tripping over themselves to point at things on the deck, while Pam repeated back the *Svenske* words for them, much to their delight. Many of the items were nautical gear she didn't even have a name for in English, so she found herself scribbling descriptions such as *rope and tackle thingie* and *looks kind of like a winch.*

There were twenty-nine sailors serving on *Redbird.* Pam made a vow that she would learn all their names, which she made a point of asking for as she went along, jotting them down in her notebook with a brief description.

There was Helge, a ten-years-older version of Pers, textbook Swede with blond hair and a big smile, and Fritjoff, a grandfatherly, but spry enough fellow, at seventy-one, the oldest in the crew, who was extremely polite to the point of being a bit formal. It was plain to see the other sailors held Fritjoff in great respect. Then there was boisterous Eskil, who always made jokes. Judging by the mortified expressions that came to Pers's face when he did, they were colorful to say the least, and most went untranslated! Åke was Eskil's polar opposite, a quiet, unassuming gentleman from the great northern forests, who was hailed as something of a wizard with woodworking. Rask was tall, quiet, and a bit shy. Hake was a giant of a fellow, nearly seven-feet-tall, boasting a head of shaggy orange-red hair and beard that all together resembled a lion's mane. Pam had never seen such enormous hands on a human being, but they were gentle hands, and surprisingly nimble with the rigging. Then there was dark-haired, olive-skinned, taciturn Lind, who to Pam's eyes didn't look Scandinavian at all. As it turned out, his mother was from Spain and he was able to speak that language. Pam tried out her high school Spanish on him which brought a broad smile to his usually somber face. There were many more, Pam knew it would take time to get to know them all, but time was something they would have in plenty on this voyage.

Eventually the first mate, sourfaced Janvik, came along. Without saying a word, he directed the men back to their work using only an exceptionally hairy eyeball. Pam smiled sheepishly at him. He nodded politely enough before turning his attention to a sloppy line, his growled order to secure it properly making young Pers jump into action as if lit on fire.

Pam decided it would be a good time to make her exit, heading belowdecks to check on her friends, who still hadn't been sighted. She found them milling about their little cabin attempting to make themselves presentable. The room was so full of bags and boxes that there was barely any room for the two of them, much less Pam. They were both still a bit green-tinged, but some of the color had come back to Dore's cheeks and Gerbald was wearing the stony expression that so expertly hid the impish joker within.

"My Pam, I am sorry we are up so late!" Dore apologized.

"It's all right Dore, you needed the rest. I'm really sorry I got us into this, I never expected we would get so seasick."

Dore clucked such nonsense away. "Think nothing of it, the captain says it shall pass."

"Indeed, he did." Pam said, trying to keep a dark expression from her face at the memory of how entertained he had been at their discomfort. So much for the charming sea captain, he was just another male chauvinist jerk!

Gerbald added in a wry tone "It reminds me of the kind of hangover one gets after mixing too much whiskey with beer. There was definitely a spinning sensation to it."

Seeing the daggers in the eyes around him he attempted to make an escape through the door, but became tangled up in the copious amounts of luggage Dore had insisted on bringing.

Pam turned to her friend with a wry smile and a raised eyebrow.

"Dore, just what *is* all this stuff? I know we are going to be gone for over a year, but this looks like a decade's worth of luggage! Surely, you don't need this many clothes?" As far as Pam knew, Dore didn't even *have* this many clothes!

Dore frowned a little, but held her chin high.

"Clothes? Do you think me some preening peacock concerned with such worldly trifles as fashion? This—" she said with a sweeping gesture at the many bags, satchels, and boxes, her voice full of righteous aplomb "Is all *food*!"

"Food." Pam repeated, then began laughing. Pam thought Dore was overdoing it by a good stretch, but there was no point in telling her that. "Of course, it's food! Great idea!" She said instead "You would never trust a bunch of shiftless sailors to feed us properly, now would you?"

"Of course not!" Dore proclaimed proudly. "It is my duty to ensure we have good nutrition in plenty! A most solemn undertaking, not that *some* people would appreciate my efforts!" A haughty glare went to husband Gerbald who was now sitting resignedly on a large, battered, dingy-white plastic up-time suitcase with only the brim of his ridiculous floppy felt hat pulled over his eyes for protection.

"I am sitting on a fifty-pound sack of flour, and another of sugar." he told Pam "One-hundred pounds of food, and just a small portion of what you see gathered here. Now, I would like to note that it was *I* who had to get it all down that ladder! My *solemn undertaking*, and I can still feel it right here in my back." he reached around to rub the sore spot with a low moan. "I am hoping for at least a *strudel* in acknowledgment of my contribution!"

Pam nodded sympathetically at the poor fellow. She scanned the piles of diverse up-time and downtime luggage. Just out of curiosity, she pointed to a particularly lumpy, large leather satchel. "What's in that bag?" she asked Dore.

"Your spice cabinet!" Dore replied proudly.

Pam just nodded and smiled. The woman was thorough!

"Well, Dore, I do admire your forethought, better to be prepared, I guess!" she told her ever-resourceful friend.

Dore beamed beatifically at *her Pam* for acknowledging her ceaseless and selfless labors.

Deciding this was his chance to both change the subject and make a break for it, Gerbald spoke up in bright tones, "I think I'm well enough now, shall we go up top?" he suggested, the chipper Gerbald of yesterday returned.

"I'm feeling pretty good, too." Pam said "Being out in the fresh air definitely helps."

Dore narrowed her eyes at her husband. "The fresh air will do nothing for this oaf's foolishness I am afraid. The good Lord knows he has had plenty of it while we lived outdoors like animals, and it has not helped any yet!" She shoved past him, clambering over the heaps of supplies with surprising agility for her solid frame, then heading to the steep, stair-like ladder followed closely by a chuckling Gerbald. Pam smiled at the warm familiarity of their banter, a comforting balm for the long journey ahead.

After a tour around the deck introducing her friends to Pers and his mates, the three of them stood watching the waves pass by. This seemed to suit Gerbald and Pam, who were practiced observers of nature, but Dore grew restless and fidgety.

"I don't know how you two can stand there and gaze at nothing all day! I'm going to go down to tidy up our cabins."

Pam and Gerbald knew that their cabins were already as tidy as could be since there had been hardly enough time to clutter them yet, but kept mum. There was no point in trying to stop Dore, who with shoulders pulled back in stiff determination marched below decks to rejoin her never-ending battle against dust, dirt, and her new archenemy, *germs*, real or imagined.

"These may be the luckiest sailors ever." Gerbald remarked.

"How's that?"

"The next thing you know, Dore will be up here swabbing the decks and polishing the brass for them. They might as well go on holiday!" The two friends laughed, their voices swiftly carried away by the North Sea's bracing breezes.

After a while, Gerbald gave Pam a big-brotherly pat on the arm and said, "I will go now to check on Dore and see if she needs any help."

Pam raised a doubtful eyebrow. "Just exactly how are *you* going to help Dore?"

"By taking a nap and staying out of her way, of course!" he answered with a grin before vanishing down the ladder below-decks.

Pam laughed and returned to her vigil, occasionally pulling her precious scope out from where it hung from sturdy leather straps under her coat, to get a closer look at the various seabirds flying and floating to-and-fro. She could recognize a few of them, such as the sea-going ducks like the eiders and scoters, but when it came to the gulls, she had to admit she was a bit out of her league. There were many, many types, and the differences between the species were quite often subtle, at best. Still, she added her observations to her notes, quietly enjoying a lovely afternoon of birdwatching.

Eventually the afternoon grew late, the sky and sea going from ash to gunmetal gray. Pam was about to go below when she sensed someone approaching her from behind—she turned to see it was the captain, a very humble expression on his (still handsome, dammit!) face, and his hat literally in hand.

"Frau Miller, may I?" he asked in heavily accented, but clear English, his tone unexpectedly soft for a well-seasoned leader of men. Pam raised her eyebrows at him a bit fiercely, but nodded politely, if stiffly.

"Of course, Captain. What can I do for you?" she replied, making no attempt to keep the disdain from her voice.

"It is rather what *I* must do, Frau Pam, which is apologize to you and your party. The behavior of my bridge crew and I was utterly deplorable, and we are all very sorry."

Pam nodded, taking a moment to consider the sincerity of the apology, keeping her face impassive. She had to admit she was still pretty pissed off about it, maybe more than she should be, but there it was.

"Yes, well, I'm sure we landlubbers losing our lunches all over the North Sea was quite amusing." she said, her tone as icy as the frigid waters surrounding them.

The captain bowed his head in shame. "Yes, that was most rude of us. Even so, please let me try to explain our behavior. It is an old tradition, you see. Greenhorn sailors are brought to the top decks the first time we hit rough seas and made to go through the discomfort, just as you did. Our experience has shown us it is for their own good, and the good of the ship. If they are allowed to wallow sick in their bunks for days on end, there is a danger that they will never adjust, not to mention the small detail that they are not getting any work done. It is to everyone's benefit they face the foul weather and get it over with, once and for all! It has happened to all of us, and it's best just to laugh it off!"

He shrugged contritely and gave her a repentant smile, but Pam just stared at him as if he were a lowly worm struggling on the end of her hook, begging not to be cast into the fishing hole.

The captain winced at her unmoved expression, but bravely continued on, "Our terrible mistake was that you are most certainly *not* greenhorn sailors, you are our very distinguished guests, and by no means should we have subjected you to our coarse customs. I'm afraid we have never before carried such esteemed passengers as yourselves, and our manners are frightfully lacking. Frau Pam, we truly are *very* sorry, and on behalf of myself and my crew, I can only hope you will eventually find a way to forgive us. I promise you we will make the rest of your voyage as comfortable as we possibly can. You have my most profound apologies." and with that he went into a very low, remorseful bow and stayed there.

Pam bit her lip, her stubbornness melting away at the captain's really very moving apology, a thing she knew did not come easy to a proud and powerful man. She waited for him to come back up, but he didn't. Now she felt embarrassed at her own lack of proper manners, not sure what she should do next. Sighing resignedly, she reached out to tap him gently on the shoulder, which was not too surprisingly very firm and muscular, the brief touch sending a kind of thrill through her that she had not felt in quite a long time.

"Come on now, stand up straight." she urged him, her own voice now brimful of repentance.

He raised his head just enough to peek cautiously at the current state of her mood with just one hopeful, sapphire-blue eye, which made her laugh.

"All right, fine, I forgive you already, yeesh!" She told him, her voice warming up about thirty degrees. "I get the tradition thing, and I know you meant well. It's just that I'm a bit of a proud old biddy and don't much cotton to being made fun of. I know ya'all didn't mean any harm, and I shouldn't have taken it so dang hard. This is all new to me, too, and believe me, friend, it has been a rough road just getting this far. Now, it's my turn to ask you for *your* forgiveness. Can we start again, please?" she asked him, her voice ringing with sincerity as she put her hand out to him. With a shy smile he took it, standing up straight again. His grip was warm and firm, just the right mix of gentleness and strength. Pam's eyes started batting and it took a conscious effort to make them stop. *Gawd, it must be the sea air, I am reverting to age seventeen! Next thing you know I'll hang a poster of him on my bedroom wall!*

"Of course, Frau Pam, and I thank you!" his former hearty, confident tone had returned to his voice "It truly is a pleasure to have you on board, my men and I are delighted! Now, please, I would like to ask you and your party to do me the honor of joining my senior staff and me for dinner in my quarters this evening. It's a bit cramped I'm afraid, and I have some concerns about the quality of the meal, but the pleasure of your company will surely shine a light upon the affair that will cause any such shortcomings to pale in insignificance."

Pam did blink a few times at that little speech, and it took her a moment to favor the captain with her Number One Most Pleased Smile. "The pleasure will be mine! I mean, ours!" she felt her cheeks growing hot despite the chill, northerly wind. "What time?" she managed to ask before her throat constricted too much to say anything at all.

The captain smiled back widely, his teeth notably white and straight for a man of the age, undoubtedly the result of clean living at sea. "About an hour from now, if it pleases you, Frau Pam. I will send an escort to your cabins. We very much look forward to your company!" he told her cheerfully, with no small amount of relief in his expression at having successfully navigated his way through the kind of rough seas he plainly wasn't used to . Then he turned away and made a beeline for the safe and manly territory of the bridge. Pam just smiled and nodded, continuing to do so for a while even after his back was to her.

Oh Pammie! She chided herself. *You had better just get your head on straight, you dope! There is too much work to do to play the part of some moonstruck ingenue on The Love Boat! You are a grown woman with big responsibilities for Pete's sake! Yeesh!* Even so, she went belowdecks feeling all warm and cozy inside, impervious to the bracing cold of nightfall on the North Sea.

✳ ✳ ✳

The fluyt, was not a terribly large vessel, and the captain's cabin was a little more than three times the size of Pam's own, while also serving as an office and dining room. She, Gerbald, and Dore joined the first mate, Mr. Janvik, *Löjtnant* Lundkvist, the leader of their marine guard, and Nils, the ship's bosun, a red-cheeked, fifty-ish gentleman who was an old friend of the captain's, all squeezing in around the cramped, yet carefully set table.

The captain poured wine from an odd round bottle, which Pam recognized as a signature of Franconia's wineries.

"I hope this will make you feel a bit more at home." the captain said to them graciously. "Now that Thuringia has joined with Franconia, I assume you share wine as well as borders? To a successful voyage!" he raised his glass in toast, being sure to meet everyone's eye, one by one in the Scandinavian style. A chorus of 'Cheers!', 'Prosit' and 'Skål' came from the diners, bringing a cheerful mood to the slowly swaying cabin.

"It's lovely!" Pam remarked, having sipped the dry, but still slightly sweet, white wine. "Thank you for your thoughtfulness Captain. You have made us feel so very welcome, and we do appreciate it."

That brought a pleased expression to the captain's windburned face. Pam smiled inwardly to herself. It was sometimes hard to believe that she, a former semi-recluse, had somehow learned to function so glibly in public. She tried again not to think about the fact that the captain was not only charming, but also rather handsome. *Business, Pam, business!* she silently scolded herself.

After another round of wine, a harried looking crewman arrived at the door bearing the first of several covered pewter trays.

"Ah, Mister Mård! Here you are with our supper!" the captain said cheerfully, almost causing the fellow to drop the trays. Mård looked to be in his late thirties, but his hair had a touch of premature gray. He currently exuded the demeanor of one who strongly wished he were somewhere, perhaps anywhere, else. After safely placing all the trays on the time-darkened oak table, he leaned over to whisper something fervently to the first mate, then made a hasty, bowing exit.

The first mate's expression was less than cheerful as he leaned over to whisper to the captain. The captain frowned and looked around solemnly at his guests.

"At the risk of spoiling our dinner before it has even begun, I must make an apology to our guests. Our former ship's cook retired after many years of excellent service to us, and it seems the new ship's cook that we hired for this voyage, a very capable fellow we were promised, is currently suffering from an extreme case of gout, which forced him to resign at a very late hour. There was no time to find a replacement before leaving port, and so Mr. Janvik here assigned the job to a much less experienced man, crewman Mård. And now I am made to understand that Mård, while an excellent sailor, feels he is even less adept at the culinary arts than we had hoped, and wishes to extend his apologies, fearing that your meals may be quite a bit less savory than desired and deserved. Mind you that ship's fare is never very fancy at the best of times. In any case I must extend all of our sincere apologies in advance."

There was a murmur of "Never mind!" and "Don't trouble yourself over us!" from around the table as the meal began. All put on a brave face, but the truth was that the food was supremely awful. The potatoes were only half-cooked, needing to be cut with a steak knife, while the meat, which may have once been beef, had been charred to a crispy lump. Everyone did their best to eat at least some of it, but in the end their plates were hardly touched. Pam looked over to see Dore poking at a bowl of soggy, salted cabbage with her fork, a thoughtful expression on her perpetually rosy-cheeked face.

SAVING THE DODO

The captain sat back in his chair and sighed.

"Honored guests, I have spent most of my life at sea, and I shall be blunt. I have eaten things that even a pig might pass up, and this is one of the worst. I can only once again offer my sincerest apologies. Tomorrow we shall signal the other ships to see if they can spare someone with at least a rudimentary familiarity with the galley to become our new cook." His face was bleak, this was the kind of captain who took personal responsibility for all that transpired on his ship.

Pam found herself admiring him all the more. She suddenly felt a rush of relief from the tension that had been niggling at her ever since they had left land; seventeenth century sailing aside, they were in as good a set of hands as could be found.

Dore looked at Pam with a questioning eye that meant 'May I say something?' in the nonverbal communication they had established over their years of friendship.

"Dore, what's on your mind?" Pam asked her, hoping it would be what she suspected was forthcoming from the doughty German.

"I don't wish to speak out of turn Captain, but perhaps *I* can be of service."

The captain raised his eyebrows at the woman who, thus far, had been as quiet as a mouse in his presence.

"Yes *Frau* Dore? Please, you may speak freely at my table!"

"Well, there's really no need to take a cook from another boat. I can do the job myself. I have a lot of experience. Please, let me try."

The captain looked at Pam.

"She sure is a great cook, Captain!" Pam exclaimed "I can vouch for that!" Pam prayed inwardly that the captain would accept her friend's offer. She missed Dore's excellent cooking already, and it would make the voyage a much more pleasant experience.

"My wife is the best cook in all the USE!" Gerbald chimed in "I'll wager in all the Kalmar Union as well!" he added with a husband's pride, making Dore blush, and elbow him affectionately in the ribs.

The captain smiled while the usually dour first mate looked on with great interest. He had barely touched his food yet judging from his pear-like shape he was a man who thought much of dinner, and missed few.

"Your offer is very kind *Frau* Dore, but surely I cannot prevail upon you. You are a member of *Frau* Pam's personal staff and it wouldn't be right to put you to work on a voyage in which you are a passenger."

"Just try to stop her!" Gerbald countered wryly, earning himself another, less gentle blow to the ribs.

Dore straightened in her chair, casting aside the meek act she sometimes put on in front of strangers. "The truth is, Captain, I would very much like to do the job. Please understand I am a woman accustomed to work. I have worked my entire life and when I pass on to the next realm my sincerest hope is the good Lord will have work for me to do there. Spending the next few months lolling around in the confines of this ship with nothing to do would bore me to tears. Please, I *need* to work! Again, I offer my services as ship's cook for the voyage, with the hope that you will accept." She fixed her gaze on the captain with determination in every inch of her robust frame.

The Captain laughed, throwing his hands up in mock defeat. "Very well then, if *Frau* Pam and your husband have no objections, I certainly don't!" Pam and Gerbald both nodded their approval enthusiastically. "The galley is yours."

"Good! Then I shall start immediately! If you would all be kind enough to amuse yourself for an hour, I shall make what repairs I can to this dinner, as well as make you a simple dessert."

She then paused to favor her husband and friend with a very arch look. "And, in the unlikely event that I find your galley to be missing any useful ingredient, we can go down to our cabin where I have laid in an extensive larder. This was meant to be used upon reaching our destination, of course, but I see no reason we couldn't break into it now if the need arose!" Gerbald and Pam just grinned, both bowing their heads slightly in apology for having ever doubted Dore's prudent foresight.

"How wonderful, Frau Dore! It is always best to be well prepared for a long voyage such as this! I am sure the continuing well being of our stomachs are now in very capable hands! Mr Janvik, by all means, escort *Frau* Dore to the galley, and send some men to bring along these trays!"

The portly first mate nearly leaped from his seat, and Pam thought the sour-pussed fellow might actually be attempting to smile. They exited the captain's cabin at a speed which must surely be hazardous in such narrow confines.

Pam and Gerbald were left behind, both grinning like alley cats picking their teeth with feathers from the bluebird of happiness. The captain laughed heartily.

"I see from your faces that I am going to be most grateful for my new cook!"

The four remaining diners passed the time in conversation, the Grantvillers telling the Swedes of life in their most unusual town, while the captain and his bosun regaled them with tales of high seas adventure. Time passed by quickly and pleasantly.

One hour later to the very minute, a rich stew of fully cooked potatoes and chunks of meat salvaged from the center of the burnt round of beef, came to the table, seasoned with onions, caraway seed, and dried thyme. It was, of course, excellent, and as the diners scraped the last molecules from their plates, Dore and a very relieved crewman Mård, brought in the dessert, a soft and chewy spaetzel in a sweet cream, simple and delicious.

Dore sat back in her chair with her quiet kind of pride, dutifully accepting the rain of compliments. After the party ended with a round of minty schnapps, they made their way up to the deck for a breath of fresh air before retiring. By the lantern light, the sailors all cheered when they saw Dore emerge, shouting praise in German and Swedish. Dore waved, then told them to shush with an embarrassed laugh. There was more than her usual rosy blush on her cheeks this night!

"Well, you certainly are the big hero, Dore!" Pam gave Dore's arm a happy squeeze.

"I fixed up the sailor's dinner for them, too. It seems they liked it well enough."

Dore making light of her contribution, was belied by the extremely pleased crinkles at the corner of her mouth and eyes. Later, Pam fell asleep smiling at the improved prospects of their crazy voyage.

Garrett W. Vance

CHAPTER 7: ALL THE PRINCESS'S MEN

The North Sea

The *Redbird* was making good time. With the English Channel currently far too dangerous to attempt, thanks to the current political situation, they had to go a bit out of their way first. Their course led them to the northwest, around the top of Scotland, passing between the Orkney and Shetland islands. The days grew a bit cooler accordingly, but no one seemed to mind, as the winds were with them, and the sailing was the best they could ask for.

Pam and Gerbald were on deck enjoying the fresh air as they watched the marines go about their routines. They were soon joined by Dore, who lately spent most of her time belowdecks, ruling over her new empire, the ship's galley. Having apparently run out of grit and grease to annihilate, she breathed in the cool North Sea air with a contented smile on her face, which Pam was damn glad to see! A busy Dore was a happy Dore. An unhappy Dore, well, that was a force that any sensible person would not wish to reckon with!

Meanwhile, the marines were putting on quite a show. One group was performing rather strenuous martial drills with their swords, while another group fussed over a fearsome-looking deck gun called a carronade. They had learned that *Löjtnant* Lundkvist commanded a platoon consisting of two squads, twenty-two soldiers in all, chosen for their military prowess and almost fanatical devotion to Princess Kristina. Kristina's marines were based on the highly acclaimed up-time American version, men who valued honor and duty as much as that august fighting force.

Dutifully catering to their beloved Princess's whimsical decree, the entire force was called the Chessmen Platoon, in reference to characters in Lewis Carroll's *Through the Looking Glass,* the very same book that had triggered the entire *save the dodo* mission. The *Löjtnant* had confided that some foolish know-it-all in her father's court had once informed her that "Platoons don't have names!" Kristina's response had simply been "This one does." Case closed!

The White Chessmen Squad was made up of eleven *korprals* and their squad leader, Sergeant Järv, a fierce warrior who very much resembled his namesake, the formidable wolverine of the Northern woodlands. They were all well-seasoned fighting men, trained in a variety of melee and ranged weaponry, now dedicated to providing security for the ship, particularly Pam and her staff. Although few in number, they were definitely a force to be reckoned with!

The Black Chessmen Squad was a team of eight *bombardiers*, an equivalent rank to *korpral,* specializing in heavy weapons and explosives. These highly-trained experts were led by Sergeant Sten, a tall, stern fellow in his late forties, easily recognized by his steel-gray mutton chops that were sometimes partially singed away. Their pride and joy was the carronade, a gleaming weapon of destruction based on an up-time design from the 1770's. Originally created for use on merchant ships, the carronade required only a small crew to operate, and was lethal over short range. God help anyone foolish enough to attempt to board *Redbird!* The bombardiers took their responsibility seriously, tending to the formidable weapon as if it were a pampered child, polishing its shining metal until it was nearly blinding to behold on a sunny day. When that solemn undertaking wasn't going on, the carronade was kept under a heavy tarp while the bombardiers joined the rest of the marines in their drills. *Löjtnant* Lundkvist saw to it that there was cross-training between the squads. All the White Chessmen needed to know how to fire the carronade in a pinch, while the Black Chessmen kept their melee skills fresh for any possible close encounters.

Gerbald, a retired soldier who had had held the rank of master sergeant during his years at war, watched the goings on with particular interest. Pam was pretty sure there was a wistful expression on his usually impassive face. Although retired, Gerbald was still very much a warrior to be respected, part of why Pam had originally engaged his services as a bodyguard. He never went anywhere without his katzbalger shortsword, the only thing that was possibly more precious to him than his rather silly-looking, in Pam's opinion, mustard-yellow felt hat. All she could say for the wide-brimmed tall, floppy thing was that it was definitely eye-catching, the kind of thing a fairy tale dwarf or wizard might wear. Dore loathed it with a passion usually reserved for sinners and shirkers.

Pers, who had taken quite a liking to Gerbald and was currently his Number One Admirer, took notice of it and asked "*Herr* Gerbald, does that hat of yours ever come off?"

"Ha!" Pam laughed "He'd feel naked without it! I would've sworn that it's sewn to his head if I hadn't seen him doff it at dinner." Along with his sage-green, many-pocketed wool longcoat, the outlandish piece of headgear was part and parcel of Gerbald's signature look, no matter how much they teased him about it.

"I insist on that much." Dore said in a much put upon tone. "He used to take it off in church as well, but his shadow rarely crosses that threshold anymore." Dore added, casting an admonishing look at her confirmed black sheep husband.

"But what about the wind? *Herr* Gerbald, do you not worry that the sea breeze will carry it away?" Pers asked him with real concern. "I've lost my hats out here so many times I no longer bother to wear one."

"No, my friend, it troubles me not. In the unlikely event that nature should take it from me, it only means that it is time for a new one, but I doubt that will happen. You see, I have worn this hat for so long that it has become a part of my body, it is as likely to blow away as my ears are!" Gerbald reassured him with a playful wink.

Pam and Dore, neither who could in any way be construed as an admirer of said appendage, looked at each other with wide eyes, which then narrowed into the slits of hunting cats.

"Nature, nothing! Get it, Dore!" Pam shouted in English. Both women lunged at Gerbald in a bid to tip the silly thing off into the wind. He dodged them both easily, of course, reflexes honed to avoid the jabs of deadly pike and sword were more than a match for such innocent sport as this. Laughing impishly, Gerbald gently kept his assailants at arm's length. He favored their fruitless antics with a beatific smile, as if they were unruly, but well-loved youngsters, until they eventually grew tired and gave up, the offending headgear still safely in place.

"Oh well, it was a good try." Dore grumbled, flushed and slightly out of breath. "Many times I have thought to burn it while he sleeps, but *oh,* the fuss he would make, I would never hear the end of it! Men are such children about their precious things!"

Pam shook her head in resignation "Well, I guess he wouldn't be Gerbald without that stupid hat. It's like his trademark or something."

"There are still a few men in the Germanies who fear the sight of this hat, you know." Gerbald remarked matter-of-factly, adjusting the wide, floppy brim to no visible effect; the felt remained as warped as ever.

"Only a few men?" Pers asked Gerbald in his still-heavily accented, but passable English. Pam had been teaching him, improving on his already fairly solid base, in exchange for their Swedish lessons. He was proving to be a quick study. The bright young fellow was still in awe of the ex-soldier, but curious.

"Yes, it is so. I once had some notoriety on the battlefield, long ago." as he spoke, his hand instinctively went to the hilt of his trusty shortsword, pulling it partially out of its scabbard to proudly show it off to Pers. "This *katzbalger* is feared by more than just cats!"

"Please excuse my forwardness, but with prowess such as yours, why *only a few*?" Pers's question held just a note of teasing, trusting in the good nature of his newfound idol.

"Because most who have met this blade are dead, young fellow! Some survived, yes, but only a few." Allowing himself one of his very rare, proud-as-a-lion-and-twice-as-dangerous-grins, Gerbald sauntered away, every inch the consummate warrior. Pers grinned after him, in full blown hero worship.

Pam and Dore looked at each other with eyebrows raised. Gerbald seldom spoke of his soldiering past, much less bragged about it.

"All hail the conquering hero! Must be the sea air?" Pam asked wonderingly.

"He rarely speaks such words!" Dore answered in a surprised tone, "Perhaps it is the close company of other fighting men." she nodded toward the Swedish marines fiercely engaged in their drills. "He is still very proud of his exploits, you know. Despite all the hardships we endured."

"I'm just glad he's on our side." Pam said and meant it. Meanwhile, Gerbald had sauntered over to the marines. After a brief, and smiling discussion with the *Löjtnant*, they watched him join in, stepping and swinging his deadly katzbalger right along with the rest as if her were born to it. He truly was something to see, his moves exhibiting the fluid grace of a dancer, despite his solid, powerful build. It didn't take long before Sergeant Gerbald, Retired, the veteran of many a terrible conflict, was giving the younger men pointers. Even the *Löjtnant* and the older soldiers seemed to hold him in awe, affording him nothing but the greatest respect.

"Oh yes, there he goes." Dore switched back to German, frowning deeply as she pointed at her husband with her chin "The great old soldier teaching these fresh-faced Swedish boys how it's done. He will be full of himself tonight." With a long-suffering roll of her eyes, she headed back to her bastion of cleanliness and moral purpose, the galley.

Pers had been standing with them, quietly watching the proceedings until the ever-surly first mate walked by and cuffed him lightly on his head, causing the lad to bend himself back to the nearest task at hand in embarrassed haste.

Pam turned back to the view over the rail with a smile to watch the gulls swoop and cry alongside the ship, her heart filled with a sudden and surprising contentment with life at sea.

* * *

The next day, as Pam tried to get used to working at a desk that felt more like a carnival ride, one of the sailors brought her a pot of tea at Dore's instruction. His name was Fritjoff, the eldest of the crew. He seemed to be in his seventies, yet still hale and hearty, which was sadly not always the case among down-timers. Tall, thin, and sporting a long gray beard, Fritjoff was a serious old fellow not given to talk much. He set the tray down gently where she motioned him to, and shyly mumbled a reply to her thanks. As he was about to leave, something caught his eye, and his face lit up in a very surprising way.

"The Princess!" he said in halting German. "Princess Kristina!" Pam raised her eyebrows at him, then remembered the photo she had put up the day before.

"Yes that's right. It's a photo of Princess Kristina."

The older gentleman's eyes were moist with adoration, they were fixed on the photo which he studied as if to commit it to perfect memory. "We love The Princess." he told her, "She is our light."

"Yes, I think I can understand that. She's a wonderful child, and she has a lot of heart." Pam watched Fritjoff stand there entranced and wondered how long he would stare. After a very long moment, he came to his senses, and began to leave hastily, apologizing profusely for having disturbed her work. Pam gave him an understanding smile. He seemed like a real sweet old guy.

"Think nothing of it, *Herr* Fritjoff. Say, wait a minute." Pam stood from her chair and reached for the photo. She pulled it carefully off the wall and studied it for a second. *You imp,* she thought, *this is all your fault, bless your too-big-for-that-skinny-body heart.* With a broad smile, she held it out to Fritjoff. "Here, I'd like you to have it. I can get another easily enough when we get back, and I can see you think so much of her. Please, take it."

"*Frau* Pam, I can't..." Fritjoff said, but his eyes were fixed longingly on the glossy image of his adored princess.

"Yes, you can, in fact, I insist. I have had the honor of meeting the princess in person, and I am *sure* she would want *you* to have it."

Pam gently opened the old man's trembling hands to place the photo on his palms. "Only pick it up by the edges or it will smudge, and don't ever let it get wet! Now take it, it's yours now!"

Fritjoff's long fingers closed delicately around the edges, careful to grip it as she had instructed. He looked at Pam as if she had gifted him with eternal life, then bowed his head deeply to her.

"Thank you *Frau* Pam, I shall never forget your generosity. I am in your debt." and with that he backed out of the cabin quickly, closing the door behind him. Pam could hear him nearly running down the narrow hall to show his mates his new treasure.

"Well, looks like I made a friend." Pam laughed to herself as she went back to work. That evening on her way to dinner, she saw that the photo had been hung high in a place of honor near the stairs. Several of the sailors were looking at it with worshipful expressions. They grinned at Pam merrily as she went by and thanked her repeatedly for sharing her wonderful photo. *Yeesh, that kid is a superstar to these people!* Pam rolled her eyes a bit once she was past the giddy sailors, but was secretly pleased at the reaction to her little good deed.

CHAPTER 8: THE MISSION

The North Atlantic Ocean

The days passed slowly as they made their way along what would, in another universe, have one day become a clipper ship route. Pam had studied everything she could find regarding her intended voyage before she had left Grantville and found the age of the great clippers fascinating. *Alas, the heyday of the tall ship won't happen here,* Pam mused as she strolled around the decks enjoying the brisk, but bright weather. Those magnificent constructs of rope, sail, and wood were destined to be passed by all together in favor of bluntly effective engine power, an almost naturally evolved technological butterfly crushed before it had a chance to fly by the hot, oily, steel of growling motors from the future.

The coast of Ireland passed by at a regal pace befitting its ancient majesty, just as green as it was reputed to be. Pam had always wanted to visit that many-fabled island, but it had just been an idle daydream. But now? She couldn't help but think it was possible in this new life in a younger world. It was slow going there as the prevailing winds and the North Atlantic Current were against them, but eventually fair Erin slipped away behind them, vanishing into the chill ocean mists.

The days passed and turned into weeks. One blustery afternoon, Pam and Gerbald walked the deck for exercise as they often did, the stiff breezes of the North Atlantic a refreshing respite from the confines of their cabins. They had finished their Swedish lessons for the day. Gerbald and Dore had soon joined Pam to learn that musical tongue of the far north. They were surrounded by eager teachers, and were picking it up fairly fast, especially since there was not much else to do! Currently, they were making a valiant effort, going so far as to use it among themselves, instead of the more comfortable mix of English and German they were accustomed to. That patois of necessity, born from the Ring of Fire, had begun to take on a life of its own. Some were even calling it *Amedeutsch*!

As they made another loop around the deck, they saw something moving in the water about ten yards off the prow, so they paused to see what it was. Two large seabirds swam along the waves, chasing fish, and occasionally calling to each other. Pam was pretty sure they were flightless as their sleek wings looked thoroughly adapted to swimming.

"Are those penguins?" Gerbald asked, having seen them in the movies and taped TV shows he enjoyed so much.

"No... not penguins, they only live in the southern hemisphere, and we haven't passed the Equator yet." Pam looked closer at the pair of large, swimming birds. They certainly resembled a penguin, about thirty-three inches long, their markings black-and-white, with a prominent white spot on the top of their heads. Still, their beaks seemed rather big for a penguin... Suddenly she remembered, another page in the sad little chapter in the back of *Birds of the World* shared by the dodo. A chill went through her that had nothing to do with the stout breeze.

"Oh my God! I know what they are . . . They're great auks! They were extinct up-time, just like the dodo was!" Pam exclaimed, her voice ringing with childlike wonder, her eyes wide at the sight of the unique creatures as if they were living unicorns leaped out of a storybook page. Pam's hands shook from the thrill as she fumbled to pull her scope out of her coat. Focusing in on the gaily cavorting seabirds, she fairly hummed with delight. They were beautiful, sleek and graceful. The great auk, a classic case of convergent evolution, and sadly another species destined for extinction. But not now, not yet, anyway.

One of the sailors, Helge, a very friendly fellow seldom seen without a smile on his ruddy face, paused from his work to join them in watching the great auks.

"I haven't seen those things for a long time, not so many as there once were. I hear they make good eating!" he told them as he looked down at the birds.

Pam just blinked at him, feeling her face grow hot, and her eyes fill with moisture. Suddenly, it was all much too big for a bird-loving former housewife stuck in the wrong century, and she couldn't stop the hot tears from coming, blurring the sight of birds that were surely doomed, wondering if she could somehow save them as well as the dodo, or if it weren't too late already. She mumbled an apology, and fled back to her cabin, burying herself under her blankets for a long cry.

Back on the deck Helge, his usually cheerful demeanor now fraught with worry, turned to Gerbald.

"*Herr* Gerbald, what have I done? I did not mean to offend the good lady!"

"It's all right my friend, it wasn't your fault." Gerbald reassured him with a sad smile. "It seems the world grows narrower and crueler with each passing year, and Pam's heart is so big she feels the pain of it more keenly than most."

Gerbald started to go, then paused. A whimsical look came to his face, then quickly turned serious. He leaned in close to poor, worried Helge, speaking to him in low, confidential tones.

"Perhaps you haven't heard! I must warn you, it is very bad fortune to kill the great auks! I saw one fellow who had eaten one die terribly, as if he had ingested poison! It was awful, just three bites, then his face turned purple and he coughed blood!" he paused for dramatic effect, then leaned in closer. "But here's the *worst* thing: the *very same thing happened* to that fellow's mates, and they hadn't even taken a bite yet! Most of them died before the dawn came. Very bad *juju.*"

Helge's face grew extremely pale even for a Scandinavian, as Gerbald nodded his head knowingly.

"If I were you, I would take those birds permanently off the menu. That is, if you want to live! You had better spread the word."

Helge nodded solemnly.

Those superstitious sailors are so gullible! Gerbald smirked, enjoying his mischievous jest as he walked back to his cabin, not realizing that he, himself, had just taken a major step toward preventing the future extinction of the great auk.

*   *   *

Pam declined the usual dinner invitation that evening from beneath her blankets, not wanting her friends to see her red, tear-stained face. She mumbled a vague apology saying that she felt a bit off and just needed a rest. Gerbald just nodded, knowing what had happened earlier and understanding that sometimes Pam just needed to work things out on her own. Dore fussed over her a bit, rearranging the blankets as best she could so that they covered her feet. Realizing there wasn't anything more she could do, she marched off to the galley to make sure all was in order for the evening repast.

Eventually Pam's good, long cry over the fate of the great auk dwindled to an occasional sniffle. She had felt hopeless and helpless for a while, composing long lists of animals that had gone extinct by her original time that might still be alive now, agonizing over the slim possibility of one woman saving them all. What could she do? But then, as the tears dried and she remembered she *was* doing something, right now, saving the dodo, and she wasn't alone in it. After all, she had a princess on her side! With a low groan, she pulled the covers off, slid the low protective rail that prevented her from sliding out of bed in high seas out of the way, and got up.

She went to the small basin that held fresh water, splashing it on her face and gently rubbing her still-puffy eyes. *Gawd, you look such a mess when you cry, silly girl!* she chided herself. Having pulled herself together as best she could, she sat at her charming little wood desk and pulled out a fresh sheet of paper. After taking a moment to use a small knife to sharpen one of the new down-time made pencils (they mostly worked, but still had a ways to go before they achieved the quality of their up-time models), she wrote at the top of the page *Animals to Save,* and began listing them, starting with the birds. *Great Auk. Carolina Parakeet. Passenger Pigeon. Ivory-Billed Woodpecker.* Eventually, nearing the bottom of the page, she ran out of birds and switched to mammals. *Quagga. Sea Mink. Stellar's Sea Cow. Aurochs.*

There were a lot of them, and the list spilled over to the back of the page. When she ran out of mammals she considered reptiles, but couldn't recall any off hand. She would find out more about those when she got back to Grantville. This little exercise could have made her despair again, but it didn't. Instead, she felt a warm glow of resolve filling her. For better or worse, she had found her purpose in this strange old world, and her work was just beginning. At the bottom of the page, she wrote, *My mission grows.*

A knock came to the door. She forced a bit more cheer into her voice than she really had, as she called out "Come on in!"

Not too surprisingly it was Helge, come to apologize, a heart-breaking expression of shame on his face. Pam stood up and beckoned him in, feeling awful herself that she had made the jovial sailor feel so bad. She should have thought of him earlier. He was carrying a tray with a small dinner for Pam. There was no way Dore would let her go without, 'feeling a bit off' or not! She motioned for him to put it on the small side table beside her bunk.

Helge looked like he wanted to speak, but his tongue was tied. Pam smiled at him and spoke first "Helge, I am so sorry for today, you did nothing wrong, nothing! Sometimes I just get upset about things, it's a long story." She used her Swedish as Helge didn't have much English. She hoped he would understand her. Her skills had improved, but she hadn't achieved real fluency yet.

Helge managed a smile then, visibly relieved that he had obtained the American lady's forgiveness. He started to speak again, but then paused, looking shy.

Pam gave him her most encouraging smile and said, "Go on Helge, you can always speak your mind to me."

Some of the tension left Helge's face, and he managed a bit of his usual smile for her before speaking.

"Frau Pam, I just want you to know that myself, and the rest of the crew, understand what you are here to do and that you have our full support. These animals that will one day disappear because of the greed and foolishness of mankind, it is not God's will. The Bible says *The Lord gave us dominion over the fish of the sea, and over the fowl of the air, and over the cattle, and over all the earth, and over every creeping thing that creeps upon the earth.* It seems we are not doing a very proper job of it. The Lord tests us and in this we are failing. Our beloved princess, so wise beyond her years, has seen this, and so she sent us on this mission. Tell us what you need of us, and we will do our very best to help you! We want you to know, we do it not just to please you and our princess, but because it is the right thing to do."

Pam felt a warm rush of joy at Helge's heartfelt pledge. She knew the working men of the ship were decent people, highly skilled at their jobs, but with little education. They had befriended her, treating her like she herself was royalty, but she had sometimes wondered if they really comprehended why they were out here. It was not the first time she had underestimated down-timers, but she was learning.

"Thank you, Helge. That means so much to me, please tell the rest of the men how grateful I am for your friendship and support. I am so proud to be serving with such fine people as yourselves, and I am certain the princess is very proud of you, too!" she paused then, and lowered her voice a bit, hesitating a moment before speaking. "I have to tell you, Helge, I was terrified to come on this voyage! I have never done anything like this before. I was an average person living in a sleepy little town, and now here I am sailing around Africa on a quest from a princess! I just want you all to know, I am not so scared any more, because I know I am in the best of hands, surrounded by men who are no longer strangers, but friends. Thank you for that!"

That brought Helge's broad grin back to his ruggedly handsome, windburned face. He gave Pam a quick salute, a gesture borrowed from the princess's marines, which Pam returned, laughing, then he ducked back into the corridor to return to his duties.

Pam sat down at her desk . Before she started eating, she paused, and did something that she had not done in a very long time— she bowed her head and gave a prayer of thanks.

CHAPTER 9: SOUTHWARD BOUND

The Horse Latitudes

The *Redbird* and her flotilla made better time as the winds came into their favor, passing near the Azores to give the Iberian Peninsula a wide berth. The fleet was on high alert for hostile sails, not just the U.S.E.'s current enemy, the Spanish, but also the famed Barbary Pirates who haunted the region. They saw nary another ship during that passage, much to everyone's relief, although Pam had full confidence the Chessmen Platoon would make mincemeat of any scoundrels with an eye to giving them trouble.

The friendly winds were in full force now, a steady hand pushing them firmly south. Pam squinted through her birding scope, hoping for a glimpse of North Africa, but alas, they would not pass close enough for much of a view. Still, it was all very exciting, with the sunny skies buoying everyone's spirits despite the long days at sea. They were following the famed clipper route, but the well-aged vessels of their modest little fleet were no clipper ships, and their progress was much slower.

Sometimes, the *Redbird* came close to the other vessels and they were able to wave and shout brief conversations. Pam's Swedish was still clumsy, but the cheerfully stoic Swedes on the *Annalise*, *Ide* and ever-watchful *Muskijl*, all congratulated her on her growing fluency, which pleased her. She found, by God, she *liked* these civilized scions of the Vikings. There was something about them that attracted her. Sometimes she would watch the captain going about his duties, only to find herself blushing. There was *definitely* something about *him* that attracted her, but she always pushed such thoughts aside sharply. *No time for that, idiot! Get back to work!* She made strides in her studies and the book she was

79

writing, *Birds of the USE*. The gentle motion of the ship's rocking as she sat at her little desk seemed to add to her momentum. Even with that distraction, the days went by slowly, and she often found herself wandering the decks, watching the seabirds while trying not to spend too much time sneaking glimpses of the captain.

Pam had made good on her vow to get to know every member of the crew, including the Princess's Chessmen Marines. They were a great bunch of guys, often reminding her of the scads of male uncles and cousins that had made her childhood in rural West Virginia so much fun, always including her, whatever they were up to, making a real tomboy out of her. Thanks to them, Pam knew how to ride horses and motorbikes, shoot bows and guns, and live off the land, things that had turned out to be helpful in her new life down-time. She missed her big, rambunctious family terribly and found some solace in the antics the men of the *Redbird* got up to when they weren't battening down hatches and hoisting up sails, and all those sailor things, which, like her jolly relatives, they were always happy to teach her how to do. She knew her way around *Redbird* by heart now, and if the need ever arose, felt confident, she could lend a hand! Despite all this, there was one nut among them she found she simply could not crack: Janvik, the first mate.

The first mate was an equal opportunity scowler. He scowled at everyone, from the bottom to the top, including Pam, who reckoned he thought of her as *That Foreign Nuisance*. There were only four people aboard he showed any deference to— the captain, the *Löjtnant*, the Bosun, and Dore, and among those, Dore ranked the highest! The only time he looked like he might even be in danger of smiling was in her presence and he always treated her with the utmost respect. To understand why, you only had to look at his waistline— the first mate liked to eat and he liked to eat a lot! It's no secret that the way to a man's heart was through his stomach, something that Dore had recognized immediately. More than once, Pam had caught her slipping Janvik a sweet bun or a meat tart when they thought no one was looking! For his part, the first mate knew who buttered his bread and he made sure to keep his cook happy! When it came to requisitioning supplies from the ship's stores, a process that required Janvik's approval, who usually made it as difficult as possible, Dore never had any trouble whatsoever! Her loyal eater simply handed the goods over to her without question. Pam found all this hilarious.

One languid day in which the ship required very little adjustment under such fair sailing conditions, Pam noticed sailors and marines playing cards on a heavy square board placed atop the flat end of a large barrel. The gaming area was mostly out of the wind, but they still used small flat stones to keep the cards on the table from blowing away in the occasional gusts. They were playing for common coins in what looked to be a pretty low stakes game, but the players still maintained a rather serious disposition.

Pam leaned over dark-haired Lind's shoulder, who obligingly raised his hand for her, and her alone, to view, all the while maintaining a stony expression that reminded her of an Easter Island statue. To Pam's surprise, the cards were rather different from those she was used to. Hearts were present, but the other suits had been replaced with what appeared to be bells, acorns and leaves! She saw his hand held four of a kind comprised of sixes, not a bad hand for poker. She had no idea if it was of any use in this game. She murmured her thanks, then stepped back to watch, keeping her own face as stony as theirs. It was time for everyone to lay down their hands. Lind let out a laugh of delight as he scooped the small pile of coins towards his corner.

He grinned up at Pam and said "Frau Pam, you bring me luck! My thanks!" Everyone groaned, and laughed, the spirit of the game was light despite their sober demeanor during play.

"What's the name of the game?" She asked them, her interest piqued.

"*Pochen!*" they cried out in unison.

A roguish smile came to Pam's face. "Deal me in." she said, which they obligingly did. She guessed under normal circumstances of the period, a woman might not be welcome at the table, but she was after all, *The American Lady,* proxy to The Princess, and could pretty much get away with murder with these fellows.

The name *Pochen,* resembling poker, was no accident. It shared many features with its future descendant, poker, but there were still enough differences to make it interesting. Pam played a few hands and lost as she learned, but then the tables turned and she went on a winning streak, all the while feigning beginner's luck.

The truth was, Pam was a bit of a ringer. She had been a card player all of her life thanks to the large band of uncles and cousins she had grown up so close to! They started her out on Crazy Eights and Go Fish, but it wasn't long until their rather precocious six-year-old cousin was sitting at the poker table with them, albeit on top of a Charleston, West Virginia phone book placed on her chair! Pam had a knack for cards and her doting uncles and cousins took a perverse delight in getting their asses whooped by *Little Pammie! 'The Game'* became a well-loved family tradition, be it poker, gin rummy, hearts, spades, cribbage or whatever suited their moods that day— they played them all, but poker reigned as the favorite.

When she became a mother, Pam taught her son Walt to play. He proved to be almost as good as she was, and the two together became a force to be reckoned with at family gatherings! It was one of the few things she and her so often contrarian son agreed upon, so she played cards with him as much as she could until he reached his teens and became too old and wise-assed to want to anymore. Pam sensed she was frowning at the sour end of that memory, so she quickly forced her face back into its well-practiced card shark stoniness.

The game went on, everyone having a lovely time. The men were beginning to suspect that Pam knew more than she was letting on, but the novelty of having her join them quelled any hard feelings they might have had if she had been just another sailor. A crowd had begun to gather as word of the game spread throughout the ship. Anyone who was off duty and a few who most likely were not, circled the makeshift table, viewing the procedures as they mumbled their own wagers among themselves. Pam was currently the favorite.

Pam relished this. It felt so good to do something familiar again and so exciting to do it in such an exotic locale. After a while, she felt a funny tingle on the back of her neck. She turned to see the captain had appeared behind her! The sailors suddenly looked nervous. They began to stand up, but the captain laughed and said "Far be it from me to stop a good game of cards! You men have more than earned some enjoyment! Now, if you don't mind, how about dealing me in?" One of the *Löjtnant's* White Chessmen, sharp-eyed Sergeant Järv, jumped up to offer his place at the crowded table. Pam started to get up to let him take her place, but Captain Torbjörn, wearing a very disarming smile, raised a hand to stop her.

"Frau Pam, surely you wouldn't deny me the pleasure of your company. It's plain your skills present quite a challenge, what say you?"

Pam smiled, nodded, and sat back down. "As you wish, Captain." *Well, this should prove interesting ole' Pammie! Just focus on the game, not the man!* she chided herself as she examined the cards dealt to her. It wasn't a bad hand and she might be able to evolve it into a winner. Trying not to be obvious, she stole a glance at the captain, to find he had a good, solid poker face in place, not too stony, with a slight smile that showed he was enjoying the game, but nothing was being given away. Pam narrowed her eyes and returned to her cards, doing her level best to focus.

Pam soon realized she might be meeting her match. The captain won the first round, but Pam won the next. They congratulated each other and kept the tone light, but Pam felt a tension rising in her. She *liked* Torbjörn, maybe even a bit more, but be damned if she were going to let him win the day!

"Best two out of three, Captain?" she asked in her cordial for company voice.

"It would be a pleasure!" he answered with his winning smile, which Pam returned in kind.

The gathered crowd watched as quietly as they could, but Pam knew bets were being placed and wondered if she were still the favorite. They were playing for the Swedish equivalent of pennies at the table, but she thought the stakes might be a bit higher on the side.

It was a close match. One by one the others folded, leaving only Pam and the captain in play, their faces impassive with only a tiny bit of beetling around the brows. At last, the final hand came down, a resounding victory for Pam. She watched to see how the big man would take his loss. With a rueful grin, he bowed his head in defeat and pushed the small pile of tiny coins, a couple of brass buttons, and a pretty little seashell across the makeshift table to her.

"To the winner goes the spoils. Well played, Frau Pam!"

"Thank you, Captain. Well played yourself, it was a close thing! I hereby donate my winnings to the Swedish Sailor's Relief Fund! Don't spend it all in one place!"

This brought hearty laughs and a round of applause from the crowd.

The captain stood and smiled that very disarming smile of his. "Frau Pam, you are a most challenging opponent! Will you do me the honor of a rematch sometime? This was most enjoyable!"

Pam agreed readily to the proposal and found herself once again admiring the Swede's gallant nature. Playing cards became a regular onboard tradition, with several matches a week, when they could find the time from their duties. Pam found a pack of up-time playing cards in the bottom of her backpack and began to teach the crew all the games she knew. 'The Game' in all its incarnations was a lot of fun for all and helped the time pass more quickly and more pleasantly.

The Equator

The long days at sea rolled on. And on. The temperature grew warmer under the increasingly sunny skies of their southerly course. Rather than hug the African coast, they would continue to take advantage of the Trade Winds, by heading for a set of way-markers, The Saint Peter and Saint Paul Archipelago. This tiny group of islands lay just above the Equator, roughly halfway between South America and Africa. Darwin himself had stopped there and described two species of bird, a booby and a noddy, so Pam was anxious for a sighting. The captain had asked her if she wanted to stop and have a look around. Pam had to take a moment to think about the offer.

Darwin had already been there and done that in her former time, so what was the point? While the idea appealed to her, it would slow their progress by several days, plus there was the danger of losing the wind in the Doldrums which could turn those days into weeks. She had a mission and would stick to it. It did, however, make her feel a bit depressed. Here she was risking her life, on an ostensibly scientific expedition, in a world where someone else had already discovered almost everything in a future that wouldn't even happen that way again. Deep down, she knew any research she did would have value, but the feeling of being a dwarf following along in the footsteps of giants, even ghostly ones who would now never even be born, made her feel a bit insignificant.

She could still birdwatch, so she occupied her time prowling the decks, peering through her scope and binoculars, in hopes of catching a glimpse of such exotic birds. So far her efforts had been rewarded with only common gull and tern species.

The area was known for storms, but the breeze that bore them along was sultry today. The men working on deck had taken off their shirts to keep cool. Panning around to the bridge with her binoculars Pam saw, to her surprise, this included the captain!

Unable to stop herself, she paused to study the man. His chest and back were a bit hairy, but it was of a fine, red-gold color, and not too long, nor curly. It was maybe even kind of attractive! He was definitely in good shape. She had seen him drill beside the marines with what looked to be considerable skill with a longsword. He could also be seen pitching in at the ropes, the kind of leader who would get his hands dirty if need be, and the men loved him for it. Pam admired his lean physique, that of a much younger man.

She was just about to turn away when he noticed her attention and flashed her a smile and a friendly wave. *Ack! I've been caught!* Pam, blushing hotly, gave him a feeble wave in return, then pretended to be interested in a handy seabird flying by, hoping the utterly fascinating Captain Nillson couldn't see the scarlet hue her face had taken on from that distance. *Gawd Pam, you are acting like a silly teen-ager!* She scolded herself. *Still,* she admitted with a tiny smile, *he is pretty hunky!*

Suddenly a voice spoke beside her, startling her when she was already as jumpy as a frog in springtime. It was Gerbald, who had used his considerable skills to sneak up beside her.

"Splendid creatures, aren't they?" he remarked in a wry tone.

"Oh, the seabirds? yes, lovely." she stammered.

"I was actually referring to the male Scandinavian in his nearly natural state."

This made Pam blush even deeper, and groan.

"Guilty as charged. For God's sake, don't tell Dore I'm playing Peeping Tom on the men!"

"Not on your life! Funny thing though, she wouldn't judge you as harshly as you think. Despite all her Christian militancy, she is still a woman of these times, and as you may have noticed, the puritans have not come into existence yet! To up-time eyes we can be downright bawdy, even Dore!"

"I've caught glimpses of that..." Pam said thinking back.

"When we get the schnapps into her, yes! Which reminds me, it's been too long, let's do that again soon! She's so much fun when she's in her cups!"

"Agreed!" Pam said and they shared a hearty laugh at the usually prim and proper Dore's hilarious antics once the booze was in her!

"You shouldn't be embarrassed, you know, my dear Pam. We have eyes and we have seen the way you look at the captain. He is a fine man and I believe of good heart and sound mind. If you have feelings for him, perhaps you should see where they lead? Life is too short to spend it wondering, without actually doing anything about it . . ." he paused then, before continuing in a somewhat more somber tone. "But, in this case, you should be aware you have competition."

Pam's eyebrows raised and her heart skipped a beat. "Is there another woman?"

Gerbald just shook his head no, then pointed out at the horizon. "The Sea, Pam. The Sea."

*　*　*

Pam was quiet through dinner that evening. It had been a long, strange day that had played across her emotions from top to bottom. After dessert, the captain asked everyone to join him on the bridge for a toast. Pam looked at Gerbald, but her friend only shrugged. The Bosun, however, had a knowing look about his ruddy face. The night was a bit cooler than the day had been, and very clear, with the stars so thick and close they could pluck them out of the sky like grapes from a vine. Once Dore arrived from the galley, the bosun passed out a cup to everyone, then the captain poured them a very fine French brandy.

"I've been saving this for a special occasion." he announced in his rich, baritone voice. "Today we crossed the equator, having come a long way on our journey. I would now like to direct your attention to the south." he pointed with his brandy glass. "Do you see those bright stars, low on the horizon, in a group? They are, I am assured, the Southern Cross, and it is the first time I have ever laid eyes upon them, perhaps it is the same with some of you? They are as beautiful as their reputation suggests, and I hope for their blessing. And so, we have arrived at an excellent time and a place for a toast," he raised his cup as the others followed suite, "Here's to the good ship *Redbird* and to all who sail on her!"

A chorus of *Skål* followed and Pam found herself feeling better as the warm night and the delicious brandy worked to soothe her soul. While Gerbald joined the Swedes in another round of drinks, Pam noticed Dore had drifted off to the rail by herself, where she gazed solemnly out at the southern sky. Pam joined her friend, giving her a playful bump, which made Dore smile.

"Penny for your thoughts, Dore?"

Dore smiled again. Pam could see the usually unflappable woman had grown a bit emotional, and needed to gather herself before speaking. Eventually she turned to her younger friend.

"I never thought I would see anything like this, Pam. The Southern Cross, the great oceans, are sights for men of adventure, for the brave, and the mad. I'm just an old washerwoman, a simple soldier's simple wife. I never thought I would be in such places as these." Her voice was thick with unexpected emotion, a sense of marvel she had never experienced before, and that had greatly moved her. Dore gazed at the winking lights of unfamiliar constellations, slowly shaking her head, her face having taken on an almost child-like look of wonder.

Pam nodded slowly. "Neither did I, Dore, not in a million years. I'm just glad you're here to see it with me, it makes it a lot easier to cope with. Thank you for coming along on this crazy voyage. It's a lot to ask from a friend, even one as dependable as you."

"It is nothing Pam, I would not have let you go without me! I just didn't expect such beauty, such thrills. I am glad I saw this, I am glad we are here, doing these things. It's . . . fun."

At that revelation, it was Pam's turn to have her words catch in her throat, so she just looked back at Dore with wide eyes, and grinned her biggest grin. After a moment, she was able to speak, and said "It is fun, isn't it? I'm just so thankful you think so, too!"

After a while, the impromptu party broke up. Pam lingered, enjoying the cool air after the heat of the day. Soon all that remained were the night watch and the captain. When the captain noticed her in the shadows, he came to join her at the rail.

"Thank you for the party, Captain." Pam told him, trying not to smile too shyly. There was always something about him that made her usual tough gal demeanor seem suddenly hard to maintain.

"You are most welcome! And please, at this hour, I am just Torbjörn."

"Of course, Torbjörn. So, none of that *Frau* stuff from you, all right? It makes me feel positively ancient."

He laughed his rich, seaman's laugh and replied, "As you wish, Pam!" He held out what remained of the brandy and two cups. "Will you do me the honor of assisting me in laying this soldier to rest?"

Pam nodded and smiled as he filled her cup and gently handed it to her. She waited for him to fill his, shaking the last drops of delicious amber fluid into it, then placing the empty bottle safely in the middle of a coil of rope where it wouldn't roll about. They both stood there holding their glasses for a moment, the silence suddenly feeling just a bit awkward.

"For once, I am at a loss, Pam." he said, pulling on his neatly trimmed red-gold beard with a small frown. "What should we drink to?"

"Ah. That's an easy one! Let us drink to you, Torbjörn! Your great skill has brought us so far, so safely, and your inspiring leadership has turned this frightened landlubber into someone who truly loves the sea! No small accomplishment, that!"

"I assure you, the pleasure was mine! Thank you, Pam! *Skål!*" They clinked their glasses, caught each other's eyes, and nodded in the ancient Swedish way, then downed the little glasses in one go.

The brandy was, indeed, very good. Pam felt its gentle fire fill her with a pleasant, lingering warmth. The gentle rocking of the ship was a delight, reminding her of the comfort of her grandmother's hand on her cradle, the waves, the sighs, and soft snores of the blissful dreamer. She was broken from her reverie by a niggle in the back of her neck. She looked up quickly to see that the tables had turned and it was Torbjörn now stealing a glance at her. She held in a giggle as he blushed, a cheery shade of red visible even in the soft flicker of starlight and lantern.

That's something new! And nice. Pam thought to herself as she rewarded him with an amiable smile, then turned back to the spectacle of the Southern sky to give the poor fellow a chance to compose himself. *So, this thing could go both ways. Don't say you don't want it to, Pammie.* She allowed herself a small grin— obviously, the balmy weather and that most excellent brandy had gone right to her head, and she didn't care .

Torbjörn cleared his throat, then proceeded to make a charmingly clumsy attempt at some conversation— whatever was in that lovely brandy had clearly had its way with him, too!

"So, Pam, I understand from Gerbald that you have a son back in Grantville. Any other, err, family?"

That almost did make Pam snort out a jolly laugh, but she was able to hold it in. Instead, she took a deep breath, and said nonchalantly, "Well, there's my mother and father, who are getting up in years now, and a hand-full of shirt-tail relatives. Sadly, most of the fun ones were left up-time." she paused then, for dramatic effect. "Then there's my EX-husband, Trent, but he's not really family anymore is he? Apart from being the father of my child, of course." she finished that bit with a radiant smile. *Find what you were looking for, oh mon capitan?*

Torbjörn nodded, eyebrows raised. His own attempt at nonchalant was a bit awkward, but it was cute, too, and kudos for trying.

"Ah." he paused there, not sure where to go next, but soldiering on anyway. "So, you say '*ex*-husband'. You are parted then?"

"Yes. Totally. Divorced. Long story short, we just didn't get on very well. He's basically a good guy, and there's no longer any real hard feelings, but yeah, we parted. It was hard on our son Walt. We waited until he was seventeen-years-old to go through with it, but it still hurt him. I'm afraid he doesn't like me too much these days, blames me, I suppose. He always was a difficult child . . . takes after his father." She turned to Torbjörn with a helpless shrug and a rueful grin. *What can you do?* "So, yeah. I had my heart broken. . . twice." She felt a tear forming at the bitter memories, but pushed it back in. She was a big girl now and big girls don't cry. Much.

Torbjörn's face was solemn as he nodded his understanding. "I am so sorry to hear. . . " another pause as he thought that one through, "You had such difficulties. It is not always easy with family, in any time, or any place." He fell silent, and Pam caught the look of pain that appeared in his eyes, not expecting to see such there. The ice had been broken, so she turned to him, and asked him in a low, gentle voice.

"Torbjörn, do you have family?"

He nodded his head for *yes*, then took a moment to find his voice. "Yes. I did. But not anymore."

Pam gazed at him as encouragingly as she could, the question remaining in her eyes. She knew some men had a hard time opening up and she was determined to be patient. After taking a deep breath of the mild, salty air he continued.

"My father was a fisherman, like all his people were, as were my mother's. They married late and had me in the autumn of their lives, cherishing me like a spring flower come to bloom in their garden. We were happy for a time, but when I was but ten-years-old they died in a coach accident, a terrible, unexpected thing, cruel fate. They were so wonderful and kind to me. I will remember them fondly always. My elderly uncle on my father's side was all I had left and he took me in. He was a good man, a bit gruff sometimes, but with a warm heart.

My uncle taught me the family trade and we fished together for many years. That was how I came to love the sea and ships. When I was just seventeen, I fell in love with the daughter of a farmer in a nearby village. She loved me as well and we were soon married. Her name was Anneke." he paused again, his expression a heart-breaking mix of both joy and grief. Pam waited for him to continue, radiating all the empathy she could muster toward him in what she hoped was a palpable wave. At last, he began again, the story spilling out of him like a breath held in too long.

"She was my joy. She was kind to my old uncle, who treated her as a daughter. When he died three years after she joined our little family, she sat with him all night, holding his hands and singing the old songs he loved. He passed away with a smile on his face, thanks to her. She was kind to all she met, and often came home with lost and wounded animals, even wild things. She would nurse them back to health, they never feared her because she had such a way about her. She was half a wild thing herself, she loved to run with me through the fields and forests, and swim with me in the summer sea. Never had I seen anyone so full of life and love!"

He paused again, a tear running down his face, catching the lantern-light like liquid amber, pausing at his cheek, the memory caught there for a seemingly eternal second before it rolled down into the night's shadows to join the sea below. Pam wanted to reach out to him, but didn't dare, not yet. He took another deep breath and continued, wanting now to get it all out, to release it into the soothing coolness of the night.

"It came as such a shock when she fell ill in our fifth year together. We had planned to start our family that year, but were robbed of that joy by her failing health. The physicians could do nothing. It was some foul disease that consumed her, that stole her away from me, creeping in the night. Like a flower in the winter garden, she withered, and crumpled, oh God, how it hurt me as I wanted to go with her! I held her in my arms as she died, her final breaths spent telling me how sorry she was to leave me so soon." His usually deep, seasoned voice sounded much like his younger self's voice must have, higher and softer, filled with pain, as he relived the tragedy.

He turned toward Pam, not trying to hide the tears on his face, owning them, letting them cleanse him as they were meant to do.

"I brought her to her people and we mourned her together. I signed over all my property and worldly goods to her brothers, except my uncle's fishing boat. With a last wave of farewell, I sailed away never to return. And so, the sea has been my home ever since, and my men my family." He smiled a little then, a small amount of relief now visible in his demeanor. He had needed to tell that story, needed to badly.

"Few have heard that tale, Pam. Thank you for listening."

Pam was moved deeply, her own heart breaking in sympathy with his. She reached out to take his hand then, squeezing softly in support, like an old friend would. It was strong and cool as he carefully squeezed back.

"Thank you, Torbjörn. I am honored you chose to share it with me. Your men are good men, the best. Gerbald and Dore are my family now, so much more than friends to me, more like the big brother and sister I never had. I am blessed."

"As am I. And now I feel I have made a new friend, a true friend, and let me say that I value her quite highly." He gave her hand another squeeze.

"You have indeed, sir, and right back at you! Just don't start thinking of me as a sister, all right?" His eyes went wide. She gave his hand a last squeeze, hard this time as if to say *I mean it, buddy*! They both laughed and she gave him a gentle sock on his arm as she left him to his bridge. It was time for bed. Much had been learned this night. Where it would lead, who could know? The trade winds would blow them where they would. Pam was satisfied with that. For now.

CHAPTER 10: BITTER WINDS

The leg of the journey around the Cape of Good Hope was a bit of a disappointment. They passed by far from shore, the vast wild of Southern Africa little more than a hazy green mass on the horizon. Pam had learned that in this time trade with the indigenous peoples of the coast had not yet begun in earnest, the bottom line being there was nothing they needed there, so why stop? Pam could think of a million reasons why they should, but the truth was none of them were directly related to their current mission. Giving the legendary 'dark continent' a last, longing look, she vowed she would set foot there one day, perhaps even on the voyage home.

Pam had come to understand their voyage had been a very, very lucky one so far. Long, certainly, but with favorable sailing conditions, fair weather, and no disasters along the way. Pam smiled ruefully at that last thought— no disasters *yet*. She could only pray their good fortune would continue to hold, especially now that, at long last, they were closing in on their destination.

The winds grew strong as they entered the famed Roaring Forties and they made excellent time. The days seemed to pass in the blink of an eye, *Redbird* fairly flying across the sparkling waves. Suddenly they were in the Indian Ocean and Pam's heart sang. They were almost there! Her joy was short-lived though, as the weather suddenly turned from fair to foul. Day after day, they fought their way through hair-raising swells. Pam felt as if she were back on the North Sea, the low, brooding gray skies a cold, wet blanket smothering the world.

Then, one magical morning, the captain announced they might sight Mauritius by afternoon, maybe even be able to land if all went well! Pam had become increasingly anxious over the long days of unpleasant pitching and rolling. The rough seas had dampened her mood, even though the sailors claimed they were happy there were such strong winds to push them along.

Pam welcomed the good news, of course, and did her best to break out of her pensive mood. Feeling cooped up in her cabin, she decided cruel waves and wind or not, she would spend the day keeping watch, unable to just sit and wait anymore. After a late breakfast from an ever-sympathetic Dore, Pam bundled up in her best foul weather gear to go stalk the decks, binoculars ever at the ready.

Topside, the crew was hard-focused on managing *Redbird* through the rough seas, except for young Pers, who was eager to climb into the crow's nest to help her keep vigil with his spyglass. The Bosun allowed it with a blithe shrug, while the first mate, sourpuss Mr Janvik, elected not to interfere, despite surely considering it a shameful waste of the lad's abundant energies. Pam looked up at the bridge to give Captain Torbjörn a hopeful smile, which he returned. He had dressed in a fancier than usual coat today, and cut a fine figure, which Pam did her best not to linger on too long— he truly was a handsome specimen of rugged manhood!

"Come on up, *Frau* Miller!" he called down with a friendly smile and wave, using her polite title as they were in public. She climbed the steep ladder-steps carefully, grateful to be that much higher above the bitter cold, splashing seas.

"I see you are eager to arrive, Pam." He switched to her first name now that she stood close, which had the pleasant effect of warming her up nicely despite the wind's chill gusts. "One hopes you have not grown unhappy with our service?"

"Oh, no, not at all, Torbjörn! You're wonderful! I mean, you and your crew, you're all wonderful!" *Gawd, you sound like a total dork!*

Torbjörn laughed, he had been teasing, and fully understood her desire to reach their destination without delay. "Of course, of course, it's been a long voyage!" he replied in a jovial tone. "I must admit I'm looking forward to some time on shore, maybe find some fresh fruit— not that *Frau* Dore's cooking isn't delicious, it's the best ship's fare ever! I don't imagine you would let me keep her on?" he asked, grinning in jest.

"No way, buddy, she's mine!" They shared a laugh, and Pam began to feel the knot of tension that had been forming in her shoulders ease. *We really are almost there! I can hardly believe it!*

"Dodos, here I come!" she said to herself, as the captain turned back to his duties.

The hours passed by slowly. Behind them, the weather from the South promised to turn surly, as black clouds built, and the temperature dropped a few degrees. The *Redbird* lagged a bit behind the rest of the fleet, sturdy *Muskijl* tread solidly along a mile ahead of them, a faithful shepherd herding the *Annalise* and *Ide* on before her. Their fleet may be few in number and made up of small vessels, but Pam now understood that they were also tough, the product of years of shipbuilding know-how in the wintry north. They were made for weather like this and took it in stride.

"That's a real demon storm brewing." The Bosun muttered when he came up on the bridge to confer with the captain.

"Looks no worse than a North Sea squall." the first mate said, his voice full of tedium.

The captain looked at the storm front slowly gaining on them and frowned. "Now it does, but this is the far south, and the weather's different down here, meaner. I've seen it like this before near Cape Horn. When she hits us tonight, she'll be full blowing all right, let's hope we're in the lee from it, behind the island."

As the weather worsened, Pam did her best to go unnoticed, hoping the captain wouldn't send her belowdecks. He and the pilot, sturdy Arne, both held the wheel steady, their eyes only for the waves. The southern sky took on a menacing darkness in stark contrast with the still-bright skies to the north. The afternoon was slipping away fast, the descending sun's rays slanted across *Redbird*, casting her in bronze as the shadows grew longer on her decks. Pam's eyes were aching from straining to see over the horizon, and she began to feel tired, regretting the foolishness of her long watch. She was just about to go find some tea, and possibly pour a little whiskey in it, when Pers' excited call came from above.

"There it is! The island! The island of the dodos!" Pam ran to the rail, fumbling to get her binocular straps untangled, the ceaseless rolling of the sea had a mysterious way of winding them up in knots. With her naked eye she saw something to the north, a blur of color above the horizon's distant curve. Focusing in with her trusty binoculars, provided a clear view of pastel lavender and green volcanic mountains rising majestically from the island's interior.

"Mauritius. At least that's what I'll call you until we give you a new name to go with your new destiny." Pam grinned up at Pers' pale face high in the crow's nest and waved crazily at him. Not letting go for a second, even to wave, he grinned back, letting out a loud whoop of joy. They were moving so fast with the blustery wind, the mountains continued to grow larger and higher above the horizon as she watched. Despite the storm trailing them, the captain deemed it safe enough, so Dore and Gerbald were summoned to join them on the bridge, where they grinned like children at the county fair, nearly half out of their minds with excitement. Gerbald brought along a bottle of schnapps to pass around, all were careful not to let the wave's ceaseless rocking spill any as they took their grateful sips.

Captain Nillson, whose eyes kept darting back to the foul weather to the Southwest, eventually caught their joyful mood. He told them in a pleased voice "Our colonists may be able to set foot on their new home this eve after all, if we can find a safe anchor before dark. We'll head up the east side. The storm is blowing from south by southwest, so we'll have more protection there. Your maps from the future show several suitable harbors, let's hope they prove right." The captain turned back to the wheel, well earned pride in his every move. Pam made herself stop staring at his broad shoulders and returned to the impromptu party at the rail. That was when they felt the ship take a jarring jolt that almost knocked the less experienced among them off their feet, accompanied by a sickening crunching sound. The *Redbird* started to heel over to port, losing speed and listing .

"*Jävla skit!*" the captain cursed, a rare event. "We've hit a snag! Get her righted and keep her steady for the west!"

"She's coming around sluggish, sir! I think whatever it was damaged our rudder!" Arne the pilot's voice was strained as he pulled on the wheel with all his strength. Arne was a very robust fellow, but showed the strain of his efforts. Another crewman, nimble Åke, leaped to his side to help.

Gerbald turned to Pam.

"We should get belowdecks, Pam, it would be safer there." He made a pointing motion with his chin, sending all their eyes to the storm that had been dogging their trail, now grown menacingly closer. Jagged streaks of lightning played across the massive wall of blackness. They could hear the thunder rumble even over the rush of the waves. The cruel, bitter winds continued to increase in force, blasting their bare faces raw and red.

"I'm not so sure about that." Pam said, her near-shout barely audible over the general din. " I want to stay here. I'd rather know what's happening than wait in the cabin. You two go down. I'll be all right."

Dore nodded. "The ship is damaged and a storm chases us. I will go to the galley and prepare emergency supplies, just in case."

"And I wish to gather up my gear and weapons. It's best if we be ready . . ."

Pam nodded her agreement. No one wanted to say what they were all thinking- *in case we have to abandon ship!*

Despite announcing their intention to leave her side, the two remained, looking to Pam for some signal they really had her approval. After a moment she figured this out and gave them both a gentle shove.

"Go, both of you! I am as safe with these guys as I would be with you. You're right, better we be prepared for the worst. Go, and be careful!"

Looking at her with worried faces, Dore and Gerbald hurried down the ladder.

The captain was barking orders, almost too fast for Pam to catch. He shouted at the first mate, "Janvik, go tell that fool Pers to come down from the rigging before he blows away!" sending the portly fellow scuttling down the ladder like an overgrown beetle.

Pam went to the rail, searching for the rest of the fleet. Pers came safely down from his perch, far too dangerous a place to be in weather such as this. He joined Pam at the rail, where she scanned the northeast with her binoculars. Pulling the birding scope out of the safety of his coat, he joined her with a young, keen eye. Behind them the men of the *Redbird* struggled with their injured ship.

"Bosun! Report!" the captain's voice was hoarse, carrying a tone of tension that Pam had never heard in it before. It was quickly becoming apparent that the situation was serious.

"Sir!" The Bosun was bent precariously over the stern rail attempting to see how bad the damage was. "It's not good, Captain! We barely have a rudder left. It's held together by splinters! The snag was a dirty big tree! Its branches are all snarled up in our keel. We're dragging the damned thing along with us!"

Inch by painful inch, the *Redbird* changed its course back to true, limping along at a sharply reduced speed.

"There! Pers shouted, "The fleet is nearing the island's southeast tip. They will be safely in the lee in a few more minutes!"

Pam tried to locate the fleet herself, but the ever-increasing power of the waves slamming into *Redbird*'s hull made it hard to focus.

"Well, that's something good, anyway!" The captain replied, his voice freighted with concern, "and damn blast our own terrible luck, there couldn't be a worst time to be disabled."

"Captain, the *Muskijl* is signaling with their lights! Just a moment . . ."

Another crewman, hulking Hake, joined him at the rail, bringing the ship's signal light with him which he handed to Pers, who was clever with such things, before hurrying to lend his considerable strength to holding the crippled wheel steady.

"The *Muskijl* wants to know if they can render assistance?" Pers' face, which was naturally quite pale, appeared positively ghostly now in the wan light of the dying day.

Captain Nillson bit his upper lip as was his habit when deep in thought. After a moment, he shook his head, his bright-blue eyes grown dark with regret.

"No. Tell them to take *Analise* and *Ide* to safe harbor. We will follow as best we can. If we don't make it to them, they must wait until this storm has blown out before searching for us. That's an order!"

Torbjörn held the position of fleet captain for the mission, making him the highest-ranking officer among them. The captain of the *Muskijl* wouldn't like it, not at all, but he would do as ordered.

Pam held the rail with one hand, the other clutching her binoculars as she strained to see if the fleet had reached safety. She was struggling to keep on her feet. The high seas grew increasingly violent as the storm caught them. The captain saw her clumsy movements and scowled.

"Blast it all, woman, put away that contraption and hold fast! I'd tell you to get below, but at least up here, I can keep an eye on you!"

Pam nodded and did as she was ordered, flattered the captain (*Torbjörn!*) would want to see to her safety personally. She was beginning to feel sick, not just from the movement of the sea, but from her own guilt. They were in real danger now, risking their lives, all for that damned dodo! The worst thing was, there was nothing she could do but watch. She fought back helpless tears as her pale and bloodless hands gripped the *Redbird*'s cold, wet rails.

The wind shrieked through the rigging like an army of lost souls now, sending a chill through her heart as cold as the Antarctic seas that had spawned this maelstrom. The sun was still up, just barely, a glowering orange disc poised to slip over the horizon at any second, but before it could, the darkness arrived, enveloping them in an instant as if a sackcloth had been pulled over them. The storm had arrived in all its terrible glory, howling and blasting them with untamed Antarctic wrath.

"We've got to find safe harbor before this gale blows us up on the rocks!" Janvik yelled over the nearly deafening roar.

"If the rudder holds, we have a chance!" The captain rejoined the sailors at the wheel, where they barely held *Redbird* on course, using all their strength.

Redbird pitched like a roller coaster, cold spray drenching them. Pam saw Mauritius drawing closer, dimly lit by the dusk, the waves pushing them toward frothing shores.

"Pam! Come to me!" The captain called to her. She left her place by the rail to stand before him, steadied by one of his strong arms grasping hers. He was dripping wet, his muscles trembling from the cold and the strain of man-handling the damaged rudder. "There is a chance we may have to abandon *Redbird*. Best to prepare for the worst! Don't tarry! Gather only what is absolutely necessary from your cabin, *quickly*! Then, I want the three of you beside the ship's first longboat, understood?" She looked over toward the rail to see the two pinnaces, longboats rigged with both sails and oars for scouting and shore excursions. They also served as lifeboats when the need arose, and as such were being hurriedly prepared by an increasingly frantic crew. Between them, there would be enough space to fit the entire crew, albeit uncomfortably.

"Yes, sir!" she shouted back over the roaring wind. Their eyes locked for a moment, summer-sky blue to wintry gray. Torbjörn managed a smile for her. "Fear not, my friend! Who knows what fate awaits? My crew and I have faced many a fierce squall in our time, and I'm sure we can weather through the Southern Ocean's rage just as well as we have the North's." Pam sensed he wasn't as hopeful as he meant to sound, but she returned his smile . That having satisfied him, he gave her arm an encouraging squeeze before releasing her, then turned back to aid in the struggle with the ever more unresponsive wheel.

Pam realized that she had wanted him to do much more than squeeze her arm. There had been something building between them for quite a while now, despite her best efforts to pretend otherwise. Unfortunately, now was not the time for such distracting thoughts, so she swept them off into the corners of her mind as she always did, but with more than a tinge of regret . To her surprise, she believed what Torbjörn had said, and she smiled again despite the grave danger unfolding around her. *We are going to survive this.... We must!*

Garrett W. Vance

CHAPTER 11: *REDBIRD DOWN*

Pam hurried down the ladder as carefully as she could. Everything was made slippery by the crashing sea and the icy rains that had come to join the winds. After a slippery journey across the bucking ship, she reached the hatchway to half-climb, half-slide down the ladder stairs to the lower decks.

Gerbald and Dore, who had been appraised of the situation by Pers, emerged from their cabin, each loaded with copious amounts of baggage—Dore's back-up food supply! Pam had thought her friend was being overzealous and a bit paranoid in dragging all that stuff aboard, but maybe Dore had been right all along. Gerbald wore a large, lumpy backpack containing his weapons and gear and held a large suitcase in each hand. Pam recalled one held two fifty-pound bags, one each of flour and sugar, which he carried as if they hardly weighed a thing! He was a strong man, and no doubt this was bolstered by the surge of adrenaline coursing through their veins. Dore had a variety of smaller bags on straps slung across her back and shoulders, while she held the big soup cauldron from Pam's kitchen clutched to her chest like a precious infant.

Pam caught her breath and told them "The captain says to wait beside the ship's first boat. I need to go get my things."

"I will go!" Gerbald told her.

"No, you stay with Dore! You're already loaded down. I'm smaller and I can move faster—three minutes! Now you two, *git!*" Pam ran down the water-slickened narrow passageway to her cabin without slipping, then ducked into her cabin just as a huge wave hit the ship. She was thrown against the wall as *Redbird* listed hard again. She hit her elbow right on the funny bone, which was never very funny at all. Gasping with pain, she pushed herself toward her desk. Things were getting worse out there. "I have seconds, only seconds," she muttered.

Her trusty rucksack waited for her, holding her most precious gear. *Good thing I thought to always be prepared for disaster! I wish I wasn't right about things so much.* She stuffed her now damp notes from the desk and her pencil box in; everything else was replaceable. Her flashlight was on her bed; she grabbed it just as the boat listed again, this time throwing her to the wet and sloshing floor. The small portal in the outer wall had popped open and rain and sea water were pouring through it at an alarming rate. She saw her grandmother's walking stick lying on the bed, sadly it would have to be left behind, there was no way she could hang onto it and get herself back topside, she would need both hands to navigate the dangerously tossing path. She shoved the flashlight into her rucksack, zipped it shut, and shrugged it onto her back. She was standing in eight inches of cold seawater now. The ship was taking on water at an ever increasing rate. It was well past time to go!

Topside the scene was mayhem. The waves were driving them closer and closer to the rocky shores of the island while the sailors scrambled to prevent that dire outcome. Dore and Gerbald had only just now finished dragging their luggage onto the deck. Their grim faces brightened with relief at the sight of Pam's safe arrival. Grabbing on to whatever they could find to steady themselves, they made their way across the bucking deck to the far rail.

As they neared the pinnaces, their path was suddenly blocked by First Mate Janvik, his scowling face resembling a puckered sour apple, slightly green in the spectral light of the storm.

"What is all *this*?" he demanded, motioning brusquely at Dore and Gerbald's baggage. "It is too much, leave it behind!" he ordered, his voice hoarse from shouting over the buffeting winds.

Gerbald started to speak, but Dore muscled her way past him to stand before the officious officer, bringing her own formidable scowl to bear just inches from his face, which now looked more surprised than surly.

"THIS, Herr Janvik, is FOOD! And if it doesn't go on that little boat, then neither do I!" Her entire, very sturdily built form bristling with outrage, she moved even closer into the hapless fellow's personal space. He was not a tall man, and her nose almost touched his as she waited for a reply.

Pam knew Dore had a way with the man. The little treats she passed to him on the sly had earned her a high place on the very short list of people the man was civil to. Blowing a puff of disgusted air from his paunchy cheeks he relented, stepping aside with a shrug.

"Very well, Frau Dore, you shall have it your way." the bluster had gone out of his voice and his shoulders slumped. Pam realized the man was close to exhaustion and felt a twinge of pity for him. "You have fed our men, and me, very well." Janvik told her, rare praise indeed! "I pray you will be able to continue to do so under whatever conditions await you on that island." Some small amount of his commanding demeanor returned and he barked "Now, get on that first boat and don't make me tell you twice!"

Dore very unexpectedly favored him with a butter-melting smile, then went so far as to pat him gently on the cheek, which turned the apple green to rosy red. "I always knew you are a good fellow Jens. God bless you!" With that she continued toward the waiting boats like a steamer under full power. Gerbald and Pam fell into step behind Dore, drawn along in her wake.

A rather nonplussed Gerbald turned to an equally surprised looking Pam.

"Jens?" he asked in an incredulous tone, hardly believing what he had just heard.

"I always thought his first name was '*Herr*'." Pam replied, shaking her head in shared wonderment. They both shrugged and continued. Life at sea was certainly full of surprises.

Gerbald helped the marines load the pinnaces while the sailors struggled to keep *Redbird* alive. Pam could barely see the captain through the rain and darkness. Another rumbling, crashing sound joined the thunder, the impact of massive waves on cliffs. Mountainous Mauritius towered over them like an unfriendly giant, illuminated by eerie flashes of blue lightning.

The Bosun arrived, his usually cheery face grim and lined with worry.

"The captain has decided!" he shouted in a voice much practiced to being heard above inclement weather "We are abandoning ship! All hands to the pinnaces!"

The sailors, their struggles pointless now, bleakly dropped what they were doing to make ready for launch. Pam couldn't imagine how this was going to work in these wild seas. She told herself to breathe, and to trust in these good souls who had befriended her on their long voyage together. She was frightened, and angry at this cruel whim of fate, but there was no time for that now. She must focus on each moment or it may become her last.

"Come, my friends, get in, get in!" The Bosun ordered Pam's group, reaching to help them into the swaying boat. Pam pushed her friends ahead of her. The first mate was holding tight to one of the lines, his face gray with the strain, trying to keep the pinnace steady.

"The captain!" Pam cried, looking back at the man who now stood alone at the nearly useless wheel, buying them what time he could before the rocks could take her. "Captain!" she shouted, frantically trying to get his attention. *"Torbjörn!"* she called again, now nearly a shriek, no longer trying to keep the rising panic from her voice.

He waved them off. "Go, go now! Pam, you must go!" His words were barely audible over the crashing seas.

Garrett W. Vance

"He has his duty, Pam, you can't help him! Now get in or we all die here!" The Bosun implored her. With a firm hand, he pulled the reluctant Pam into the swinging pinnace. The small craft bucked and leaped on its lines. Dore grabbed her struggling friend in a bear hug and forcibly dragged her the rest of the way, using all her strength and considerable mass. They collapsed into a heap in the boat's bottom on top of the baggage. Gerbald arched himself over them, trying to stay out of the way of the sailors as well as using his own bulk to prevent the women from being pitched out. Pers arrived next, clutching his precious spyglass, his young face pale and full of fear.

They were lowered swiftly into the fast-moving water, which caused them to bounce even more. The sailors and marines who had handled the ropes on deck now clambered down them into the pinnace, while others readied themselves at the oars, their movements fluid and confident despite the raging waves. Having finally freed herself from Dore's frantic embrace, Pam, tears running down her face, looked up at Janvik, who was still on deck, but backing away from the rail— he made no move to climb down the rope to join them. Now that he had seen the boat and its precious cargo safely lowered, Pam knew what he was going to do. *Down with the ship! That's what they do, isn't it? Down with the damn ship!* He looked at Pam and favored her with a smile, the first she had ever seen upon his thin lips.

"May God be with you, *Frau* Miller. Make our dear princess happy, she has suffered much." With a swipe of his knife, he cut the last line connecting the pinnace to *Redbird* .

Seeing the true courage in the man revealed for the first time, Pam called back to him as loudly as she could as the waves carried the pinnace away from the *Redbird*, her voice fraught with emotion "Thank you, *Herr* Janvik! I will do as you ask! Dore is right, you are a *very* good man!" The first mate smiled again, then with a sketch of a wave he hurried to join his captain at the wheel.

The nimble craft moved rapidly, steadier now that she was free of the ship and fully manned. They rowed fast in well-practiced unison, carried along by the marching swells, surfing the waves like the outrigger canoe in that old crime drama, *Hawaii Five-0*. Perversely, the show's catchy theme song began to play in Pam's mind, and she wondered for a moment if she would wake up on her sofa in front of the TV, all of this just an awful dream.

"Thank the Lord! The cliffs stop here, there's a beach. Make for it!" The Bosun shouted. The sailors and marines rowed for their very lives, silent and determined to beat the hungry sea.

Pam grasped the gunwale and pulled herself up for a better look. The other pinnace was close behind them. She could see *Redbird* through the darkness and sheets of rain, flash after flash of lightning illuminating her in a spectral light, some of her lanterns still lit despite the gale, looking like a ghost ship from the old tales. As poor *Redbird* spun about and rolled precariously, she caught a glimpse of the massive, water-logged tree that had fouled its gnarled black roots in her rudder, then bludgeoned a gaping hole in her hull's bottom. No wonder she had grown so sluggish! It was a bullet through the very heart of her.

The captain and first mate were still trying to steer the damaged vessel away from the rocky point toward the same possibility of safety, but an unseen rock caught her, and to Pam's utter horror, sent her over on her side. Pam couldn't see if the two courageous men had time to leap free or not. With the next mighty wave, the *Redbird* rolled completely upside-down. The sound of her wood scraping and splintering against the rocks was the screeching din of all the damned in Hell. Pam screamed over the gale, her voice lost in the curtains of rain that now mercifully hid the wreck of the *Redbird* from view. Gerbald and Dore held her tightly in their strong, loving arms.

Pam willed herself to breathe. *Get back in control, woman!* some strangely cool part of her mind ordered as she gasped and shivered in her friend's protective embrace. Grief would have to wait. Their troubles were not over. Sweeping twelve-foot rollers pounded against the narrow beach. Landing would be dangerous.

The Bosun shouted to the frightened passengers and crew, "We are going to try to bring her all the way in, but it's ugly—if we go over, you'll have to swim to shore !"

Pam looked down to see Dore's face was white and filled with fear, a sight that Pam would have given anything never to have witnessed.

"I can't swim!" Dore blurted out, a trace of sob in her voice that brought a gush of fresh tears from Pam's eyes. Thankfully, Dore couldn't see them as they were lost among the ceaseless raindrops.

"I can swim for both of us, don't worry!" Pam shouted back, injecting a tone of confidence into her voice. Pam was in the grip of clutching fear, fear of an intensity she hadn't felt since she stood between a badly wounded Gerbald and an evil man wielding a bloodstained sword, with just her grandmother's walking stick to defend them both. She lived through that, won that battle—maybe she would live through this, too. The thought helped quell the worst of the terror.

The pinnace and her frightened passengers sped toward the shore, its white sands lit by cobalt lightning like a haunted dance floor under a phantasmal strobe. The Bosun ordered the men to row harder as he used the tiller to guide the craft over the treacherous waves. Pam clutched Dore, and Gerbald clutched them both, grimly ready to swim if they must. The Bosun let out a whoop that had something of joy in it, as he turned the pinnace quickly to starboard.

Through the rain and darkness Pam could see the shore at that edge of the wide
cove was somewhat protected by a jutting wall of rock, another arm of the same
rocky point that had destroyed the *Redbird* farther out. If they could make it to
the calmer waters, the chances of landing the boat would improve. If they
didn't, they would crash against the very rock that could save them.

"Get ready to jump if I say so. It's going to be close!" The Bosun bellowed
over the storm and hollow booms of the waves slamming onto the shore. The
sailors heaved mightily on their oars at the Bosun's hoarse commands, now
surfing again along the face of an awesome wave, growing menacingly taller as it
reached the shallows. The rock wall loomed ahead of them, waves crashing
against it in foaming white fury.

"Steady . . . steady . . . Now, hard to starboard, men, *heave!*" The nose of
the pinnace jumped to the right, well away from the approaching rocks. The
boat bounced dangerously across an area of roiling, white-streaked water
deflected from the rock face. "Now, hard port!" The Bosun shouted with all his
might to be heard over the crashing waves. With a roller coaster flutter in their
stomachs, they slid over the hump of a smooth swell and into a patch of
relatively calm water in the lee of the rock wall. "Brace yourselves!" The prow of
the pinnace hit this gravelly section of beach hard, but stayed upright. "Jump to
shore, hurry!"

Gerbald pulled Pam and Dore up by their arms and guided them to the
prow, Pam leaping first. There were larger rocks mixed in with the gravel. She
felt one scrape the side of her leg and knew it had drawn blood. She turned to
help Dore, still clutching her wicker basket. She landed with a heavy "*Ooomph*",
but managed to stay upright. They were up to their knees in clutching, fast-
moving water that almost knocked them over, but Gerbald had arrived, and he
used his solid strength to keep them on their feet. Pam was towed along, her
arm in his powerful grip. Soon the three of them were above the tideline,
standing amongst driftwood and the hearty kind of low brush that thrives along
the edges of beaches. Gerbald ran across the gravelly sand to help the men
secure the pinnace. The sailors had lines out and were dragging the boat safely
away from the angry sea.

As they worked, the second pinnace came in, running aground at almost
the same spot. Pam blew out a held-in-breath in relief. Both boats had made it
safely to refuge. She squinted through the rain at Gerbald, and the sailors and
marines at work, almost grateful for the eerie flashes of lightning that played
across the scene. She wanted to help, but how? She realized with relief, she still
had her rucksack and doffed it, fumbling until she found the flashlight. She
handed the bag to a still-stunned Dore and said, " Find shelter in those trees just
above the beach!" She ran to the waterline, following the narrow, but powerful

beam through the driving rain. Reaching the men, she tried to aim the flashlight at places she thought would help the most, feeling heartened by their thanks. Eventually, they had both boats just past the high tide line, secured to the sturdiest trees and rocks they could find.

With this vital matter accomplished, they opened water-tight compartments containing emergency supplies. Mård and Pers delivered Dore's food-filled baggage where she sat hunkered under the fronds of a young palm tree. This brought a small smile to her exhausted face, a good sign to Pam's eyes. Dore was strong and she would be on her feet again shortly! With a determined look on her face, Dore began to dig through her portable larder, no one would go hungry this night!

The men gathered in a relatively flat area of grass among the wind-twisted shrubs and small trees that lined the shore beneath rows of towering palms swaying like hula dancers in the howling wind. After a short conversation as to its merits, it was decided they would erect their shelter there. Pam and Gerbald did their best to help the sailors set up camp, using one of the pinnace's spare sails draped over lines tied between trees as a rain tarp. An oil lamp sprang to life, lighting the surroundings in a heart-breakingly warm glow. Pam could now see the faces of the sailors and soldiers she had come to count among her friends. They were exhausted and fearful, but there was relief there, too; they would live to see the dawn. Suddenly, Pam remembered the captain and the first mate left behind. She came to her feet, feeling saltwater still sloshing in the toes of her boots.

"Get up! Get up! We have to search the shore for the captain and the first mate!" Pam told them. The weary men looked at her for a long moment. There was little hope in their eyes. Some of the marines started to stand even before their officer, *Löjtnant* Lundkvist could growl at them. The sailors stirred, but it was plain they were exhausted.

The Bosun's gravelly voice cut through the noise of the raging storm. "*Frau* Pam is right. Move your arses, you lazy sots! We have a duty to perform." As one, the sailors rose to their feet, stifling groans. If there were any chance of finding the first mate and the captain alive, it must be now.

Dore stood and announced "I will make us a supper and keep Mård to assist me. You will all need something to eat to regain your strength after a night like this."

The wet, weary men gave her a grateful murmur of thanks as they shuffled back out into the night's cold rains. Pam favored her friend with an encouraging smile as she ducked out from under the tarp. Her doughty Dore was back and working, a glimmer of good in all this night of loss and pain. *Better to be like Dore and stay busy, Pammie, because if you start to think too much about what's happened here you will lose it, and not be of any help to anyone.* The thought of the captain, her friend, and possibly the beginning of something more, sent a knife of regret into her heart, but the painful slap of the cold, rain-filled gale made her keep moving. *Please, oh please let him be alive!*

* * *

The cove was about a mile long. The gravel turned to softer sand as they left the rocky edge where they had landed. The waves had calmed, but were still dangerous. They made their way slowly through the darkness, fighting the fierce wind, forming a line from as near the pounding surf as they dared, up to the highest elevation the storm waves had reached. Two men carried lanterns, one at the high tideline, and one halfway down to the water. Pam, walked between Gerbald and the Bosun, as near the rushing waters as they could, scanned the surf with her flashlight. Pam tried not to think about the long-handled spade the Bosun carried, and what its purpose might be.

Flotsam and jetsam from the wreck of the *Redbird* were beginning to wash up on the shore. Anything that might be useful, such as planks and pieces of rigging, the men placed on the coarse grass out of the tide's reach. A brief cheer went up as they recovered a large cask of potent Swedish *snaps* liquor. The far end of the beach ended in a jumble of massive volcanic rocks, making further exploration this night impossible. On the way back to camp they found a few more odds and ends, but no bodies, much to Pam's relief. Maybe the captain and the first mate had escaped the wreck and survived, safe elsewhere up the island's coast. It was a faint hope, but better than none at all.

At their makeshift camp, they were surprised to find a roaring driftwood fire blazing a safe distance from their shelter, being carefully fed by vigilant Mård. The storm had almost blown itself out and the rain had stopped. Dore was clucking over the old cast iron skillet Pam had given her so long ago. It sizzled on a bed of coals. The heavenly scent of pancakes wafted toward them, mingled with the fine perfume of wood smoke.

"Good gravy, Dore, how on earth did you get a fire started in all that rain?"

"Oh, that was nothing, Pam. Remember that I was once a camp follower. I have lived outdoors for months on end thanks to that oaf there." She gave a haughty tilt of her chin to Gerbald, who returned it with his usual shrug of guilty-as-charged resignation. "I always keep flint and steel in my apron pockets and we found plenty of dry tinder under all that driftwood. It was a snap!" The last line was in English, and she snapped her fingers loudly to punctuate her American vernacular. "Now, you men gather round and get dry, but don't kick sand on my cakes or I'll have your hides!" There was a murmur of assent as the exhausted men encircled Dore's bonfire. Soon they were eating the simple pancakes Dore had concocted with the help of her big wicker basket and the prodigious portable pantry she had rightfully insisted be brought along. Dore was not a woman to be caught unprepared! The pancakes were a little brown on the outside, and a little mushy on the inside, and absolutely delicious.

After dinner, all the men, sailors and marines, huddled together under the sail's shelter to begin a rigorous cleaning of their weapons and metal tools. It was vital to remove any sea salt from the firearms right away. From somewhere in the infinite secret pockets of his sage-green Jäger's longcoat, Gerbald pulled out an up-time gun cleaning kit, which he shared with the grateful Swedes. Pam watched him deftly clean the "Snakecharmer" pistol-grip shotgun her son Walt had given him. His touch was noticeably tender. Pam had seen it before, the fanatical love men had for their guns. As she listened to the wind whisper through the fronds of the shore palms here, so far from home, on an unexplored shore at the other end of the planet, it was a comforting sight.

The important ritual of gun cleaning accomplished, and with a hot meal in their bellies, they all found places on the matted grass beneath the sail tent to curl up. Despite the chill damp, most soon slept the deep and silent sleep of those who have faced death and lived.

Pam stayed awake sitting by the fire, watching the flames dance in the wavering breeze still blowing in from the unquiet sea, occasionally feeding it with another gnarled piece of sun-bleached driftwood. Under decent circumstances, she would have reveled in spending the night on an exotic island, but now she just felt lost, a castaway in a hostile environment. Even surrounded by her closest friends and a group of highly trusted men, a desperate loneliness overtook her. Deep down in her heart she felt she was still a woman out of time and out of place.

CHAPTER 12: ON THE BEACH

Pam awoke just before sunrise to find Dore preparing breakfast. She had cleverly arranged a pile of black, volcanic stones into a simple oven and was using it to bake what looked like muffins. Pam decided the woman was a miracle worker. Nearby, Gerbald, *Löjtnant* Lundkvist, and the Bosun conferred about their situation while the sailors and soldiers slowly roused themselves. Pam, her legs and back stiff from the lack of a mattress, lurched over to join them. The Swedes greeted her warmly, glad that she was up and about, while Gerbald flashed her a grin.

"Look, Pam, it is just like in *The Swiss Family Robinson*, isn't it? We are marooned on a desert island! How thrilling!" Gerbald told her in a far too chipper tone, obviously hoping to cheer her up, but only succeeding in annoying her thoroughly.

"Back off, Man Friday, I ain't had no coffee." Pam answered in a menacing croak. Gerbald nodded solemnly at her caffeine emergency, but didn't lose his smile. He always seemed delighted with adversity, often to Pam and Dore's chagrin.

Dore gave Pam a very apologetic look. "Pam, I am so sorry. All the coffee was in the galley and is now lost in the storm."

"It's not your fault, Dore! You have gone way beyond the call of duty! Look at this breakfast, it's fantastic!" All those gathered murmured their sincere agreement. Dore went back to her ceaseless work, satisfied that she had done everything she could to ensure they had food to eat, and under very dangerous circumstances to boot.

Pam turned to the Bosun. "Any idea where we are, *Herr* Bosun?"

The stout, windburned Swede scratched at his gray-streaked, red beard. He used a stick to draw a rough map in the sand.

"Not with perfect accuracy mind you, *Frau* Pam, but I have some idea. We were approaching the southern tip of our destination when the storm struck. Our progress was slowed by the snag and we were taking on water. So, we are somewhere on the south coast of Mauritius, not far from its western side. Even after looking at the up-time maps I can't tell exactly where. They show very little of the island's topography. We might be somewhere between the up-time towns of Souillac and Le Souffler, but that is just a guess." The sun could now be seen poking its head above the green hills that stretched along the coast to their east.

"What do you think became of the rest of our fleet?"

The Bosun hesitated, giving the impression he didn't even dare to hazard a guess. *Löjtnant* Lundkvist saw this and stepped in to assist.

"*Frau* Pam, when last sighted the colony ships were fleeing the storm, heading for the island's east coast. They would have been looking for a sheltered harbor and there are several possibilities on the maps . . . we can hope they made it that far."

The unknown fate of the fleet caused them all to fall silent, concern for the colonists weighing heavily on their minds. Did they make it? Were they better or worse off than lost *Redbird* and her crew? Would they be able to find each other in this wilderness? It was a large and wild island. It might be another year or more, before anyone friendly came visiting, if ever, and for the moment they were very much on their own.

"What if we sent a pinnace up the coast to search for them, Nils?" she asked the Bosun.

The man sighed sadly. "Of course, we have considered this, *Frau* Pam. The problem is we are at the change of the seasons here, and the weather is highly unpredictable. It's safe enough for us to tool around our cove, yes, but embarking on a longer journey would be very risky. What if a storm blew up while our little pinnace was up against a rocky coast? More lives lost, I would fear. My best advice is to wait at least a few weeks for the storm season to die down before we try such a thing." Nils shrugged a helpless shrug, his mournful expression made bitter by its out of place appearance on his usually jolly, round face.

Pam nodded her understanding, politely, before falling into a deep brooding. She was filled with a helpless anger at their situation, her entire mission had been thrown completely out of whack, possibly even doomed. She made herself unclench her fists and looked around at the three men. She realized they were waiting for her to say something more. Why were they waiting for her? The Bosun's melancholy, hazel eyes watched her. Yes, this was a man awaiting orders, a man ready to go to work. More surprising, she felt the same vibe from the *Löjtnant*. It occurred to her that with the captain and first mate missing, it was *she* who was ostensibly in charge, the brilliant up-time lady scientist appointed to lead the expedition by their beloved princess. *Oh, Hell! I don't want this job!* All Pam wanted to do was curl up under a tree and cry herself to sleep. With a kind of mental shove, she made herself look up, knowing it was up to her to *do* something.

"All right, then. Thank you, gentlemen. We must hold on to hope that *Muskijl, Analise,* and *Ide* found safe harbor. We may be shipwrecked, but we aren't completely lost. At least we know what island we're on! At some point, either our comrades will come find us, or we will go find them. For the moment, let's remain calm and do what we must to survive while we ponder our next move." *That actually sounded pretty good!* "First off, I think we should make another sweep of the beach to see if anything else has washed up overnight." She had hung on that word "anything" for a second longer than she wanted to, thinking of what things might have arrived with the tide that she might not want to see. "We are going to need fresh water. Gerbald, can you take that on? This sure isn't Germany, but you're the best woodsman we've got."

"Of course, Pam. We may be far from home, but this is still the world of our birth, and where there is greenery, there is water. I will find it."

"Good. As my daughter-in-law Crystal would say, 'You the man.'" They shared a quick smile and Pam began to feel better. It was a small, weak kind of better, but still a step in the right direction. The Swedes were already heading off to organize the search party. She called after the Bosun.

"*Herr* Bosun, can we take one of the pinnaces out to see what's left of the *Redbird?*"

"Yes," he said, coming back to her side "but we must wait for a better tide. Right now, it is too shallow. See the coral reefs out there? In a few hours, the tide will come in and we can go. While we wait, I will send the men down the beach."

"Taking the pinnace out to the wreck, that's exactly what they did in *Swiss Family Robinson!*" Gerbald was back to his ridiculously boyish delight in being marooned. "I do wish I had that book with me now." He sounded like this was all a cheerful Sunday picnic, earning him a roll of the eyes from both Pam and the Bosun. Gerbald had been trained as a forester in his youth, so for him this was nothing to worry about, just one big campout. Compared to his later years as a professional soldier in a terrible, blood-drenched war, she supposed it was.

Pam turned to the grizzled seaman. "Thanks, *Herr* Bosun. When you go, I want to come along. I have to see how bad it is with my own eyes . . . it was kind of my ship, too, you know?"

"I understand completely, *Frau* Pam. I am so sorry we lost her for you. It is a shame I and all our men feel most strongly. Today the seas are calm and I believe it will be safe enough. And now, to work." The Bosun, with tasks to accomplish before him, sounded almost like his old cheerful self as he rousted the still-sleepy men to give them their orders.

Gerbald stayed with Pam a minute longer, his always startling blue eyes regarding her calmly from beneath his monstrous mustard-colored hat, which had unfortunately survived the wreck along with him. Pam met that stare with her own stormy gray eyes and asked in a bit of a surly tone, "What?"

Gerbald, either oblivious or immune to her dark mood (likely a side effect of his marriage to the often fearsome Dore), flashed her a truly sunny smile. "I am pleased to see you are adjusting to these unfortunate new circumstances so quickly, Pam! You are truly the toughest, and most resourceful woman I have ever met, excepting Dore, of course. There is no one else I would rather be shipwrecked with . . . except perhaps Ginger and Mary-Anne." he added with a dreamy look on his face and a wishful sigh.

Pam flipped him that singular bird one doesn't find in any field guides and marched off to join in the search.

CHAPTER 13: THE FLOOD MAY BEAR ME FAR

Not long after dawn, the sailors raised a shout from down the beach. Pam and the Bosun rushed over to see they had discovered an old shipwreck high above the tideline. There wasn't much left intact, just a rotting, wooden skeleton. Nearby, pieces of it looked like they might once have been removed and used to make a temporary shelter.

"Apparently we are not the first to sail or wreck on this shore," The Bosun said, looking around the scene carefully.

"How long do you think it's been here?" Pam asked, a note of concern in her voice. Did they have neighbors?

"I have seen a lot of ships and a lot of wrecks in my time, too many of the latter I regret to say, but it's impossible to say for sure. The vessel's wood might be cedar, which could explain how well-preserved it is. From the overall condition, I'd make these pieces to be around a-hundred-years-old. Just a guess, mind you." The Bosun cast his eye around the scene with a worried expression on his face. "Still, we can't be sure we are alone here. No one should go wandering off, although I don't see any signs of recent activity. Best to play it safe, though." Pam was not comforted.

After a bit of digging around the decaying hulk, Pers let out a whoop of discovery. Full of youthful vigor he soon unearthed around two hundred pounds of wax bricks ensconced in a hollow under a heavy beam. To their surprise, each bore some kind of inscription.

"This looks like Arabic to me, but I'm no expert." Pam said. The Bosun nodded, squinting at the strange script.

The men made a thorough search of the area, but nothing else of use or interest was found. The Bosun ordered the men to carry the bricks and whatever lengths of wood that might still be usable to camp. Looking back at the abandoned shelter, he told Pam "Perhaps they were rescued!" with a well-meaning attempt at good cheer.

"There's a good thought. We must think positively." *Easier said than done. I have to stay busy or I'm going to go nuts.* Pam put six of the odd wax bricks into her own bag, feeling they might prove useful. Having been too uptight to eat earlier that morning, she returned to camp to see what kind of miracle her friend had produced for breakfast.

First, Pam gave most of the wax to Dore to see if she could find any use for it, keeping one brick for herself as a souvenir. Dore was well pleased. "Candles!" she exclaimed and began to bustle about looking for the right pot to melt them in and something to use for wicks.

"There's a lot more where these came from, the men found them on an old shipwreck. Nothing else there, nor any signs of life."

"Still, a lucky find, we shall have light through the night now, if we wish it."

Pam sat down cross-legged in the sand under the sun-dappled shade of the palms, studying her mysterious prize. *So, others have been here before us.* She wasn't sure if that was a comfort or not. She also mused they were most likely going melt an important archaeological find, but pushed the thought aside. Their survival came first. Dore handed her a muffin on a plate of plantain leaf. At the moment, none of the various fruits growing in abundance around the camp were ripe, but Pam looked forward to the day. She had loved plantains since her holiday in the Caribbean and there weren't any to be had in Thuringia-Franconia. *The plus side of being marooned, I guess.*

Pam ate her muffin slowly. It was utterly delicious, seasoned with a bit of sugar, nutmeg, and cinnamon, just enough to fill her growling belly. She had to laugh a little, as she had thought Dore mad for dragging the contents of Pam's kitchen spice cabinet along on the voyage. Thank the Lord she had! The only real problem was coffee, or the terrible lack of it. Her head still felt fuzzy inside even though she had been up and about for hours and there was a dull ache at her temples. These were the same telltales signs of caffeine withdrawal she had experienced in the first year after the Ring of Fire, before Grantville had come into a fairly reliable supply of the blessed bean. It would take a few more days, but the feeling would pass. There was always the hope they would be rescued by the rest of the fleet by then, but she wouldn't let herself think too hard about that.

Pam stood up from her place near the fire and tied the red cotton handkerchief from her back pocket over her head. The sky was the extra deep cerulean seen after a storm has passed and the climbing sun promised to be hot. It felt like it was already around eighty-degrees Fahrenheit, and it couldn't be much later than ten in the morning. The sea glowed the intense aqua of tropical waters. The sapphire sparkles at the surface were nearly blinding to behold.

At least it was beautiful here, which made Pam begin to feel just slightly better, the awesome pageantry of nature pushing her many worries to the back of her mind. *Its a nice day, just enjoy it for what it is.* She made herself get up, thank Dore, then wander down the beach to rejoin the sailors in the ongoing search and salvage operation. Down by the water's edge, the sea was as gentle as a lamb now that the lion winds had ceased their roaring, so she took off her socks and boots and walked barefoot across firm pale sand, wading through the lapping wavelets.

From Pam's point of view the pickings were fairly slim, but the men seemed pleased by every broken barrel and tangled mess of rope they recovered. The sailors found a saw and wood-working tools packed in a water-tight wooden crate that had washed up. They held a brief, whooping celebration at such excellent luck.

The tide was all the way out now and just beginning to turn. They could now pass by the jumble of boulders at the cove's far end and go on to the next stretch of beach beyond. The low tide revealed a wide muddy flat dotted with slippery black volcanic rock. The upper beach here was made up of a coarser salt-and-pepper sand composed of tiny volcanic pebbles and bits of broken coral. Neither surface was particularly conducive to walking, Pam definitely didn't like the feel of the mud oozing between her toes. After rinsing her feet in the sea as best she could, she put her footwear back on, taking a moment to be thankful she had brought her best waterproofed boots along.

Shortly, Pam herself whooped aloud when she saw a small barrel floating along the water's edge. The sailors got there first and were checking its contents as Pam ran through the splattering muck to join them. *Please be coffee, please be coffee, please be coffee!* she prayed earnestly. It turned out to contain sugar, which was no bad thing, so Pam did her best to hide her disappointment.

Pam continued to follow the waterline closely, scanning the shallows. There were countless black crabs scurrying about the rocks. Pam thought they might make a decent meal if they could be caught. She was startled for a moment by a long, brown, tube-shaped object half hidden in a clump of kelp. A sea snake? She approached carefully, then let out a peal of delighted laughter as she realized the menacing looking creature was in fact, her grandmother's oak walking stick! After flicking off sticky bits of seaweed, she found the tough old thing damp, but no worse for wear. Pam clutched the familiar item with both hands and held it to her breast.

Memories of her grandmother flooded her mind, the long birdwatching walks they had taken through the peaceful West Virginia countryside, her grandmother's gentle voice listing the many birds and animals they found for her attentive grandchild. That was where a love of nature had been firmly planted in her heart. What would her grandmother have thought of Pam using it as a weapon in the seventeenth century? Pam had once broken a man's jaw, thus saving Gerbald's life with the dear old thing. It was almost beyond imagining. That incident had begun with rescuing a family of up-time wood ducks from poaching. Why? Because she had to save the natural world, that's why! Pam Miller, Mother Nature's Protector, "The Bird Lady of Grantville." She shook her head, thinking of the dangers her obsessions had led her to, as well as the friends she had made because of them. Now, she had led those friends into even greater danger.

She looked around at the men combing the beach, every floating piece of civilization they could find increasing their chances of survival just a bit more. Everybody was putting on a brave face, but she knew they were really in trouble. The bright burst of joy from recovering a personal relic from a lost future faded as the depression which had been whispering to her, biding its time at the edge of her consciousness, finally asserted itself in her mind, a dark cloud spoiling her sunny day. All the parades and good will speeches meant nothing now. Their ship was sunk, their expedition was over before she had even *seen* a goddamned dodo, and they were marooned on a remote island in the seventeenth century with no such thing as search-and-rescue planes. Pam fought back tears. They had been waiting their turn too, now threatening to spill. That was when she saw the line of sailors farther up the beach had gathered in a circle around something floating in the shallows.

Her recovered walking stick proved helpful as she made her way across the muddy flats toward the now silent sailors. Young Pers saw her coming, and quickly ran to cut off her approach. As he drew near, Pam thought that he didn't look quite so young anymore. Where was the happy fellow who had helped her pass the hours on the long journey around Africa? His rosy cheeks looked dim even in the bright Southern sunlight.

"Pam, please, you must stay back. This would not be good for you to see."

Looking past him, Pam saw Lind and Helge dragging a soggy mass from out of the shallow water. Ever so cheerful Helge's face was ashen and sorrowful. Their movements were strangely gentle and spoke of a deep respect. She saw a boot had come free revealing a bare foot, its color an unnatural shade of white, with a tinge of palest blue. Pam looked away.

"Who was it?" she asked in a small voice.

"Our first mate, *Herr* Janvik. We must give him a proper burial now. It is better to do it quickly . . ." Pers paused, his face full of worry for an obviously upset Pam.

The tears that had been waiting impatiently behind her eyes burst loose now, as she tried her best to swallow a terrible sob. Her grief was made worse by a sharp sense of guilt that she hadn't liked the man much in life, only because he was just doing his job, keeping his men at their tasks, while she flitted about the ship like a silly school girl, distracting them at her whim. Tears ran hard in a hot cascade down her tanned face, their salt and moisture joining the great Indian Ocean in tiny splashes.

Pers reached out to tentatively pat her on the shoulder. Pam stepped into the young sailor's strong arms, and clung to him, unknowingly pressing her walking stick painfully against his back, but the big, solid youth didn't mind. He did his best to comfort his distraught friend, who now felt she had added a death to her list of responsibilities. Maybe two, if she counted the missing captain. The thought made her cry so hard she shook. Pers patted her back gently, as a son would his weeping mother.

"There, there, *Frau* Pam. We who go to sea know death well. He sails silently behind us, waiting until he is called upon to bring us to the next world. It is just the way of things. Please, you mustn't cry so." His voice was soothing, and so mature for his age. Pam felt a burst of motherly love rise in her heart for this orphan of the world, grateful for his natural kindness.

"It's all my fault, Pers. All of this fucking disaster is my fault."

Pers clicked his tongue to negate that statement. "You cannot think such things. Can it be your fault we struck that awful snag, your fault such a terrible storm blew in when it did? You must not make this *your* burden, *Frau* Pam, *Herr* Janvik did his duty, just as Captain Torbjörn did, and none could command them otherwise."

Pam stopped her tears and slowly drew herself out of her young friend's comforting embrace. She nodded and sniffed sharply. Finally, after doing her best to wipe her face dry on her sleeve, she asked him "How did you get so wise, anyway, kid?"

"I listen to those around me and I remember what they say when it is of value. I only hope my words, simple they may be, are of some comfort to you. You are also my teacher, and I am grateful to have met you. I have learned so much. We men of the *Redbird* all think the world of you, *Frau* Pam, don't you know?"

Pam smiled bravely as she gave him an affectionate squeeze on his arm. "That is very, very good to hear Pers, I'll remember what you said. Thanks for being here for me, it means a lot to me to have such fine friends." This pleased the young sailor, who even as he blushed, smiled in his infectious way. Pam's personal storm having blown itself out *(for now, for now)*, she joined the gathered sailors. It was time for the solemn and timeless ritual of laying a comrade to his final rest. They chose the top of a grassy hillock for the site, well past the high tide line, with a fine view of the sea. She watched solemnly as the men dug the grave with the Bosun's spade which had unfortunately come into service after all. Such sad toil taking place on a sun-drenched tropical beach seemed incongruous, like an odd twist of plot in a confusing dream.

"I'll go get everyone at camp and bring them back for the service," she told them, needing some time alone to pull herself together.

"It will take about an hour to finish our task here. We will wait for your return before we say any words," the Bosun replied, sweating from his turn with the spade.

Pam nodded and walked slowly back toward the distant white rectangle of their sail tent, leaning heavier on her grandmother's walking stick than she had ever remembered doing before. She eventually arrived at camp, feeling as if all the wind had been knocked out of her. Dore, ever busy in her makeshift kitchen, looked up to greet her, but then saw the ashen look on her face. She stopped what she was doing and slowly approached Pam, who was having a hard time meeting her eye.

"Pam! What has happened?" she asked in a worried tone, reaching out to take her friend's free hand. Pam let her walking stick fall to the sand and took a moment to wipe the unruly strands of tear-damp hair from her face. At last, she found her voice, but the most she could produce was a kind of hoarse whisper.

"I have real bad news, Dore. They found *Herr* Janvik... he didn't make it."

Dore's face fell from worry into grief as tears began streaming down her perennially rosy red cheeks. Without a word she pulled Pam into a firm embrace. They held each other for a while, both letting their tears have their way. At last, Dore let Pam go, proceeding to wipe her eyes on her sleeve. She took a deep breath and let it out slowly.

"Poor, poor Jens. No one understood him the way I did. He was gruff, yes, but his heart was good."

"I know, it took me a while to see it, but I did. He sacrificed himself to save us all. *Herr* Janvik was a true hero. . . just like his captain." Pam choked on that last word and began crying again, so it was back to the comfort of Dore's embrace.

"There, there my sweet Pam, we still do not know what became of *Herr* Torbjörn, he may very well have survived, a hearty man such as he! Do not give up hope yet."

Pam nodded, even attempting a small smile. "Of course, you are right, Dore, thank you. Now we must do what we can to honor our fallen."

Dore gave Pam a final, firm pat on the back, then turned her attention to prepare for the service. With the kitchen seen to, she produced a simple black shawl from her baggage. Pam thought about changing into the little black dress she had brought along in her bag on a whim, but decided not to, it wasn't the right kind of formal for the solemn ritual they would attend. She traded her sweat-soaked cotton shirt for a clean, dark-gray sweatshirt and tied her mass of rebellious, wavy dishwater-blond hair back in a pony tail. It would just have to do.

*　　*　　*

By the time everyone had gathered for the funeral, the grave had been filled, a fresh mound of sandy loam beneath which their sailing mate's mortal form was be returned to the earth. The ceremony was simple and sincere. The Bosun said the Lord's Prayer in Swedish, and Dore sang a Lutheran hymn in German, *Wie schön leuchtet der Morgenstern*, which Pam translated as "How Brightly Shines the Morning Star." Pam marveled at the beauty of her friend's strong, alto voice. Over the years she had come to think of this woman as an older sister, but this was the first time she had ever heard her sing. All held a respectful silence once the last thrilling notes of Dore's voice fell away with the sea breeze.

Pam clutched a simple bouquet of wildflowers she had scrounged together on her way back down the beach, weeds most likely, but pretty enough. She was about to place them on the grave when she looked up to see all eyes on her. *Oh no. They want me to say something!* The great woodsman Gerbald hadn't returned from his mission to locate a freshwater source yet, and Pam felt vulnerable without his reassuring presence, the older brother to match Dore's role as sister to her, the two forming a much-treasured set. She realized she would eventually have to answer their silent request. Her mind suddenly slipped down into a seldom used gear and she found herself stepping forward, miraculously speaking up in a somber tone worthy of an ordained minister.

"I want to share with you all a poem I learned when I was a schoolgirl. It's by a man named Tennyson, who might never be born in this world. He wrote it for sailors. I only know how to recite it in English, but I hope the sound of it will still bring some comfort to us. The poem is called *Crossing the Bar*.

> *"Sunset and evening star,*
> *"And one clear call for me!*
> *"And may there be no moaning of the bar,*
> *"When I put out to sea,*
> *"But such a tide as moving seems asleep,*

"Too full for sound and foam,
"When that which drew from out the boundless deep
"Turns again home.
"Twilight and evening bell,
"And after that the dark!
"And may there be no sadness of farewell,
"When I embark;
"For tho' from out our bourne of Time and Place
"The flood may bear me far,
"I hope to see my Pilot face to face
"When I have crossed the bar."

Pam looked up to see the men around her nodding their approval. Even if they hadn't understood all the words, they had felt the emotion of the piece. Dore regarded her with a quiet, beaming pride. Pam gently placed her simple bouquet at the foot of a stout, red- painted plank from *Redbird* the men had placed there as a marker, on which the first mate's name, nation, ship and the current year were carefully scribed with the wax they had found that morning. They hoped the water-resistant substance would tell his story for many years to come. Pam turned away first, and they all walked together back to camp seeking relief from the stinging noonday sun.

CHAPTER 14: *REDBIRD'S* LAST GIFTS

An hour later Gerbald arrived in camp carrying several full water skins, which were met with great cheer by the thirsty castaways. Their meager and stale supply from the pinnace, augmented by what little rainwater they had been able to capture in the confusion of the storm, had nearly run out, so Gerbald was just in time. After hearing the sad news and paying his graveside respects to the deceased first mate, Gerbald led them to a delightfully clear spring about half-a-mile back in the forest that would provide more than enough water for their needs. If it ever failed, he had also found an actual river a few miles farther on, so they were no longer in any danger from dehydration. Everyone felt a piece of their overall tension fall away. The presence of potable water was crucial to survival. Even if all else was hardship, their thirst would be quenched.

Pam turned to the Bosun. "It looks like the tide has come in. Have your sailors got enough strength left to go check out the wreck?"

"Why of course we do, *Frau* Pam, we are Swedes! Stronger than any ten other men, *ja*, boys?" The men all brought themselves to their feet with a creaky chorus of *ja*s, mustering smiles for the brave Lady Scientist.

Dore took Pam gently by the arm. "Pam, you must promise me to be careful, yes?"

"I will be, Dore. We all will be." Serious-faced Dore looked mostly satisfied at this assurance, then clutched at Pam's arm again. "I know you go to look for things we can use from the broken ship. Please, if you can, and only if it is not dangerous, try to find me some more pots and pans! I can make do with the few I have, but if I had more to cook with, I could provide better comfort for these poor men, and we three as well."

Pam smiled at Dore's always earnest desire to help and gave her a quick hug. "I will, Dore. That's first on our list—I'm sure the men will all agree. You are the best, Dore, always the best."

Dore blushed at the praise and hid it with her usual bluff sternness. "Yes, well, I'll be that much better with a proper soup pot in my hand! Now go and be careful. All of you!"

The salvage party, including the Bosun, all murmured their "Yes, ma'am"s to the feared and revered Most Excellent Cook, as they went to drag the pinnace back into the water.

* * *

Pam sat in the prow of the long, narrow craft where she could use her birdwatching trained sharp vision to locate any floating prizes while keeping out of the oarsmen's way. Gerbald had declined to come along, preferring to continue his scouting of their new, and hopefully temporary, home. The water was incredibly clear, the tide having swept away the roiled murk from the storm. Below them a kaleidoscope of fantastical fish darted about, frolicking among branches of coral in an undersea garden of fancy. Pam looked back at the horizon, resisting the siren call of the mysterious realm beneath. She wished she had thought to bring along a mask and snorkel and regretted she could put a name to only a few denizens of these exotic seas, such as the elegant Moorish idols, and the hearty little clownfish guarding their anemone homes. Maybe some day there would be time to study the aquatic world as she wished to, but for now she had other, more pressing matters.

The twin pinnaces carefully approached the rocky point that had taken the *Redbird* in its crushing embrace. Pam's heart sped up as she waited with dread for the first view of her wrecked ship. She knew it had sustained heavy damage, but maybe, just maybe, they could fix her up, and she could sail again. That hope was quickly dashed. Pam bit her lip as she saw what little remained of poor *Redbird*, the broken spine and ribs of her hull surrounded by splintered wood and damp scraps of torn sails. The men landed her pinnace on a relatively flat stretch of sand from which they clambered up slippery rocks to view the devastation firsthand. The other continued further out to scout the area and gather any useful floating remnants. Pam stood at the water's edge, gazing at the place where her great mission had come to its grievous end.

"So much for rescuing the dodo." she mumbled to herself. "Now *we* are the ones who are going to need rescuing." Shaking her head in resignation, she gingerly made her way up the tide-bared volcanic rocks. Most of the ship's contents had been smashed into unrecognizable bits of flotsam and jetsam by the power of the storm.

A flash of bright color against the dark stone caught her eye, a canary-yellow plastic toy whistle, still intact. It had been the captain's, a prized possession from the future world he had come across in his travels. It made his absence all the more painful, but she tucked it safely into a pocket of her rucksack, holding onto a wispy hope that she might one day return it to him. She heard one of the sailors, kindly old Fritjoff, the princess' number one fan, calling to her, so she made her way to him. He grinned with his few odd remaining teeth as he pointed down into a wide shallow depression in the rocks filled with lukewarm seawater left behind by the tide.

"Look, *Frau* Pam! It is your special bird wire!" Just under the surface lay one of the rolls of chicken wire that her old friend Willie Ray Hudson, Grantville's very own *Farmer in the Dell*, had managed to scrounge up for her. It was in perfect condition except for a festooning of seaweed. She hadn't thought of Grantville for days, and the memory of afternoon lemonades on the much-loved old gentleman's wide front porch flooded her with nostalgia. Suddenly, she missed Grantville, badly, and wondered if she would ever see it again.

"You want us to retrieve it, don't you?" Fritjoff asked her shyly, having seen the sad look pass across her face.

"Yes, please do. It could still be of some use. We don't know how long we'll be here . . ."

Fritjoff nodded respectfully, then climbed down into the depression to manhandle the heavy roll up out of the pool. Pam was astonished at his strength and agility, considering his octogenarian looks. *He's probably only in his sixties! This world is so hard on people.* Soon he and another sailor, sturdy Arne, were hauling it down to the pinnace. Little by little as they sifted through the broken remains of *Redbird,* they found other small prizes; a length of good rope here, a box of copper nails there. To their eyes it was fair salvage. They would by no means be coming back empty-handed. Pam saw the Bosun and a few of the sailors standing near one of the ships' surviving ribs, a curved finger of wood pointing at the bright southern skies. Pam made her way over to see what they were up to.

"It is the ship's gun, *Frau* Pam!" The Bosun announced with a bright tone of excitement in his voice, hoarse from shouting orders at sailors. "The new *carronade* made with the Grantville designs! It looks to be intact! We just have to gather up the balls scattered about here, and we brought plenty of gunpowder with us on the pinnaces!"

Pam looked down at the big metal weapon, still connected to a section of broken ship's wood. It shone brightly in the sunlight, retaining its polish despite the rough handling.

"Okay . . . but what good does this do us? We don't have a ship anymore."

The Bosun nodded. "Even with no ship, this gun can protect us. We can mount it on the shore. If an enemy ship comes to our cove, then *boom*! It is better than throwing coconuts!" This made everybody chuckle, even if a bit grimly.

"Can we get it back to shore?"

"Yes, I think so. It is very heavy, but we have tools. Tomorrow we will come back with the experts, Lundkvist's *Black Chessmen* bombardiers. They have all been moping about something terrible since its loss. This fancy big gun was their main reason for being along on the voyage! Alas, now the tide is returning and we must leave it for now. I am not too worried, though, I think it won't be floating away!" And so they left the elegant, but thoroughly deadly carronade behind for later retrieval, tying a line with a red-painted cork buoy attached to it, to mark the spot in high water.

The men didn't wait to round up the ammunition that had rolled here and there. They would take no chances there. By the time they finished that task, the water was up around their knees, so it was time to go!

The sturdy little boat rode lower in the water on the return trip, burdened with the weight of their prizes. Pam smiled, looking down at the variety of metal pots, pans, and cutlery they had recovered. Most fortunately, the large, stainless steel up-time soup pot from Pam's kitchen was included in the galley salvage, that would make Dore very happy. *Maybe our luck will change?* Pam mused, but she didn't dwell on the thought, not wanting to jinx it.

That night the everyone gathered around the bonfire to pass around a big bottle of spiced *akvavit* that had miraculously survived the storm, raising the men's spirits. The gathering began solemnly as they drank a traditional toast to their fallen comrade, First Mate Jens Janvik. With that duty performed, the day's salvage operation came under discussion, which had been a welcome success. The bombardiers were ecstatic to learn their carronade was still intact and recoverable. Their joy was infectious and all the men were soon in a festive mood.

Pam stood a bit back from the crowd at first, going over recent events in her mind for the thousand-and-second time. They were not in a good situation, not at all, but it could have been much worse, and they were all doing their best to improve it. The question of what had happened to the rest of their fleet weighed heavily on everyone. The fact that none of the other ships had yet come looking for them did not bode well. Pushing that unpleasant thought aside, Pam tried not to think of the dodos she had come to save and the very likely end of her quest to forge a colony that might truly coexist with nature, having learned from all the terrible mistakes of her own time.

Ultimately, there was no point in fretting about it all just now. Her beleaguered mind badly needed a rest so she joined the party, swallowing as much of the powerful caraway-and-dill-flavored liquor as the men did, laughing and singing along with them until she drifted off into an exhausted slumber. If she dreamed that night, she knew not.

CHAPTER 15: CRAZY FOR COCONUTS!

The next day Pam woke up late, her head aching a bit from the potent liqueur of the night before. Except for a small group of well-armed marines keeping vigilant watch over the camp, the men had gone to retrieve the carronade, including Gerbald, who had a knack for jury-rigged mechanics. Dore gave her a simple breakfast of soft dumplings in a salt-pork broth, the most welcome results of her being reunited with her soup pot and remarked that they were going to need to do something about getting more food, soon.

"The men cannot live on flour, water, and sugar indefinitely!"

Pam nodded, feeling hazy and disconnected. *Mild hangover coupled with severe caffeine withdrawal, blech.*

Dore took one good look at her exhausted friend and understood Pam's condition. She ordered Pam to down a large cup of water, still cool from the spring and told her to take it easy for a while. Pam obeyed, lounging in the shade, watching for the men to come back from their mission. She felt drained, like a balloon with all the air out of it, just a floppy piece of limp rubber— it was not a good feeling. After a long, boring while, she got up, having decided to make herself useful, but ended up just wandering aimlessly around the camp. That soon evolved into collecting seashells. Once she started, there was no stopping. By the time the men came back, she had a nice little collection, lovely, and entirely useless, or so she thought. Later that evening the men, hoping to revive their shipboard tradition, asked her if she still had her deck of cards, which she did, safely tucked into her knapsack. In lieu of coins, the seashells made a perfect substitute for poker chips, and if anyone began to run low a quick trip down the beach brought back a fresh infusion of wealth.

There not currently being anything she could do to help, Pam watched as the men hauled the heavy carronade up from the beach with a system of ropes and makeshift pulleys. Gerbald, who had a knack for that kind of thing, had helped rig it up. The Black Chessmen bombardiers, who had been moping about with nothing that goes "BOOM!" to play with since the wreck, looked like a bunch of kids on Christmas morning, bursting with glee at having received their best present ever! Once the formidable weapon was safely ensconced above the high tide line, everyone gathered for lunch. Dore had something special for dinner in mind, but they had to make do with the hard bread and dried meat from the ship for now.

"We need fruit!" Dore announced, looming over the shady spot where Gerbald, Pam, the Bosun, and the *Löjtnant* held council. "Pam, you have studied these islands. What can we eat here? I have learned about the need for certain vitamins during my time in Grantville. I am going to exhaust our stores sooner rather than later with all these hungry men to feed, a bottomless pit! We can't survive on just bread and water, especially since we are about to run out of bread!"

Pam felt a bit put on the spot, but understood her friend's concern perfectly.

"Well, Dore, during my library research I made a list of every edible plant that grows or might grow in this region. I was going to encourage the colonists to learn to use native species along with all the seeds and starts we brought with us. I'll go through my notes, but off hand, we have plantains, they just aren't ripe at the moment. There's probably breadfruit here, too, I think I'll know it when I see it. These palms along the beach have coconuts, and there should be a variety of palm species further inland, including date palms. Oil palm could be useful, although some types might be inedible. There are Indian gooseberries growing near the spring, an excellent source of vitamin C, so we should be safe from scurvy.   All in all, I suppose coconuts would be a good place to start."

They all stood to scan the camp. There were a few coconuts lying around, but they looked as if they had been there a bit too long as some were even beginning to sprout fronds. They could see what they thought might be several likely specimens still attached to their trees, but they were quite high up.

"Someone must climb a palm tree and cut those down," Dore decreed after careful scrutiny.

"And who is going to do that?" Pam asked a bit testily, still feeling worn out, and maybe just slightly irritated with Dore's bossy attitude.

"I know who." The Bosun answered, smiling. "*Pers!*" he shouted.

The youth came running, looking around with wide eyes to see what might be required of him.

"Congratulations," Pam told him. "We have just elected you to be our resident *Gilligan*." Gerbald and Dore, well versed in the world of up-time television, both laughed, but the Swedes could only smile politely, very much not getting the reference.

"It is a *high* honor." Gerbald told the boy in English, trying to keep a straight face even as he glanced up at the coconuts dangling at a dizzying height above their heads. They had been teaching the ever-curious Pers to speak English and German throughout the voyage, and he was getting pretty savvy. He gave his older friend a suspicious look.

Pam snorted. "I'm sure an enterprising young fellow like you can climb your way to success!" she added, then burst into a fit of giggles.

By the time they had explained their up-time humor to the uncomprehending Swedes, who still didn't really get it, but could understood someone like Gilligan's role in life well enough—a low-ranking youth, who is a bit of a buffoon, and who gets stuck with all the crappy jobs no one else wants.

Before they knew it, Pers had shimmied all the way up one of the trees, an accomplished climber by nature. "How about this one?" he called down, pointing at a large, light-green sphere one-size-again bigger than a bowling ball.

"Sure, send it down!" Pam shouted back. With a couple of whacks of Pers' knife the coconut plummeted, causing the Bosun to jump out of the way.

"Sorry, *Herr* Bosun!" Pers called down.

The Bosun grumbled something about having other things to do, and began ordering the rest of the men, who were taking their sweet time, finishing their lunches, while watching the entertainment at hand, to get back to work.

"Important safety tip: Never fall sleep under the coconut trees and mind your heads!" Pam called out to the gathering. "Are there any brown ones?" she shouted up to Pers.

"Well, try this one. Look out below!"

After a while, they had a collection of coconuts of varying ripeness. After opening the outer husk some were still green, while riper fruits were the more familiar brown. Pam knew the green ones were edible from visits to the Thai restaurant in Morgantown and was pretty sure she had eaten a ripe brown one at some point, or had at least drunk a piña colada out of one.

It was a study of trial and error. Gerbald sliced the first one in half with his *katzbalger* shortsword as if it were an enemy's head, splashing the juice all over the place. That taught them to poke a hole in it first, using an auger from the ship's tool chest, then pouring the juice, or *milk*, into one of Dore's prized pots. It tasted a bit sour, but there was sweetness there, too. Pam thought she might grow to like it. The meat was delicious, and research continued as they gorged themselves. The ripe brown ones were even better, meatier, with a creamy juice that much more closely resembled milk. Once the meat was removed, Dore suggested they clean and save the sturdy brown shell halves for soup dishes.

Pers was sent on several more missions up the trees to make sure there would be enough for everyone's dinner.

Pleased with their progress, Dore bestowed them all with an affectionate smile. "Now we will survive." she stated matter-of-factly and returned to her makeshift kitchen.

CHAPTER 16: KEEPING BUSY WITH BAMBOO

The following days were spent working to improve their situation. They didn't know how long they might be here, but the men needed something to focus on, so they formed work crews. First, they picked a relatively clear spot to build a much more substantial camp, well past the high tide line, and hidden from the beach by a belt of tall grass and the stately row of palms that stretched all down their cove.

By unanimous consent, the first project on the list was a sand-floored, palm frond-roofed "galley" constructed for Dore, featuring a sturdy bamboo worktable, and a bamboo latticework hung from the ceiling to hang utensils and keep their food safely off the ground. There was a large grove of the versatile tree that was really a grass nearby. It was truly a marvelous building material. The galley's walls were grass thatch woven between bamboo frames. A few yards outside the kitchen door, they built a primitive, but functional, oven and stove from volcanic rock, then placed a thatch roof over it, high enough to avoid sparks. Dore was pleased with it all, considering she had worked with far worse in her years following Gerbald to war.

Despite her protests she shouldn't be given special preference, next came a simple bungalow for Pam. The small structure, which she called *The Professor's Hut,* was raised five- feet-high on bamboo stilts to avoid creepy crawlies, and provided a safe, dry place to sleep and store her things. It was nothing fancy, but at Pam's shy request they added a sitting porch out front, with a basic bench and desk in the shade of the roof's extended eaves, a comfortable spot for her to do her reading and writing.

A similar structure went up for Gerbald and Dore, which Pam dubbed *The Howell Mansion,* and the men built a communal longhouse for themselves. On the tour, Pam was pleased to see that Fritjoff had lovingly hung his slightly water damaged photograph of the princess on a beam near the entrance.

Weapons and ammunition were carefully stored in cabinets fashioned from the best lumber salvaged from *Redbird*.

At a proper distance from their dwellings, they dug two outhouse latrines, each with bamboo walls and a palm tree roof, the fairly capacious *Gentlemen's Commode* (there were quite a lot of gentlemen), and the much smaller *Lady's Powder Room*. Pam used her art supplies to paint yellow crescent moons on each door, a touch of home that reminded her of childhood summer visits to her uncle's rural West Virginia cabin.

Just behind the tall grass above the shore, the men erected a well-camouflaged platform where they mounted the carronade to greet any unfriendly visitors with a nasty surprise.

The Bosun was pleased with the progress.

"The sailor's general wisdom upon becoming a castaway," he told Pam, "is to think long term and hope short term. Besides, the men are happier if they are kept busy."

"Great work *Herr* Bosun, please tell the men we are grateful for their hard work!" Pam said, appreciating the increased comfort. It was beginning to feel more like being at summer camp than been stranded on a desert island! In any case, the weather was still too unpredictable to send the pinnaces out to explore the coast, so they would simply have to bide their time. Pam figured they might as well bide it in style. It was everyone's fondest hope the remainder of the expedition were hunkered down somewhere safe doing the same and would send rescue once the weather was safe for sailing again.

Gerbald and the sailors were fishing in earnest and bringing in a very tasty haul. They were also digging clams and catching crabs in bamboo traps Gerbald tinkered together. One day, Dore pulled a slightly rusty red-and-white tin of circa 1983 McCormick brand curry powder from the bag that contained Pam's spice cabinet.

"What will you make with that?" Pam's mouth was beginning to water, it felt so long since she had eaten anything exotic or spicy.

"Do you remember when we dined at Crystal and Walt's home a few days after their wedding? She served something called a 'fish curry' I found quite tasty. I remember it also contained coconut milk. Well, we have that, and fish, so I thought I'd try it. Is it a good idea?"

Pam hugged her so hard she almost knocked the sturdy woman over. It was indeed a good idea and such a huge hit that the men argued over who should get the last few spoonfuls! Dore laughed, pleased her meal had been such a success. Eventually, the much-revered Fritjoff stepped in, putting the matter to rest by ladling the remnants of the delicious soup into Pam's bowl, a kindness she didn't resist. It was truly wonderful!

All in all, Pam couldn't help but think things were getting better. She tried to put the real danger of their predicament, and the question of the fate of the rest of their fleet, out of her mind for now. Violent storms still shook their camp frequently, so for the indefinite future, until the seasons changed, there simply wasn't anything more to do than they were already doing.

Pam decided that meanwhile, she and Gerbald would scout around on foot. There were mountains rising a few miles behind their cove and by the looks of them they weren't much higher than those of West Virginia that she had climbed so many times over the years. They would offer a broader view and Pam was getting bored and depressed hanging around camp, anyway. She needed to walk.

After conferring, they decided to head out the following morning. Whistling an old *Looney Tune,* she arranged her ever-growing shell collection decoratively around the edge of her front porch to pass the time. *Well, Mauritius is definitely* not *better than the Bahamas, but today is a pretty good day anyway.* Satisfied with the results of her art project, she rested in her hut until dinner, still feeling antsy to get hiking. There was another thing fueling her urge to go walk about, something that she didn't dare think on too much, due to the still fresh pain of losing her ship, and possibly all hope of accomplishing the expedition's goals. The fact was, despite everything else, she was dying to see a dodo.

Garrett W. Vance

CHAPTER 17: A LAND THAT TIME FORGOT

E arly the next morning, Pam and Gerbald donned their rucksacks and left camp, promising to be back before dark. Rather than trying to follow the difficult terrain along the shore leading northeast, they headed due north, inland, planning to gain the summit of the closest mountain, a fairly easy day's hike for them if the lay of the land cooperated. So far, it wasn't much worse than a West Virginia woodland, some thorny underbrush, but mostly easy walking through a beautiful forest. There was a plethora of amazing birdlife at hand but Pam resisted stopping to take notes and make sketches. They were on a mission. Despite the natural wonders revealing themselves at every turn, Pam grew morose.

"I'm no Darwin, not even an Audubon. Everything I do has been done," Pam muttered. "I'm just following in their footsteps."

Gerbald, familiar with this negative train of Pam's thought, tried to encourage her. "That was a different world, a different time, Pam. Darwin and Audubon probably aren't even going to be born thanks to the butterflies. I am told there is an awful lot of uptime knowledge that isn't in your library. The Ring of Fire brought back only a small amount of all the information collected in that other future. Right here and now, there is still much to learn! Someone must seek out the discoveries waiting to be made on *this* world, in *this* time. Look around you! I don't see any human tracks here, do you? We are possibly the first people to visit this forest. *This* world needs a trailblazer, a scientist, a dreamer. We don't have Darwin. We won't need him because we have Pam Miller."

Pam laughed aloud despite her dark mood. "Gawd, Gerbald, when did you come up with *that* speech? You sure know how to polish an apple!"

"I have been working on it, knowing the need for it would come. Were you moved?" He was grinning at his great cleverness now, which made it impossible for Pam to maintain her funk.

"Yeah, I was moved. I reckon I'll never know how or why I ended up here, but I have pretty much come to terms with it. I do feel I have purpose in this century, call it fate or destiny, or what you will, there are reasons for me being here. It's hard to stay focused when everything turns to shit like it has lately. Perhaps you may have noticed my most recent purpose ended in disaster."

"Well, you know I am no religious man, but Dore is convinced that you were sent by God to help us improve this world. I see no reason to disagree."

"Thanks, Pollyanna, you can knock it off now, I'm cheered up." Their laughter mingled with the cries and songs of unknown birds.

They took a break before noon near a small, spring-fed creek. The water was cold and delicious.

"We've been walking for hours and still no sign of a dodo." Pam looked around the open forest, searching the leaf-littered floor for movement.

"Perhaps we did not land on Mauritius after all? Could this be Reunion or some other island?"

"No, we passed Reunion the day before we wrecked. It was far enough away I didn't get much of a look, but I trust in our navigators. This *must* be Mauritius."

"Pam, as a hunter, I have spent days on end in the bush without seeing a single example of whatever game animal I was hunting. It is not unusual. I believe the American phrase is *getting skunked*."

"Yeah, well, I suppose. I'd just like to see a dodo, is all. I mean, we came all this freaking way! Remember, there aren't any left up-time, so it's special. I will be the first person from my former century to see one, and yes, despite everything, I am pretty damn excited about it!"

"My eyes are peeled, Pam. If there are any dodos around here, we will find them." They drank their fill of water and continued on. The trees were getting bigger and more numerous. With mutual sighs, they made their way through an unexpectedly deep valley they hadn't known stood between them and their intended hill climb. The massive trunks with their chaos-patterned fretwork of high branches blocked out most of the sunlight so they walked through a deep-green gloom. In the distance, something squealed, the sound taking on a sinister ring in the primeval setting.

Pam began to get jumpy as they passed through the ancient groves. The raucous cry of an unseen bird high in the canopy startled her, causing her to miss her step. She sprawled clumsily onto the forest floor, face down into a bed of moldering leaves and twigs. Gerbald hurried to help her up. She clutched at him for a moment, her eyes wide with fear.

"Pam, what is the matter with you?" he asked in his most soothing voice, gently brushing the leaves off her.

"Sorry! I can't help it. Damn!" Standing now, she took a deep breath and tried to get ahold of herself. "I'm getting the willies out here, Gerbald. I mean, this isn't Thuringia. We're on a weird, remote, and uninhabited island looking for what I was raised to believe was an extinct species for chrissakes! I know it sounds crazy, but what if there are still fucking *dinosaurs* out here in these jungles? I mean, this place has been untouched since time began!"

"Now, that would be something to hunt, a true challenge!" Gerbald the jäger sent a piercing gaze out into the foliage, his face full of melodramatic wonder and avarice. "I could be the first man from my century to track a dinosaur! I would not kill it, of course, unless it was a big predator like the fearsome T Rex and it was trying to eat us! "

"Oh, Christ, I wish I'd never let you read those Edgar Rice Burroughs books Walt gave you."

"*At the Earth's Core* and the rest of the Pellucidar series are fantastic, but I'm most fond of Sir Conan Doyle's *Lost World*. The movie was great, too, although the dinosaurs were men in rubber suits."

"Not to mention all those other hokey old movies you like so much. There were scads of film masterpieces we didn't have with us when we went through the Ring of Fire, but some dork had five years worth of schlock he taped off the Channel 13 Friday Midnight Thrill-fest, and the Saturday Afternoon Matinee. What was that one you liked so much? Oh yeah, *Valley of the Gwangi,* featuring cowboys versus dinosaurs. Give me a break! How many times did you watch that ridiculous thing anyway, twenty-five?"

"Thirty-two. A brilliant film! Ray Harryhausen was a genius! The Tyrannosaurus Rex menacing the town, prowling through the shadowy church—stupendous! I don't care what anyone says, Harryhausen's work was far more gripping than that silly *Jurassic Park* flick, ha! Oh, Pam, if only we could get a Hollywood going in Grantville, I would so like to be in the movies. People say I have a talent! Just think of it, *Gerbald, Dinosaur Hunter!*" Gerbald struck his most heroic pose.

It was true, Gerbald was one hundred percent pure ham at heart. The guy probably could have gotten at least some bit parts up-time. He did have charisma. Pam just laughed at him, concentrating on navigating the uneven forest floor. She paused before a unpleasant-looking pile of still-moist animal spoor. Seeing that she was ignoring his audition, Gerbald changed his patter down to a lower, but still melodramatic key.

"You know, Pam, I sometimes wonder—" He paused to look suspiciously at the leaf-screened sky, then continued in a somehow familiar creepy voice, while giving her a penetrating look of dread. "*What if* the event that happened to Grantville had taken you all even further back into history or even *pre*history? What if you had fallen *much* further through the depths of time, say, to the Cretaceous period, when dinosaurs ruled the Earth? What would have become of you then?" He stood staring at her intently as if this nightmare might occur at any second.

"Knock it off, Rod Serling. You're already weird enough without talking like that guy. I'd probably be safer out here with a velociraptor than a nutcase like you." Pam, as usual, couldn't help but smile at Gerbald's antics. Once he got started it was hard to stop him. His goal wasn't really to frighten her, just playfully freak her out a little. Goofing around like an overgrown kid was just his way of passing the time on a long trip. She knew he also did it to distract her from her *moods* and couldn't help but love him for that.

"You got it! That *was* Rod Serling! A master raconteur. I do miss TV shows and movies. One day we will have another of those festivals where we drink beer, eat pizzas and watch TV all day like we used to."

"Yeah, that wouldn't be half bad. I miss the beer and pizza, anyway." While humoring Gerbald, Pam had inserted a stick into the still mushy turd. It was full of smashed seeds and what might be crushed nutshells. "Although, one day we will probably look back at this jungle and say "Ahhh, the good old days.""

Gerbald's face took on a wistful expression. "I would be glad if you were to one day think of our adventures together in that way, Pam. I certainly will."

"Yeah, we do have fun, Ivanhoe, just don't get all misty on me. Let's see if we can find a damn dodo along the way while we are out here. Here, check this turd out, it's very exciting. It might be dodo scat, it's big enough and has the right consistency for a large-billed terrestrial vegetarian. Say, here's an idea, we can co-host a thrilling nature series, *In Search of Wild Bird Poop*."

"Always the romantic soul, our Pam, a woman who lives for adventure." Gerbald started humming the National Geographic theme loudly as they made their way through the underbrush. Pam joined in until they were laughing so loud it hurt their sides.

"I know! We shall do a remake of *The Valley of the Gwangi*! We could film it here on this very island! I will portray the heroic cowboy, naturally! Lacking Ray Harryhausen, we will cast live dinosaurs, of course." he stopped abruptly and pointed at a tree, his face a model of terror. "My God, its an allosaurus! Flee!"

"Pipe down, I'm trying to think of what I will tell Dore when I come back without you tonight." Pam's scowl was fierce enough Gerbald went back to his silent woodsman mode, but a hint of a contented smile still showed on his lips. He had cheered Pam up after all, always a good thing.

Garrett W. Vance

CHAPTER 18: PAM'S POT O' GOLD

Leaving the forest behind, Pam and Gerbald arrived at a wide stretch of grassland, their planned climb rising before them. It was larger than it looked from a distance, but they decided to try it anyway, as there was still plenty of daylight left. The slope was gentle and soon they were high on the grassy mountainside. Reaching the mound of the summit, they were rewarded with panoramic views, including their first look at the interior. It was a big, rugged, volcanic island, and reaching the north end of it by any route on foot would be hard going for even the most experienced hiker.

Now that they had accomplished their task and weren't in such a rush, Pam wandered about the mountaintop, pausing to make sketches of the views and various new species of birds they came across. It was sunny, but cool at this altitude, the breeze sweetly scented by the many wildflowers dotting the sub-alpine heaths.

Suddenly Pam let out a shrieking whoop. Gerbald rushed to her side to see what the matter was, his hand ready to unsheathe his trusty *katzbalger* shortsword.

"Pam! Are you all right?" He found Pam running around hugging the shrubbery, her eyes flashing with intense joy.

"All right? Am I *all right*? Oh, hell yeah, I'm all right!" She kissed a leafy branch and began to perform a pagan celebratory dance through the plants as Gerbald looked on, thunderstruck.

"Pam, what in the world is going on?" He asked, as her delirium showed no signs of stopping.

"Don't you see it? Here, *here*! Look at this little tree! Do you know what it is?" She hugged the one closest to her.

Gerbald took a moment to study it closely It was a pleasant enough looking shrub, with glossy green leaves, and yellow-shading-to-purplish berries. He had never seen one before in his life.

Pam stopped her crazy dance to stare at him. He shrugged his shoulders in defeat. Pam laughed, the merry sound echoing around the hills.

"Gerbald, this is the most wonderful plant in the world. This, *this* is *coffee*! *Coffeeeee*!" She turned back to the shrub and hugged it again.

"*Coffee*? Coffee! Great Caesar's ghost, Pam, you found a coffee tree here at the ends of the earth! Are you sure?"

"Yes, I'm sure! I studied the hell out of this stuff before I left, trying to find crops for our colonists to grow. I couldn't get my hands on any viable beans before we left, but look! Coffee trees are growing *wild* here and they are all over the place!" She swept her arm around and Gerbald realized there were hundreds of the pretty little coffee trees thriving on the slopes of their antipodean mountain, all heavy with berries.

"Are you sure you can drink it?" Gerbald liked coffee well enough, but his knowledge of the subject didn't extend beyond asking for "*A little cream, no sugar.*"

"Sure, why not? There are some different species, but they're all drinkable. I'm not sure what type this one is, but it looks like the berries are in season! Sweet jumping Jesus, I have coffee again, hallelujah!" She returned to her ecstatic dance while Gerbald searched through his many-pocketed, sage-green coat to locate a cloth bag suitable for berries.

The two of them got back to camp later than expected, well past sunset. The extra weight had slowed them down since they had stuffed every hollow and pocket of their clothes and rucksacks with beans. Gerbald's coat was visibly lumpy with the things. They were just about on their last legs when they reached camp, a very worried and somewhat irritated Dore and the men gathering to greet them. Once Pam explained what had kept them and showed Dore the beans, her friend's eyes lit up. Dore wasn't quite as big a fan of the wonderful bean as Pam, but had taken quite a liking to it, and regretted not managing to secure their supply before abandoning ship. Pam couldn't wait until morning, they were going to drink some, and drink it now! Her exuberance was easy to catch, and soon everyone watched expectantly as Pam and Dore went to work on the treasure trove of beans. They roasted them as carefully as they could in Dore's makeshift stone oven, then ground them with the back of one of the sailor's axes. Pam used a cotton handkerchief wrapped over a bamboo tube for a filter, and soon enough a black brew simmered in the cookpot. Pam, no longer caring that she hadn't seen a single damn dodo all day, took the first sip of the newfound coffee from a coconut shell cup. She held the hot, bitter, liquid in her mouth for a moment before swallowing, as all eyes watched and waited for her reaction.

"Oh. My. God. This is the best thing I have *ever* tasted. It's coffee here in the middle of no-effing-where! It's coffee for castaways! Yippie-kay-yay!"

The men all smiled, pleased to see Pam so happy. Dore refilled her cup, followed by cups for herself, Gerbald, and all the crew. The Bosun determined adding spirits recovered from the late *Redbird* would make it taste even better and the sounds of laughter and good cheer echoed around their little cove late into the night.

CHAPTER 19: BIRDWATCHING

Castaway Cove, South Coast of Mauritius

The days flew by on their stranded shore, becoming weeks, and now just over a month. The survivors of the wreck of the *Redbird* busied themselves with projects to increase their comfort and safety. The sailors continued to use the tools and materials recovered from the shipwreck, along with bamboo and other native plants, to improve their shelters. Dore and Pam gathered fruits and nuts they were sure were safe to eat, while Gerbald searched for gamebirds (with Pam's rare blessing for such activities) and fished the cove to keep their minds off their situation. Despite the distractions, they all felt the world was leaving them farther and farther behind with each passing day.

Just as he had onboard, ever-respectful old Fritjoff had taken it upon himself to be Pam's caretaker. He cut all the underbrush from under her stilted hut to make sure there were no creepy-crawlies lurking there. He cleared a sandy trail from her door down to the beach and swept it clear of leaves and debris every morning before she woke up, not before leaving a coconut bowl full of cool water from the spring on her porch. Pam was embarrassed by the attention and told him he didn't have to go to all that trouble over her, but the white-haired gentleman shyly nodded and continued to look after her.

"It is no trouble for me, *Frau* Pam. It is good for a man to have work to do and even better when it is in the service of a fine and important person such as yourself. Don't fret now. You are doing the princess' work, and I serve you as I would her. Just call on Fritjoff if you need anything. I will be here for you."

Pam was touched by his eagerness to please and thanked him profusely, asking if there were anything she could do for him. Fritjoff smiled with his few remaining teeth, his blue eyes still bright and sparkling in his heavily wrinkled by long years and weather face.

"No, no, I am a simple fellow and have few needs. But, if it were no trouble to you, one day when you meet again with Princess Kristina, I would be greatly honored if you would pass my humble respects on to her. That would be a true kindness to a faithful servant of the Vasa."

Pam promised to do so. She didn't say it aloud, but intended to make sure that on that future day Fritjoff would be right there with her to give his respects himself. *That would be a real treat for the old guy. I'm going to make that happen. He can get that precious photo autographed in person!* The thought gave her a very warm and pleasant feeling. She had grown quite fond of these stouthearted men of the north, knowing it was a blessing to be caught in such trying circumstances with such capable and trustworthy people around her. *Someday I might even look back on this castaway life and miss it . . . but not too much.*

One overcast morning, the weather still too rough and unpredictable to attempt further exploration of the rugged coast with the pinnaces, Pam and Gerbald determined they were stocked up with enough food to last several days. Utterly bored with life at camp, they decided to follow the river into the interior. They had been too busy foraging to explore further since the triumphant discovery of coffee and Pam was absolutely itching to get back to her search for the elusive dodo.

The going was fairly easy. They followed a corridor of grassy meadows between the river and the forest's edge. The sun burned the clouds off around eleven, at which point it became hot enough to chase them into the shade of the woods. The forest floor was clear of thick underbrush, a mossy parkway through ancient tree trunks. Pam kept her eyes open for new birds along the way, occasionally stopping to observe and sketch one of the myriad species that inhabited the island. She had decided her best bet on finding any dodos was to simply stop looking for them, contenting herself with the many avians that inhabited the isolated island. She wondered how she would ever manage to catalog them all. It would take ages to do it right . . . but then again, she might have that kind of time, if rescue didn't come. She wondered if she could find natural substitutes to replenish her diminishing paper and art supplies.

That thought made her mood sour despite the beauty of the venerable groves, until she was just slogging along in a funk, not paying attention to her surroundings at all. Just as she was sinking into a really, really bad mood, Gerbald let out the low whistle that meant "*Look at that,*" one of the signals they had developed in their years spent birdwatching in the wilds of the

Thüringerwald. Pam froze, scanning the tree limbs for a choice specimen. Gerbald gave her a nudge with his elbow and pointed downward with a small movement of his head.

Pam followed his gaze to a large, odd-looking bird standing just six feet away from them on its sturdy legs and thick toes. At first glance, she thought it was a very large, gray turkey, but then it cracked a nut with a loud snapping sound, using its grotesquely large and powerful bill. The bird regarded them with a bright yellow eye turreted in a beak that covered nearly all of its head. Overall, it was awkwardly-shaped, and a bit comical looking, with fluffy white tufts of feathers puffing out at its tiny, useless wings and arched tail, exactly as in all the illustrations she had seen although it stood a bit more upright and was slightly thinner had been portrayed. Pam's eyes went wide and her pulse raced as she marveled at the creature before her, its breath moving the downy gray feathers of its chest, its beak clacking softly as it swallowed the nut. It was the strangest bird she had ever seen, a bird she had at one time *never hoped she would see*, a bird lost forever in her former world. The poster child of the doomed and extinct, *alive,* right in front of her: The Dodo.

The three of them stood still for a long time, content to stare at each other. At last, the dodo gave them a dismissive coo *(just like a dove!)* and dipped its plated head to search for another nut. It soon found one, the powerful beak going back to its noisy work. Pam felt her face grow hot and wet. She realized she was crying, crying the joyful tears a child might if, through some happy magic, she found herself in the presence of the *real* Santa Claus, stepped out of the chimneys of legend in jolly flesh and blood.

"It's so ugly!" she exclaimed with joy, "and it's also the most beautiful thing I've ever seen!" She took Gerbald's hand for confidence, then together they took first one, then another step closer to the dodo, which simply ignored them as it continued its nut-cracking. At last Pam reached out with trembling fingers to gently touch the downy gray feathers. It watched her out of the corner of its bright-yellow eye, but gave no reaction other than to continue eating. "It's real." she whispered. "This is really happening." She gasped as she noticed two more dodos foraging nearby, blithely paying no attention whatsoever to the humans among them.

"Congratulations, Pam," Gerbald told her in the awed tones of one who has witnessed something truly extraordinary. "Now we know they still live and our sacrifices were not in vain. One way or another, we will find a way to save the dodos from the fate they suffered in your up-time world. Your mission *will* be a success, Pam, I swear this."

The two of them spent the rest of the day hanging around with the dodos, studying their habits, seeing what they liked to eat, watching their interactions.

Pam did a few sketches, vowing to return with her paints. Eventually the shadows grew long, so they made their way back to camp with smiles on their faces and a spring in their steps. Despite everything, they had now seen dodos with their own eyes. They were real, they were alive, and for the moment, that was more than enough.

CHAPTER 20: DODO DO'S AND DON'TS

The news of Pam finally meeting the elusive dodos face to face was met with cheers back at the camp. The sailors and marines well understood how important finding the odd-looking birds was to Pam and to their princess and Pam's joy at the discovery was infectious. All the men offered whatever services they could give, in supporting Pam's efforts to study the creatures, although Pam couldn't think of much they could do beyond the daily task of making sure they had food and shelter, which they saw to with stoic Scandinavian good cheer.

Pam and Gerbald set about a definitive study of the creatures, leaving camp early in the morning and arriving back well after dark, often having to face Dore's annoyance at their being late for dinner. A week went by in this way until Pam called a break, needing time to sort out her notes and artworks while Gerbald gleefully rejoined the marines in their daily training rituals. As she went about the camp, Pam noticed something that worried her, worried her very much. Although they were trying their best to hide it, the men were growing frustrated with their isolation. She realized they were keeping quiet about it to give her time to study the dodos now she had found them, waiting for her to satisfy her needs before making any attempts to leave their encampment in search of the colonists, and possible escape from the island. The storm season had nearly passed so that excuse no longer held much water. For her part, Pam felt guilty at letting her desire to observe the dodo supersede looking for the colonists, but it was a guilt she decided she would accept, at least for a little while longer. They had, after all, come all this way! Rationalizations well in hand, Pam and Gerbald marched off into the woods again the next day to continue the studies.

Pam was in a state of bliss as she observed the odd, flightless birds go about their business. It was as if beloved cartoon characters from her childhood had come to magical life before her eyes, their antics all for her own, personal entertainment. She sometimes shook her head in wonder that she was seeing living, breathing dodos. *Finally, something good about time travel!* Following quietly along behind the humorously waddling creatures, Pam observed their behavior with delight. Their rare cries reminded Pam of geese, and they chuckled to themselves while foraging, a sound much like a pigeon makes. Increasingly, Pam thought they might be descended from, or perhaps cousins, of the pigeons and doves.

"Pam, are the dodos eating pebbles?" Gerbald asked, no longer bothering to keep his voice low, since the dodos ignored their presence. As long as they didn't make sudden movements, the dodos were unconcerned at having large bipedal primates in their midst.

"They don't actually eat them, they swallow them into their gullet to help digestion. The stones aid in grinding up the food." Pam answered, watching a young specimen in hot pursuit of a stumbling beetle.

"I should try that the next time we have dried squid for dinner." Gerbald remarked with his usual, wry drawl. He had really taken to the hillbilly culture. Pam figured it must come naturally to him from his days as a jäger, being a kind of mountain man to begin with.

To their surprise, the dodos could move quickly in pursuit of scuttling prey. Like many bird species, they were opportunists, consuming whatever they could manage to get their ponderous beaks around. A sudden lunge, and the dodo's sharp bill might snap up a juicy frog, or wriggling worm. Pam was sure their amazing appendage could deliver a nasty wound if a dodo was provoked, so she stayed well clear of it, always moving calmly and not getting too near its business end. As far as the dodos were concerned, Pam and Gerbald were about as interesting as a big, gray rock. The humans were ignored as the clucking, contented dodos went about their endless, and not very difficult, search for food.

Gerbald managed to find out just how powerful those beaks could be when he accidentally passed to close to a dodo nest. The nest was rather unimpressive, a shallow depression dug into the mulchy forest floor, lined with a bit of down and twigs, but it was home to a magnificent white egg as big as a softball. The mother of said egg, who was eating some nuts nearby, let out a shockingly loud whistle, like a tea kettle on the boil, and charged Gerbald with shocking speed, her beak clacking loudly, and downy feathers fluffed out to give her a more menacing appearance. She was a lot larger than a turkey, if not nearly as big as an ostrich, and her head rose nearly to his abdomen. Gerbald shouted "Yikes!" one of his vast vocabulary of American slang and backpedaled away from the angry creature.

Pam watched all this from the safety of a nearby tree. As soon as the ruckus started, she had gone up the nearest one, standard procedure for non-climbing critter attacks in the Thüringerwald, good for wolves and boars, but not much help against bears. As Gerbald turned to break into a run, the outraged mother stretched her neck out farther than Pam would have guessed possible, to close her beak sharply around his booted ankle. Gerbald yelped even louder, then managed to shake the dodo loose with a twist. Pam thought the bill's sharp tip might have pierced the leather. The dodo seemed satisfied at having exacted her toll in flesh and doubled back to make a big scene of stalking around the nest while squawking loudly, a clear message that anyone else wishing to disturb her precious egg was going to get the same treatment *that guy* got! By now Gerbald himself was up a tree, massaging his ankle.

"Jesus crippled Christ on crutches cut from the cross!" he cursed loudly. Pam couldn't say her friend had been afraid during the encounter, Gerbald didn't do fear, but this was as discombobulated as she had seen him in a long time.

"Good gawd, Gerbald, where did you come up with that bit of blasphemy? Dore would pop a vein!" Pam suppressed a laugh, not wanting to further injure the great woodsman's pride.

"Thanks, it's a Gerbald original. That hurt like hell! Mother Dodo put a hole in my boot, she even broke the skin!"

"Consider it a sacrifice for science. Ya know, I never would have gotten to witness that nest protecting behavior without you along because I'm not dumb enough to actually piss a mother dodo off." Pam laughed despite herself. The whole thing, from her safe vantage point, had been nothing short of hilarious. "Channel Thirteen Mega Monster Afternoon Presents: *Gerbald the Fearless Dinosaur Hunter vs the Menace of The Mad Dodo Mama!*"

Gerbald laughed along with her. It really was only his pride that had been in any danger. The dodo, despite its bluster and fearsome beak, hadn't been any kind of real threat to him, beyond a bit of a bruise.

They stayed in their trees for a while, watching until the mollified hen settled down on her lovely big egg, from which vantage point she favored them both with stern glares until, ruffled feathers at last relaxing into their normal downy softness, she fell asleep.

On their way back to camp that evening, Pam looked back on the mother dodo's defense and began to feel sad. Gerbald had been caught off guard, but if he had really wanted to, he could have dispatched the creature with ease. She realized all his actions had been to avoid having to injure the dodo rather than to protect himself. Pam now felt a bit bad about teasing him. Even an inexperienced woodsman, say a sailor, or a farmer, would ultimately prevail against the big, flightless birds. Just as they had in her former world . . .

A darker thought came then, something she knew she must eventually face. Even if she could control human depredations against the dodo, there was still the danger posed by introduced species. Humans had killed their share of the poor creatures, evolved with no natural predators present, and completely unequipped to deal with any real danger. But from all Pam had read and surmised, the major threat to the dodo's future would be the foreign animals that would inevitably arrive with humanity, whether by design or not.

Yes, she would try to stop that invasion, and she would make some difference. After all, she had not allowed her colonists to bring along any mammals other than horses, cattle, sheep, and some very well-trained herding dogs (no cats!), but there would be rats on that ship, too, they were simply unstoppable. Even immaculate *Redbird* had carried vermin, despite her and Dore's dedicated efforts to eradicate them. How many rats had swum ashore during the wreck? Would they find today's nest and break that pretty shell into a hundred sticky pieces, while the poor mother squawked and chased them about in vain?

Listen Pammie, she thought, *there is no point in fretting about this now. We haven't even gotten from Point B to C yet in this mess, and here you are worrying about P and Q.* She smiled, deciding to chew on the problem a little more anyway. *Well, it's going to come up eventually. Might as well have a plan.*

Rats, along with feral dogs, cats, pigs, and, according to the books, monkeys, would be her enemies in the future and she would have to come up with ways to first prevent, then when that battle was inevitably lost, control their presence on the island. She shook her head knowing if she lived to see it, the day would come when she would find herself in the role of the island's animal control officer, and did not relish the prospect. Getting the bats out of the Baptist church belfry had put her off dealing with mammals of any sort. She had been able to manage that episode humanely without resorting to killing the poor little things, but it would be otherwise with stray invaders on Mauritius. She would have to be ruthless.

Satisfied with her initial studies, Pam was now spending most of her time painting accurate portraits of the dodos. This was for scientific purposes, of course, as well as the genuine pleasure the art gave her. She was no Audubon, but her technique had improved since she painted her first *blaukelchen* as it frolicked in her garden's bird bath. The problem was, despite their general appearance of ungainliness, the big birds covered a lot of ground in a day, sometimes traveling many miles on their sturdy, yellow, four-toed feet. Upon finding them in the morning, she would get her bamboo easel (a hand-crafted

SAVING THE DODO

gift from the Bosun), and her precious watercolors all set up in a nice, sunny clearing, but before she could even finish the initial sketches, the dodos would plow through the area's edible matter, then wander off, leaving Pam to repack her gear and follow. This happened again and again and she was beginning to get frustrated until she hit upon an idea.

She and Gerbald spent the next morning gathering nuts, seeds, fallen fruits, beetles, and whatever else they could find for dodo treats. After they had a sizable store in hand, they caught up to the dodos at their latest hangout. Overall, the birds seemed to move in a very loose, but discernible flock, groups and subgroups working over their various territories in what Pam thought must be a slow, weeks-long, loop, allowing the freshly foraged areas time to replenish before coming around again. Pam sat up her paints and got to work. A while later, just as the dodos were about to move on, Pam reached into her bag of goodies and threw a healthy handful of dodo treats across the clearing to the ever-hungry birds.

"Here you go, sweeties! Eat it up, yum, yum!" Pam called and cooed while Gerbald just shook his head. The dodos looked at Pam with their uncanny yellow eyes, then looked at the treats scattered at their feet. With what Pam felt for sure was a shrug of their tiny wings, they began pecking at the unexpected offering.

"I don't think this is a good idea," Gerbald muttered. "Didn't you say we don't want to make pets of them?"

"I'm not! I'm just feeding a few pigeons in the park, that's all! Look at this sweet afternoon light, it's perfect for painting!" Whistling a merry tune, she went back to it. A quarter of an hour later, the dodos had eaten all of Pam's treats and were beginning to move off again, when Pam called out a friendly "Yoo-hoo!" and threw them yet another double handful. This time, the dodos began to eat without pause while Pam continued to work on her latest masterpiece. After several more repetitions of the new ritual, Pam beamed at what was turning out to be quite a nice work of art, and she did say so herself! It might even be the one to use for the happy little afterward she would add to her book, *Birds of the USE*, detailing how the dodos *would not* be going extinct in *this* world, thank you very much!

After several hours, Pam decided any more work on the piece would just be fussing, so she set about getting her gear ready for the hike home. The dodos were finishing up their latest treat as she woke Gerbald from his nap, not part of his standard bodyguard and look-out routine, but they had determined they were in no danger. Mauritius, despite its rugged remoteness, was safer than Grantville's town park. During their time wandering the wilds of the Thuringerwald, Pam developed nearly as good an eye and ear for human-type

153

intruders as Gerbald. Besides, in the highly unlikely event any did show up, the seasoned warrior woodsman would be on his feet in an instant. She swore he slept with one eye open., Gerbald got plenty of extra sleep in the way of old soldiers from time immemorial, wherever and whenever he could.

"Come along, Rip Van Winkle. It's almost the eighteenth century. Let's get back."

"Wake me when its the twentieth century, or as soon as everyone owns a TV." he mumbled drowsily from beneath the wide and warped brim of his floppy, mustard-colored hat. With a groan, he rose to his nearly six-feet and stretched like some gray-whiskered, but still deadly, jungle cat. Pam marveled at his ability to sleep anywhere, as she finished packing her gear. As she made ready to leave the clearing, she noticed the dodos, although finished with their snacks, hadn't moved on. Instead, they all stood around staring at her.

Pam smiled, a bit surprised at this new behavior. She laughed a bit as she realized what was going on.

"Oh, I see, you want another treat! Sorry, kids. I gave you all I had. You're on your own again!" She turned away from them, pleased with her cleverness and the nice piece of art it had yielded, and began to walk toward the trail leading home. Out of the corner of her eye, she noticed that Gerbald had not fallen into step with her, and was still watching the dodos.

"Um, Pam? You best have a look," he told her, a wry grin on his face.

Pam turned around to see that the dodos, rather than melting back into the forest in search of food, had all moved closer to her, a group of six adults and a couple of youngsters, now just a few yards away. They stood in a loose clump, their somehow disconcerting yellow eyes all trained unblinkingly upon Pam. Frowning a bit, Pam took another two steps toward the edge of the clearing. The dodos did the same.

"Shit! They think I'm going to give them more treats."

"One dares not utter the phrase 'I told you so.' Oops. I uttered it!" Gerbald commented in an uncanny Bugs Bunny imitation.

Pam screwed up her face to stick out her tongue at him. She took another step, and the dodos followed. Exasperated, Pam waved her arms around in front of her, in what she hoped would be seen as a gesture of discouragement, and called out "Shoo! Go on now, I don't have any more for you, now *git!*" The dodos' heads bobbed around watching her arms gesticulating, then sniffed around their leathery feet to see if more treats had been let loose by those actions. Not finding any, their gaze returned to Pam. It occurred to her how large the dodos really were and she began to feel a bit unnerved by their bright-yellow stares.

She looked to Gerbald for support, but he just shrugged his shoulders.

"Don't look at me! You're *the bird lady*," he told her. "Let's just try walking away. They will get bored eventually."

Nodding nervously, Pam turned and headed down the trail at a brisk-but-not-too-brisk pace, followed closely by Gerbald. The dodos came along after, one-by-one down the narrow path through the forest. Even though she knew it was silly, Pam worried the large birds might try to rush her, which could possibly prove dangerous with their powerful beaks and claws, but the dodos were content to politely wait for more treats, and following the treat-giver seemed their best bet. Pam forced herself not to run, as she knew that despite their ungainly appearance, they could match her speed.

An hour later, they emerged along the shore near their encampment. Pam and Gerbald, followed by a neat line of dodos. Pers saw them first and whistled up Dore from her kitchen to come have a look. Soon, all the men stood watching the bizarre procession.

"I feel like the Pied Piper," Pam grumbled.

"More like Mother Goose, I should think." Gerbald teased her, enjoying every second of his friend's well-deserved discomfiture.

Pam grimaced, but managed a calm smile for those assembled, looking for all the world as if she were completely in control of the situation. As soon as she stopped moving, the dodos formed a circle around her, waiting for their next snack.

"Are these the famous dodos?" The Bosun asked, regarding the unusual creatures with wide eyes.

"Yes, indeed they are. Dore, do you happen to have any nuts stored away?" Pam's voice held just enough desperation to send her friend hurrying into the kitchen to find some. Dore returned with a leather bag full of nuts, which she passed over the dodo's heads to Pam's outreached hand, never once taking her suspicious eyes off the gathered birds.

"Gawd, I really hate further associating humans with food, but at this point I have to do something." Pam told Gerbald.

"I'm not sure why you are so edgy, they are just pigeons in the park after all!" he said, unable to stop himself from chuckling at Pam's predicament.

Pam vowed to have her revenge, then turned to her flock.

"Here, chicky-chickies, have some more nuts!" she called, throwing a heaping handful at Gerbald's feet. The birds ran to him, gobbling up their prize with a loud clacking of their bills.

"Here, hold this!" before Gerbald could think, Pam had thrust the bag into his hands. Just as he began to make his protest, she slipped around behind him, making a rapid beeline for her hut, leaping up the stairs, and slamming the door shut behind her with a loud slap of bamboo. In the meantime, the dodos had finished their latest round of snacks, and were now staring at Gerbald and the bag of nuts in his hands.

Dore began laughing, as did the gathered men, all of whom were now carefully backing away from the strange, hungry creatures in their midst.

"Ha!" Dore called out to her flummoxed husband. "It looks like Mister Funny Man is the one left holding the bag! It serves you right, buffoon!" she teased him, laughing aloud in righteous mirth before disappearing into the safety of her grass-roofed kitchen.

Gerbald shook his head at being so easily duped. With a sigh, he smiled at the dodos surrounding him.

"Come along then, my feathered friends. Let us see if clever old Gerbald can give you the slip." The dodos followed him as he led them away, back into the twilight forest. Pam wouldn't even come out for dinner that night, so eventually Dore brought something around for her to eat, growling she finally understood why the up-time phrase *for the birds* denoted something foolish or worthless.

The next day, the dodos had found their way back out of the forest and were hanging around the beach, scavenging the tide flats for bits of seaweed and snails. Pam watched from what she considered to be a safe distance, through her birding scope, as one of the larger dodos managed to catch a scuttling crab. Gerbald was taking the day off from scientific study, to lick his wounded pride. He had been up well after dark playing a game of hide-and-seek with his erstwhile followers and had little use for Pam at the moment. Pam just smiled. She knew he'd get over it sooner than later, understanding no trickster ever enjoys being among the tricked.

And so, the dodos decided to make the beach their home for the time being, sleeping under the palms, wandering through camp in search of treats, and getting underfoot. Although Pam warned everyone not to feed them, they inevitably did anyway. The ugly-cute critters were just too hard to resist! The lonely sailors enjoyed the novelty of having pets about, even ones as odd as these. The only member of the party who was immune to the dodo's charms was Dore, who had no fear of their sharp beaks, and who shooed them away from her kitchen and gardens with the fearsome might of her bamboo-handled, dried shore-grass broom.

From the time of their arrival, the *Redbird* castaways had been relying chiefly on seafood for their protein. There were few birds present that might be considered game-worthy. Gerbald had snared a few black-feathered marsh birds along the river which Pam thought might be moorhens, but they tasted pretty much like the mudflats they had come from, with little meat on their sharp bones. They had tried eating several species of sandpiper and gull, but the rubbery flesh stank of rotten fish and was so unpalatable, they ended up using it all for crab-pot bait.

The dodos had been among them for a week and their novelty was wearing off. Pam realized, to her horror, the attitude of the men toward their pets had subtly changed. Pam now saw a look of hunger on their faces as they watched the chubby dodos wander around the camp, nicely fattened up from their regular treats. Dodos were the largest, and juiciest bird they had seen since being marooned, resembling in many ways a plump turkey. They no longer were feeding the dodos for amusement's sake, she suspected, but rather to fatten them up for the cooking pot! Even Dore was sneaking a predatory look at them as she worked on the crab-and-coconut curry they were having *yet again* for the noonday meal.

Pam decided she had better head this disconcerting development off, right at the pass. As the men finished their breakfast, she walked out into the morning sunlight and *harrumphed* for their attention.

"All right, everyone," she announced in her now well-seasoned Swedish, "I know you all are hungry for meat. I've been watching what's happening lately, and I *know* what's been going through your minds, but just let me tell you one thing: don't even *think* about eating a dodo, not even *one*! Anyone who does is going to be in big trouble with me, and you better believe that is a place you do not want to be! I shudder to even think how Princes Kristina would react! Besides, the books all say they taste terrible!" She was really getting mad now, and stomped around among the stunned sailors and marines, making sure they all got a good look in her eyes, and that each one fully understood that she meant business! Finally, she rose up to her full less-than-a-third of their average height, crossed her arms self-righteously, and said "You lot know how to fish, right? Well, get off your butts and start fishing! *Now*! *MOVE!*"

The men, hardened seamen all, leaped up at her fiery command, rushing off to prepare the various fishing tackle they had contrived, whatever other tasks they had planned falling to the wayside as they beat a hasty retreat to the water. Meanwhile, Gerbald disappeared into the underbrush to gather materials to weave a new fish trap. Dore hunched over her coconuts with a guilty expression, while Pam continued to stalk up and down the beach keeping a watchful eye on the oblivious dodos. *We had better get out of here before history repeats itself,* Pam thought, refusing to admit to herself she, too, was beginning to wonder what a nice, juicy dodo leg might taste like . . .

That evening the men presented Dore with a record catch, which she went to work on, barbecuing some, putting some in soup, and salting and drying the rest. Pam looked on from her front porch, her face stony, lost in deep thought. Right before their communal meal began, she stood up and politely asked for everyone's attention, wincing as those gathered looked up meekly, bracing themselves for another possible tirade.

"Gentlemen, and lady" she said with a nod toward Dore who watched from her kitchen door with a carefully inscrutable expression on her red-cheeked face, "I owe you all an apology. I am sorry for yelling at you this morning, it wasn't fair, and I was out of line. I am also sorry for much more. I have been selfish making you all wait here while I study the dodos. I've already learned as much as I need to know for now, but it became something of an obsession, the prize at long last right there before my eyes, I just couldn't stop watching them. I ignored the fact the seasons have changed and the weather is now fair enough to launch the pinnaces in a search mission for the rest of the colony. Gerbald and I could have been, *should have been,* scouting up the coastline instead of messing about in the interior, seeing if maybe there is a way to go overland. I must add that in no way is Gerbald responsible, he was merely following my whims as the dear and indulgent friend he is." She paused to see Gerbald smiling at her, relieved she had at last come to her senses. "I am sorry, and I am grateful for your patience. I feel like you are all my brothers now, thank you for your kindness, and for your patience, it means so much to me!" This brought smiles from the entire crew, their faces brightening under the flickering light of the tiki torches.

Before Pam could go on, the Bosun spoke up. "*Frau* Pam, you need not apologize to us. We are here to serve you as our Princess decreed, really, we are just doing our jobs. But more than that, and I know I can speak for everyone, we have also come to think of you as our sister. We simply think the world of you and want to please you!" There was a murmur of agreement from the gathered men and Pam felt a happy tear form in her eye. "Whatever you need from us, *Frau* Pam, it will be our continuing pleasure to provide it." The men all voiced their agreement with the Bosun and many encouraging words were said much to her relief and delight.

Pam was choked up, but managed to reply "Thank you, Nils, I am truly honored. Thank you all!" She took a moment to collect herself before continuing, her voice strong and brimming with positive energy "All right then! Here is what I propose. Tomorrow morning, Gerbald and I will scout up the coast as far as we can in one day to see what the conditions are like, then we will report back in the evening. Meanwhile, I would ask you all to make preparations for the search expedition by sea, which will launch as soon as you feel ready, even the day after tomorrow if you so determine! It's time to go find our friends!"

This brought a round of hearty cheers, all the men leaping to their feet to applaud while Pam grinned and blushed.

Dore snorted and rolled her eyes at all the hubbub, but there was a grudging smile on her too oft dour face. "Hopefully," she spoke up over the crowd, immediately gaining the men's rapt attention, "when we find the colonists, they will have a nice, plump chicken or two to spare. I have done the best I can here, but I think we have all had our fill of seafood!" This brought laughter and a round of cheers for their revered chef, followed by the men declaring they adored her cooking, and would never grow tired of it! Boisterous Eskil, who always had a clever word to say, exclaimed "*Frau* Dore, you could stew an old boot in a pot of seaweed with a pinch of gunpowder and it would taste good!" Everyone laughed while Dore smiled, pleased by the praise, but trying not to show it. "*Ja, ja*, very kind of you to say. Now, let's eat before it gets cold!"

Garrett W. Vance

CHAPTER 21: STRANGERS COME TO CALL

J ust after first light the next morning, Pam and Gerbald were climbing over the rugged, rocky bluff separating the cove from the adjacent stretch of beach to the north and east. Pam hoped they would be able to learn something useful about the coastline where they had last seen their fleet before their seaworthy, but small and somewhat fragile pinnaces began their search mission. It was hard going, the dark, volcanic rocks sharp and unforgiving. Far below, she caught a glimpse of the wave-lashed rocks that had claimed *Redbird*, a painful memory Pam did her best to push aside. She needed to focus on the task before her *right now*, where an unexpected slip might prove deadly. They paused to catch their breath on a natural terrace before attempting the next difficult stretch, when an unexpected splash of color out on the water caught Pam's keen, birdwatcher's eye.

"Gerbald! Look!" Pam called out in a tense stage whisper, as she dropped to her belly in the tall grass, then began crawling toward the cliff's edge. Gerbald slithered up next to her with practiced grace. There was a ship coming into the cove, its startling red sails a bright flame burst to life on the calm, azure sea. The highly unexpected visitor began striking her sails around two-hundred yards offshore, followed by an anchor dropping with a crystalline splash.

Pam pulled her precious birding scope out of her shirt by its sturdy neck-strap. She cupped a palm over the outer lens to prevent any reflection from the glare of the southern sun that might give away their position. Focusing, she gasped in surprise. The vessel was brightly painted in very vibrant colors. Elegantly carved dragons, sea turtles, and cranes adorned the woodwork, so vivid they seemed ready to leap into life at any moment. The fore and aft of the ship were both high-set, and the sails were an unusual rectangular shape, ribbed like a folding hand fan.

"Hmmm." I think it's a junk," Pam said.

"Really?" Gerbald scratched his chin and squinted hard at the vessel below. "I am no seaman, Pam, but it looks like a perfectly seaworthy boat to me, although shaped rather oddly." He remarked in a cautious tone.

Pam stifled a laugh. "No, not *that* kind of junk! I mean a *Chinese* junk, a type of ship from the Orient."

"Ah, another one of those *homonyms*. A rather annoying feature of English, I must say."

"I agree. Christ all mighty, we have to get back to the camp. Do you think they've seen it, too?"

"*Herr* Bosun always sets a watch. The Swedish sailors and marines are resourceful and well-trained men. We are lucky to have them."

"Darn tootin'! If you're going to be shipwrecked with someone, a friendly band of resourceful Vikings is definitely the way to go!"

Pam watched the men on the junk's decks go about their tasks. It was hard to see much detail at that distance, but in general they had black hair and sported sharp, pointed beards, their complexions ranging from light-olive to a swarthy brown. Many wore turbans or various types of less elaborate cloth headgear. For the most part, their garb was loose fitting, some quite colorful, the officers perhaps, whereas most of the crew wore simple whites, grays and tans.

"They don't look Chinese," Pam whispered, even though it was very unlikely they could be heard against the wind at such a distance. She handed Gerbald the scope.

"Indeed, they don't, at least not any such as I have seen on TV or at the movies, although I think some of those were actually white people in poorly-done make-up."

"I think they're Arabs, or maybe Indians." Pam said, squinting against the sea's nearly-blinding diamond sparkle for a better look.

"Perhaps, or some relative. Turks, possibly?" Gerbald scanned the decks with Pam's scope, the retried soldier ascertaining the visitor's potential as a threat. "They are well-armed with those curved blades. They look strong and are quite possible able fighting men. Several have firearms, although those look rather primitive, even by the standards of my century. Oh— oh my!" His tone turned dark, his eyebrows knitting in sudden concern.

"What?" Pam asked, growing uneasy, not yet sure what her friend had noticed that had made him so pensive.

"It's ugly, Pam, I wish I could shield you from this. But, given the situation, I feel you had best see for yourself." He handed the scope back to her. "Look, hanging from the bowsprit."

Pam looked, and to her utter horror, beheld a line strung with severed heads, grisly trophies swinging in the sea breeze, many with long, silky, black hair. Despite the advanced state of decay, she was sure their features were Asiatic.

It took Pam a moment for her to catch her breath from the shocking sight. In a hoarse, dread-laden voice she croaked, "My God, Gerbald! They slaughtered the Chinese who owned the junk!"

"Indeed. These guys are pirates! This is not good."

"Have you ever fought any like them before?"

"There were some such as these among the Spanish. They were fierce fighters. Don't worry, though, they will bleed just as any other man." he told her, an oath, really, his voice taking on a hard, cold edge.

Pam looked at the former soldier, still fearsome in his fifties, his hand resting instinctively on the hilt of the deadly *katzbalger* shortsword attached to his belt. Gerbald didn't talk about his life as a soldier in the Thirty Years War much, but Pam had gleaned a few things from over the course of their friendship.

Gerbald had a strong moral compass, holding himself to a strict personal code of honor and justice. He was one of the few who always tried to dissuade the other men from raping and pillaging the unfortunate local populace, sometimes even coming to blows with his own comrades in arms. It had made him no few enemies, one of which Pam had struck down with her grandmother's oak walking stick, shattering his jaw while she defended an injured Gerbald. It was her own first taste of war, and it had made her admire Gerbald's courage even more.

"No doubt they will bleed, and from the looks of it they will have it coming to them. Now we gotta' git!"

They slowly eased themselves back from the cliff's edge through the grass, not wanting to draw attention to their movements, leaving little trace of their presence. Clambering back into the shadowed wood, they made haste back to what Pam had come to think of as *Camp Castaway*. They arrived to find Dore clutching her biggest cleaver, waiting near the hidden path which was their designated escape route, leading to a refuge in the forest they had prepared for such emergencies. Seeing her loved ones arrive, she puffed out her typical exasperated breath. Before they could begin to tell her what they had seen, Dore addressed them in hushed and serious tones.

"You are late. We know about the boat. We were not seen, and the *Löjtnant* has already set up his men in an ambush. They think those men out there will come ashore for fresh water. They are no Christians by the looks of them. *Herr* Bosun says they are murderous pirates!"

Gerbald nodded, allowing himself a grim smile at the prospect of combat. Pam leaned on her grandmother's walking stick, catching her breath, and calming her nerves as she watched Gerbald slip silently into the brush to confer with the men, becoming invisible to any onlooker within an instant. Thanks to his training, she knew how to do that, too, and in a situation like this, she was glad of it.

"Come on, Dore, let's get undercover. This is one time where I am more than happy to let the boys do their macho warrior thing and stay out of the way."

"And such boys they are! They relish this, you know. Fools."

CHAPTER 22: PAM HATCHES A PLAN

P am led her friend down the escape route, a narrow trail with an entrance imperceptible to any who didn't know it. Dore followed with remarkable grace. For the first time, it occurred to Pam that Dore had lost a lot of weight since their voyage had begun. Her sturdy, buxom build had taken on an almost youthful slenderness. She moved as silently as Pam did. Having been a soldier's wife and camp follower for many long years, Dore was no stranger to slipping behind cover when the weapons came out. They paused at a fallen log in the shade of the trees, not far from the hideout, and waited there, listening for any sounds of struggle from back at the camp. An hour passed, and then two, according to Pam's self-winding, waterproof Timex, more valuable than a chest of precious jewels in this century. They began to get restless.

"What if they don't need fresh water?" Dore asked.

"Then they won't need to come ashore. I sure would like to take that ship from those bastards, but I don't think our guys can win an attack by sea, even with the pinnaces. By the time they got it in the water, the pirates would have plenty of time to either pull anchor and scram, or prepare to hold them off. They would have a huge advantage." Pam rubbed her chin and began to think about the problem at hand. If they didn't do *something*, the ship might just sail away without giving them any opportunity to capture it, which was beginning to seem like an important goal. Pam was sure they were all ready to take a chance to escape in a seaworthy craft at this point, even if the risk was high.

The unfortunate truth was, the pinnaces just wouldn't cut it on a long voyage. According to the Bosun, they were only supposed to hold half their current number safely, being designed as shore-hugging ship-to-shore ferries and fair weather scouts. The pinnaces were made for the shallows and mild seas, seaworthy, yes, but not really meant for the rigors independent seagoing vessels might face. Short of being rescued by a friendly ship, which was unlikely to happen any time soon, they needed to get their hands on something big enough to carry all of them away from this lonely coast. Ideally, something big enough to mount that lovely up-time inspired carronade, which would give them a fighting chance if they encountered bad guys. The junk might be just the thing. The question was, how to capture it from the band of blood-thirsty pirates currently in possession? Pam squatted on the fallen log, going into what she thought of as thinking cap mode, working the problem in her head.

After a while, a grin came to her face. "Oh, goodness . . ." she mumbled.

Dore's ears pricked up. "You have an idea." she stated, knowing Pam's nuances well by now.

Pam nodded carefully, as if afraid to lose it. It was ridiculous, of course. It was *utterly* ridiculous, which just might be its greatest strength. She took one of Dore's strong, wash-worn hands in hers.

"Yes, Dore, I have an idea. I saw it in an old movie, or maybe on *Gilligan's Island*, that old TV show Gerbald likes so much. Now, it's pretty crazy, you are going to have to trust me on this, but it's going to work. It's going to work because it *is* crazy!" She leaned closer to her older friend and outlined her plan while Dore listened, eyes growing larger and larger.

"*What*?" Dore almost shouted when Pam had finished, then caught herself and hissed, "You want us to *what*?" Dore's face had an expression of stunned astonishment Pam had rarely seen before, the look of a very conservative Christian woman who has asked to do something beyond the pale, far, far beyond the pale. Pam continued to nod, now surer than ever.

"Listen, Dore honey, it's the only plan I've got, and I know it sounds bad, it's totally nuts in fact, but we have to do it. There's not much time. The guys' ambush isn't working. It needs bait. It's time for us girls to step up. I know you are made of strong stuff. Now please, put your misgivings aside and help me do this. I *need* you, Dore. I need you to do this with me."

Dore narrowed her icy blue eyes at Pam, her best friend, her adopted little sister, in some ways the child she never had. The formidable, all-purpose, soldier's wife harrumphed mightily, and fiddled with her apron strings, lost in thought. Disapproval and mistrust showed in every twitch of her meaty, yet deft fingers. Pam waited for her to work it out, hoping Dore would realize the necessity of her bizarre proposal. Seeing the look of fading hope on Pam's face, Dore gripped Pam's hand hard and said, "For *you*, my dear Pam, for *you*, and only because *you* would have it! May the Good Lord forgive us."

Shortly, she and Dore were in a huddle behind the camp with Gerbald, the Bosun, the *Löjtnant*, and Pers, while the other men kept their positions. The anchored ship's crew seemed to have finished doing whatever it was they had stopped to do and looked as if they were ready to set sail.

Having heard Pam's plan, the Bosun exclaimed rather loudly, "You want to *what?*" His face was a study in astonishment. Young Pers had turned a whiter shade of pale, his eyes big as China plates. Gerbald laughed into his hand, his entire frame shaking with mirth, until Dore slugged him hard on the bicep, but *not* on his sword arm Pam noted. Gerbald let a laugh escape. There were tears in his eyes, he was so struck with the pure outrageousness of what Pam proposed. Barely controlling his hilarity, he announced, "I *like* this plan!"

Dore glared at him. "As you would, you disgusting goat. To see your own women folk half-naked, like these *harlot dancers* would appeal to an impious sinner like you. May God have pity on your black and shriveled soul!"

"Not *harlots*, Dore, *hula! Hula* dancers. Big difference. It's a cultural thing. They live in a warm climate, so they just don't wear as many clothes as we do!"

Gerbald continued to chuckle at the proceedings, making Pam snarl at him with uncharacteristic vehemence "That's enough out of you, dumbass! I need her calm, and you are *not* helping!" She slugged him in the arm, hard just like Dore had for good measure. But n*ot on the sword arm, we're going to need that,* she thought. Pam was sure he was immune to any physical pain she could inflict, but her fierce tone and epithet silenced him, his mirth replaced by a pitiful, chastised look, which still smacked of insincerity. The man could be infuriating when he got into his teasing mode. *Boys!*

Pam turned to the Bosun and the *Löjtnant.* "Gentlemen, I must humbly request your participation. I would like to have the men ready to get between us and them *fast.*" They nodded their understanding, accepting her lead. The idea of her, Pam Miller, The Bird Lady of Grantville placing herself in charge of a military maneuver, especially one as preposterous as what she proposed, seemed hilarious to her, and she let out a nervous laugh that lowered the pressure in the group. "I know it sounds crazy, but it's all I've got. Are you fellows with me?"

The men looked at each other for a moment, then came to silent agreement. "We are with you, Pam." *Löjtnant* Lundkvist spoke for them, and they all nodded.

Pam favored them with her best and brightest smile, then took Dore by the hand. "Come on Dore, let's go get dressed. It's time to lay the bait."

Pam ushered Dore away, Dore dragging her feet, but following along, her face a study in misery. Pam led her into the cool dimness of their camp's main hut, where they held meetings, stored food, and ate their meals during inclement weather. It would now serve as their *costuming department.* Pam looked at Dore's deep frown and felt bad, but there was nothing to be done for it.

"You need to buck up and get into character. Smile, relax! We need to be good actors." Her voice was full of false, but hopefully convincing, cheer.

"*Actors?* Those sin lovers who appear in all manner of immodest garb in your up-time entertainments? Oh, Dear Lord, strike me down where I stand!" Dore looked up at the thatched ceiling of the hut.

Pam lost her patience. There wasn't much time, and the stress was becoming too much to bear. She grabbed Dore by the arms and shook her with quite a bit of strength, Dore being a solidly built individual. Pam raised her voice as loud as she dared. "Damn it all, Dore, *listen!* We are *not* sinners! We are doing this to save ourselves and get off this fucking rock, got it? God is merciful, right? He would want us to fight for our lives, right? So, whatever we do today, He's going to forgive us! Now *grow up* and help me pull this off!"

Dore's eyes focused on Pam with startled wideness. Her dear Pam, shaking her and lecturing her as if she were a stubborn child was an unpleasant first, the latest of what was shaping up to be a very long day of unpleasant firsts.

Pam released her grip to hug Dore tightly as she would have her own mother or sister, and spoke in a shaky small voice, all trace of anger gone. "I'm so sorry, Dore, but I can't think of *anything else to do!* This is all I've got and it *has to work!*" Dore hugged Pam back, then untangled herself from her friend's frantic embrace.

"It is I who should be sorry, dear Pam. Sorry for questioning your sincere efforts and being such a pious old fool. I know you would only ask such of me in desperate times, as these are. It is indeed time I 'grow up' and be a help to you." Dore took a deep breath and let it out. She even managed a small smile. "Now tell me, what must we do to appear as *harlot dancers?*"

That made Pam laugh, her tone a little desperate, but warming to the intrinsic hilarity of their situation. She stepped back and eyed her old friend who now stood ready for Pam's orders. Pam, much relieved, got started. "Well, first you have got to lose that apron. It's *so* last century."

CHAPTER 23: HARLOT DANCERS

A s Dore began untying the many clever knots that made up the tightly braided bun her husband had to navigate through in their private hours, Pam reached up to set free the ponytail she usually tied her flyaway hair with an effort to keep it mostly under control. She shook her head to loosen the wavy, dishwater blonde locks, *fly, be free!* then mussed it all up with her hands to make it look even wilder. Next, she emptied her pockets of any valuables such as her scope, and put them into her trusty rucksack, which she hid behind a rafter in the shadows of the grassy ceiling. She took off her shirt and stood a little self consciously in her bra, careful not to let Dore see her own shyness. Dore looked at her with approval as she hung her apron on a branch of one of the hut's primitive support beams.

"You are such a lovely girl, Pam, and still so young. If I were your age and still single, I might let the men know it, in a properly modest way, of course. You are a candle that hides its light."

Pam was forty-five years old and didn't consider herself either *lovely* or a *girl,* but smiled at Dore's praise. She had never been a bombshell of any sort, but she was attractive in a step-or-two-ahead-of-Plain-Jane sort of way. Her years tromping around forests and fields downtime had trimmed away any trace of the extra pounds she felt had made her so unattractive in her late thirties and early forties, the self-pity-cherry-bon-bon-eating-years that had followed her divorce. She took a deep breath, sucked in her hourglass waist, and stuck her ample-enough-for-another-look chest out. It seemed things were still holding up well there. She allowed herself a rather pleased grin.

"Maybe I do still got something, huh? Let's hope it's something an Indian Ocean pirate might appreciate." She took a careful step toward Dore. "Now it's your turn, darlin'." Dore stood still, nodding to Pam in a *do what you must gesture,"* so Pam reached out and began loosening Dore's untied braids. To Pam's great

169

surprise, long, lush locks of auburn laced with strands of silver fell nearly to Dore's waist.

"Talk about holding your light under a bushel! Good golly, what I would give to have hair like yours! You keep it tucked up so tight, I had no idea!" Pam reached out and felt a lock, it was thick and smooth, nothing like the frizzy feel of her own hopeless mane. Dore blushed a little, and admitted Gerbald was quite fond of it, and that's why she kept it long, for him, despite the nuisance of its required care.

Pam nodded. "I'll bet he likes it. It's gorgeous. *You* are gorgeous, Dore!" Pam shunted aside the bit of jealousy that crept into her mind and said in what she hoped was a firm yet comforting tone, "Okay, next we got to free up your bosom. Take off the smock." Dore complied, and the drab, gray piece of utilitarian clothing came off.

Like many down-time working women Pam had seen, Dore kept her bosom tightly confined. Accomplishing this was a wrap made of sturdy canvas. At Pam's nod, Dore loosened the straps on the dour down-time version of a modesty-defending brassiere. Pam's eyes widened. She knew Dore had plenty in the chest department, but the reality was, well, larger than expected, the envy of any Hollywood starlet. Dore's liberated assets thrust out like those of a mighty warrior queen, nothing at all like she had expected. Dore, bare to the waist, with her hair down, had ceased to resemble the humble washer-woman Pam had grown accustomed to, and was revealed as a Wagnerian goddess, a lovely and fearless Valkyrie. Dore was solidly built, certainly, even after the island diet the hourglass was perhaps a bit thick, but now that her true buxom, healthy beauty was revealed, the effect was something close to ravishing.

Pam let out a long, almost catcall of a whistle. "I'm going to call you 'Wonder Woman' from now on. You are a hottie!"

Dore blushed even harder. "Gerbald, he tells me I am beautiful, but you know him. His sweet talking is shameless. When I was a young girl in my teens, I remember the village boys thought well of me, and I often felt their lustful looks, but that was so long ago."

"Girl, I'm here to tell you, you still got it, and then some! Gawd, Dore, you look fantastic, and not just in a 'for a woman your age' kind of way. You could make the village boys get down on their knees and beg right now! Shit, I guess that makes me Mary Ann 'cause you got Ginger nailed."

Dore's face burned the scarlet of a summer sunset. At last, she smiled in a way that Pam had never seen before. A day for firsts indeed. A bright bit of Psychology 101 popped into Pam's head and she put it to *The Plan's* advantage right away.

"Look, Dore, just pretend you are a silly seventeen-year-old again and these pirate types are the village boys! It's perfectly all right to be a bit naughty in a situation like that. We are just pretending, to save our skins. So just let go and be a little more flirtatious than you would have allowed yourself back then. Well, a *lot* more flirtatious. We need these clowns to want our bodies badly!"

It was Dore's turn to laugh now, in a shy, but pleased way. "The village boys! Yes, I was a flirt sometimes, oh, the shame. Very well. I can do that, Pam. We will make this work."

"Right. Now, off come the skirts." Dore's face changed from glowing sunset to kitchen flour again. Pam thought she heard her mumbling a prayer for forgiveness under her breath as she began to unclasp the ties of her exceedingly modest dresses.

A short time later the women emerged sporting their hastily improvised costumes, chests wrapped loosely in torn bedsheets, bedecked with hastily picked flowers from the garden Dore had planted around the hut, and grass skirts over their under-garments made from materials reallocated from the hut's walls, making sure to show quite a bit of leg. Dore's legs were those of an athlete, well-muscled from years on the road, and standing at work for long hours, but still shapely. The strings of seashells they had made to decorate the place while fighting the sheer boredom of their existence, were now draped around their necks, and more blossoms firmly woven into their free-flowing hair. Each carried a large basket full of that evening's dinner fruit and Pam had used some of the berry juice to brighten up their lips.

"We are some glorious and sex-starved hula harlots in need of some male attention and we always get our way!" Pam announced, and they both nearly lost control to a fit of nervous giggles.

"Now, Dore," Pam said breathing deeply to retain composure, "remember these pirates are dangerous. We don't want them to get too close. Let's try to lead them back up the trail where our guys can get the jump on them and the fight can't be seen from the ship. When the killing starts, we run like hell, okay?"

"Got it." Dore resembled a seductive and dangerous heathen chieftainess. If Pam had a mirror, she would have been both shocked and proud of her own wanton and wild appearance, a veritable tigress of lust. She figured she at least somewhat resembled a Caucasian Hollywood extra made into a faux-Polynesian girl, last seen throwing flower petals in the path of *Fantasy Island's* latest guests. A ridiculous, counterfeit *wahine*, but still easy on the eye. A sudden burst of confidence filled her, *Goddamn it, we actually look pretty fine!*

As they sashayed down the path to the beach as seductively as they could muster, Pam began to feel eyes on her. She tried not to look right or left to avoid giving away the mens' positions, but out of the corner of her well-trained birder's eyes she could make out sailors hidden in the bushes, their mouths open in pure astonishment, tinged with a bit of dawning appreciation. *Sailors! They are forgiven! But those goofballs better keep your eyes on the pirates when we come back this way!* All too soon, they left the cover provided by the last line of palms perched along the high tideline and sauntered onto the still hot sand. Pam stifled a grimace and whispered, "Remember, we want them to come ashore. We must be alluring sirens. Let's get their attention now."

Dore called out in German, "Come, oh wretched and lustful goats from yon ship. Come and feel my ample breasts in your greasy, godless hands!" Pam almost lost it again, but realized they would be better off not revealing their identity as Europeans beyond the paleness of their skin, which she hoped would pass for exotic in these latitudes. She stage whispered to Dore, "Don't speak German or English. We want them to think we are natives."

Dore's brow knitted below her wreath of exotic blossoms. "What should I say then?"

"Just use nonsense talk, like to a baby. Boo-loo ooh-loo gaga waga! But make it sound sexy!"

"Boo-loo-ooh-loo! Rhumba, rhumba, rhumba!!" she crowed back with unfettered heathen delight. She whispered to Pam, "A *rhumba* is one of those shamelessly suggestive dances from up-time. I saw it on TV."

"That's perfect, Dore. More like that!" Pam whispered back. "Calypso bistro, bongo wongo marimba hoochi-koochi!" Pam shouted at the top of her lungs while performing her best imitation of a parade float beauty queen's welcoming wave. In the distance, she could see the junk's crew beginning to rouse to the racket.

About halfway to the water's edge they came to a stop. Pam squinted to see if they had the pirate's attention, and found, oh yes, they did. The sheet-wrapped goons were beginning to chatter excitedly as they stared and pointed at the spectacle unfolding on the beach. Pam motioned to Dore to follow her lead. They set the baskets down slowly to make sure there was a nice long view of their cleavage, then began motioning to their abundant offerings with alluring gestures of invitation that would make a pro blush.

"Ooga, beluga! *You swarthy schmucks!* We got's-a some big-a froota-loopas for you-a!" She turned again to Dore who was mimicking her gestures. "And now, we dance!" Pam announced to her blushing, but gamely seductive, friend.

"You start!" Dore hissed at her.

"Koo-lookoo-kookoo-lookoo-koo!" Pam yodeled at the top of her lungs as she began to shake her belly and her breasts as hard as she could in a move she had seen on a Don Ho TV special when she was a kid. She continued to vibrate, as she slowly turned around to give them a three sixty degree view of all the available goods. Dore followed her lead, turning in the opposite direction. Her shaking was a speed or two slower, but she added a warbling bird-like cry in her powerful church choir alto. *Go, girl, go!* Pam grinned at her as they came back around again. Next, Pam stopped shaking and began a circular swaying of the hips while her arms lithely made come hither gestures toward the boat.

To both Pam's relief and growing trepidation, she saw their ploy was working. The junk's pirate crew were slapping each other on the backs in what was surely an exchange of lascivious dares. Several more worked to untie a small craft lashed to the deck, a sleek longboat they lowered into the water. *They've swallowed it, hook, line, and sinker! Time to reel in!* Pam and Dore continued to shake and gyrate their scandalously half-clad bodies as if trying to stay upright in a fearsome earthquake.

An older, corpulent, and well-dressed fellow emerged from the upper decks. He sported an enormous, white handlebar mustache, and a over-sized turban from right out of a storybook. *The captain, I presume?* Whatever he may be, Pam was sure, he was the guy in charge. Upon seeing what was happening, his round face turned scarlet, and he began shouting at the crew. The men shrugged their shoulders, pointed at the beach, and looked back at him with shamed, but imploring grins. The captain-type narrowed his eyes to have another look at the distraction across the water, so Pam and Dore both waved and blew kisses to him. With a disgusted snort and a dismissive wave of his hand, he marched back into his cabin. Whatever happened next would be no responsibility of his.

The men began arguing over who was going to get to go first, which soon escalated into a scuffle. After a few moments of chaos, the winners began crowding into the longboat, stepping on and over each other as they vied for a spot. There was another contingent who remained on the deck, their faces scowling, either unimpressed by the beach-side burlesque show, or under strict orders to remain on watch. They would have to deal with that fun bunch of fellows later, but at least most of the moths were flying to the flame.

"Oh shit, here they come!" Pam hissed out of the side of her mouth to Dore, who had really gotten into the spirit of the thing and was beckoning to the oncoming boatload of hormones. Pam's eyes widened at this impressive display of wantonness, and not to be outdone, she began a snaky, pelvis-thrusting, dance that included some low front bends complete with jiggling. It was all mortifying, but she silenced that unhappy voice in her head, they were doing what had to be done. The pirate types were now rowing faster, looking like something out of a corny old adventure movie. Pam couldn't deny the comical aspect of the proceedings, she held back a laugh that could too easily turn hysterical. *This is so dumb, but it's working!*

When the boat hit the shallows, the pirates began clambering out into the gentle surf, tripping over each other in a continuing race to reach the prize first. Pam and Dore began their retreat to the trail. They left the fruit baskets where they were, hoping to slow the oncomers a bit. Walking backwards as rapidly as they dared, while still beckoning and cooing, they reached the line of palms just as their admirers reached the baskets. Pam and Dore both began pantomiming eating, and a fair number of the men paused to fill their hands with the offering, biting into the luscious fruit with sly smiles that anticipated more delights to come, their eyes never leaving the women for long. *Good, now some of them have their hands full of nice, juicy, slippery fruits instead of on their weapons.* Pam had caught a good look at the wicked scimitars, daggers, and several exotic-looking pistols they wore shoved into their belts and lost any doubts she might have had they were facing dangerous pirates, or whatever passed for a seagoing scourge in these parts.

Pam winked at Dore, their mission almost accomplished, and began to edge back into the trees, still cooing and beckoning to their prey. *Come on, you ass-holes, follow the pretty ladies!*

There was a discussion among the pirates, undoubtedly, as to whether to proceed into the trees or not. This didn't last long, as they appeared to feel they were in no danger, if any unfriendly "natives" appeared, they seemed confident they would be able to make short work of them. Such overconfidence and lust proved to be just the right combination. The pirates assumed they were being led to where the real party would start, and gamely followed along.

Pam and Dore had not quite reached the spot where the ambush awaited. Unfortunately, some of the pirates had grown impatient, and were catching up to them more quickly than expected, their hands eager for offerings more alluring than fruit. Pam gave Dore a small push, a signal to move faster. A pirate caught up to Pam just then, grabbing her wrist, hard. Pam felt a note of panic ring through her, but kept smiling. Dore paused, to look back, worry creeping onto her face. Pam gestured with her chin for Dore to move on, but she knew her friend wouldn't leave her behind. A second pirate was closing fast. The plan was in danger of falling apart and Pam's heart began to race. The one holding onto her used his free hand to grab one of Pam's breasts, causing her to yelp. In retaliation, Pam gave him a solid sock in the jaw that would have ended any bar brawl, but this was a hardened brute, it only made him laugh as he tightened his grip while she struggled to break free.

That was all the signal Gerbald and the Swedes needed. Pam watched in amazement as a large, sage-green and mustard-colored blur came rocketing out of the brush. Suddenly, the man pawing Pam was sporting a bright red gash where his throat had been, the work of Gerbald's deadly *katzbalger* shortsword.

Pam brushed the dying pirate's still clutching hands away from her, all that was holding him upright. He collapsed into a growing pool of his own blood, limp as if all the bones had gone out of him. An identical fate met the pirate closest behind, who hadn't even had time to begin to think of pulling out his own weapon before the *Löjtnant* drew an ornately-decorated longsword across his throat. *Good!* Pam thought, her blood running cold, a deep current of icy wrath. The decaying, tortured faces of the beheaded Chinese sailors flashed in her mind, evaporating any shreds of guilt she might have had about orchestrating the deaths of these men.

Pam and Dore began running, Pam pushing Dore ahead of her as much as Dore was pulling Pam into the tall grass, away from the action. From a relatively safe distance, she saw Gerbald cut down a third pirate with his *katzbalger* as the Bosun shoved his cutlass deep into the gut of a fourth. The *Löjtnant*, not to be outdone, skewered another through the chest. As planned, no one fired a shot, keeping the inland action a secret from the remaining pirates at anchor. One or two of the pirates managed to get their weapons out, but Gerbald and the Swedes made quick work of them. It was finished as rapidly as it had begun. The sailors dragged the pirates' bodies off into the brush to hide them, then scuffed fresh sand and scattered leaves across the trail to cover the drying pools of blood just in case anyone else came looking. Pam hoped they would, since the same fate awaited them as had befallen their brother pirates.

Pers, with his keen eyes, and Rask and Torgir, both experienced marines, remained on watch at the ambush site while the rest went back to the camp to regroup. The Bosun was a hearty man in his early fifties, although aged prematurely by years of sea-winds and the relentless sun. He was doing his level best not to stare at Pam in her 'harlot dancer' get-up, and losing that battle. This was possibly the most female flesh he had ever seen, outside of a dimly lit dockside brothel, and the poor fellow was obviously shaken. Pam smiled at him, causing him to snap out of it. The Bosun, scarlet with embarrassment, quickly turned   his focus to what must have been a fascinating nearby palm tree.

"Good job, everyone!" Pam praised them, "That worked really well! I have an idea for part two, so tell me what you think." All the men listened to Pam's next plan, mostly managing not to stare at the ladies' exposed expanses. Dore stood unashamed beside her, a lioness proudly standing with her brave and clever young companion, head, and other assets, held high. Gerbald couldn't stop grinning to the point that it must certainly hurt, he was so pleased to see his Christian soldier wife of many long years standing before him in unfettered heathen glory, a warrior queen of old! Dore saw his goggle-eyed look, and rather than become annoyed as she once would have, favored her husband with a serene smile. Pam saw this exchange out of the corner of her eye. *Oh gawd, what have I unleashed? I just hope he doesn't want her to dress up like Princess Leia next!* When Pam finished outlining her plan, the men, heads down, all mumbled their agreement before fleeing the sight of so much female flesh. Pam giggled as she and Dore retired to the main hut to get ready for their next show.

CHAPTER 24: BOARDING PARTY

The shadows had already grown long. Dusk followed, so they didn't have much time to prepare. The pirates onboard the anchored ship had grown agitated, but it seemed there was only one landing craft, and it was out of reach on the beach. So far, no one had volunteered to swim ashore to check how their comrades might be enjoying their shore leave. The mustachioed, and ornately turbaned captain was close to having a conniption fit. He stomped around the deck, shouting at the empty shore with a menacing bellow.

Just after sunset, a procession of the island's inhabitants came down the trail to the beach carrying torches and more baskets of fruit. The two women were joined by a slender male youth dressed in the same grass-and-flower style, whose downcast face was a study in red. The captain shouted himself hoarse in his unintelligible language, but all they did was wave, as the youth pushed the pirates' longboat back into the water. The women climbed into the front, while he sat in the back, paddling the unfamiliar craft toward the junk, canoe style. The women stayed seated so as not to tip the odd craft, but put their upper bodies to good effect in a shimmying and swaying dance, all the while crooning sweet nonsense. Slowly, they drew nearer to the larger craft. The youth's piloting was unskilled, but they were making headway. It looked like the crew aboard were gathered at the rail to observe the bizarre shore party's approach, hopefully including whoever was supposed to be standing watch!

"It's working, it's working," Pam said just loud enough for Dore and Pers to hear. The giddiness that had helped her get through the first act had faded. Fear ran through her, a cold tingling in the balmy night. She had washed the spattered blood from her face, but she still felt unclean. Her smile was forced, and she began to worry the enemy would see through their act too soon. She jiggled her scantily-covered breasts a bit harder in an effort to distract these frightening, ruthless men from the terror that was threatening to creep across her smiling face. Whatever mad confidence had taken hold of her earlier, had now fled. She was literally half-naked and felt completely exposed.

I can't believe this is really happening, it's a nightmare, oh God, oh God! As they drew nearer the boat, she took a deep breath, forcing the inner voice of her fear to stop its nattering. Now was when it mattered the most she stay cool. She could see Dore reflected in the water, waving the torches in a graceful arc. The more distraction the better, plus the light might blind the pirates to the darkness beyond. They were only a yard away now. Pam fluttered her eyelashes at the captain, whose outrageous, curled mustachios dripped with sweat. She regretted that as it sent the already upset fellow into a rage, eyes bulging, his face cartoonishly crimson, reminding her of the garrulous Nome King from the Oz books of her childhood.

With a nerve-jarring bellow, the corpulent old pirate captain vaulted over the rail to climb down a rope ladder with a grace that belied his awesome girth. He jumped the last few feet to land in the front of their longboat, his prodigious weight causing the craft's back end to rise dangerously out of the water. Dore dropped one of her torches over the side while scrambling to take hold. Pam was bounced upward and back, landing painfully on her bottom between her and Dore's bench seats. She received another nasty jolt when the pirate captain began making his way toward them, causing the craft's rear to fall back to the surface with a splash. Suddenly, Pers leaped over her, placing himself between the women and the invader, armed only with his paddle. Pam looked on in horror as the enraged captain knocked the paddle from his hands, then began pummeling poor Pers with meaty fists. The youth got a few good shots in, which only made the horrid creature angrier, laying into Pers with increased vigor. Pers was knocked backward, as Pam had been and was in a bad position to defend himself. A kick of the pirate captain's boot knocked the wind out of him, and Pers slumped into the boat's planked bottom.

Pam felt something hard and cold jam painfully into her shoulder blade. She knew it was the butt of the up-time Smith and Wesson .38 caliber revolver Gerbald had insisted she bring for this part of the mission. Dore had hidden it in her fruit basket. She thrust the revolver into Pam's hand.

"Shoot, Pam, shoot! I *know* you know how!" Dore hissed in her ear.

As Pam's eyes narrowed, a chill and powerful anger rose in her like a sudden winter squall. Her fierce maternal instincts contributed to its growing force, Pers was no more than a boy! *So much like my own Walt!* She had grown fond of the lad and his sunny disposition. The fat captain had stopped beating the boy now and was reaching for a nasty-looking curved long-knife at his belt. The storm in her, partially physical sensation and electrified emotions that buzzed through her blood and brain, finally broke. *You really do see red!* she thought as tiny red stars began to sparkle in her vision. She gripped the revolver, felt its weight, and pointed it at the approaching foe's chest.

I've shot this weapon a hundred times back at Uncle's farm. Hold it steady, get your target in your sights, deep breath, squeeze. . . Pam felt as if she were moving in slow motion, the pirate captain, angling his knife for a murderous stab, paused when he saw that Pam was armed. His cruel eyes widened, and for a brief eternity, he was caught like a fly in amber. There was a flash and loud crack as if lightning had struck.

Pam watched, half in horror, half in glee, as the pirate captain looked at the bright-red stain on his chest where a bullet had pierced his heart. Favoring them with a final angry scowl on his now bloodless face, he died, tipping over into the water with a kind of preternatural grace, turban first and producing a sizable splash. The heavy revolver had kicked back into Pam's hands hard when she fired from her awkward position, jarring her muscles, but she kept it under control as her uncles had taught her, ignoring the pain. Even so, she realized then, she needed to scream.

"ARGGHHH!!" Pam's wordless, primal wail was lost in a wider cacophony. The bitter gun smoke stench helped clear her head. With a twist and a heave, Pam began to extricate herself from between the seats, keeping the revolver pointed away from her friends. Dore helped lift her as best she could with her free hand, holding the last torch with the other, its light flickering across the longboat as it swayed and bounced with their frantic movements.

Pam looked up at the junk's rails to find only a few pirates remained, and they were distracted by something happening elsewhere onboard. With a rush of relief, Pam realized the second part of their ruse was in full effect. During the noisy show they had put on, Gerbald, the Swedish sailors, and marines launched the pinnaces under cover of darkness, circling to the seaward side of the anchored junk. They had succeeded in boarding and were now locked in close combat with the Arab pirates.

There was a loud *boom* as Gerbald downed one charging pirate with one barrel of his pistol-grip Snakecharmer shotgun while sticking his *katzbalger* shortsword deep into the gut of another. He moved around the deck with the practiced grace of a ballerina, dodging and killing with silent precision. Another *boom* from the next barrel, and two more charging pirates fell, screaming, and pawing at their shot-destroyed faces before dying. This is what Gerbald trained for, how he made his living from his youth to just a few years ago. War was nothing new to him and he was damn good at it. *I'll have to remember to thank my boy Walt for giving him that crazy shotgun pistol,* Pam mused as she watched him reload. The Snakecharmer soon fired again, killing one pirate and maiming another, which the *katzbalger* finished in a single, swift stroke.

Not to be outdone by *The German Sergeant,* the *Löjtnant* parted a burly-looking fellow from his head with a swift slice of his elegant longsword, sending the appendage rolling across the deck like a ghastly, black-bearded bowling ball. The Princess's White Chessmen took the lead in the battle on the main deck, fronted by Sergeant Järv, who was snarling just like his namesake, the fearsome wolverine, as he hacked his way through one hapless foe after another. The sailors, refusing to be left out of the fray, found their target, a group of pirates attempting a stand in the stern. Howling a bone-chilling battle cry, giant Hake led the charge, the Swedes falling over the enemy like a great North Sea wave. Gazing about with wide eyes, Pam realized she was witnessing the fabled *Fury of the Norsemen* in living, bloody color, playing out before her very eyes, and shuddered. The night was filled with the sounds of clanging metal, angry shouts, gunshots, and death.

Dore grabbed Pam's shoulder and pointed — above them a pirate trying to flee the battle, was halfway over the rail, poised to drop into their longboat. Pam shot. His lifeless body struck their bow on its way down with a sickening *thunk* before splashing limply into the water. Pam let out a long, low stream of curses under her breath.

Dore gripped her shoulder harder, bringing her face close behind Pam's ear. "It is good, Pam, you help our men! There, shoot that one!" Dore pointed at a pirate closing in behind the Bosun, who was occupied with another opponent, his cutlass clashing and clanging against a blood-streaked scimitar. Pam focused for a split-second at the wet, red blade in the sneaking enemy's hand. *That's the blood of one of ours.* She took aim, supported by Dore's firm grip on her shoulders. Her finger squeezed. Having grown accustomed to the bang and flash, she didn't flinch. She watched as the pirate fell to the deck like a sack of wet sand, a bullet through his neck. *My shot went a little high, but he's still dead as a door nail.*

The Bosun separated himself from his momentarily distracted dueling partner with a mighty shove. The taller, thinner pirate skidded backward on the blood-drenched deck. The Bosun glanced a question at Pam, and with a barely perceptible nod, she drew on the Bosun's opponent as he regained his footing, and shot him in the gut. Pam looked away from the messy results, her own gut sinking, as if meeting a sudden drop on a roller coaster. The deck went quiet but for the moans of the dead and dying. No pirates were left standing. *Löjtnant* Lundkvist looked down to see Pam still holding her smoking revolver. He saluted her. Pam's hands lost their strength and she laid the revolver down on the seat in front of her as Dore eased her grip on her shoulders.

"It is all right now, Pam. It is over," Dore told her. "You did well, my friend. You helped turn the battle's tide! You never missed once!"

Pam thought of each man she had shot, fought throwing up. She had barely eaten a thing all day so it wouldn't have helped much anyway. She looked to the deck where Gerbald had finished hurrying the enemy injured along on their journey to hell with a quick slice to their throats.

"Let us leave none alive." he said to *Löjtnant* Lundkvist and the Bosun as as if he were ordering a hamburger at the Freedom Arches. They nodded their solemn agreement. The Swedish marines took the lead in searching the ship, entering the captain's cabin, then the lower decks, weapons ready. While Dore went to the aid of injured Pers, Gerbald motioned for Pam to join him on the deck. Somehow, she managed to climb the rope ladder with nerveless fingers until Gerbald dragged her over the red-lacquered rail. Dore clambered up onto the deck next. Pam saw bodies in the flickering torch light. Not all were dressed in bloodstained white robes. Gerbald looked at Pam proudly.

"Nice shooting, Tex! Four shots, no misses! It was you who ensured our triumph!" he told his ashen-faced friend, who just blinked at him, half in a state of shock. He saw where Pam was looking, and his voice took on a serious tone. "Rask is injured very badly. We have already lost poor Mård. Fritjoff is sure to follow him soon. He is asking for you, Pam."

Pam felt a knot tighten in her stomach. *Not the nice old fellow who loved that photo of "The Princess" so much!*

"You are sure about Fritjoff? Not making it, I mean?"

Gerbald nodded. "I am sorry, Pam. He fought bravely. Please, follow me. Dore, see what you can do for our wounded."

"Pers has also been hurt, but not too badly. I shall tend to Rask first," Dore replied, being used to aftermaths such as these.

Gerbald led Pam to where Fritjoff lay, his head cradled by an exhausted bosun. Fritjoff's face was pale except for a line of blood trickling into his white beard. Someone had placed a cloth over his wounds. Pam could see that it was dark and soaking wet. Her gorge wanted to rise, but she forced it down.

"Fritjoff, *Frau* Pam is here to see you," the Bosun said into his ear. The old man's eyes opened, bloodshot and wild, darting about in search of her.

"I'm here, Fritjoff," Pam told him, kneeling next to him and taking his hand. Although they were cold and bloodless, his long, thin fingers grasped hers with surprising strength.

"*Frau* Pam, thank you, thank you. I haven't much time now. I am no longer the fighter I was when I was young, but I take two of these dogs to their graves with me."

"You are very brave, Fritjoff. I am so proud of you. I know the princess will be, too." Pam told him, tears forming in the corner of her smoke-stung eyes.

"The princess. Will you tell her? Will you tell her that I served her to my last?" His sentences were now punctuated with heaving gasps as his punctured lungs fought a losing battle for every breath.

"I will. I will tell her all about you, Fritjoff! How brave you were, and how you loved her and how you kept her photo. I will tell her of our good Fritjoff, loyal friend and fearless soldier!" Her voice caught, and she fell silent, trying not to lose her composure, not yet. Fritjoff tried to say more, but his gasps were coming rapidly now, stopping him from further speech. Pam took the damp cloth from the Bosun and began to wipe his face, tears streaming now, mixing with the cool water and drying blood. The touch of her hand seemed to calm him, and he was able to speak again.

"Thank you, *Frau* Pam, thank you. I see the faces of my ancestors now. They have come for me in the ships of the old times. I see their sails, red and gold. Soon I shall join them." His grip on her hand tightened, and his eyes were able to focus on her for a moment. "You were always kind to me. It is you who are the brave one, *Frau* Pam. All we men see it. It was *you* who captured this prize. I am glad to have you as my captain here at my end." Before she could answer, Fritjoff convulsed, a final ragged breath, then silence. His grip loosened, and his hand fell limply to the deck. Pam let out a low wail, still wiping his forehead with the cloth. The Bosun gently pushed her hand aside and closed the old sailor's eyes.

"Fritjoff lived a long life, *Frau* Pam, longer than most who go to sea," the Bosun told her, his voice rich with utmost kindness. "He is with his people now in the next world. Don't weep so."

Pam somehow ceased her keening cry and took a deep breath. She wiped her tears with her arm, her hands shaking.

"Come, good lady. Let us now help those who stay with us in this world of trials and troubles." The Bosun stood, his movements those of one bruised and battered in cruel battle, but still filled with strength. He took her trembling hands in his and lifted her to her feet. Pam embraced him fiercely, nearly knocking the wind out of the poor fellow, then released him to peer about the deck with tear-burned eyes. She shook herself, then spoke from an icy, calm place in the maelstrom of grief and disgust heaving about her mind.

"I'll go check on Pers. I think he's all right, just badly bruised."

The Bosun saluted her, then turned to place a cloth over the face of their fallen comrade.

Pam returned to the rail to see Pers was beginning to come around in the junk's longboat. The boy was black and blue, and he had a bloody nose, but his eyes focused on Pam, and his pupils weren't dilated.

"How do I look?" he asked cheerfully. Pam let out a laugh, more of a growl really, and told him, "You look like an elephant stepped on you, but you'll live. Stay put there and pinch your nose shut until I come back and tell you to stop." He did as she ordered while Pam went to join Dore where she ministered to Rask.

"Oh, dear. It is not good. A deep cut to the thigh here, and a gash to the side of the belly. I must find out how deep." No stranger to battlefield medicine, Dore went about her examination with the same deft swiftness she would preparing a chicken for the boil, ignoring the man's gasps and moans of pain. Pam was impressed that Dore had developed such sophisticated first aid skills during her years as a camp follower. She knelt to assist however she could. Under Dore's direction they made quick progress and stopped the bleeding.

Pam cursed under her breath and wished for up-time antibiotics. Back at camp she had a precious plastic bottle of Bactine, an over-the-counter antibacterial and mild local anesthetic she kept in her birding pack's tiny medkit for cuts and scrapes on the trail. She had been hoarding it, using it only sparingly, but she would give it all if needed to help this man. With Rask stabilized and resting as comfortably as they could make him, they stood.

"I have antibacterial medicine in my hut." Pam told Dore.

"Good, we will use it. Here come the men. Let us thank the Lord we have prevailed and pray He welcome the souls of our brave men in His heavenly kingdom." Dore lowered her head and clasped her hands in silent prayer, a common pose for the upright German lady made utterly unearthly by her half-naked condition. This night Dore was a grass skirted, savage warrior queen with flowers in her hair, blood spattered and brooding as she sent the power of her unwavering faith to aid the souls of their fallen on their journey to Paradise.

Garrett W. Vance

CHAPTER 25: THE PRIZE

Captured Oriental Junk, South Coast of Mauritius

Pam watched while the sailors cleaned the blood from the decks of their prize. The flickering light of the torches made their shadows leap and dance, lending the scene an eerie, otherworldly quality. An hour had passed since their success in capturing the junk, its original, presumably Chinese merchants having perished at the hands of an organized gang of pirates she thought must certainly be Arabic in origin. She based that guess on their clothing and behavior, but most of the denizens of the seventeenth-century Indian Ocean were still a mystery to her. She had a hunch she would be learning a lot more about this part of the world in the days to come, and, based on what she had experienced so far, doubted it would be pleasant.

Just twenty minutes ago, she had watched her men cut down the severed heads of the junk's former owners from where they had been hung as trophies, a gruesome display courtesy of the now dispatched pirates of the Indian Ocean. It was a grisly task. Pam felt pity they had died in such a horrible way. She had asked they be wrapped in a sack and given a Christian burial at sea. No one had any idea what their religion in life might have been, so Lutheran would have to do. Having borne witness to the brief, but dignified ritual, she now waited to be returned to their beach refuge.

The uncomfortable feeling none of this was real that sometimes swept over her came again. She felt as if she had wandered into some live-action period drama, a terrible tale of fighting seamen and ruthless brigands of days gone by. Any minute now, the lights would come up, and the actors would shed their costumes. She closed her eyes hard, wishing with all her might she would wake up back in the future age she had been born to. But when she opened her eyes, she was still there on the blood-splattered deck. *Damn!* Forcing herself to stay calm and make the panic subside, she thought *This is* not *"days gone by." This is* now *days! These are* new *days, these are* my *days and I must* live them, *like it or not!* Gritting her teeth, she felt her head begin to clear. The scene came back into focus. Although lacking in sophistication, the current age brimmed with action.

A watch of marines under the command of *Löjtnant* Lundkvist was assembling on deck. All the sailors could fight, and fight well as she had seen, but these men specialized in it. They would stay aboard to guard their new ship, a bizarre, and brightly painted three-masted vessel that dwarfed lost *Redbird* in size and complexity, while the rest of the tired crew and Pam's personal staff, returned to the beach camp. There was a lot of clean up left to do, but once the gory decks had been swabbed, the rest could wait for morning. The slain pirates were to be thrown overboard with the outgoing tide just as they were, with no wrapping or ceremony.

"Those poor Chinamen were one thing, but these lot don't deserve any such respect." The Bosun said, his voice cold. "Let the crabs have them, the murdering sons of dogs."

Pam nodded, trying not to look at the sheet-wrapped body of their friend Fritjoff lying nearby. Fritjoff and the Bosun had been close, sailing together for many long years. The injured look on the normally jolly Nil's face was enough to make Pam cry. She considered weeping again, but the tears wouldn't come. She was all cried out for this night. Maybe in the morning. Meanwhile, dark thoughts like *I've killed men with my own hands!* and *More good men have died for my cause this night!* tried to push themselves into her consciousness, but she was too tired, so she ignored them until their shrill accusations fell away. She knew they would return, demanding to be heard in the early hours of the morning when she would stare at the shadow-filled ceiling of her hut and remember. But *not* just now.

Looking around the deck, she saw not all the men's faces were grim. Some were beginning to admire their prize and clap each other on their backs in celebration of a hard-fought victory. Pam made herself smile for them. She knew for some reason they looked to her, so she allowed herself to share some of their pleasure. They had won, they had a ship, it was foreign and weird, but seaworthy. Now they were *free* and able to take action! Pam turned her gaze away from the flickering orange glow of the torch-lit deck to peer at the dark mass of the coastline. Her colonists were out there, somewhere, and they were certainly in trouble.

"We'll come for you," she spoke into the night in a voice beneath a whisper. "We're ready now, hold on!"

A few minutes later, Pam sat in the rear of the pinnace as the exhausted sailors rowed through the tranquility of a windless night. She was heading back to the simple comforts of her bamboo hut with her most trusted friends, Gerbald and Dore, as well as young Pers, injured Rask, and the earthly remains of poor Mård and Fritjoff. Mård had been a shy fellow, the hapless sailor who had ruined dinner their first night out. Pam hadn't really gotten to know him, but she recalled that he had always spoken gently to Pers, even when the lad was being a teenaged idiot, and so she thought highly of the man for that. He had been close with Dore, often helping her in the galley, and Pam knew despite her stony expression her friend was taking his loss hard. She would miss Mård's face, and dear old Fritjoff's. Their places would be empty at breakfast. These fallen heroes would be given a proper burial on the grassy mound beside the first mate in the morning.

Dore turned to see Pam looking at the shrouded corpses with an expression that held all the world's cares. She reached for Pam's hand and squeezed it. Pam returned the squeeze, and the two of them looked back at their prize. The vivid colors of the junk's lacquered woodwork and fanciful carvings under the flickering torchlight made her seem like something come sailing out of a dream, a phantasmagorical craft from beyond the edge of the world.

"What a day." Pam said, while Dore nodded in agreement.

CHAPTER 26: BREAKFAST OF CHAMPIONS

Castaway Cove, South Coast of Mauritius

Pam slept like a stone. The marvelous aroma of coffee brewing wafted through her little window and summoned her from slumber half an hour after dawn, bringing her forth to blink at an already too-bright sky, filled with enormous cotton clouds. She managed to stagger to the cookfire to join the men waiting for breakfast. The Swedish crew always treated her with deference, but this morning they leaped to their feet, except Rask who was still nursing his injuries. He looked much better as he smiled widely at her. They made much fuss about finding her the most comfortable seat next to the fire. She leaned over to Gerbald and quietly asked him in German, "What's up with these guys? Since when do I get the star treatment?"

Gerbald smiled his best "You have asked the Fount of Wisdom" smile at her. "Pam, do you mean to tell me you really don't know? Think about what you did yesterday! It was *you* who lead them to victory! You even killed four of the enemy yourself, more of those bastards died at your hand than by the hand of any one of us! You are their hero!"

Pam blinked at this revelation, and then smiled, though her brow remained furrowed.

"Well, Howdy Doody," she muttered in English. "Now I'm a hero. I just wish I felt like one." Dore handed Pam her coffee, but she just stared into its steaming darkness for a while, savoring the aroma along with a growing feeling of pride.

Dore seemed unfazed by the wild events of the day before and was going about her tasks with her usual efficiency. As Pam began to sip the wonderful native coffee from her coconut shell mug, she was pleased to see her friend had concocted a culinary miracle from the final remnants of *Redbird*'s food stores, ingredients Dore had been guarding, doling them out over the months of their isolation.

"No point in saving all this now! Much longer and it would have all gone bad anyway," she said, stirring a rich broth of salt pork, beans, dried onions, and butter, thickened with the last of the flour, and seasoned with a variety of herbs and spices. Everyone was beginning to crowd around the cookpot, staring at it with hungry eyes.

"Stay back now, you fellows. There's enough for everyone, and we need to save some for the men on the ship!" Dore chided them, but in a tone set at a less stern pitch than usual.

Pam, beginning to achieve caffeinated consciousness, now noticed that Dore hadn't put her beautiful auburn and-silver streaked hair up in its usual severe bun. Instead, she wore it in a loose braid over her shoulder, tied with a string to keep strays out of her eyes. Pam smiled to see this development. Dore was wound a bit less tight today. Evidently a little "harlot dancing" had been just the thing for her ever-serious friend.

After filling themselves with the delicious and hearty soup, they all stood, stretched, and made ready for the solemn duty they had to perform this morning. Singing a Christian hymn that was ancient even in the seventeenth century, many of the words of which Pam couldn't catch, the Swedes carried their dead down the beach with all the respect one might have afforded the kings of old.

The dodos followed along behind the procession, forming a peculiar kind of honor guard, cooing and chuckling softly, but keeping a polite distance instead of engaging in their usual snack begging. Pam thought they must be able to sense the somber mood, and once again was surprised at their intelligence. The dodos really were not dummies. They had just evolved in a place where there was no need to fear bands of roving carnivorous apes. The sight of what to Pam was almost a mythical creature, alive and thriving right before her wondering eyes, made her heart race yet again, and brought a modicum of good cheer to her heavy heart. *All this fuss, all this trouble is really for you, funny birds!* she thought at the exquisitely odd creatures.

At their lonely little seaside cemetery, Pam saw two graves had been dug already. Getting up early for hard work was nothing new to sailors, and Pam respected them all the more for it.

There were four grave markers now, all made of sturdy boards salvaged from *Redbird,* their epitaphs neatly painted by Pam with her waterproof acrylics, and further protected by a coating of amber-tinted tree pitch. Each bore the name and rank of their fallen and, if known, their birth date and birthplace, followed by their country, *Sverige,* the date and, lastly, the name of their ill-fated ship.

The fourth marker had gone up this morning along with Fritjoff's and Mård's but there was no grave at its feet. It was a memorial to their captain, Pam had put off looking at it now it was in the ground, and finally decided she would just have to face it. The marker read: *Torbjörn Nilsson, Captain of the Redbird.* After the official names and dates, Pam had added, "*He stayed behind to save us all. Lost at sea, we pray this brave man yet lives.*" She had done the work alone in her hut, not wanting the others to see her tears as she painted this memorial to their lost friend, a man who, if still with them, maybe, just maybe, would have become something more to her. Now, standing among her band of castaways, all gathered for a funeral yet again, she sent a brief thought across the rolling waves. *Torbjörn, if you are out there somewhere please know we haven't forgotten you! I haven't forgotten you! Please be alive!*

Dore wept as they lowered poor Mård into his grave. They had become close friends as he assisted her in the galley during the voyage and continued to do so in her makeshift island kitchen. Pam did the same for her special friend, kindly old Fritjoff. The burial ceremony was brief, but emotional. The Bosun spoke the Lord's Prayer and the twenty-third Psalm in Swedish, his voice cracking, the loss of his long-time friends and shipmates having hurt him deeply. Pers stood beside him, lending his quiet support. The Bosun then asked Pam to recite Tennyson's *Crossing the Bar* as she had for First Mate Janvik. She managed to get through it in a calm, clear voice, despite the great sense of loss within her. Pam brought along the photo of Kristina that Fritjoff had prized so much. She considered burying it with him, but decided the fine old gentleman would have been more pleased to have it hanging proudly in a place of honor on their new ship. Holding it to her breast, she spoke quietly to her fallen friend as he was lowered into the sandy grave.

"I won't ever forget you, Fritjoff. I will do as I promised and tell the princess of your bravery in battle, and your dedication to her cause. I will tell her of the great love you felt for her, and how you served her so well, just as soon as I see her again." An unwelcome thought intruded. *If. If you see her again.* Pam looked out at the captured Oriental junk floating in their lonely bay, its vivid colors glowing ethereally in the morning light. *Our chances have improved by a lot.* She left a small bouquet of wildflowers beneath each of the four markers, whispering "thank you" to each. Then she walked down the beach, trying hard not to think too much on all they had lost, and to concentrate instead on what they might now hope to gain.

Gerbald caught up to her, and gave her the look that said "*Is this a good time?*" He knew Pam's emotions ran deep and that sometimes she just needed to be alone. She saw his cautious approach, smiled, and took his arm, something she rarely did. He patted her hand in an awkward, big brotherly way, glad that she wasn't taking things too hard. They walked together in silence for a few minutes. Gerbald said, "Pam, this morning the Bosun told me it will take a day or two to make this *junk* ready to sail. They 'need to figure out if this fancy-painted Oriental contraption can be sailed by Christian men.' I believe those were his words." They both laughed. Pam had watched the Bosun studying the junk from the shore during breakfast. She couldn't tell from his expression if he felt love or loathing for the strange new ship that had become his responsibility.

"He's a smart guy. They all are. They'll figure it out."

"Indeed, I have the highest confidence. In any event, the search mission has been delayed while we study our prize. So, it seems we have a little more time to spend here, and I thought of something you might like to do."

Pam's eyebrows arched up at him, her gray eyes sparking with curiosity. "Ooh, what, do tell! Do you have a box of chocolate cherry bonbons and a bottle of *kirschwasser* hidden away for me?"

"Nothing so immediately gratifying." He laughed. "We are getting low on coffee and who knows when we might come across it again? I thought we might hike back up the mountain and resupply ourselves. We can bring back some live specimens to grow in pots on the ship until we find a more permanent home for them. That is, if you feel up to it." Gerbald's face was perfectly straight, but she detected the tiny wrinkle around the corner of his mouth that revealed he was terribly pleased with his idea. Pam tried to keep her own face straight, but a grin was doing its level best to break out.

"I take back everything I said about you, Gerbald. You are a real stand-up guy, a real pal." Pam kidded him, slapping him on his sturdy bicep with her free hand. They both grinned, Gerbald knowing the teasing praise was sincere.

Pam noticed the dodos had fallen in around them, cooing with contentment, spread out around their path in search of sand fleas and bits of seaweed.

"I have an idea that will go well with yours," she said, nodding at their avian companions "Let's take *them* with us. I don't want to leave them hanging around the beach looking like dinner to the next ship that comes this way."

"I'll get some nuts and dried fruit from Dore for the bait. I'm sure she will be happy to provide. She won't be missing what she has come to refer to as 'those flightless pests!' It is only her deep respect for your wishes that kept them out of her stew pot." Gerbald grinned.

CHAPTER 27: UPS AND DOWNS

A while later, as Pam gathered supplies for their trip, she found a rather depressed Pers carrying odds and ends from the sailor's longhouse down to the beach for transfer to the ship. He was still bruised from his encounter with the pirate captain, but had been deemed fit for light duty. Pam stopped him as he hurried by without so much as a greeting for her.

"Hey, Pers, are you all right?" Pam asked, first checking to make sure they were out of earshot of his boss, the Bosun.

"Oh, yes, Pam, I'm fine." The boy managed to give her a small smile, but still didn't look fine. Pam figured he was tired and feeling bad about losing two more comrades, as they all were. Pers was a good kid, and had been very brave, not to mention a good sport, dressing up for their friendly natives act, and Pam wanted to do something to cheer him up.

"Well, maybe so, but you look like you could use some fun anyway. Gerbald and I are going to hike up to the mountain to get more coffee today. Would you like to join us? We could use your help carrying the beans back. That is, if you're up to it. You took a pretty good beating last night!"

Immediately, Pers face lit up. "Oh yes, I feel a lot better this morning! I'd like to come with you very much!"

"Great! It will be a good chance for you to work on your English and your German, too. We haven't had much time for your lessons lately. Let's go talk to the Bosun."

Pam led Pers straight to the busy gentlemen who was about to board the pinnace to be rowed out to their gaudy new vessel.

"*Herr* Bosun, I wonder if you can spare me Pers for the day. Gerbald and I are going for a resupply of coffee and could use some help carrying it back."

The Bosun smiled, having become an aficionado of the bitter drink himself. "We are likely going to be all day figuring out how that floating fancy is sailed. I think we can spare the lad." He turned to Pers, who was looking brighter by the minute, and told him "Now, you mind *Frau* Pam, young fellow, and stay out of trouble!"

"Yes, sir!" Pers looked like his usual happy-go-lucky self again.

"Thanks! We'll be back by sundown," Pam told the Bosun. He gave her a salute and stepped into the pinnace which immediately pulled out into the gentle surf. Pam was sure it was the first time the Bosun had ever used that particular gesture with her and it made her feel a bit uncomfortable.

A few minutes later she, Gerbald, and a much cheered-up Pers, were heading down the beach to collect the flock of dodos that had decided to become their permanent neighbors. The problem was their current humans were leaving and future visitors were not likely to be so gentle.

"I can't leave them here on the beach," Pam said as they handed out treats to the now nearly tame animals. "The next people who land here might put them on the menu. We have to lead them back up into the forests where we found them and then throw them off our trail."

"No problem," Gerbald said.

The dodos, having determined these three humans were today's most promising food source, followed as they left the shore for the interior, encouraged along the way by frequent treats.

"I have heard dodos are supposed to be quite foolish," Pers mused. "But they don't really seem so to me. They know who has food and who is likely to give them some!" He chuckled as a dodo took the nut he offered with its massive beak, yellow eyes bright with what Pam took for pleasure.

"We have made them into terrible beggars," Gerbald added. "I wonder if it was situations such as this that helped lead to their extinction back in that other world you came from, Pam. The dodos getting used to people, coming around for handouts, until one day they find themselves in the stew pot."

"Well, based on what we have observed, it all fits. It was very selfish of me to give them food just so they would sit still for a portrait. No true wildlife scientist ever baits their subjects. I feel awful that here I am trying to save them and ended up putting this flock in more danger instead." Pam's face drew down in a deep frown.

"Now, now Pam, you mustn't think that way!" Gerbald told her, knowing it would be best for them all if he could improve her mood quickly. "No one else on the planet cares about these creatures as much as you do, and ultimately, it will be you who prevents their loss in this world. I am confident in your abilities."

"As am I!" Pers chimed in "You will save the dodos, Pam, it is your destiny!" Pers' exuberant sureness in her made Pam laugh, the frowns forgotten for now.

"Well, it feels like we're making progress again. Maybe we can still give the dodos their second chance."

"Come along, you second chance birds!" Pers called, starting to walk up the trail with the dodos in tow, waving a banana in his hand like a parade baton. Several of the larger dodos crowded around in front of him, stretching their necks up after the banana, and blocking his way up the path. Pers had to push past them and scowled at the insistent panhandlers. "Argh, you stupid creatures! I take back the nice things I said about you! You are too greedy!" Pam and Gerbald enjoyed a silent smirk at the youth's expense. They had both had the same thing happen to them after all.

Soon enough, they were sorted out and on their way again. After conferring with experienced woodsman, Gerbald, they decided to lead the dodos to a similar, but different part of the forest than where they were found. Hopefully, the dodos would be disoriented by the convoluted journey. Better yet, if the same kind of foraging were available in the new territory, the ever-hungry birds would be distracted enough to make finding the beach again, not worth the bother. Reaching the top of the first rise, a couple of miles from camp, they looked back to see the junk sailing around in a tight circle in the bay, the small forms of the sailors running about her decks like angry ants beneath the red sails.

"Shhhh, listen!" Pam told her companions as she leaned on her walking stick and pointed toward the misbehaving ship. The wind was blowing inland, and even at that distance, it carried a faint stream of curses from the Bosun. She put a hand over her mouth to stop from laughing.

"Sounds like they are having a wonderful time," Gerbald whispered, unable to keep from chuckling at the foul language. "The Bosun could make a career in the opera. His voice certainly carries well."

Pers gazed at the humorous scene with a wistful expression on his face even though he chuckled along with Gerbald. Pam saw this, and knew something was still eating the kid. She vowed to find out what, before the day was done.

*　　*　　*

The temperature grew uncomfortably hot as noon approached. The near-daily rains seemed to have spilled themselves dry for a spell, but Pam suspected they would be back. Today it felt like high West Virginia summer in the Tropic of Capricorn. They were grateful when they finally entered the moist depths of the forest. The shade of the great trees was a cooling balm. The dodos became excited, scuttling through the underbrush, and squawking in what sounded like happy tones to Pam. She sighed despite the pleasure at escaping the too-bright sun, remembering back in her original century, Mauritius had lost nearly all of its original vegetation through rampant logging and uncontrolled agriculture. *Not this time,* she vowed. *The colonists agreed to follow the modern sustainability practices I researched. We can't let that happen again!* then another darker possibility entered her mind. *It will only work if my colonists are still alive.* She pushed the thought away. She knew better than to start stacking up her cares too high. It just made her feel overwhelmed. *One step at a time,* she reminded herself and breathed deeply to stay calm.

To further distract herself from her endless list of cares, Pam set about identifying what trees she could. While Grantville had by no means contained a plethora of information on such a remote place, Pam had found out quite a bit about the Mascarenes in her studies, surprisingly more than she had thought she would. She spoke aloud as she led them across the forest floor, sharing the knowledge with her companions.

"Let's see, what tree have we here? I think this is *Foetidia mauritiana.* It's named for the strong smell of its oil. Straight trunk, gray bark, a bit of red in the leaves. I'm sure that's it. This fellow over here must be *Diospyros tessellaria,* one of the ebony trees. It's nearly twenty meters high, black bark, long glossy leaves. If we're careful, and harvest its wood wisely, we can make a lot of money for the colony. It's perfect for piano keys and from what I've seen there's going to be a booming business in those things back in the USE."

"It's beautiful," Pers commented, running his fingers across the bark. "I've always hated cutting down trees, but I know we must sometimes."

Pam favored the youth with a beatific smile. "A necessary evil. If things go our way, we will protect a great many more trees, such as these, and those we do harvest we will replace with new. That way we can have wood for generations to come instead of just lopping them all down and leaving nothing for later, as so many fools have done. That's what happened in my other history, here, and a lot of other places, before people wised up to the concept of sustainability. Even once we knew better, far too many people continued clear cutting, only interested in what they could get for themselves, not about the future. It was awful. We made our world ugly and sick."

Gerbald nodded his solemn agreement. "There are many hunters in the Germanies such as myself, who would see it done your way. But every year, the forests shrink. Unfortunately, greed wins and the trees come down. If it continues there will be no animals left to hunt as there will be no place left for them to live."

"Well," Pam said with a sigh, "and I do hate to say this, it's probably already too late to save much of what's left of Germany's old growth forests. In an ideal world, the arrival of Grantville might have slowed things like uncontrolled logging. But from what I see, most of us Americans are dancing around the fires of industry as if they were the Golden Calf. The people concerned with the ecological impact of our industrial revolution, I can count on one hand, starting with me."

"Well, that's a start," Gerbald said. "If you add me, you will have six. As a hunter, I'd like to see the Thüringerwald preserved. Surely, we can do better."

"And I seven!" Pers chimed in. "I don't believe that when God gave man dominion over the Earth He intended for us to destroy all in our path, yet I have seen such in every port. It is shameful."

Pam's eyebrows rose high on her forehead at such an erudite statement from their young 'Gilligan'. Pers, though still in many ways a carefree youth, was paying attention to the world around him. Her fondness for the boy deepened and she allowed herself a bit of pride in knowing she had played a significant role in his education. She gave them both a big smile as she sat on a large round rock to take a breather.

"Well, looks like I've made two converts to the Pam Miller Tree Hugging and Marching Society. A good start indeed." After taking a quick look around to make sure the dodos weren't close by, she reached into her pocket to pull out the shaved coconut, dried fruit, and nut gorp trail mix she brought along, unwrapping its banana leaf container so as not to spill it.

"Here, help yourselves!" she invited her companions, lifting her open hand up in offering. Pers and Gerbald both took a step forward, but stopped, eyes wide. Even though neither of them were anywhere near her palm, she felt a pressure there and heard what could only be a chewing sound. Shifting her eyes to her hand, she was stunned to see a very strange face--a wide beak of a nose shaped like a rounded ship's prow, two holes for nostrils beneath, with a wide, lip-less mouth chewing gorp. Dark, liquid eyes regarded her from behind droopy lids set in thick, scaly gray skin. This startling visage was at the end of a long neck that snaked down into a horn-like saddle heading a large, smooth, green-gray plated shell. A shell she happened to be sitting on!

To her credit, Pam didn't panic, conquering her first instinct to jump up with a startled shout. If she had been in any real danger, Gerbald would have taken care of it, with his warrior's reflexes, long before she could react. The creature was obviously harmless.

"What is it?" Pers asked in a hushed tone.

"It must be a dinosaur!" Gerbald answered, laughing with delight.

Pam felt the large "rock" beneath her shift slightly as the long-necked creature took another gentle mouthful of trail mix.

"Gentlemen," she announced with some bravado, "meet the giant Mascarene tortoise. I remember reading about them and wondering why they weren't as well known as the Galapagos version. The answer was, of course, they had become extinct along with the dodo, but the dodo got the starring role in the tragedy."

"The dodo is a most engaging creature," Gerbald said. "But this fellow has personality as well. I am a hunter by nature, but I confess I wouldn't be able to kill such a soulful-eyed beast unless I was in utmost need of sustenance."

"Yeah, he's pretty cute, huh?" Pam slid off her living seat to kneel beside the placid creature, offering it more gorp, which it took from her palm with a wide, bluish-hued tongue. "Unfortunately, a lot of hungry people who aren't as kind as you, will end up here in the years to come, unless we get control of things first." Pam stroked the tortoise's shell. "This must be the saddle-backed version. They were . . . or, I'm pleased to say . . . *are,* inhabitants of the forests, adapted to stretch their necks in search of leaves and fruit. There's another closely-related type with a shorter neck and rounder shell that lives in the grasslands." Pam gave the tortoise the last of her gorp as she rubbed it gently on its scaly skull, which it seemed to like. Its heavy-lidded eyes half closed in delight.

After a long minute of deep thought, Pam stood and looked at her friends. Her face was pale in the arboreal shadows and filled with cares.

"Ya know, guys, sometimes it just seems like too much. This island is so complex, we are barely scratching the surface of understanding how these ecologies work and now we are introducing human settlers, even earlier than they came here in my other history. I hope I've made the right decisions. I hope I can make all this work. It's really a lot on my plate. Sometimes I just feel overwhelmed." Her shoulders slumped, and she looked at the tortoise with a helpless expression.

"Pam, you must not forget that we are with you in this. You do not face these burdens alone." Gerbald told her. "Can you not see myself and Dore, this fine lad Pers, the Bosun, and all the men of the *Redbird* support you wholeheartedly? You carry too much on your shoulders. We lend you our strength. Please, take it."

Pam took a deep breath before speaking in a low, but controlled tone. "I know you do. I'm stupid for forgetting that. It's just that sometimes I get scared by my new life here. If you had seen me up-time in Grantville, you wouldn't have recognized me. I was a failure as a wife, as a mother . . . it seemed like no matter how hard I tried nothing worked. The only thing I ever got right was science, so I got education and went to work, and that helped, but now I'm not a lab tech. I'm the lead scientist. I'm the one who has to make the big decisions, and it's freaking me out! I hold the lives of all these living creatures, the lives of all these people who came here with me, in my hands. And so far, I've sucked at it." She had started calmly, but by the time she finished her voice was freighted with emotion.

Pers had a good grasp of up-time American English vernacular, thanks as much to Gerbald's wise-cracks as Pam's lessons and knew what "sucked"' meant.

"Pam, you do not *suck*. I can assure you none of we Swedes think that. We *admire* you. We think of you as the brave lady, our wise woman, a warrior! You must not think of yourself in such a bad way, please. Listen to *Herr* Gerbald! We will all help you succeed!" There was no mistaking the deep concern and sincerity in Pers' young voice.

Pam visibly pulled herself together, rubbing her flushed face, and clearing flyaway locks from her brow. She nodded, favored them each with a tiny, but sweet smile, gave the giant tortoise a final pat on the head, then turned and started walking. Pers and Gerbald watched her go, giving her the time and space she had silently asked for. After a minute Gerbald clapped a still worried Pers companionably on the back.

"Well done, my boy."

Pers stood tall, feeling as if he had just been knighted.

Garrett W. Vance

CHAPTER28: FAREWELLS AND BEGINNINGS

Pam's mood improved as they left the gloom of the forest behind to begin the ascent into higher country. The sun was still bright, but there was a cool breeze dancing across the rocks and shrubs that made the afternoon heat bearable. Gerbald and Pers picked their own paths nearby. They traveled in a silence she knew would be up to her to break, but not just yet. She paused, looking back to see that the dodos had stopped at the edge of the forest. Apparently, the open hillsides were not to their liking, or maybe the long walk had tuckered out their stocky legs.

This was good-bye to the flock Pam had gotten to know so well. They would return by a different path so the birds couldn't follow them to the perils of the beach. She took a long, last look, a kind of mental photograph she was sure she would never forget. In her heart she had a feeling it wouldn't really be the last time she would see these birds. Satisfied, Pam gave the dodos a smile and a farewell wave, then turned away to continue her climb up the gentle slopes of what they had dubbed Coffee Mountain. A mile or so later, she looked back once more. The dodos were gone, returned to their former life hunting for nuts and grubs among the great trees of this island paradise. Pam envied them.

Upon reaching the top, Pam opened the picnic lunch she and Dore had concocted, which included a small flask of *snaps* to celebrate with.

"Come and get it, fellas!" she called as she lay the offerings out on a broad, flat boulder conveniently placed near the summit. They would enjoy their meal with a fabulous view. Somehow, Dore had managed to bake a simple bread in her stone oven. They filled each loaf with crab meat, thinly sliced Barbel palm hearts, bamboo shoots, and a generous helping of spices mixed in melted butter from Dore's larder. The results were delicious. Pers liked his so much, Pam gave him half of hers. The portions were more generous than she could handle anyway.

Around them the lush, green mountains of the island's interior marched into mists in the north. To the south, they could see the sapphire sparkle of the sea. They passed the flask around while enjoying the spectacular views, and then lay in the soft grass to take a short nap before gathering coffee beans. After an hour passed, Gerbald estimated it was around three in the afternoon. It would take them at least an hour to gather the beans, as well as some young trees. They would begin the long walk home, reaching camp at dusk. Time to get to work.

Pam gave Pers a lesson in coffee-bean picking. The trees bore a variety of ripe and unripe fruits, making it a bit tricky, but the youth was a quick study, soon filling his sacks with the purple-yellow coffee beans faster than Pam and Gerbald. Seeing his progress, they turned their attention to bringing young trees back alive. Gerbald brought along a short spade from the *Redbird*'s toolchest, which made the work go faster. They placed the roots in moist canvas sacks surrounded by native soil, wrapped the leaves in sailcloth, and tied them in a bundle, easy to carry down the narrow forest trails.

With all their bags and pockets bulging with beans, they began the long walk home.

"Ugh. This stuff is heavier than I remember it." Pam groaned. Her shoulders ached from the unaccustomed weight in her rucksack.

"Well, you were about out of your mind with joy last time," Gerbald reminded her. "That must have made the burden feel lighter."

"Now I think I'm just out of my mind," Pam muttered.

"Yes, I recall you pranced down the mountain like an alpine goat in spring." Gerbald chuckled, stifling a groan of his own at his even heavier share of the burden. "I'm sure you will find it all worthwhile, months from now, when you still have coffee to drink." he added, trying to sound encouraging.

"Here, *Frau* Pam, allow me to take some of this." Pers came beside her, reaching for the extra sacks she carried draped over her shoulders.

"Naaw, come on, I loaded you up like a pack mule, Pers. You're already carrying a lot more than your share, even taking the age difference into account. I know how strong you are, but I don't want you to get injured."

Pers grinned and took the sacks from her, ignoring her protests.

"Nonsense! This is nothing compared to the tortures the Bosun has put me through. Believe me, as far as I am concerned, this is still a 'light duty'!"

Pam gave him a grateful smile. "Well, at least it's all downhill from here." she said as brightly as she could manage. Pers stepped into the lead, walking with a spring in his stride that belied the many pounds of coffee he carried.

Gerbald and Pam looked at each other, silently admitting that they were both already tired, and knowing they had a long way to go.

"Youth. If only there was a way to steal it from the young." Gerbald said as they watched Pers stride down the trail. With a tandem sigh, they followed, placing one well-worn boot in front of the other.

Just before sunset, they were back on the familiar trails near the beach camp with less than half a mile to go. They paused again at the rise where they had observed the junk ship, to watch the sun go down. The junk now lay at anchor on the high tide, once again resembling a fanciful toy more than a real ship, its bright colors darkened to deeper, eldritch hues in the evening glow. Lanterns were lit one by one. Pam thought she could hear the quiet murmur of the men on deck in the evening hush. As twilight surrounded them, Gerbald started walking and Pam began to follow. After a minute, she realized Pers was still standing on the rise, his head hanging low, and his face long in the dim purple light.

Pam tapped Gerbald on the back, speaking to him in a low whisper. "Hey, something's wrong with the kid. I knew something was bugging him this morning, he put on a brave face all day, but now . . . I'm going to stay and talk with him. Do you want to join me?"

"Hmmm. I know he looks up to me, which is very flattering, but I also know sometimes a young man needs the comfort of a woman instead of a man. Lord knows when last he saw his mother, or if he ever has. Go see what's troubling him, Pam. It would be good for him." He carefully didn't add *and for you,* but he certainly thought it as he started walking again. The last mile was easy even in the dark, but he would wait in the brush below the rise until they passed by, then follow them back, just in case. *The bodyguard's job is never done.* He smiled with satisfaction despite his earnest wish to be back at camp and in bed.

Pam walked back up the rise to Pers. He saw her and started to walk, but she motioned for him to stop. He tried to look cheerful, but she could see plainly enough in the remaining light, he was troubled.

"All right, you can't kid a kidder, pal, so tell me what's wrong." Pam gave him her best sympathetic smile.

Pers smiled, but his brow was still downcast.

"Well, it's nothing really . . ." he paused, tongue-tied.

Pam waited, continuing to smile. Seeing there was no escape, the young man went on.

"Well, I shall have to tell you a little about me. My parents were poor farmers on the coast near Norway and, already having several sons, they sent me off to sea when I was but nine."

"Just nine! Jesus!" Pam was appalled, but had heard far worse since her arrival in the 1630s.

"Please, don't think badly of them. They could barely feed us all. Besides, I was glad to go. I wanted to leave that stupid village and see the world! The work turned out to be harder than I thought, but the men usually treated me kindly. It's just that life on a ship, well, the faces change, and once you get to know someone they die, like poor old Fritjoff, or move on to another ship . . ." He stalled for a moment, but Pam nodded her understanding, signaling for him to go on.

"My dreams have changed. I've seen a lot of the world. You may be surprised how much. I want a home now, to stop traveling, to know a place. And the truth is, even though we got stuck here against our will, this is the first time since I was that boy of nine that I've lived in a *home* instead of a ship, here on this island with all of you. And now, we are all leaving . . ."

Pers was struggling to keep smiling, but Pam could see he was upset. She took his hand, afraid the simple act might make him lose his composure and start to cry, a terrible thing for a proud youth becoming a man.

"Pers, I'm sorry. I didn't know you felt this way. I want you to know I understand. When Grantville came through time I was all alone. Like I told you earlier, I was divorced, so no husband. I still had my son, but he doesn't like me much anymore. If I hadn't met Gerbald and Dore, I don't know what would have become of me. Well, I'd probably be living as a shut-in and weigh fifty pounds more than I do! At least until my supply of cherry bonbons ran out. Anyway, everybody needs a home sometimes, and Gerbald and Dore gave me one."

She paused, trying to gauge if what she wanted to say would be the right thing, the thing Pers needed and wanted. She had all his attention and knew that he looked up to her far more than she had realized. *Well, you have never been Miss Congeniality, that's for sure.* She took a deep breath and placed a hand on Pers' wide shoulder.

"Pers, I'm sorry I didn't see how strongly you felt sooner. I want you to know that you will *always* have a home with me if you wish it. You have been my special friend all through this voyage, proving your love and loyalty a hundred times over. I have already come to think of you as another son. I swear to you, it's true! When that pirate was beating you, that was what made me mad enough to shoot him. He was hurting *my boy*! In my heart, *you are* my boy, you've earned your place! Whatever you want, I will make it happen for you. If you want to go to school, I will see to it. If you want to work with me, I will have a place for you. If you were to think of me as your family, why, it would make me very proud." Now it was Pam who was in danger of tears. The hope dawning on Pers' face, still a boy as much as a man, made her heart beat double time.

Pers stuttered a bit, and then, in a small, shy voice said, "I'd like that very much, if you will have me. I would like to have a mother again."

"Awww, come here, kid." With that, she grabbed Pers, who was a good two feet taller and gave him a bear hug. "Let old Pam be your momma. I'll try my best, but I'll warn you I'm not always too good at it. I'm not sure where all this is going from here, but you just stick with me, we'll figure it out together, all right, son?"

Pam could feel Pers shaking. He was weeping, but she could tell from the vibration that these were good tears, the tears of relief and discovered joy. She joined right in, and they stood there for a while, a mother and son, not by blood, but in all the ways that really mattered. After a time, Pam stepped back from the embrace to look at the bright, lovely youth who had entered her life. She patted him gently on the cheek.

"Don't worry, Pers. I won't tell anybody what a sweet kid you are. They already know anyway. Now, let's go home. I'm so hungry I could eat coconut crab curry!"

"Yes, ma'am . . . er . . . *Mom*!" He gave her a happy salute, his usual grin back in place and a size bigger.

CHAPTER 29: THE LAST DAY OF CAMP

It was their last day at the beach camp. That evening they intended to dine on the junk and spend the night aboard before sailing with the dawn. The Bosun, despite an initial raft of complaints about the many oddities of their new vessel, had deemed her seaworthy, and ready to go. Toward the end of their conversation around the dinner fire the previous evening, and with more than a bit of liquor in him, the Bosun had began to wax so poetic on the junk's capabilities, Pam suspected he was beginning to fall in love with the thing, and thought that must happen between all sailors and their ships eventually.

After an early breakfast, Pam sat on the porch of her hut, sipping her third cup of coffee, all delivered by a very attentive Pers. He couldn't linger, though. The Bosun had work for him, and plenty of it. She gave him a motherly peck on the cheek as he set off for the beach, exactly like she used to give Walt as he left for school. It made Pers blush, but he positively radiated happiness. *Looks like I'm a mom again, well good for me! I missed having a kid to dote on!* The thought filled her with a deep, comfortable warmth. Pers had come to think of their beach camp as home and she realized she had, too. She would miss her funny little bamboo shack at Castaway's Cove and wondered if she would ever come this way again. They had been lucky to make a safe landing here when the *Redbird* went down. All in all, they had enjoyed a much higher level of comfort than could be expected, thanks to the island's natural bounty and the many skills of her companions. At times, it had felt more like she was on summer holiday than marooned, especially during the heady days that followed her discovery of the dodo flock. Those were good times and she wouldn't forget them.

"Maybe someday we can make this a research station and spend some time here again," she said to herself, a habit she was careful not to let others overhear. "I would like that. Yes, we shall." The sailors had built to last, and she thought the buildings could survive a few seasons without human care.

Finishing her coffee with a gulp, she went inside and put the coconut-shell cup on a shelf, leaving it there for that possible someday. The tiny room was almost empty, now. She had already sent her baggage out to the ship, and only a few island gewgaws remained; a shell collection along the window sill and some unimportant sketches left hanging on the walls.

One piece of art, placed in a prominent place over her cot, was a message to any who might take shelter here in the future-- a large canvas featuring a painting of a dodo and the words *"Protected Species! Do not kill this bird! Not only is it illegal under Swedish Colonial law, but terrible misfortune follows any who do! And, if you are stupid enough to eat one it will make you very, very sick, often fatally! You have been warned! Signed, Pam Miller, Representing HRH Princess Kristina Wasa."* The message was written in English, German and Swedish. "Can't hurt!" she said, chuckling at her own cleverness. Assuming they could read, sailors were by nature superstitious, and she had no bones against using a bit of psychological warfare in her cause. *In fact, I should probably do that more often.*

As she was leaving Pam brushed against some of the shell necklaces hanging from a peg beside the window, the very ones she and Dore had worn with their native getup. On a whim she took one down and put it on, a bit of beach-camp style to remember the place by. Pam took one last look around, backed out onto the porch, then closed and latched the door against the wind. It was time to go.

She found Gerbald and the Black Chessmen bombardiers had already moved the heavy carronade from its log mount and were now loading it onto one of the pinnaces with a complicated affair of poles, ropes, and pulleys. Gerbald had proven, many times, to have a knack for that sort of thing, even impressing the sailors who worked with such tools on a daily basis. Had he been born up-time with the opportunities available there, he would have made a highly talented engineer. They had made him the foreman for the task, and he was basking in the glory of leadership, one of his few foibles.

"Show off." she teased as she sauntered by the proceedings. Gerbald just grinned, as pleased with a ribbing as he was with positive attention. Pam thanked the Lord she had found such a good-natured friend. She knew he had become an expert in deflecting the worst of her moods and she usually allowed him to do so with silent gratitude.

Pam wandered to the kitchen to see if she could help Dore with her cooking things. Not too surprisingly, the incredibly efficient woman was already packed up and had drafted sturdy Arne and quiet, dark-haired Lind into hauling the boxes and bags down to the beach. Pam was given a fairly light basket to carry. By the time she got there, the pinnace had already gone to deliver the precious carronade to the new vessel, and her sister boat hadn't yet returned, so

Pam put her basket on the pile of goods waiting for the next trip and decided to take a walk. She thought about it a moment, but decided she didn't want to go by way of the cemetery. Her good-byes had been said, and the pain was still too fresh, so she went the opposite direction, ending up on the high cliff lookout where she and Gerbald had first sighted the junk, just a few days days ago. It felt like weeks! Pam sat with her back against a gnarled, wind-tortured tree to watch the proceedings. The job of getting the carronade onto the junk and mounted looked like it was going to take a good long while. Gerbald and the dedicated Black Chessmen swarmed around it like a colony of ants wrestling a particularly large and tasty prize into their anthill, while the *Löjtnant* and the White Chessmen cheered them on from the upper decks. Seeing that all was going smoothly, Pam let herself drift off into a nap.

Garrett W. Vance

CHAPTER 30: AN UNEXPECTED PROMOTION

After an hour of dozing filled with dreams featuring swords, blood, and the screams of the dying, Pam shook herself awake with a sour taste in her mouth, feeling unrested and anxious. She hurried down to rejoin those at the beach, comforted by their dependable presence.

The Bosun and two of the more senior sailors, Vilfrid and Hake, were waiting for her on the shore along with Dore. This was the last trip out for *Redbird's* pinnaces, which the sailors would then haul up onto the junk's wide deck, where they would hang at the ready, over the starboard and port sides. The versatile small crafts were quite dear to them, having proven their worth time and again. It took her a while to realize, but the sailors were once again especially polite and deferring to her. Of course, they always had been, but there had been a change since they captured the Oriental junk. Perhaps, now that they were going to be at sea again, they felt they must restore some kind of shipboard formality with their important passenger. Pam frowned at the thought. She much preferred the informality of the cove where she was the adopted little sister to a bunch of doting big brothers.

"Are you ready to board, *Frau* Pam?" the Bosun asked. *Humph. Back to Frau, is it? Oh well, they are just doing their jobs.*

"Yes, just let me take one last look." Pam scanned their home for all those long months. Their stay in this remote place had come to an end. A fierce joy filled her. *We did it. We are getting out of here!* She climbed into the pinnace, where she was ushered to a seat in the prow. She watched their beach recede until they began to draw in close to the junk. After one last, long, look she turned her back to the shore, ready to resume her interrupted journey.

Pam looked up to see all the sailors and marines were lined along the gaily painted rails. As the pinnace drew close the men sent up a cheer, whooping and hollering with hearty gusto. The passengers and the men crewing the pinnace quickly joined the merriment, waving and whooping back at the cheering crew.

They clambered aboard with the help of many friendly hands, accompanied by the high, keening tune of the Bosun's whistle. Their entire company now stood assembled on the capacious deck of the fanciful junk they had acquired at such bloody cost. The men opened a space around Pam and her staff, all the while clapping and cheering. After a while, the Bosun raised his hands and brought the noise down to a hush. Pam smiled at all of them, these men who had brought her to the far side of the world, these men who had worked so hard to make her safe and comfortable during their castaway days, these such very good men who had become as brothers to her.

"*Herr* Bosun, you fellows shouldn't make such a fuss!" Pam said, her West Virginia twang creeping into her Swedish. She was beginning to feel shy and a bit overwhelmed, as she sometimes did when finding herself in the public eye.

"It is from our hearts that we do!" the Bosun told her, "We have been delivered from our sojourn on that wretched shore and are in possession of a fine craft. All of this is because of the great courage and many skills you, *Herr* Gerbald, and *Frau* Dore have lent to us. We never would have been able to live as well as we have while lost, or to have captured this vessel without *your* leadership, *Frau* Pam."

The men broke out into a cheer again, clapping their hands for Pam, who was deeply moved by their gesture, but also felt as if she wanted to dissolve down into the deck away from all this attention.

The Bosun nodded happily and fixed a toothy grin on her. Before she could make a break for it, he said, "In the tradition of the sea, a captured vessel becomes the property of the victors, in particular the leader of the victors, their captain. Pam, *you* made the plan which ensured our success. *You* led the attack like some warrior queen out of the old tales!" He paused to dramatically sweep his arm across the decks in a gesture that included all the grinning men standing at attention. "This is *your ship,* we are *your crew* and *you* are *our captain.* We await your orders, *Captain* Pam!" He gave her a long salute, his eyes meeting hers with glowing admiration. Ending the salute, he made a polite bow, then took a step back to join the men now waiting silently at attention.

Somewhere, a seagull cried, and the sound of gentle waves lapping against the red-lacquered hull became loud in the silence. Pam's eyes were as wide as porcelain plates, their steely-gray having attained a glazed cast. After a while, Gerbald reached out and poked her in the arm, a deep chuckle coming from beneath the shade of his ridiculous mustard-colored hat's floppy brim. Pam looked at the men, *her* men, and managed a kind of stunned half-smile. She nodded a few times, taking it all in. Somewhere inside the turmoil of emotions whirling through her brain, she heard a calm, clear voice, the one that only came when she really needed it: *You have earned this honor, Pamela Grace Miller. Now acknowledge their faith in you. It is yours by right!*

Suddenly, her eyes came into focus, she drew back her shoulders, and in an unexpectedly loud and commanding voice bawled, "Make ready to sail!" The crew jumped at her order, dispersing through the ship to their stations. Tired of life ashore, everyone was delighted to be back at their chosen profession, and so they bent to their tasks with relish. The Bosun stepped forward to pump Pam's hand in the American-style Gerbald had taught him.

"Was that the right thing to say?" she asked, relieved the show was over, and reeling from the ramifications.

"Absolutely! Well done, Captain Pam. I knew you had it in you!" the Bosun beamed at her.

"Look, I'm not so sure about this 'captain' thing, Nils." she said in confidential tones, leaning into him and using his Christian name, which she rarely did. "Isn't it a job better suited for you, or the *Löjtnant?* The extent of my boat piloting experience is rowing a rubber raft around a lake as a kid. I have only a basic idea of how to sail a ship, much less captain one."

"No, ma'am, I wouldn't have it. This ship is squarely *yours* and *you* command her. There's a lot more to it than the sailing, leave that part to us! You just tell us where you want to go and we will take you there! This is your expedition and we will follow your lead."

Supremely touched by the confidence these brave men had put in her, Pam's eyes were moist. The Bosun saw she needed time to let it all sink in, and motioned toward the aft cabins.

"If I may be so bold, Captain, might I suggest you and *Frau* Dore have a look around the ship?" He started to go, but stopped, with a bemused expression on his face. "Perhaps I have grown a bit rusty. You ordered us to make sail, but what is our destination?"

Pam looked out at the sparkling azure sea to think for a moment. "Well, the plan was to anchor here tonight. We know its a safe harbor. Why don't you just take us for a spin up and down the beach, a little demonstration of what we feel like under way. Then let's anchor back here and give everyone a rest. I think the men need one before we set off into the unknown."

The Bosun beamed. "Very wise, Captain, very wise. Now, you leave it all to me, and make yourselves at home. What I believe serves as the captain's cabin is at the top of those stairs, and meaning no offense, ma'am, but you might find more comfortable clothing there, although it will be of a foreign cut."

Pam looked at what was left of the clothes they had landed in, barely rags now, held together with grass stitching in places.

"I think that's the best idea I've ever heard, *Herr* Bosun! We look a mess. We'll try to find some new clothes, and some for you and the men as well. We are all a bit worse for wear."

"Well, then, I'll get back to work. May I ask *Herr* Gerbald help with raising the pinnace? He has an eye for rope work and is the only one of us who can make some sense of this foreign tackle." Then, he and Gerbald just stood there looking at her. After a long moment it dawned on her. *Oh good Lord! They're waiting for you to say yes, dummy!*

Pam muttered her captainly assent. "Yes, yes. . . carry on!"

"I would be delighted, Captain Pam!" Gerbald answered. "I have always loved a good puzzle." Gerbald had been in Pam's service for years, and knew the high quality of her leadership well, even if she herself didn't see it. Even so, as he left, he didn't neglect to give his friend and employer a wry smirk, much amused at her obvious discomfiture with her new position. She stuck her tongue out at him as he walked away.

"Ever hear of walking the plank, buster? Yeah, *you* in the funny hat!" she called after him. She turned to see Dore was smiling broadly, face bright with pride and excitement. This rare sight filled Pam's heart with a shiny kind of joy and she grabbed her friend's hand.

"We need new clothes, sister. Let's go find some booty!" Pam said to her.

"Yes, ma'am, Captain Pam!" Dore replied in English with her thick German accent, coming to comically straight as a board attention while making a snappy salute. This made them both start laughing, and so, in high spirits, they started their exploration of the exotic and alluring, gaily-painted foreign ship.

CHAPTER31: GALLEY OF CELESTIAL DELIGHTS

They began their tour below decks, deciding to save the captain's cabin for last. No point in putting on something new, then getting it all dirty down in the holds. The junk was certainly unusual looking on the outside, but a ship was a ship, so the belowdecks offered a layout not too different from those built in Europe. In Pam's opinion, it was more spacious and well thought out in its design. The cabins were larger and the hallways surprisingly higher. None but the tallest of the men would have to crouch as they moved about. Everything was clean and dry, the wood well-caulked, painted with a preservative stain. They found a large storage bay with its deck doors open to let in the bright southern sunlight. Pam walked around its shadowy recesses, lifting tarps, and poking at oddly-shaped barrels marked with the wispy brush strokes of strange languages.

"We should find out what all this cargo is." Dore said, peering into the shadows at a plethora of crates and sacks neatly made fast to the walls and floors. "We may have something of value here. It's likely we will need to trade for supplies in the voyage to come."

Pam made a slow turn, the light from above catching her hair and bringing out flashes of silver among the dishwater blond locks. She was smiling and Dore thought she looked like an angel. Dore was pleased to see her friend happy after such a long ordeal.

"There's enough room here to make a pen for a flock of dodos." Pam said. "They would have fresh air and light when the weather is good and be well-protected when its not." Her voice was filled with a hope she had not felt in a long time. "We have another chance. Maybe I can still save the dodos, bring a breeding population back to Europe, if we accomplish nothing else."

"Of course, you can, Pam. We will help as always." Dore encouraged her.

They left the cargo hold to continue aft. After climbing steep stairways that could have passed for ladders, they arrived in a room that made Dore emit a gasp of delight. It was the ship's galley and it was . . . wonderful! There was a brass pipe built into the wall from which either stored or freshly caught rainwater could be drawn from barrels on the deck with ease, to fill a deep, porcelain sink. Next to this was an open window, its square panes made of a thick, ivory-colored laminated paper that would let in plenty of light to work by, even when closed. There were fat candles for after dark. Pam and Dore entered the seemingly cluttered, yet actually highly organized space, not sure where to begin their exploration.

Hundreds of small drawers and cabinets dotted the walls and filled the spaces under the wide, wooden counters. A peek revealed dry goods, what might be flour, sugar, and dried herbs and spices. A variety of unusual pots and pans hung from a rack above an iron woodstove. Pam recognized a wok and a steamer. Even though their shapes were strange, she knew Dore would be able to put them to use. Latched drawers held a dazzling array of cooking implements and tools, including ladles, skewers, meat forks, and items whose purpose was a mystery. The room was filled with a delicious aroma of woodsmoke, strong scented herbs, and fresh salt air. Immediately adjacent, lay a pantry chock-full of dried meats, fish, fruits, vegetables, and as yet unidentified items. There were even pots with live herbs growing on a shelf beneath a window. Dore and Pam both clucked over these, and watered them with a teapot. It was obvious the plants hadsuffered under the pirate occupation.

"Good gawd, Dore, it's like a modern kitchen! More like a restaurant kitchen than something you'd have at home. It has everything but an electric dishwasher!" Pam exclaimed, overwhelmed after months of coconut-shell soup bowls and clamshell spoons. She didn't say it to Dore, but vowed to herself she never, *ever* wanted to eat the Castaway Cove staple coconut and crab curry again. *Ever!*

The galley of the *Redbird*, despite the addition of several up-time style conveniences, was a greasy hole in the wall compared to this. Pam noticed a cylindrical ceramic pot filled with what must certainly be chopsticks. She pulled two of them out to study them. They were about eleven inches long, one quarter of which was squared and the rest rounded, cut flat at the ends, made of a smooth, yellowish wood that had been stained darker on the rounded, food grabbing end, presumably by use.

"Hey, Dore! I wasn't sure, but I think I now know what country this boat is from— China, or, whatever they call it in this century." Dore looked at her friend with eyebrows raised in interest. "These are called 'chopsticks' and they're used for eating. When my son Walt got old enough to behave reasonably well for an hour or two, we started going out to eat once a month and we tried a lot of different kinds of restaurants. There were lots of Chinese places around and even a couple of Japanese joints over in Morgantown. Once we tried Korean food up in Pittsburg, but it was a bit too spicy for the guys. Anyway, I'm sure these are Chinese-style chopsticks. The Japanese versions are shorter with pointy ends and the Koreans make theirs from metal. I have no idea why because they sure were tricky to use. That metal was slippery!"

Dore looked on with a certain amount of amazement. "It's sometimes hard to believe that you lived in such a world, Pam. You make food from the Far East sound commonplace, available just down the road, when in our time most people know little about the world beyond a few miles!" She reached over to the holder to pull out two of the slender wooden rods herself. "I don't see how these could be used to eat." she remarked after giving them a careful study. She ended up holding one in each hand like drumsticks with a mystified expression on her face.

"I'll show you!" Pam began to demonstrate. "You put them both in one hand like this and pick up the food between the ends. It's tricky at first, but you get the hang of it pretty fast. Especially when you're hungry!" She opened a few drawers until she found what must certainly be dried peas. "Here, watch!" Pam deftly picked up one pea at a time and made a row of six across the counter as Dore looked on, wide-eyed. "I think we left all the clamshell spoons back at the beach, so I guess I'll have to teach everybody how to use these. My ex-husband never could get the hang of it. He always had to ask for a fork." With several flicks of her wrist, she returned the peas back to their drawer and slid the chopsticks back into their container with a satisfying wooden click. "Yup. Must be Chinese. They like their food all right, pretty fancy stuff! I'm not surprised they had this nice a setup even in these times. Well, lucky us!"

She turned to Dore, who was allowing herself a tentative smile at the prospects of cooking in such an odd, yet practical galley.

"Welcome to your new kingdom, Chef! I can't wait to see what you come up with first!"

Dore grinned at her enthusiastic young friend.

"Well, I can promise you one thing, my dear Pam— it will *not* be coconut and crab curry!"

Garrett W. Vance

CHAPTER 32: ONE MAN'S JUNK IS ANOTHER MAN'S TREASURE

Captured Oriental Junk, South Coast of Mauritius

Pam and Dore climbed out of the cool shadows of the lower decks to stand blinking beneath the Tropic of Capricorn's blazing sun. Squinting against the glare, Pam saw Dore looking down toward the galley — a paragon of luxury and abundance after their long sojourn marooned on a remote shore. Pam smiled at Dore's almost child-like eagerness to play with her new toys and motioned her to follow. "Okay, pal-o-mine, you'll have your chance to do your thing in there soon enough. Let's go check out the upper cabins."

The junk was cruising slowly down the length of the cove, pushed along by a summery breeze filling her slatted crimson sails, engaged in another practice run. Sailors rushed to and fro, sometimes pausing to puzzle over her unfamiliar designs. The Bosun's voice could be heard on the foredeck, by turns roundly cursing any man who was slow to grasp the intricacies of the foreign rigging, then damning the mad heathens who had built such an unusual craft in the first place. Well, all romances had their rough spots. Pam had full faith her crew would manage. They were moving forward in any case, which must surely be a good sign. Now that they had a ship, she didn't want to dally. The question of the fate of the colonists weighed heavily on her, as it did on all aboard, and all possible haste would be made to find them. But not tonight, tonight they would take a rest. They had certainly earned one.

Their eyes now somewhat adjusted to the brightness, she and Dore headed to the high aft tower Pam thought of as "the castle deck." Standing in its shade, they peeked into the bottom cabin. The windows had been opened to freshen the air inside, which was a bit stuffy. Earlier, the sailors had reported they had performed a thorough cleanup, removing all evidence the pirates had ever lived aboard. The foreman of the cleaning-crew, always helpful Mård, a meticulous fellow, had remarked the heathen pirates had been unexpectedly neat and clean, except for bloodstains here and there, likely from tortured captives; "Once they've dried, they're hell to remove." Pam had grimaced at that, but didn't fault the fellow for his honesty.

"Let's go inside!" Pam said, Dore nodding agreement.

The cabin was no disappointment even after the delights found in the galley. These were the quarters the Bosun had suggested for Gerbald and Dore. The door opened near the bottom of the castle deck's ladder. As the only married couple of the expedition, they would be given the second-nicest room on the ship, the first being reserved for the captain. They found a spacious, wood-paneled apartment, elegantly furnished with the same kind of heavy, ornately carved, and lacquered wood furniture found in the lobbies of fancier Chinese restaurants. It most certainly had been reserved for distinguished guests or perhaps used by high-ranking ship's officers. They found fresh bed linens neatly folded and ready for use in sandalwood scented cabinets. Pam was pleased to see they were made of silk. The bed was, much like the *Redbird*'s, built into the walls. It was wider, yet a bit shorter than what they were accustomed to. There were plenty of large cushions and pillows if they needed to spread out onto the carpet strewn floor.

After the initial inspection, Dore wrung her hands and exclaimed, "We can't possibly stay here!" She was shocked by the level of opulence. "This is a room for a prince or a duke, not a washerwoman and her old soldier husband!"

"Nonsense," Pam replied. "You're the ship's chef and Gerbald is my personal bodyguard, as well as an acting sergeant in our fighting force, so you get the good stuff. Enjoy it!" Dore looked unconvinced, but Pam added "That's an order!" and gave her friend a playful grin.

Pam wasn't surprised when the upper quarters were double the grandeur and four times the space, occupying the entire floor of the tower. Pam looked around, deciding she would make the area near the door, the dining room and office. The back third of the capacious room would be made private, since that was where the bed was, as well as the bathroom. Placed along the dark-stained, wooden walls were beautifully painted, movable screens perfect for dividing the room. She was pleased to see the bathroom facilities were more advanced than on the ships of Europe, and to Pam's great delight featured an actual porcelain bathtub! *Calgon, take me away!* The elegant stateroom was more than enough space for her needs and she looked forward to doing some serious basking in its luxuriousness.

The two friends grinned like fools at their change of fortune. To go from roughing it, stranded on a deserted shore, to occupying ship's quarters that oozed with comfort was a pleasant shock. Pam shook her head, gazing at the opulent space as if she were in a dream, daring it to be real. Pam and Dore began rearranging the place to suit Pam's needs, taking one of the screens from the wall and placing it in front of her bunk, to make a sleeping alcove. This took some work ,the wood bases of the five-foot screens were quite heavy, designed to stay upright even in the worst storms. Pam was pleased to find this ship would provide a gentler ride than poor old *Redbird* had. They were under way at a fair clip now and she could barely feel it. As they went for another screen, Pam bumped into a pile of pillows leaning against the wall and knocked them over. When she bent to straighten them, she noticed there was an opening in the wall—a thin, dark crack running from the floor to a height of about three feet.

"Hmm, what do you suppose this is?" She pushed the pillows away and felt along the crack with her fingers. To her surprise, it was a small, hidden door slightly ajar. *So, our lovely craft has secrets. Wonderful!*

"Dore! Try to find a knife or something we can use to pry this open!" Dore began to scurry around the room in search of a suitable implement. Pam kept tugging and pushing here and there until she discovered a tiny spot the size of a man's thumb that appeared to have been worn smooth by years of touch. She pushed it, and the door popped open as neat as could be. "Never mind, Dore. Bring a candle!"

Dore, well-practiced with the flint and steel she carried in her apron pockets, had a candle lit faster than Pam could strike a match. She handed it to Pam, and they both got down on their hands and knees to peer into the space.

To Pam's amazement, there was a deep closet, a secret room. Among the various items within the dark space, the one that caught her eye above all, was a large wooden box reinforced with metal bands. Crawling to it, she tried to pull it toward the door. It wouldn't budge. There was something about the thing. . . . The very heaviness of it made the teeny-tiny hairs at the nape of her neck stand up and do the mambo. Sticking out of an ornate-looking brass lock was the back end of a tarnished silver key. Apparently, its last user had left in a hurry, possibly the ill-fated original owners, or the fat, mustachioed pirate captain they had sent to his rightful reward in Hell. The box was built like a safe, massive, and thick. It was age-stained and covered in a faded, but flowing white script. She didn't dare think the words that were screaming to be heard in the back of her mind. It simply couldn't be . . .

"Open it, Pam! Let us see!" Dore urged her on, her voice a bit higher pitched than normal, more that of a child than a serious-minded, middle-aged woman of God. Pam marveled once again at the amazing youthening effect adventure was having on her friend. They knelt in front of the mysterious box, both giggling, holding on to each other for support.

Pam hesitated, her hand trembling near the key until Dore gave her a gentle push. They both jumped a bit, their nerves as taut as guitar strings.

"Oh, we are so silly!" Dore said, laughing "It's probably full of ship's papers, all written in that ridiculous squiggle these Easterners use instead of decent letters." Even so, her face was full of expectation.

"Right!" Pam agreed. "It's not like we would find anything valuable on a real pirate ship! This isn't a movie, right? I'll bet it's empty." They both laughed while Pam turned the key. There was a muffled click deep within the mechanism, then the lid popped up a few inches as it released from a spring. Pam and Dore's eyes were as big and round as harvest moons as they gazed at the rainbow of colors glinting within.

"No, it's a treasure chest!" Pam announced with comic nonchalance. "Holy shit." she murmured as she raised the chest's heavy lid until it caught and held open. "Holy shit." she said again as her hands touched cool metal and smooth stone. Despite her amazement at such an unexpected discovery, Dore managed to give Pam a quick look of disapproval over her blasphemous language. Pam's mouth was a bit too dry and she croaked, "I can't *believe* this!"

Dore murmured something incomprehensible as she peered over Pam's shoulder. This was replaced by a funny kind of squealing noise and she held onto Pam to steady herself. Scarcely believing what she was seeing, now *touching*, Pam filled her hands with a shining mixture of gold and silver coins, glittering jewels, and pearls. The box surely held a fortune, a small one perhaps, but a fortune, nonetheless. As if to make sure it wasn't a figment of her imagination, she pried one of Dore's hands from its painfully tight grip on her arm and poured lucre into it. They knelt, staring into the chest's contents for a long time.

"It's real. A real treasure chest on a real pirate ship. Yo-ho-ho." Pam's voice was hushed and full of wonder.

"One might say our fortunes have changed," Dore said, her head shaking as if to dispel her disbelief.

"Go fetch Gerbald!" Pam told Dore, now feeling dizzy as if she were on a carnival ride, the thrill switching to terror and back to thrill again. She dug deeper, scooping the contents to pile them on one side. Besides the coins and gems, there were some larger pieces buried within: tiaras, combs and other less easy to identify objects, all a-glitter with precious stones.

Dore ran so fast she might have shot out the door and off the top floor like a cannonball if she hadn't caught herself. Pam had never seen her friend move like that, but chalked it up to her years surviving in the rough, following Gerbald in and out of battles. Dore was full of surprises, but then these days, surprises had become the norm.

A huffing, puffing Dore returned with an amused Gerbald hurrying after. His ever-present goofy mustard hat was knocked from his head by the low door casing as Dore pushed him through. Before he could bend to retrieve his precious chapeau, he froze, seeing Pam holding a double palmful of treasure. His eyes widened, and he just stood, staring, while Dore picked up his hat, long the object of her scorn, taking care to scrunch and twist its seemingly indestructible mustard-yellow felt between her strong hands with malicious intent. Failing to make much of a dent, she stood on her tiptoes and plopped it back onto his head where it looked no worse for the attempted wear and tear.

"There, he is speechless! If only we had one of those video cameras to record the moment for ages to come." she said, laughing at her husband's flummoxed state.

Pam smiled to see a bit of the feisty old Dore back in play.

Gerbald straightened the much abused and well-loved hat over his salt-and-pepper hair, taking a moment to digest what he was seeing. With a regal sweep of her arm, Pam escorted him to the closet, which he crawled into with easy grace. He pushed the box to gauge its considerable weight and was able to move it a quarter of an inch. He scratched his chin and grinned.

Pam grinned back. "I think this might have belonged to that fat, old pirate captain. The writing on it looks more like swirly Arabic script than Chinese characters. This wasn't the first ship he'd captured, I'll bet. We are looking at years of plunder. I guess you really can't take it with you."

Dore, who had managed to compose herself, quoted scripture in her old, familiar Christian soldier's tones: "*Treasures of wickedness profit nothing: but righteousness delivereth from death. The Lord will not suffer the soul of the righteous to famish: but he casteth away the substance of the wicked.* Proverbs 10:2-3."

Gerbald nodded in sober agreement with his pious wife, buying always useful good will with the gesture, then turned to Pam.

"Pam, when your luck changes, it *really* changes. What do you intend to do with all this?"

"I've decided already," Pam said, while letting a handful of gleaming coins fall back into the chest with a musical tinkling. "We should divide it equally among everybody on this ship."

Dore nodded in staunch approval.

"That is the right thing to do, my Pam!" Dore told her. "We are all in this together. Shall I summon the Bosun now?"

"Allow me to tell him," Gerbald cut in. "After all, I missed out on the thrill of first discovery. I would very much like to see our good friend's face when he hears of this windfall. I will keep it between we four for now. We can divide it all up and then pass it out to the men before tonight's party. I'll wager they will be over the moon!"

"Tonight's party?" Pam asked. She saw Dore deliver what must have been a painful blow to the small of her husband's back.

"Oops!" Gerbald said in English, followed by a long-suffering sigh.

"Spiller of the beans!" Dore growled at him, also in English. After many years together they used English and German interchangeably, and sometimes mixed the two together in one sentence, despite their best efforts not to. This dubious habit was rampant in the USE now, evolving into a creole some were calling 'Amideutch.' Dore continued in German, which would always be the most comfortable for her, "It matters not. We have all had enough of surprises by now. We have earned a bit of fun after our many troubles and so tonight is for celebration!" she said, her face alight with pleasure.

"Who are you, and what have you done with Dore?" Pam asked, but Dore didn't seem to hear. She was pushing her husband toward the door. "Go now, oaf! We must make ourselves presentable. Now that our Pam is a captain, she can't go about dressed in these rags! Out with you!"

Gerbald didn't resist. This time he was careful to duck and keep his hat on.

"Maybe you can afford to buy a new hat now!" Pam called after him. It never hurt to hope.

"What? Waste such riches on everyday items? No, I shall use my share to do something wonderful. I shall buy my own television set."

"Not until I have a decent house you won't, foolish man. If the Lord has seen fit to gift us with riches, we must use them wisely!" Jumping, Dore took a swipe at the much-hated hat, but Gerbald was too fast. Her hand flew through thin air as Gerbald disappeared, launching himself out the door and dropping from sight in a blur. No crash or injured call for help came, so Dore and Pam returned to their fun. They laughed like schoolgirls as they rummaged through the room's many drawers and cabinets, laying out exotic garments on the bed and divans as they went.

CHAPTER 33: COUNTING THEIR BLESSINGS

Soon after, the Bosun was brought in to view their unexpected bounty. He let out a long whistle as he squatted in front of the brimming chest. "I've sailed the seas since I was ten years old," he said, "and never have I seen this kind of wealth. I will be able to buy some land on the coast and retire now. Truly, your generosity is great to share it with us, Captain. We would never ask it of you." His eyes glistened.

"You've earned it, my friend," Pam told him. "You all have. Let's count it out, the four of us, and the *Löjtnant* as witness, equal shares for all." The Bosun nodded, but Pam still had some idea she would somehow end up with more. The men of the sea had ways of doing things, and she knew the captain traditionally got a larger share of the booty, a much larger share. She intended to protest, of course, but wheels were already turning. Pam had projects lined up for years to come, and now she had that most critical of all resources: funding. One thing was certain, the first thing she would do with her share of the take was to make damn sure her colony succeeded, which went hand in hand with saving the dodo.

When the *Löjtnant* arrived, he tried, in his gentlemanly way, to eschew receiving a share of his own, but Pam told him to just accept what was coming to him and be happy. Capitulating, he smiled, and replied, "As you wish, Captain. My sincerest thanks!" No doubt he was as glad to get his hands on such a large chunk of change.

Together, Gerbald and the *Löjtnant* managed to drag the chest out of its closet, and bring it to a massive, teak table Dore had cleared of Oriental knickknacks.

"Okay, here's what I think we ought to do," Pam said, after considering the situation for a few minutes. "Let's start with the coins. We will group them by types first, and then the ones that don't match any others, we can group by material and weight." She reached into the chest to scoop up a double handful of coins which she piled onto the table's surface.

"Here, these two are the same, they look like copper, and they have square holes in the middle. Chinese, maybe. I bet they're not worth much." She pushed them off into their own area. The next coin she held up to the light and made a long whistle. "If this isn't a gold doubloon, I'll eat Gerbald's hat. I always think of the Spaniards hanging out in the Caribbean, but I remember reading something about the Philippines as I was getting ready for this trip. Let's hope there's more of *these*."

It turned out they weren't able to recognize most of the coins but the Bosun had an old sailor's eye for metals and was able to make what Pam thought were pretty good guesses about the value of each. Gerbald, as an ex-soldier, had seen his share of foreign coins, and did his best to help make identifications. They sorted the coins into gold, silver, and other less identifiable blends of metals. Piles sprung up around the table as they worked. Pam could scarcely believe they were engaged in such a project. Once they finished the coins, they turned their attention to the loose precious stones.

"Could this be a ruby, Pam?" Dore held up a red gem the size of her thumb.

"Well, maybe. I really don't know much about this stuff." As it turned out, no one else in the group did, either. "Where the hell is a jeweler when you need one?" she muttered. They ended up grouping the gems into pretty little mounds by color. Overall, the coins were more numerous, but they still ended up with a respectable amount of precious stones.

Next came the jewelry. The *Löjtnant* handed Pam a fanciful gold tiara encrusted with what must surely be blue sapphires. Pam placed it on her head and grinned.

"Look, I'm Wonder Woman! Now we just need to find the gold lasso and the bullet-proof bracelets!"

Gerbald, a dedicated student of American pop culture, laughed. Dore just rolled her eyes to signify *How much of such foolishness must I endure?* while the Swedes wore the painful smile of wanting to show approval for a joke they didn't get. Pam tried to explain Wonder Woman and the concept of a superhero to them in Swedish. She was fully conversant in the language but would need more time to become as fluent as a native speaker. After several minutes of word searching and a bit of gesturing, the Bosun and the *Löjtnant* both nodded with the satisfaction of understanding.

"We see now," the *Löjtnant* said, "This is just like the sagas from the old days! This woman is as strong as Thor, she can fly like a bird, and she has enchanted accouterments to aid her in battle. It's obvious! Wonder Woman was one of your gods before you Americans became Christians! It's just as in our Norselands, where the stories of the old gods still survive in the tales we tell children!" The Bosun agreed, nodding sagely while Pam just smiled.

"Close enough," she said, and remembered to take the tiara off, feeling like an idiot for having it on throughout her explanation. She held it in her hands, admiring its sparkling beauty. "Hey, I know who we should give this to. Princess Kristina! Look, it's even in the Swedish colors, blue and gold." The Swedes clapped their hands at this suggestion. The lion's portion of the treasure in the form of jewelry was put aside to add to the princess's crown jewels, a gift from her admirers. A pang of sadness came to Pam as she thought of poor old Fritjoff, and how much he would have approved of such a gesture. Even so, Pam didn't give everything to her patron. There was a certain pearl necklace that called to her in a siren song and she claimed it without apology.

"I heard there's a party tonight and a girl has got to have something to wear!" she exclaimed as she fastened it around her neck. It looked good, and it felt good, too.

It took another hour to divide all the shares out of the various piles. As Pam had expected, the Swedes insisted she take a larger portion.

Since it was harder to gauge the value of the gems, she took a greater share of those, figuring some of the pretty stones might be worthless, while others might be worth more than the entire find, who knew? She would have to wait until she found a qualified jeweler, and that would likely be a long while. And so, despite her many protests, Captain Pam ended up with a larger pile of loot than the rest. She felt a bit guilty about it.

"Look, I know you mean well, fellows, but really, I wanted everybody to have an equal share."

The Bosun listened to her, but his answer was always the same: "You are the captain, you get more. It's tradition."

Finally, Pam conceded. "Fine, but I want you all to know I'm going to use most of my take to help make this colony work. I don't need this much money for myself. I'm already well off."

This was met with warm smiles from her companions, which made her feel better. Smiling, she dropped her take into the chest next to Kristina's jewelry, locked it, and put the key in a zip pocket of the knapsack that held her most precious things.

The Bosun summoned the men. One by one, they filed past the table receiving their share, their eyes bugging at the size of the unexpected windfall. Apparently, sailors of the day were not well paid. The shares weren't really that big. It hadn't been that large a box. Even so, each seemed overjoyed, and thanked her profusely before making way for the next.

When the task was all finished, Pam shooed everyone out of her cabin and fell onto the bed, ready for an afternoon nap.

It's better to give than receive, but it's lot of work, too.

CHAPTER 34: THE CAPTAIN'S BALL

As the breezes died with the evening calm, the junk was anchored back where it had started, not far from their camp on Castaway Cove. Dore had come back to wake Pam and help her get ready for the party. After some fussing, they stood on the narrow deck outside Pam's door, both dressed in fine Chinese silks.

Some of the garments they had chosen were most likely designed for men, but they made do, with pleasing results. Dore found a long skirt which she belted with a sash and a simple tunic top, all in deep reds which suited her well. The tunic must have belonged to a large man as it had plenty of room for Dore's buxom figure. Pam, who was slight in comparison, wore a pair of knee-length black silk pants, a simple black shirt that buttoned at its collar-less neck, and a cerulean blue silk jacket ornately embroidered with gold pheasants and cranes, with large gold buttons, and teardrop-shaped clasps. She left the jacket open to show off the lovely pearl necklace from the treasure chest.

"Look, I'm wearing the Swedish colors!" she said to Dore as she preened in the jacket. "The men will definitely approve. Plus, it's got birds!" She felt as if she were sixteen again and headed for the high school's spring dance.

"Really, Pam, these garments are far too fancy. I am embarrassed to be seen in them! Tomorrow I shall have to find something simple that can withstand the galley. It would be a shame to ruin such finery as this."

"Yeah, yeah, tomorrow, fine, but come on, tonight's a party! Live a little! I now know that you *do* know how." Pam gave her friend a sly, knowing grin which made Dore blush. Pam took her by the elbow and guided her toward the ladder. At the bottom, Dore told Pam to go ahead, she would check on her foolish husband before joining her.

On the main deck, the men had placed a long, low table near the second and largest of the three masts. It was covered from end to end with food, a collection of dried meats and fruits found in the galley, fresh fruits from shore, and a row of large fish they had barbecued with spices. The aroma was utterly delicious and drew Pam closer. She thought the seasoning might be a mix of garlic, Chinese five spice, cloves, and black pepper. *Is that sesame oil and a dash of rice wine splashed on, too? Heaven!* Pam's mouth watered. She was impressed that the men managed such an ornate dinner without Dore's help! It had been a long time since she had smelled such a savory meal and she felt delightfully hungry.

Pers saw her and hurried over. He slowed when he noticed Pam's change of clothes and smiled.

"You look very nice!" he complimented her, despite his obvious shyness about such things.

"Why, thank you, Pers! You look very nice yourself!" He was dressed in a canary-yellow version of what Pam wore, but without the jacket. The pants were too short on the long-legged youth, riding well above the knees, but he still looked handsome in the exotic outfit. Pam took his arm to give it an affectionate squeeze. She nodded toward the table "It looks like you fellows found your way around the galley! Well done!"

Just then, Dore joined them. Pers gave Dore, the indisputable ruler of all things to do with food, a nervous glance and hurriedly told them, "We wanted to give *Frau* Dore here a night off from cooking. We men of the sea are not wholly without talent in that arena. I hope you like what we have prepared. We were very careful not to make a mess."

Dore scanned the table, sniffing warily at their offerings. After a long, tense moment she smiled, finding the sailor's efforts to be to her satisfaction. After all, it was nice to have a night off, and now, she need not feel guilty for it.

"It looks fine, Pers," she told the youth. "You men have done a good job. I thank you."

Having met Dore's approval, Pers brightened and led them to the place of honor, a line of five comfortable chairs placed on a temporary platform raised three feet above the deck. Behind the stage, the clever sailors hung a variety of flags and banners decorated with fanciful motifs, to very festive effect. Pers ushered Pam into the middle seat, which was practically a throne. Intertwining ebony serpentine dragons with ruby eyes and ivory teeth framed a plush velvet cushion in scarlet-and-gold trim. Found among the cargo, it had been undoubtedly headed for some exotic sultan's palace.

The men were still going about their tasks under the watchful eye of the Bosun although many a glance was stolen in the direction of the food. Pam arrived a bit early, but no one seemed to care. She was delighted to see they all managed to trade their island rags for new clothing from the hold. No two were dressed the same and they looked more like a band of circus performers than a ship's crew. Pam smiled at the bustling scene so widely her face began to hurt. She turned to Pers, who was assigned to be their maître d', and asked, "You got any booze?" Pers smiled his sunniest smile and disappeared from her side in a Pers-sized gust of wind.

He returned with two elegant ceramic bowls garnished with fresh flowers, full of fruit juice, and a generous shot of what tasted like rum. "I believe *Herr* Gerbald called them mai-tais. He says he will be your bartender tonight," Pers told them as they each took a careful sip. Even Dore smiled at the delicious taste and took another, bigger quaff. Pam looked at her friend and grinned. *No teetotaling for the Christian soldier tonight. Looks like we won't have to play our usual game of "Let's get Dore drunk." She's leading the charge for a change! This is definitely going to be fun!* Pam thought with glee. She was fairly vibrating with excitement and drank again, deeply, with intense pleasure.

"Tell Gerbald he's a genius and to keep these coming," Pam said. "I intend to get loaded. Party on!" Pers had enough English by now to get the gist of her meaning, and smiled with professional grace as he vanished again, taking on the role of attentive head waiter like a duck to water. Despite her proclamation, Pam tried to pace herself. She knew she was going to have to give a speech or two, and wanted to be well-relaxed for that, but not to the point of word-slurring wasted. She could do that after the speeches were done.

The sun was setting, and various torches and lanterns were being lit. The men were assembled on the deck, ready to commence the official celebration. Someone had found a large gong which Lind struck with a cloth hammer, a rare look of boyish delight on his usually serious face, the deep, vibrating tone signaling everyone to be quiet. By now, Gerbald had joined them, having passed the torch of bartender on to the eager to please Pers, a quick study as always. He sat next to Dore, who was on Pam's left. The Bosun and *Löjtnant* Lundkvist joined them, sitting to Pam's right.

The Bosun stood, causing the crew to settle into silence.

"Good evening to you all. Here at last, we find ourselves delivered from our isolation, aboard a ship that, while strange looking, is a nimble and sound vessel, worthy of the Swedish Navy!" He waited while a hearty cheer went up from the men, Pam, and her retinue. After a few moments, he silenced the men with a subtle gesture and continued on. "And though some of us gathered here are not Swedes by birth, they have earned their place in our ranks through their great courage and dedication to our beloved princess! All hail Gerbald, Dore, and our esteemed Captain, Pam Miller!" The cheers were louder this time, which Pam didn't think was possible. The attention made her face flush an embarrassing pinkish red as usual, but she smiled, and took another big gulp of cocktail to steady her nerves.

The Bosun, once again cutting the cheers off with an effortless gesture, turned to the two Germans and the American, a woman from a country that didn't exist in this world and probably never would. "As far as we are concerned, you three are every bit as Swedish in your hearts as we are, and I welcome you as our brothers and sisters. Hurrah!" The men went wild this time, and the three of them found themselves urged to their feet to take their bows. Gerbald and Dore returned to their seats, but the Bosun beckoned for Pam to join him at the front of the stage, just as she had dreaded.

"And now let's hear it for our fearless Captain Pam! Three cheers!" Gerbald must have coached them in the English-style he'd gleaned from watching old movies, as "Hip-hip-hurray!" sounded across the deck. When the traditional cheer finished, the Bosun, who was proving to be quite the expert master of ceremonies, gave Pam a courteous bow and asked her, "Please, Captain Pam, a few words for your men, if you would." He stepped back then, leaving Pam in the figurative spotlight.

She smiled at all around her, surprised to find the butterflies had faded away. She was comfortable here. These were her people, as much as any she had ever known. There was nothing for her to be shy about. She spoke out loudly and clearly, "My beloved brothers and sister, my dearest friends in all the world. You are the best of the best. It is my supreme honor to be chosen as your captain. I will work my hardest to earn your trust in me and to lead us to victory. In Princess Kristina's name, I swear!"

She paused and another cheer went up, everyone clapping as loudly as they could. She felt as if she were a rock standing in a sea of love, each wave that washed over her filled her heart with perfect joy. Deep in her mind, she took some of that feeling and put it away for safekeeping. She knew she would need it someday when the doubts returned. The love she felt tonight would be a talisman against the darkness that sometimes tried to steal her few joys. *Maybe that won't happen so much anymore. Things have changed. I have changed.*

With what she thought might be the sweetest smile she had ever worn, she raised her hands and shouted over the din, "Let the party begin! I order every man aboard to drink as much as he likes and then some more. Let's raise some toasts!" She felt like a rock star.

There was a bustle about the deck, and soon she saw everybody was holding a cup. They had quite a bit of their rationed rum left, almost an entire barrel, which she figured they would finish off this night. Gerbald told her they had also found large ceramic jugs filled with a palatable alcoholic beverage he thought must be rice wine, stored in the ship's hold, along with a collection of jugs and barrels containing strange and less reputable liquors. *We aren't going to run out of booze in any case, God bless us one and all! We'll be needing His mercy when the hangovers hit tomorrow!*

The crowd was quiet now, waiting for her lead. Pam held her cup aloft, and in what she had been taught was the Swedish way, made a point of meeting the eye of every single person aboard. Once accomplished, she shouted "Skål!", and downed her cup in one swallow, followed by everyone else. As soon as the cups were refilled, she began working through a long list of toasts, to the men, to their country, to their king and princess, to the lost men of the *Redbird*, and finally to their new ship. She paused, looking a bit perplexed. She turned to the Bosun who was beginning to list a little to the side, thanks to the quick succession of shots. There was little doubt that everyone was starting to feel pretty darn good.

"*Herr* Bosun, what is this ship's name?" her voice had grown just a tad thicker, but still could be heard clearly across the deck.

The Bosun stepped over to her and scratched the back of his head as if it would help him think. "Truth to tell, Captain, I have no idea. I think that's it painted there on her aft, but none of us can read it!" Then he laughed, and everyone joined in, the raucous sound echoing all around the bay.

Once the hilarity had subsided, he said, in as serious a tone as he could muster, "Captain Pam, she's your ship so you must name her," and gave her a slightly wobbling, but deferential bow.

Her mind a sudden blank, Pam turned to Gerbald and Dore for help. Those two had been drinking almost double time and were already about two sheets to the wind and starting to let out the third. They both broke into fits of laughter when they saw Pam looking at them so seriously. That almost made Pam start laughing, too, but she kept in control.

"This is serious, you guys, we need a name for the boat, and we need it quick!"

"How about *The Hungry Dodo*?" Gerbald offered, trying hard to keep a straight face. His goofy hat was tilted nearly sideways on his head, and Pam figured the only reason it hadn't fallen off was because of the longtime bond of affection they shared. The hat, in combination with the incongruous fuchsia silk blouse he wore, made him look like something straight out of a Dr. Seuss cartoon. Pam struggled to keep a straight face.

"Hmm, well, they certainly are, and we are here because of our fat, feathered friends after all, but I think it's a bit too silly . . ." she replied. She turned to Dore, whose rosy cheeks blazed like fire engine lights on the way to a three-alarm fire.

Seeing that it was her turn, Dore sat up nearly straight and said, "How about *Chinese Chopsticks*?" with sincere earnestness, except it came out sounding more like "Shineeze Shopstigs." She waited for Pam's certain approval, her big, blue eyes wide and glassy.

Pam had to look away from the two of them before she lost it. Meanwhile, Pers had come onstage bearing yet another round of drinks, (someone should tell him to stop . . . well, maybe later), and her face lit up. An idea was coming.

"Pers! The other day, when we were taking the dodos back to the forest, what was it that you called them?"

"Ummm, 'those stupid creatures'?" he blurted out, too late realizing that wasn't likely the answer Pam was looking for. He looked embarrassed.

Pam had to laugh then but stayed in control. Everyone was waiting on her decision.

"No, no, something about them being lucky or something." Pam stared at Pers, putting the pressure on him to deliver.

Pers, who quite sensibly hadn't been drinking at all, being sentenced to take the night's watch after the party, thought hard for a moment, then raised his hand. "Do you mean when I called them the 'second chance birds'?" he asked in a hopeful tone.

"That's it!" Pam rushed over to hug him. If not for his quick reflexes and fast feet, she would have knocked him, and the small drink staging table he had set up, right off the stage. After a good squeezing of bear-like strength, no doubt augmented by the high octane alcohol content of her blood, she let go of the scarlet-cheeked Pers and turned to those assembled.

"The *Second Chance Bird*." She worded it in English as Pers had. "That's what we'll call her!"

Pers translated this into Swedish and another great cheer went up. Pam took the fresh cup Pers held out and raised it. "Here's to the *Second Chance Bird*! God bless her and all who sail on her!"

Pam thought the sound of the cheering had grown a bit hoarse, but they bellowed away at full volume once again anyway. Feeling her duties had now been performed, she gave everyone a deep—almost too deep—bow, managed somehow not to pitch headfirst over the side of the stage, and returned to her seat amid thunderous applause. She was smiling so hard and so wide that her face would have hurt had she been able to feel it.

The *Löjtnant*, who was seated beside her and who rarely said much beyond that which was required by the ever-diligent performance of his duties, turned to Pam, and addressing her in the most genuine and admiring tones, said: "Captain Pam . . . you sure know how to party!" Pam raised her cup to his and they knocked them together with a sloshing clunk, drank them down, and in unison, signaled for more.

Off the hosting hook, Pam began to relax and enjoy the festivities. She was pleased the usual butterflies in her stomach had been vanquished, and laughed at the thought they must have perished, drowning in rum. The *Löjtnant* asked her what she was laughing about, and she tried to explain, but just got more and more mixed up until they were both snorting with laughter, him still clueless as to the phrase's meaning. Gerbald pitched in, trying to help, and soon they were all laughing so hard they could barely speak and weren't even sure why.

Pers looked on, frowning with a mother-ish kind of concern, wondering how he was going to get them all to bed, and praying no enemies would come across them in such a debilitated state.

During their exploration of the *Second Chance Bird*'s many holds and storage rooms, the men had found a variety of musical instruments which they were now bringing out. Pam saw something slightly resembling a violin, but round-bodied and with only two strings, what might be a hammer dulcimer, some long-necked apparatus that could be distant kin to a guitar, oddshaped drums, cymbals, and other unidentifiable noise makers. Apparently, the junk once boasted a small orchestra, very likely for the entertainment of its august owners and their distinguished customers. Many of the Swedes could play an instrument, a seaman's tradition, but their own fragile pieces had been lost with the wreck, except for a tin flute or two.

The men started warming up with the foreign instruments, creating a cacophony that would make an alley full of amorous cats cover their ears with their paws. After a few minutes, it transformed into something resembling a tune. Soon, they were playing a rollicking sea shanty Pam could recognize as one she had heard many times on the voyage around Africa, a real foot-tapper made somehow thrilling by the unusual sounds forming its melodies and harmonies. Now that the band was in full swing, the five luminaries managed to get down from the stage without falling, to go dance. Soon, they were joined by anyone who wasn't playing an instrument. The *Second Chance Bird* was a floating festival, the long-suffering crew indulging at long last in the comforts of civilization.

Pam clapped as she watched Dore and Gerbald spinning about in folk dance. Dore grabbed Gerbald by the scruff of his neck and dragged him into a passionate kiss. Gerbald's eyes went wide, but sensing there was nothing to do but enjoy this shocking public display of affection from his wife, he embraced her and kissed her back. When they parted, both looked as embarrassed as kids caught necking in the library, while the men raised a ribald, encouraging cheer for their performance. Pam felt like the Queen of the May, surrounded by a bunch of merry men, some of whom were not bad looking at all, no sir, all eyes on her, and appreciative of her charms in a delightfully non-threatening way.

Ahh, what fine gentlemen, she thought as she took turns whirling about the deck with every hand on board. *Another good thing about time travel! In this century they still make them like they used to.*

The festivities were winding down as the hour grew late, the revelers tiring out, or in some cases, becoming incapacitated. It was well past midnight, and Pam thought she should probably have passed out by now, but she had somehow fed on all the positive energy surrounding her, filling her with a giddy joy. She felt drunk, but also calm and aware. She turned to the Bosun, who she had been talking with just a moment or three ago, to find him curled up under the mainmast, like a big gray tabby cat. It was time to admit the party was over.

Head held high, but beginning to feel drowsy, Pam allowed the ever attentive and long-suffering Pers to escort her to her cabin. She walked with the careful, mincing steps of one intoxicated, but trying hard not to show it, stepping over the snoring sailors who hadn't made it to to their bunks. As she climbed the stairs with Pers bringing up her rear, sometimes with a gentle shove, Pam chuckled to herself it was the only teenager in the group who had got stuck with taking care of all the drunk adults. *What a fine example we are setting for today's youth!* Pam thought with pride. *Someday I hope Pers has children of his own to put him to bed when he gets shitfaced.*

Pers guided her to her bunk, aiming her so that when she fell her head was near the pillow and most of her body off the floor. He picked up her dangling legs and placed them on the bed, then located a light blanket to cover her. Even a balmy night could get chilly before dawn.

Pam was still awake, or semi-conscious, at least. She reached to take Pers' hand and squeezed it.

"Yer a goo'boy, Perzzz." she mumbled, eyes closed, her face the very portrait of pickled contentedness.

Pers smiled at her and gave her hand a squeeze, which he doubted she could even feel.

"I didn't know my real mother very well," he told her as he lifted her head and slid the pillow under it. "I was so young when I left . . . but I do know one thing: You are a *lot* more fun than she was. Sleep well, dear Pam." He stroked her hair for a moment, then headed for the door. Before he closed it behind him, he could hear the gentle breathing of the fast asleep.

A little while later, Pam opened her eyes, awakened by noises nearby. Listening carefully, she heard muffled thuds and giggles coming from the cabin beneath hers. Gerbald and Dore's cabin. *Dear Gawd!* She grabbed a couple of pillows and crammed them over her ears to shut out the far too intimate sounds emanating from below. It must be their second honeymoon. No, it was probably their *first* honeymoon. Pam looked up at the cabin's ceiling, lit by dim starlight reflected off the waves and through the open windows. Yes, she was happy for her friends, and yes, maybe just a tiny bit jealous. To distract herself, she reviewed the day's triumphs. Memory became mixed with dream as the waves rocked her to sleep and the last clear thought she had before drifting off was, *I'm Perilous Pam Miller, pirate captain! Who'd have ever thunk it?*

Garrett W. Vance

CHAPTER 35: ANCHORS AWEIGH

The decks of the Second Chance
Bird at anchor in Castaway's Cove

Nobody was up early the next morning except the few unfortunate marines assigned to the watch. Pam woke to a splitting headache, and after some debate, swallowed a couple of her precious aspirin with the carafe of water Pers had left for her.

"I'm giving that kid a promotion." she mumbled through dry lips.

After a while, the drum and bugle corps marching around in her head settled into a less driving beat, and she decided she might be able to get dressed. This took much longer than usual, considering the clothing was of an unfamiliar design, and her hands felt like she was wearing oven mitts.

"That's the last time I drink that much." she growled, ignoring the annoying voice in her head reminding her she said that every time she drank that much. Finally managing to pull her new boots on, Pam made her way to the door. She opened it, allowing a shaft of bright sunlight into the room, then closed it as quickly as she could. The beam of light still seared in glaring orange across her closed eyes.

"Dear God, I swear, I'm going on the wagon." She sat, cursing herself for not thinking to bring her up-time sunglasses on this little jaunt. Looking around, she found a floppy hat with a wide brim that resembled the ones she had seen Dutch merchants wear. She put it on, trying not to think about how it had ended up here. It was a bit large, so she tied a scarf around her head to make it fit better. She caught a glimpse of her red-eyed, exotically clothed self reflected in a silver platter on the table, and laughed aloud.

"I'm either a pirate or a pimp! Grandma would be so proud." Pushing her hat's brim low over her eyes, she made her way out the door into the late morning sun.

The decks below resembled a zombie movie. Everyone seemed to be stumbling in slow motion, their tanned faces bleached a deathly shade of gray. Except for Gerbald.

Gerbald was the proverbial cat who had dined on canary. Pam watched him swagger around the decks, grinning as only a guy who had gotten laid the night before can. She rolled her eyes at him as she brought him under tow and went to look for the Bosun. They found him running his hand over the junk's delicately curved, crimson lacquered railing. Pam wasn't sure, because of the surf's sussuration, but she thought he might be softly cooing. He looked up with a grin that made Gerbald's giddy expression seem droopy in comparison.

"Captain Pam, *Herr* Gerbald, good morning! What are your orders, ma'am?" The Bosun, a cheery sort to begin with, was as bright as the new dawn, in the highest of spirits. Apparently, he was immune to hangovers, and Pam stilled an annoyed twinge of jealousy.

"Well, we ought to discuss that. Let's have a meeting." Pam saw the Bosun was now distracted by the sails, which resembled giant Venetian window blinds to Pam's eyes. "So, *Herr* Bosun, what do you think of our new ship now that you've gotten to know her a bit?"

"Oh, Captain Pam, she's lovely." and then he really did coo, making Pam and Gerbald's eyebrows arch in surprise. "Sure, she looks ungainly at first glance, but there is a swan hiding within this duck. See that high aft deck? I thought they were mad, but now I think it's there to keep us dry in a following sea. The bottom is flat, but she's got a kind of a wedge keel, we can go shallow with her, and even beach her with ease, but she should go confidently in high seas as well. I'll wager she's watertight, too. The hull is a sealed box. I'm not sure yet how they did it, but they're a clever lot, all right! And look here, these paneled sails and rigging are going to give us far more control than a regular rig once we master their ways. We haven't sailed her as much as I'd like, nor have we had any foul weather to try, but I'm sure she's the best damn vessel I've ever set foot on! We've nothing like her in the North Sea, and I'd take her into those cruel waters with no fear."

Pam nodded, catching a bit of the Bosun's boyish enthusiasm, despite her hangover. She understood most of the nautical terms from her hours pacing the decks of the *Redbird* on the long journey around Africa, watching, and listening to the sailors at their work. She was pleased the Bosun had a new love in his life and left him to his bliss to go find the *Löjtnant*.

Eventually, the senior crew all gathered on the dizzy heights of the junk's castle deck. It was time to make serious decisions. Pam felt calm, despite the mantle of authority that had somehow fallen on her shoulders, *not* something she had ever expected, nor wanted.

"Okay, we've got a real good ship, the Bosun tells me. We can sail her?"

"Yes, Captain Pam!" the Bosun's pride in his shiny new vessel resounded in his voice. "Our men are learning her ways quickly. We shall master her."

Löjtnant Lundkvist spoke up, "Captain, you should know this vessel is not without teeth. If we are attacked, we can fight back. There are two guns of Chinese make on each side. They are unusual, of course, but they look well made, and operate on the same principles as our own. With your permission, Sargent Sten and his bombardiers would like to test them."

Pam nodded her assent.

"Also," the *Löjtnant* continued, "The Black Chessmen have mounted the *Redbird*'s carronade to the foredeck on a swiveling turret we were able to improvise. Its range is short, but its firepower is devastating."

"Excellent work! And yes, please do your tests, but maybe wait until the afternoon. I think everyone's ears might be a bit sensitive this morning." This brought a rueful chuckle from the *Löjtnant* who looked about as ragged as she did. "It's good to know we can give somebody a bloody nose if need be. There's always a chance we will encounter more foes while we search for our friends."

Despite the mean hangover they shared, this was the happiest Pam had ever seen the fellow, a military man with shiny new weapons.

She gave them all a determined smile despite her self inflicted discomfort. "All right then, gentlemen, which way do you think we should go?"

The Bosun rubbed his chin, considering.

"Well, Captain Pam, the colonist fleet was last seen headed northeast up the coast. No one has come back this way to look for us since we fell behind, and those ships would have had no trouble handling the rough weather that grounded our pinnaces. To fear the worst, they may have wrecked or been damaged in the storm. Another unpleasant possibility is they, too, were captured by heathen pirates. I would suggest we follow that course, looking for signs of wreckage, and hoping to find our folk in good health in a safe harbor. On your maps of the island from up-time, there are several places to check. The site of Vieux Grand Port will be the first we meet, followed by Poste de Flacq. Until we can establish what the situation is, I think it would be best if we laid low. "

Pam nodded her approval, if pirates had indeed captured the expedition, horror of horrors, they would want to keep the element of surprise on their side.

"Sounds good to me, *Herr* Bosun. Let's do it. Slow and steady."

Suddenly, despite everything, they all grinned at each other. Some of the tension of the last months was melting away, replaced by a healthy excitement. They were back in control of their destinies, free men and women, with a good ship to carry them on their mission.

"All right, let's get going! Anchors aweigh!" she shouted at the top of her lungs into a rising antipodean wind. On the decks of the *Second Chance Bird* the men, beginning to feel a bit better thanks to the fresh air, smiled as they made ready to sail.

SAVING THE DODO

CHAPTER 36: SMOKE ON THE WATER

They followed the coast, always prepared for the possibility of more pirates. They kept a constant watch for signs of human activity along the shores, Pers spending all day up in the rigging, scanning with his spyglass. There was a good chance the other boats had been wrecked by the storm and the survivors now castaways just as they had been. They took their time, anchoring at night in what safe coves and cover they could find, keeping their lights dim and their voices down. The *Second Chance Bird* was on the prowl.

On a overcast morning, they saw their first hopeful sign of people. They had set sail at dawn, heading for the large, natural harbor at Poste de Flacq, one of the proposed destinations for the colony ships. Pers knocked on Pam's door to summon her to the wheel. She put on one of her new Chinese suits, and arrived on the bridge sleepy, but resplendent in red-and-gold brocaded silk. Before she could greet the Bosun, Pers reappeared with coffee, served in a deep, ceramic bowl decorated with stylized pine trees. She took a long, grateful sip before trying to speak, a ritual everyone knew not to interrupt.

"Good morning, *Herr* Bosun. Report, please."

"We've sighted smoke coming from behind that point, Captain. It could be from cook fires or maybe someone clearing land. It's possible. it's just a natural brush fire, but my gut says there are people there. Plus, we are fairly certain this is the site of Poste de Flacq on the up-time maps. A good, safe harbor to hole up in."

"Okay. Yeah, that could be good or bad, depending on just who is having a cookout over there." The caffeine, in somewhat less concentration than the coffee up-time, began to kick in. The discovery of a possible human presence made Pam's heart race with excitement.

The *Löjtnant* spoke next. "May I suggest we row the longboat we captured with this ship along the shore and have a look around? We can keep close in

245

and stay hidden among the rocks along the point. The seas are fairly calm today." He was obviously eager to find out what was coming.

"No, I think it's too risky. You'd be seen. My gut is screaming to be cautious. Gerbald and I will go have a look overland. You can put us in behind the point. It's wooded and will give us plenty of cover."

The Bosun didn't look happy at that prospect.

"Don't worry, friend. *Herr* Gerbald and I are good at staying hidden in the woods. If it's bad guys, they will never know we were there."

Gerbald nodded his assurance, his eyes gleaming at the opportunity to do some scouting in his favorite environment, the forest.

After a quick breakfast—which Dore insisted on, and to which there was no saying no,Pam and Gerbald arrived on deck ready to head out on their reconnaissance.

Pam was dressed in whatever green and preferably not-too-shiny clothing she could find among the ship's unusual collection. Unfortunately, it was all pretty gaudy. With a grim smile, she strapped on the leather gun and ammo belt Gerbald had fashioned for her from materials found on the junk. The Smith and Wesson .38 caliber revolver was heavy, but as usual, Gerbald insisted she bring it. To her surprise, she liked the feel of its deadly weight at her side and knew she would not hesitate to use it again, when and if, the time came.

Gerbald, of course, had on his perennial outfit of sage-green wool long-coat, a black T-shirt featuring a faded Lynyrd Skynyrd band logo, brown breeches, knee high leather boots, and his perennial crazy old mustard hat, along with his trusty *katzbalger* shortsword and pistol-grip Snakecharmer shotgun hanging from his wide belt. He was the very picture of a new-fangled USE bad-ass, a bonafide *Lefferti*, the toughest stuff from up-time and down-time, rolled into one dangerous package. He took a look at Pam's bright green silks and laughed aloud.

"You can fly, you can fly, you can fly!" he singsonged as he pointed at her undeniably elfin-looking outfit.

"That's pretty funny coming from a guy who looks like he's just come from *Beyond Thunderdome*. By the way, Dr Seuss called, and he wants his hat back."

They shared a brief laugh, then boarded the fleet Chinese longboat, much smaller and easier to launch than their trusty pinnaces. They sat quietly, their minds focused on the mission ahead, feeling ready and able as they were put ashore.

"Remember my friends, give us a week before you come looking for us. If you need to retreat, do it, we will head south along the shore watching for you." Pam reminded them.

Their rowers, Vilfrid and Lind, were worried about their much-loved new captain and ever-popular Gerbald. They nodded in assent, managed a rather sad salute, and in hushed, but fervent tones, wished them luck and a safe, speedy return. The somber sailors watched in silence, until their reconnaissance team had vanished into the trees, before rowing back to *Second Chance Bird,* faces frowning with worry.

CHAPTER 37: CONTACT

Near the site of uptime Poste de Flacq, Mauritius

"This is not good." Gerbald peered through the scope, scowling while Pam did the same with her binoculars. They were atop the high bluff that formed the point, lying under the cover of ferns while watching the harbor below, deep, with an impressive set of docks in place. The worst had, indeed, happened, much to their shock and dismay. As they scanned the scene, the pieces began to fall into place, one bad break after another. Their would-be guardian, dated, but still doughty *Muskijl*, was tied up to the dock, heavily damaged, but still afloat. Looming behind the defeated Swedish warship they saw a much larger light frigate flying the French flag, most certainly the foe that had claimed *Muskijl*. There was also a squadron of medium-sized lateen-rigged boats of the style preferred by the denizens of these far seas. Their hearts sank even deeper as they saw the *Annalise* and *Ide* at anchor nearby, with several foreign soldiers, undoubtedly French, standing guard on the otherwise empty decks.

There were more unpleasant surprises to be had as they continued their surveillance, grief and anger beginning to smolder in their hearts. Construction was taking place on a gently sloping hillside behind a five-meter wall of heavy timbers running some twenty meters from the shoreline, the beginnings of what would be an imposing fortress. To their horror, they could see sturdy Swedish men tethered together in work crews, doing the heavy work. Now they knew how so much building had been accomplished. Swedish slave labor. Pam blinked in disbelief when she saw their overseers looked like black Africans, dressed in white robes with their heads covered, nearly the same garb worn by the Arabic-looking pirates they had defeated to take *Second Chance Bird*. Pam was no history expert, but like many Grantvillers, she had become a lot more interested in the subject since she had been thrown backward through time. She knew the African slave trade was largely run by Africans themselves and that must have been where the French had found these fellows. Pam bit her lip as the slavers shouted at the colonists in what sounded like broken French. The snap of a whip echoed across the quiet bay, making her cringe. Out on the end of the dock, she saw French soldiers passing around a wineskin and enjoying a little fishing, while their mercenaries oversaw the work for them.

"The *French*." Gerbald muttered under his breath as if it were a bad word.

"Apparently, we are still at war." Pam muttered. "I'm surprised to see the French here now, in the uptime history they didn't get here until 1721, a good ten years after the Dutch colonies failed."

"What is it they say about the wings of the butterfly? Much has changed and is changing since Grantville arrived in this time."

"I'll bet the French got word of our colony plans and that sly old weasel Richelieu sent these guys to usurp our claim. He wouldn't have even needed spies, our expedition was public knowledge, and I've heard he subscribes to all Grantville's newspapers."

Gerbald frowned. "I have also read the uptime histories, Pam, especially those focusing on this region, just as you did before embarking on our voyage. Yes, Richelieu was, *is* ruthless, but would even he dare to enslave other Europeans?"

"If it was for his view of the good of France, he would do anything. Occupying an important stop on future shipping routes is part of what sold our colony to Gustav, so it's not surprising the French would want to get the jump on us." Pam paused, shaking her head. "I am surprised at this level of brutality, though. Maybe I shouldn't be, the French certainly made much use of African slaves in this region in the old timeline, supplied by African slave traders like these. I figure they think this far away from Europe, they can get away with it."

"Gerbald scowled. "Scum. Let's make them pay."

"In spades. How many of them do you think there are?"

"At least two hundred of the enemy all together, is my guess."

"We'll need help, then." She bit her lip as she scanned up the sloping clearcut area rising behind the harbor. Her blood boiled as she saw men and women, *her colonists*, carrying barrels and performing menial tasks, their feet bound or chained. "We have to free the colonists and the crew of the *Muskijl* and use them against their captors." Gerbald looked doubtful. Pam gave him an encouraging nudge with her elbow. "Come on, that's how they do it in the movies! It's worked for us so far."

Gerbald gave her an unconvinced smile.

"A risky proposition at best." he cautioned her. "The Swedes will be tired and weak from ill use. Just trying to contact them at all, while they are under guard, will be risky. They are bound. The ropes we can cut through quickly, but the chains will require either more time, or a key. It will be difficult." Gerbald's expression was grim.

"Okay. We told *Second Chance Bird* to give us a week out here in the field before taking further action. Let's take our time, lay back, and watch for a while. Once we know more about the routines here, we can make a move."

Gerbald grinned at her with wry amusement, despite the dire situation. His adopted little sister was simply unsinkable. He had best follow suit.

"Yes ma'am, Captain Pam!" he stage whispered in his best West Virginia drawl. He was full of pride in his mastery of the accent and American slang and seldom missed a chance to show it off. "And when we're ready, we can open up a king-sized can of whoop-ass all over them bastards! KA-BLAMMO!"

Pam rolled her eyes as the two of them vanished, back into the shadowy forest, sly and silent as foxes.

* * *

Pam and Gerbald watched the slave colony from various vantage points over the next three days. The Swedish colonists looked fairly healthy, despite their ordeal, at least from a distance. They were a robust lot, weathering the hardships as well as they could. At night they were housed in makeshift huts, in an open meadow fenced with an imposing array of ten-foot high bamboo stakes. The few children they had brought along were kept in the enclosure all day, tended by the expedition's small number of elderly. Pam saw even this group was given work to do, weaving rope and baskets. The sight of the children and the old folks put to work by their new masters made Pam see red.

Oh, I'm SO going to put the hurt on those assholes just as soon as I am able! she thought, a part of her shocked at the depth of her own wrath. She took a deep breath to help herself focus on the situation. They now knew most of the men had been put to work logging and constructing the growing fort. Many of the women were sent out to the fields to tend newly planted crops. Other small groups of women were made to forage for fruits, nuts, and firewood along the forest's edge, always under the watchful eye of a slaver.

Pam and Gerbald decided it was one of the latter groups they would approach. The women were all bound by a short chain between the feet and were the least heavily guarded. Since they worked along the wall of forest that had, so far, escaped clearcutting, there was ready cover nearby. The experienced woodsman and his talented protege were confident in their ability to remain unseen among the trees and brush. Gerbald stayed back, prepared to distract, or even kill the guard, if necessary. Pam, now a bit chagrined she had dressed like a silken Peter Pan, rummaged through her pack for something to help disguise her as a colonist. She wrapped her head in a gray cotton towel from *Second Chance Bird*'s galley and draped a brown wool blanket from *Redbird*'s pinnace over her shoulders— it would have to do.

Walking slowly, as if bound herself, she made her way from the deeper woods to the forest's edge. Slipping out of the underbrush, with the practiced stealth of a long-time birder, she slipped in behind the unfortunate foragers, at the trailing end of their group, farthest from the bored-looking slaver guard. She stayed low, endeavoring to be seen, but unseen, just another slave. She scanned the beleaguered women for the right one to approach. Her gaze settled on a tall, statuesque woman in her late twenties, fair features now deeply tanned and careworn, golden-blond hair tied back in an unkempt ponytail. Pam studied her for a while before making her final decision. The young woman looked like the calm sort, not someone who would react loudly and stupidly to a stranger in their midst. Pam, following her gut, came up behind her, keeping the tall woman's larger frame between her and the guard who stood some twenty yards off.

"*God dag, vän.*" 'Good day, friend', Pam greeted her quietly in Swedish, her months practicing with the sailors serving her well. "Please don't turn toward me, just keep working while I talk."

Startled by an unexpected stranger's voice, the woman instinctively looked over her shoulder, one sea-green eye regarding Pam, for a brief moment. Grasping the situation, she looked forward again, shrugging as if she had simply been distracted by the call of a bird. She nodded her head while continuing to pick small berries. Pam wondered how they knew they weren't poisonous, but didn't want to think much on the likely answer.

"I will listen." the woman whispered just loud enough for Pam to hear. Proving herself to indeed be the right choice, she slowed her pace to let the other women get a little bit, but not too far, ahead of them.

"Good. I'm Pam Miller, the American from the United States of Europe, who led this expedition on Princess Kristina's behalf. Do you remember me?"

"Of course, I do! The American Bird Lady!" she answered, fighting to keep her voice down.

Pam grimaced at the ridiculous moniker.

"That's me! There are more of us who remain free. Can I trust you not to betray us?"

The woman nodded, her shoulders tightening under her ragged, once brightly floral patterned vest.

"Good, good, I knew I could. We have soldiers, and we intend to free you, but there aren't enough of us. We need find a way to set your men free, to fight with us when we make our move. We will want you to create a diversion to distract your captors while we do that. Are there those among you who are brave enough to help us?"

The woman turned back toward Pam and hissed under her breath. "*All* of us! We will do *anything* to be free."

"I've come to learn Swedes are just as tough as us West Virginia hillbillies! I need you to spread the word that we are coming, but only to those who need to know. You can let the rest in on it when the time comes. We will make our move in a few days. I'm not sure yet how, but I will get word to you, the same way I am now. Make sure it's you taking up the rear of your foraging expeditions from now on."

"It will be so. I can hardly believe it, *Frau* Miller, you and the others, still alive! We thought the worst."

" Call me Pam, please."

"I am Bengta. I am so pleased you made it, truly a blessing."

" You, too, Bengta. We are going to do our best to get everybody out of this, I promise."

"Thank you, thank you so much!" the woman's voice was quiet, but filled with emotion. Suddenly, she lowered it even further, a furtive hiss, "Pam! The guard comes this way, go!" Bengta continued to pick berries, keeping her head low, trying not to attract the surly man's gaze. No answer came, and she soon realized, Pam the Bird Lady was already gone.

The joy produced by Pam and Gerbald's safe return faded quickly, as the gathered men heard the terrible news of the colonist's enslavement, their countenances darkening as they fell into a seething rage. The senior staff adjourned immediately to the high castle deck for a strategy meeting.

Löjtnant Lundkvist, commander of their small, but highly capable military force, spoke first.

"It sounds like *Muskijl* was badly outgunned by those bastards, and though our new vessel may be better armed than *Redbird*, she can't possibly match a French warship of that size. A direct confrontation at sea is beyond our capabilities, I'm afraid. So, where does that leave us? We must do whatever it takes to rescue our people. We may be small in numbers, but we have proven ourselves in combat! Please, Captain Pam, allow me to lead my men on a surprise mission by land. We can hit them hard and fast, and they won't be expecting us." Flanking him, his top sergeants, Sten and Järv nodded in agreement, their usually formidable expressions made even more so by a cold, implacable hatred for their newfound foes.

Pam nodded. "I am in complete agreement with you, *Löjtnant.* Gerbald and I have been working on a plan. Trickery has worked for us so far, so we intend to stick with it. We *will* liberate our people and we *will* make those assholes pay for this!" Pam's voice was charged with a fiery eagerness, a newfound thirst for vengeance.

"It seems it is our turn for a masquerade, gentlemen," Gerbald told the men with a wicked smile. "Beware Greeks bearing gifts."

✳   ✳   ✳

The next morning, Pam and Gerbald were rowed to the shore again. They made their way through the forest to the foraging party was along the freshly cut forest's edge. Pam winced at the destruction of so much timberland. The invaders were not following her zoning plans. She spotted her contact trailing along at the end of the group. Pam came up behind her, hidden in the underbrush.

"Hello again, Bengta. I have news."

"As do I."

"Tell me."

"We have done as you asked. We are prepared to make our break. We have hidden weapons, tools, stones, whatever we could manage. When your signal comes, we will fight."

"That's great! What became of the *Muskijl*'s crew and soldiers?"

"The sailors are building the fort. The officers and marines are being held captive on the French warship. We fear for their health. No one knows what condition they are in. Those filthy French bastards and their foreign dogs care nothing for our lives. If we weren't useful, I doubt we would have been spared." Bengta's voice was thick with a long-pent-up anger. " See that heathen devil who guards us? When the signal comes, I intend to stove his skull in with a stone, may God forgive me."

Pam nodded. "I shot four like him a few days ago. First time I'd killed anyone. It was necessary. God forgives. Be careful." Pam reached into her rucksack and pulled out a bundle, filled with sharp knives, a few hammers, and

254

some chisels she had collected from the *Second Chance Bird*. "I've brought these. Can you keep them hidden? They may help."

"Yes, indeed they will! I will make sure they get to those who can use them best. Thank you, Pam, you are our savior!" The woman broke protocol to gaze upon Pam with her captivating sea-green eyes, flashing bright with hope after long suffering.

Pam blushed at the woman's fervency and flashed an encouraging smile.

"I'm just doing my duty, friend. I got us all into this mess, and I'm going to get us all out. So, here's what's going to happen. Make sure only your most trusted leaders hear this. Tomorrow afternoon, you are going to see a strange ship with red sails pull into the dock. It's called a Chinese junk. You won't be able to miss it . . ."

As Pam outlined the plan, the woman's face grew bright beneath the grime of the brutal captivity she suffered.

Pam finished up. "The signal to raise holy hell is going to be 'Save the dodo!' When you hear that, go to work."

"'Save the dodo!' Yes, the princess' funny-looking birds. We have seen them from time to time, they look just like the paintings you showed us. They are rather cute, in an odd sort of way I think, and we know they are so important to her! We have done as you asked, and try to protect them, shooing them back into the woods when we find them, so our captors can't eat them."

This bit of news almost made tears of joy erupt from Pam's eyes.

Bengta stole another quick glance back to smile at her. "It shall be as you say. We will be ready. You have our gratitude, Pam Miller. You are a very brave woman. We have seen that these swaddle-headed fools underestimate the true strength of women and they shall die regretting it." Bengta turned to check on the guard, who seemed to be dozing at his post. When she turned back, Pam was gone.

"Go with God, Pam." Bengta whispered into the trees.

Garrett W. Vance

CHAPTER 38: HAIR TODAY, GONE TOMORROW

"**Y**ou want to *what?*" The expression on the Bosun's face was a mixture of horror and astonishment. Pam had expected this and repeated herself in a calm voice.

"I want you men to shave your beards, hair, and eyebrows off." Looking at the incredulous faces of the sailors and marines gathered in the early dawn on the main deck, Pam realized while she didn't quite have a mutiny on her hands, what she had to say was not at all popular. *Tough*, she thought, feeling firm in her resolve.

"Look, I know it sounds awful, but honest, it grows back! If I'm going to make you look the part of Easterners of any stripe, we have got to lop off those golden locks, like it or not! We are stretching the boundaries of believability to their limits. This is the only way I can think of to fool the enemy into thinking you are visitors from a far away, exotic land! Hopefully, the make-up will finish the job and we can pull this stunt off." Pam paused to take a moment to convince herself that this would work. *Yul Brynner be with us!*

A sea of faces glared at her, even the sound of grumbling emanating from their midst, a sound rarely heard during their long time together. She looked to Gerbald for support, but found he had made his way to the back of the crowd, where he was attempting to hide behind the mast. Now that he was having to go through with the plan he had helped hatch, it seemed his enthusiasm had taken a powder. Pam grimaced, taken aback by the men's strong negative reaction. The Bosun and the *Löjtnant* were just about to quash any rebellion when Dore stepped past them, her expression dark and menacing.

"That's enough whining, you silly boys! What are you, fancy little dandies afraid to lose a bit of their pretty hair?" Dore bawled at them so loudly, it made them all take a fearful step back. "The captain has given her orders! Now line up and get ready for your haircuts! You, there hiding in the back, who is that?" An eager, crocodilian grin came to her face when she realized, it was her husband "Oh, well if it isn't the celebrated German sergeant, always a shining example of courage! Front and center, Gerbald, you shall be first! Make a good example for these men, or you might find my hands become shaky!" she ordered him, brandishing the straight razor a bit wildly in front of her, with a maniacal look in her eye.

The men parted to make a path for Gerbald, whose unflappable face had turned a flushed red. He nodded, and came forward, head held high, to sit on the chair placed on the deck for the day's barbering.

"Here, let me take your hat!" Pam offered a little too eagerly.

"I think not, I shall hold onto it myself," he replied, giving her a wary look while clutching the misshapen monstrosity safely to his breast.

"It was a good try, Pam." Dore told her as she set to work. Gerbald kept his salt-and pepper-hair close-cropped, and he shaved regularly in the up-time style, so the task didn't take long. When Dore came to the eyebrows, he flinched.

"Must you, Delilah?" he asked in a pleading tone.

Dore couldn't help but chuckle as she patted him on the arm. "Yes, Samson. It will make you look incredibly odd and that is the point. Perhaps it will be an improvement!"

Pam stepped up to remind her reluctant partner of the necessity for the sacrifice of his usual appearance, "We need to do all we can to convince the French and their lackeys you are Asian traders. Look at it this way, Gerbald. You are playing a part in a play, and simply doing what is needed to complete the costume. You'll be a real actor after this, just like Yul Brynner! Hollywood could be next!" Most of the actor's best-known films could be found in Grantville and Pam knew Gerbald, a bonafide film nut, held them in high regard.

That seemed to mollify him, and he closed his eyes tightly as Dore shaved his eyebrows off. When she was finished, there was no trace of blood, and Gerbald resembled a shiny new dodo egg. Some of the gathered men couldn't resist a chuckle, including the Bosun, who had drawn near to watch— a bit *too* near as it turned out.

Gerbald gave them all fierce glare, then smiled at Nils.

"Ah, *Herr* Bosun." he said, "I'm sure *you* will want to go next, as an example for the crew, of course! Here, have my seat."

258

All good humor evaporated from the Bosun's face as he realized there was no escape. He managed a weak smile for the benefit of the other sailors, then slumped into the barber's chair, looking for all the world as if he faced the gallows. It was Pam's turn to do the deed. She started by snipping the usually cheery old fellow's chest-length gray beard right to the chin. She thought he might cry, so she moved in front of him and was as gentle as she could be. When she was done, she paused to admire her work.

"My goodness, Dore, doesn't he look like a younger man now?" she asked her friend with just the slightest eyebrow twitch in her direction.

Dore, long-practiced in such subtleties, caught the signal and nodded her agreement. "Oh *yes*, Captain Pam! You have cut at least twenty years away along with all that fur. *Herr* Bosun, you are truly a handsome fellow!"

The fact of the mater was, they weren't kidding. The Bosun had a good, strong chin, and he did look younger without the gray hair. He pointed that masculine chin forward, and grinned as he rubbed it, his cheeks a brighter red than their usual cherry flush. He stood and bowed to the gathered men, who gave him a reluctant cheer as they fell into line. The rest of the operation went smoothly, except for giant Hake, who did cry as his prodigious ginger mane fell away from his massive face. Pam patted him on the back as if he were a small child, while reassuring him, it would grow back in no time.

A couple of hours later, the entire crew stood for inspection as Pam and Dore admired their work. At first glance, they faced a collection of strangers, a good start indeed.

"All right, take a break and get something to eat. In half an hour, be back on deck for your makeup, and don't be late." Pam ordered.

She and Dore took their leave, retiring to Pam's cabin. Once the door was closed, they both broke into helpless fits of laughter.

"You thought that was fun," Pam managed to gasp, "just wait till we put on the makeup!"

CHAPTER 39: MAN DOWN

Pam would never forget the sound of the scream, followed by the sickening thud. Her heart stuttered a beat as an intense chill arced through her body. She tried to run to the door, but her legs felt like rubber. Something terrible had happened and she thought she recognized the voice behind the terrified shriek. She hoped she was wrong, and felt guilty for it, but if it was the boy . . . Pam felt as if she were trapped in a nightmare and knew there would be no waking up.

Somehow, she managed to make it to her door. She wrenched it open to find the men gathered below, surrounding a still form on the deck. She tried to shout, but could only muster a painful croak. The Bosun stood up, and looked at her, his face ashen. Summoning his own voice, shaky, and pitched too high, he called out the answer to the question on Pam's stricken face.

"It is Pers! He has fallen!"

"Dear God, not Pers!" Pam whispered and found it hard to breathe. She climbed to the bottom of the ladder and made her way toward the men. They opened a space for her, all of them wearing the same pale look of fear as the Bosun.

There was Pers, lying on his side, blood leaking from his ear. His right arm lay akimbo, broken. Beside him was a shattered ship's spyglass, its shards gleaming in the sun. To Pam's amazement and relief, the boy was alive, breathing in ragged gasps. Pam knelt beside him and touched his forehead, but Per's eyes were rolled up into his lids, he was, perhaps mercifully, unconscious.

She turned to the Bosun. "How?"

"He was climbing the mainmast to spy ahead for us, you know what a monkey he is! His foot became tangled in the unfamiliar rig, and as he was trying to get himself loose the line slipped. He fell . . ."

"How far?"

"From up there, just above the third sheet. A good thirty feet at least! His feet landed on that coil of rope there first, which took some of the impact, but his head hit the deck pretty hard, and his arm is broken. Damn my old eyes, I was the one who sent him up there." The Bosun was starting to tear up. Pam fought the urge to cry as well, but a part of her she was coming to think of as 'Cool Captain" stayed in control.

"Bosun, go get Dore, now!" she ordered him, partly to give him a chance to pull himself together and not be seen weeping by the crew. Without a word, he jumped up and headed for the galley where Dore was preparing the skin dye they would apply to the sailors after lunch.

Gerbald appeared over Pam's shoulder. With remarkable gentleness he took the boy's pulse and pulled back his eyelids to view his pupils. They were dilated as big as saucers.

"He is concussed. I've seen symptoms like this in men thrown from horses or hit with blunt weapons. His pulse is good, but blood from the ear is bad."

Pam could barely speak. "Will he live?"

Gerbald took her shoulder in a firm, encouraging grip.

"I won't lie to you, Pam. It's hard to say just now. The head injury may be serious, or it may not be, only time will tell. I have seen men, with injuries like these pass away suddenly, without ever waking up, and I have seen some up and about within a few hours. We must think positively for him. There is plenty of hope. He's young, and the rope helped break the fall. I saw the whole thing with my own eyes. There is hope."

Dore arrived, plowing through the crowd like a bulldozer. Although they were trying their best to get out of her way, the men couldn't move fast enough, and the unlucky were bowled over by her fast-moving, low center of gravity and sturdy mass. She knelt beside Pers, clucking and praying under her breath as she gave him a thorough check. She was no trained nurse, but years following a soldier had taught her many first aid skills. Her methods were homespun remedies, but effective. When she moved Per's broken arm, he moaned, and his legs kicked, as if to flee the pain.

"He can feel the pain, and move his legs, that is good. His neck isn't broken, thank the Lord!" she announced. "But, I am most worried for what may be damaged inside his head." She had brought her homemade first-aid kit with her and began to splint the boy's arm with expert skill, Gerbald assisting her. Pam stroked Pers' flaxen hair as they worked, telling her dear, sweet boy he would be all right, and trying her best to believe it. Sailors arrived with a makeshift stretcher, and many hands lifted Pers onto it, as softly as a cloud.

"Clear that storeroom two doors down from the galley. It will be our sickbay." Dore ordered. The men jumped to the task without question, knowing in a situation like this, Dore held supreme authority with the captain's blessings. For her part, the captain was beginning to cry and feel shaky. She let Gerbald steady her as they followed Dore and the stretcher-bearers into the cool shade belowdecks.

* * *

An hour later, Pam called her senior staff together for a meeting on the castle deck. All the fun and excitement of the last few days had drained out of her. She was left with a bleak sense of foreboding. Her life had started to feel like she was the star of some wacky adventure show, but the sight of Pers lying bleeding on the deck brought home to her the real desperation of their situation. The truth was, she wanted to go curl up in her cabin and wait for it all to be over, but these people had come to rely on her. She accepted their allegiance and now she had to be strong for them. Physically pulling herself together with a deep breath, and unclenching her fists, Captain Pam Miller turned to those gathered around her, waiting for her to speak.

"How is Pers now?" Pam asked Dore.

"He is sleeping and his breathing is normal. I think it's best we just leave him be for now, and let his body do what it must to heal."

"Thank you, Dore. That's good." Pam let out a long whoosh of breath. She was terribly worried about her adopted son, but they had done all they could, and there were a host of other problems to face this day, all of them deadly dangerous.

She turned to Gerbald, the Bosun, and *Löjtnant* Lundkvist. Despite the gravity of the situation, she did allow herself a small smile at their shaven heads and faces, they looked like three cue balls lined up in a row. She almost didn't recognize Gerbald, who was making a rare appearance without his silly hat.

"Gentlemen, we were going to make our attack today. After what happened to Pers, I'm not so sure. We haven't had a very auspicious beginning. Should we wait another day? *Löjtnant* Lundkvist, you are our military leader, please tell me, am I out of my mind? Do you think this plan will work?"

Her earlier confidence had faded away. Pam felt like she was participating in vitally important events that she was highly unqualified for, but somehow, she had ended up in charge.

"Well, Captain Pam, it's highly unorthodox, reckless, perhaps even quite mad. But, as you have said, that's precisely why it might work. In this situation, normal military strategy has no chance. Our only real hope is the element of surprise your trickery gives us. So, yes, I think we should go ahead. Despite today's misfortune, our men are ready to fight and are clamoring for battle. We should use that to our advantage. I say we go in today."

The other two nodded their agreement.

"In addition,," Gerbald added, "I can already feel my hair growing back. If we wait too long, you will have to shave us again." Gerbald's face was a perfect picture of distaste at the thought.

They shared a quiet laugh, humor so often being the best way to deal with stress. Pam was thankful to her old friend for his good cheer in the face of danger.

"All right then, let's do it." she told them, feeling her resolve grow. "Dore, let's get the makeup ready."

The three men moaned in unison, dreading further torture at the hands of these formidable Valkyries. Despite their disdain, they put on resolute expressions as they went to round up the crew for their makeup session. Dore motioned for Pam to wait. She produced a folded cloth, one end of which she handed to Pam. Together, they opened it to reveal a hand-sewn flag.

Pam gasped with delight. It was made from silk, from plentiful variety and supply found on their captured Chinese junk. The base was a rich sky blue and over it was sewn a golden cross, in the Scandinavian style, the flag of Sweden. Behind the cross a black saltire ran from the corners with two gold stars on each band, just like the flag of the United States of Europe. Finally, to Pam's great delight, a gray dodo outlined with black thread occupied the center, complete with a shiny, gold button for an eye.

"Wow!" she exclaimed in English, then switched to German, which Dore was more comfortable using. "Dore! It's fantastic! How did you manage this?" Pam asked her grinning friend, who was aglow with one of her rare demonstrations of pride.

"I have some talents beyond the galley, you know. That oaf of a husband of mine was always tearing up his clothes in battle or while running down some poor creature in the woods. Someone had to mend them! If left to his own devices, he would go about in nothing but rags. Just look at his hat! I became handy with the needle and thread." she said. It was plain she was pleased with her work, which was perfectly executed.

Pam hugged her, the flag squished between them. "Thank you, Dore. It's wonderful! We needed something like this, it will help morale. A fine flag for our new colony. Really, you are a wonder!"

Dore took it from Pam to fold it again.

"Today, when the time is right, we will raise it from this deck," Pam promised. "Then, we will fly it over the colony once it has been liberated! Dore, you have outdone yourself, you are the best!" Pam was moved at her friend's thoughtfulness and felt some of the fear that had been building throughout the day ease. "Now, let's go paint our men yellow."

CHAPTER 40: A RUSE BY ANY OTHER NAME

Pam and Dore stood before their first unhappy subject, Gerbald, of course, whose sad, hound dog face was now a rich, yellowish-orange, not quite what they had in mind, but it would have to do.

"It goes well with his hat." Dore remarked, enjoying her beloved husband's discomfort.

Pam studied their victim.

"I think a bit more turmeric paste around the ears. He looks more like a *Star Trek* alien than an Asian, but I think it will fool the French long enough."

"My people are declaring war on your Federation." Gerbald grumbled. He had, of course, seen every episode of the classic 1960's version, one of his supreme favorites in the Grantville Library's video preservation archives. He made an effort not to flinch as Pam applied powdered turmeric, found among the galley's spices, which they had worked into a soupy paste with rice flour and water. She prayed there wouldn't be any rain this afternoon.

"Just be glad I decided not to color you blue and glue antenna to your forehead. There now, it's staining nicely," Pam exclaimed, pleased at her handiwork. "I think it will last a few hours, maybe even a few days!"

Gerbald groaned. "Must you do more? Am I not heathen enough yet?" he pleaded.

"Ha!" Dore interjected "Why *not* look like a heathen? You have always lived as one! Those such as you, who have turned their back on Our Savior, deserve far worse than this bit of discomfort!" Dore's face became the very embodiment of self-righteousness. "Pray The Lord doesn't strike you down, at the very sight of you!"

Tuning out his devout wife's pious haranguing, Gerbald sighed as Pam painted a realistic Fu Manchu mustache on his long, moping face with an ash and ink paste. It was too bad something couldn't be done to hide his blue eyes, but Pam just didn't have that kind of technology available. She shuddered at the thought of trying to maintain a set of contact lenses down-time. Since she knew any pair of glasses in her possession would end up lost or irreparably broken within a few days, contacts would have been her choice. In her opinion, maybe the Lord hadn't given her all that much, but she was truly grateful for her excellent vision.

Two hours later, Gerbald was not alone in his oddly colored misery. He stood nearly indistinguishable from the crowd of orange-yellow-skinned Swedes. Pam laughed, thinking they looked like spear carrying extras, wandered away from the set of that goofy old movie *The Conqueror*, an expensive flop which had miscast an unlucky John Wayne as Genghis Khan.

"Okay, Jason and the Argonauts, it's time to get dressed!" Pam announced, pointing at the pile of cloth and clothing they had assembled from the foreign goods aboard their prize.

The men went to work pulling on colorful silk robes embroidered with glowing scenes of cranes and sunsets. The best of the finery and some sparkling jewelry from the treasure chest went on Gerbald, whom they had unanimously elected to be their great and powerful Khan. He was a good choice. With his gift of mimicry and natural penchant for hamming it up, Pam was confident he was their best chance to carry this charade off. Besides, he was the only one among them who could speak a smattering of French, something he had picked up back in his soldiering days.

And so, Gerbald The Great and Powerful was to be carried on a beautifully carved palanquin they had found, no doubt belonging to the wealthy merchant who had once been this ship's master. Its satin pillows would be the perfect place to hide his shotgun pistol, the deadly *Snake Charmer*. According to Gerbald, when Pam's son, Walt, had given it to him, he had asked him to protect his mother with it. She and her son were not exactly on good terms, and she thought that might be a polite fiction, but she was quite glad to have the lethal little weapon along. Pam hoped that its services would not be required, but knew in her heart, they would.

Pam and Dore added the finishing touches to the costumes. Soon, they stood facing a mysterious envoy from what Pam declared to be "*The Far-Out East*".

"I would not recognize them if I didn't know them so well! Dore exclaimed "Even that foolish husband of mine!" She was well pleased by their handiwork, cleaning her hands on her apron in a gesture of job well done.

"Gosh almighty, don't you fellas look a picture!" Pam gushed, lapsing into West Virginia hillbilly-ese for a moment as a rush of excitement coursed through her. *I can't believe we're doing this. It really is like something out of some crazy old movie!* Her giddy grin turned serious as she thought of poor, badly injured Pers, lying unconscious below, and what might happen to these men, her friends, in the coming hours.

"All right, we all know what to do. Good luck, my brave brothers!" she regarded them with an intense pride, then shouted, "Battle stations!"

Pam and Dore kept a low profile on the castle deck. They were both wearing white linens draped over their clothes, with their hair tied up under makeshift turbans. They had decided against dying their own faces and hands since they were going to be far enough back from the action. Truth to tell, they couldn't bring themselves to do it out of simple vanity, although they would never admit it, even to each other. Pam felt the heavy weight of her revolver at her belt, the weapon she had used so effectively in the capture of her ship. It both terrified and comforted her.

On the foredeck, Sten, the top sergeant of the Black Chessmen, his crack gun crew, waited eagerly beside the formidable carronade deck gun salvaged from *Redbird*. It was hidden beneath a tarp and Pam hoped that they wouldn't have to unleash its deadly force. If all went well, little blood would be shed this day. The marines and sailors not needed to sail *Second Chance Bird* to the harbor's wide dock stood in attendance of the Great Khan Gerbald, who sat in his palanquin, regally fanning himself with a hand fan while wearing a bored expression.

Every man had a sword, and most had pistols, all concealed within the folds and sashes of their outlandish garb. Around them were placed brightly lacquered boxes and barrels of rice wine, the 'gifts' they had prepared to lure out the renegade French officers. Pam shook her head and frowned in a moment of doubt. Yes, it was a variation of the old Trojan Horse trick, hopefully these guys had never read Virgil. *Beware orange-skinned weirdos bearing gifts.* Pam knew they were taking a desperate gamble, but no better choices had presented themselves. It was completely nuts and it had to work.

The Bosun brought the junk in slowly, giving everyone on shore a nice long look. The captive Swedes paused in their work for a moment, while their captors gaped at the gaily painted ship's approach. The enemy had erected a grass-roofed sun shelter on the long, wide dock. Several sailors loafing there began making their way out to the T-shaped starboard side facing the shore. Pam saw that both the *Annalise* and *Ide* were still anchored out, out of easy reach by any would-be escapees.

The Bosun, guiding the crew with gestures and whistles alone, skillfully piloted *Second Chance Bird* against the dock with a light groan of timber. He had chosen a position lateral to the shore which gave them a tactical advantage. Their hidden deck gun, as well as their Chinese cannons, had a clear sweep of the dock and shoreline, including the warship tied up, stern out, some twenty yards inland.

At last, they could read the enemy ship's name, *Effrayant.* Tied up just past its bow, the much smaller and badly damaged *Muskijl* floated, mostly hidden behind *Effrayant's* massive bulk. Hopefully, if cannon fire started, her crew was imprisoned aboard their own vessel, rather than the enemy's. Down the left side of the dock, the slave-master's graceful lateen-rigged crafts were tied up in a line, looking like a scene from out of the *Arabian Nights.* Their guns would have a nice, clean shot at them. Pam was pleased with whatever advantages they could get.

Five French sailors, who Pam noted were armed with, what looked like flintlock sidearms, arrived at the end of the dock and were shouting at them. Pam was pretty sure they were ordering them to cast off and leave. She smiled to herself, because that was definitely *not* what was going to happen. Several of the African slavemasters began to venture toward them from the beach, but the sailors waved at them to stay back. The slavers were curious about the newcomers and reluctant to retreat.

Not for the first time, Pam felt sickened by the horrors mankind could inflict on one another for a profit. She knew there had been slaveowners in her own ancestry, among the Virginians on her mother's side. The very idea disgusted her, but she still tried not to think of these men as monsters. These were terrible times she had been thrust into. She knew she would likely have to do things, on this day and in the days to come, that would have appalled the old mild-mannered Pam Miller. There was nothing for it, but to accept that, and act as she thought best. She would try to minimize loss of life on all sides, but in her gut, she laughed at her own naiveté. *You're a killer now, Pam Miller, and you're gonna do it again! Admit you like it, you love the power!* a sly inner voice teased her. She shook her head to clear her mind, almost dislodging the ridiculous turban nesting there. Exercising a strong force of willpower that had been growing within, she made herself concentrate on the events unfolding. There would be plenty of time for probing self-analysis of the inner demons she had let loose. Right now, she was too damn busy leading a hostage rescue mission and slave rebellion, thank you very much! *I'm one of the good guys damn it, just let me work!*

The men of the *Second Chance Bird* remained silent as the sailors gesticulated at them. It was agreed, Gerbald would do *all* the talking and that time hadn't come yet. Completely disregarding the protests of the lowly dock crew, Gerbald waved his hand lazily, signaling the disguised Swedes to throw lines at the surprised sailors, who now found themselves, quite against their will, tying the junk up to the dock. The Great Khan Gerbald motioned he was ready to disembark. Two of the strongest men climbed over the rail and waited on the dock, ignoring the confused and increasingly nervous sailors gesturing at them to stay onboard their vessel. The palanquin was lowered to the waiting hands, passed down by two more men stationed on the junk's narrow step-ledge, halfway between the rail and the rough-hewn, uneven planks below.

Watching the scene unfold as scheduled, Pam patted her Smith and Wesson .38 caliber revolver where it lay waiting in its holster, hidden under a sash at her hip. She had tried to make Gerbald give the weapon to one of the men going onto the dock, but he had insisted she keep it, saying she was a better shot than most of them, and it was best she have it just in case things went badly. She prayed the revolver would not prove necessary, while the new, and bloodthirsty part of her that had made itself known in recent days, was downright gleeful to have it. Pam rolled her eyes to the heavens, lamenting it was bad enough to go into a conflict, without being conflicted about it to boot.

The disguised Swedes had begun passing the various prepared offerings down to the dock. This caused the sailors to cease their frantic fussing and become interested in the arriving packages accompanying their bizarre visitors. They whispered among themselves loudly, pointing at the brightly colored wooden boxes. They were especially interested in the barrels and casks. Perhaps they had run out of whatever rotgut a French sea-dog prefers.

Once the entire shore party was assembled on the dock, Gerbald harrumphed loudly for attention. He pointed at the sailors, and commanded in a deep, resonant voice, "*Sous capitaine!*" The sailors stood there staring, wondering what they should do, not quite sure they had heard the leader of these strange folk speak French. Gerbald repeated the order forcefully, adding a jabbing, pointing finger. "SOUS CAPITAN!" Then, with a sweep of his arms to their "gifts", he said "*Sous capitaine!*" in a cordial tone, while smiling. Acting as if everyone had understood him, he clapped his hands twice and folded them across his chest, waiting for the French to get moving.

A brief discussion followed, the highest-ranking of the French dock contingent shook his head in resignation, and sent someone go find their captain. Seeing this, Gerbald let out a loud grunt and pointed at the man leaving, a clear signal to his palanquin bearers to follow the messenger, while the rest of his men gathered the packages and fell in behind. This brought a fresh hail of protests from the French, but they didn't reach for their guns, and soon found themselves escorting the determined strangers toward their own ship.

Pam started to laugh at their consternation, a kind of giddy, hysterical laugh, then forced herself to stop.

"Thank God, it's working so far. Please let us pull this off, please!" she prayed under her breath, joined by Dore doing the same in German. Pam looked over to see Sergeant Sten and his Black Chessmen, ready to man their precious carronade on the foredeck. If that kind of shooting started, the Great Khan Gerbald and his loyal minions had orders to hit the deck and hope the cannon shot sailed past safely above them. Pam hunkered down behind the rail, peering through her scope to see what was happening ashore.

Up on the hillside she could see women working in the fields while their men were busy expanding the town. The French and their allies intended to make this a long-term base, and why not? They had free labor, and all the supplies necessary, captured along with the colonists. This would be a golden opportunity for an enterprising officer to create a little kingdom for himself, far from the eyes and ears of his nation. During her research, Pam had read about pirate havens sprouting up on Madagascar and Isle St. Marie off to their west in the century to come. It occurred to her then, rather than being the plot of a hostile French government, perhaps up-time tales of lucrative piracy in the 1700s had inspired this bunch to start the game on their own, a century early.

"Well, whatever brought you here, *mes amis,* I am about to throw a big wrench in your plans!" she hissed.

The palanquin was a few yards away from the *Effrayant's* long, steep gangplank. The procession came to a silent stop at The Great Khan Gerbald's raised hand. They wanted to be close enough to storm the enemy ship if they must, but still have some room to duck if it came to cannon fire. Gerbald waited with an impatient expression as several officer types emerged from a shady spot on the ship's main deck and began yelling with much gesturing, at the French sailors on the dock below. Said unfortunates yelled back, also with much gesturing, recounting the story so far. After a minute, the yelling stopped, and the original welcoming committee stepped back, relieved that their superiors were coming to rid them of the problem. Gerbald took the opportunity to announce his intentions to the officers. *"Sous capitaine!"* he bellowed, full of generosity and good cheer, sweeping his arm toward the enticing boxes his servants bore.

After another long moment of consternation, one of the officers nudged a junior, likely sending him off to fetch the captain. The fellow chosen for the task had a unenthusiastic expression on his face, which Pam thought spoke volumes about the personality of the captain. After angry shouting emanating from the captain's cabin, a grouchy fellow swaggered to the rail, an expensive sword at his belt, and a many-plumed hat on his head. He looked annoyed, but couldn't hide his interest as he squinted at the bizarre envoy assembled below. The officer who had remained at the rail announced with proper respect, if little love, *"Capitaine* Leonce Toulon!" while the sour-faced man paused in what he must think was a heroic pose. Pam thought he bore more than a slight resemblance to Captain Hook and fought back a snicker. Sometimes it all just seemed unreal and she had to remind herself, their lives were very much in danger, even from such an unlikely character.

"Capitaine! Gerbald exclaimed with glee *"Por vous, pour vous! Mon ami! allez, allez."*

Pam stifled another nervous laugh. Gerbald's fractured *Francais* was funny to hear, plus it was working.

The captain cocked his head at the insistent potentate, who had so unexpectedly appeared, but favored him with a thin smile. Giving those gathered a curt nod, he stalked down the gangplank, followed by his chief officers. Pam whistled in relief, so far, so good. Dore took hold of one of Pam's shaking hands, pushing all the blood out of it with a single squeeze. The sailors and marines of the *Second Chance Bird* stood perfectly still, a set of bronze statues in the late afternoon sun.

Having seen the enemy leadership, Pam now leaned heavily toward her warship gone rogue theory. The sneering officers were no gentlemen, but pirates, through and through. They stepped onto the dock, then sauntered to Gerbald and his men, all of whom bowed in unison at Gerbald's unspoken cue. The officers smiled and chuckled to themselves, smug in their superiority. Gerbald the Great Khan swept his arms once more toward the gathered gifts. With an openly condescending nod of acceptance, the captain bent down to open one of the boxes filled with part of the treasure they had found aboard the junk. A gleam of avarice came to the captain's scheming eyes. His officers opened other boxes to find more of the same. As the greedy marauders became engrossed in their unexpected windfall, the odd visitors began to surround them, cutting them off from retreat to their ship.

Garrett W. Vance

CHAPTER 41: ALL HELL BREAKS LOOSE

One of the sailors who had first met the contingent from *The Far-Out East* when they arrived, realized what was happening. He placed a hand on the back of one of the disguised Swede's to push him aside, but it slipped on the sweaty skin, leaving a smeared trail. With an expression of astonishment, he held up his palm to show it was stained the same shade of orange-yellow. There was a moment of silence as everyone stared.

"The jig is up." Pam sighed to Dore, her heart sinking.

The man with the stained hand began to shout at the top of his lungs, presumably to rouse reinforcements. Pam realized the Swede he had pushed was *Löjtnant* Lundkvist. Thanks to their disguises, it was hard to tell them apart at this distance. The *Löjtnant* calmly produced his razor-sharp saber from within his loose silk cloak and stopped the shouts by slicing the man's throat wide open. He pushed the corpse backward, to fall into the other sailors who had started to follow him. They hesitated at the sight of so much blood. Even so, it was too late. An alarm bell began to sound on the *Effrayant*. Within moments, about forty surly French soldiers surged onto the deck, all armed to the teeth. The Swedes were outnumbered.

"Christ, they have a freaking army with them!" Pam exclaimed. She thought fast, ignoring her terror.

"*Carronade*! Sweep that deck," she screamed at the top of her lungs. Sergeant Sten grinned through his swarthy makeup as he and his Black Chessmen unleashed the carronade's deadly force. Her men were ready for the signal. All of them dropped to the dock. Gerbald leaped from his palanquin, knocking down the French captain and landing on top of him, having decided they wanted to keep him alive if they could. The other officers, realizing what was happening, flung themselves onto the dock as well. Sergeant Sten swept the cover off the carronade and aimed it directly at the enemy heading toward their gangplank. Not a second later, its load of anti-personnel shot sprayed death and destruction across the *Effrayant's* deck. Half the enemy fell dead or dying to the deck, their moans of agony awful to hear. Still, that left at least twenty alive, who hurried across the gangplank or swung to the dock on ropes.

Knowing it would take time for the Black Chessmen to reload, Lundkvist and his Swedish marines, who had been stationed near the front of the procession, leaped to their feet and opened fire on the advancing soldiers, along with any sailors who had dared to draw their arms. Several were mowed down while crossing the gangplank, while others were parted from their ropes as the bullets ripped into them. Dead or dying, they fell into the water with a great splash.

Pam gasped as a musket ball hit the *Löjtnant*, shattering half of his left knee in an explosion of blood and white bone chips. He started to fall, but was buoyed up by two of his White Chessmen, who continued to fire their uptime-make pistols into the charging soldiers even as they dragged their commander backward, to the line the men were forming around Gerbald. Stunned by the amazing rate of fire, the enemy hesitated long enough for the *Löjtnant* to reach safety, before finding their courage and mounting a charge. The determined French soldiers closed with the White Chessmen, who stood fast, Seargent Järv giving a defiant snarl of challenge to their attackers. Soon the dock rang with the clang and crash of close quarters sword fighting.

Meanwhile, Gerbald had pulled out his *Snake Charmer* and had the nasty little shotgun pointed directly at the captain's head. The rest of the palanquin bearers had their swords and pistols aimed at the prone officers. The prisoners were relieved of their weapons, while the Swedish sailors bound their hands behind them, and their ankles together. They wouldn't be going anywhere for a while. The captain was pulled to his feet by giant Hake, who held him with his toes barely touching the floor, Gerbald's shotgun-pistol jammed under the villainous Frenchman's chin. Given the chance by the line of engaged marines, the circle fell back to the *Second Chance Bird* with their captives. Pam could hear Gerbald taunt the captain over the din of combat.

"Surprise, surprise, surprise!" Gerbald exclaimed in his best Gomer Pyle imitation, the skill of which would be lost on the captive captain. "I'll bet you speak English better than I do French, eh, mon *capitaine*? Well, don't you?" Gerbald gave the trembling man a painful prod with the barrels of his weapon. "Speak up, quickly! German will also do." he added in his native tongue.

"I speak English. What do you want, you stinking buffoon?"

Gerbald smiled at the insult, respecting the man's courage for uttering it, before slapping him so hard across the face that Hake lost his grip, so that the man fell to the ground and had to be hoisted up again. Now Gerbald brought his face within a few inches of the captain's, and his voice turned as cold as Germany's winter skies.

"Call your dogs off, now! If they don't surrender immediately, I will take great pleasure in killing you, you son of a jackal. I may yet. It's best to do as I say. Understand? Now tell them, tell them to lay down their arms if you want to live!"

Pam suppressed a groan, she could hear *The Terminator's* Austrian accent loud and clear in that last line. *We really do need to get him an acting job someday, he has truly missed his calling.*

"Yes, yes, I will do it," the captain cried, cowed by Gerbald's menacing presence and the shotgun barrels now resting against his cheek. With panic in his eyes, he began to scream orders. Some of the enemy paused at the sound of his words, but the battle continued. Pam saw to her horror, two Swedish marines had fallen to the dock's knotted planks, undoubtedly beyond help. Even so, their side's weaponry was superior. The dock was littered with enemy corpses, rivulets of blood running off the edge to make pretty little crimson waterfalls, expanding into billowing red clouds in the clear waters below. The captain continued to shriek at his troops to stand down, and slowly the combat ground to a halt.

Pam had been so caught up with the action nearby, she had completely forgotten about the colonists. She looked to the shore to see they had another problem. Two dozen of the African slavers had arrived, each wielding a nasty looking scimitar. They were running down the dock, straight toward *Second Chance Bird*.

"Gerbald, look!"

"Tell them to stop!" he ordered the captured captain. The captain shouted hoarsely at the charging slavers, but they ignored him, bloodlust glinting in their dark eyes. The White Chessmen had disengaged from the French soldiers once the fighting stopped, and had fallen back. They formed a line around Gerbald and the sailors gathered at *Second Chance Bird's* lowest point, and were reloading their weapons. The men at the carronade were frantically trying to do the same, but were having some kind of trouble with the weapon. As usual, Murphy's Law was in effect. Sergeant Sten's curses echoed around the bay. Never taking their eyes off their foes, the Swedish marines braced themselves to defend their comrades and their ship.

Seeing the slavers making a charge, the French soldiers who had been ordered to pause, started to advance again, but the terrified wail of their captain made them stop, albeit reluctantly. Whatever power their *capitaine* had over them was slipping. Although they wore the colors of France, they were little better than pirates. Unhappy with the situation, the French soldiers were backing toward their own ship, disgusted with their leaders for getting captured, but unwilling to sacrifice them for a certain victory, either. They stepped aside as the slavers trampled past them, whooping an eerie war cry.

Dore grabbed Pam and shook her. 'Your gun! Shoot them, Pam!" she implored her friend. Pam nodded, pulling the heavy revolver from its holster as quickly as she could. It tangled on her sash for an agonizing moment, but she managed to free it. Below her, Gerbald kicked the captain's knees out from under him, sending him crashing face-first to the dock, along with his officers, and out of the way. He stepped over the prisoner into the front of the line, unleashing the *Snake-Charmer* with one hand, while pulling his *katzbalger* short-sword out of its scabbard with the other. The two leading slavers fell beneath the shotgun pistol's wrath and the third had his scimitar knocked out of his ruined hand before receiving the *katzbalger* in his gut. The Swedes immediately entered the fray, pistols firing and swords flashing.

Pam decided to shoot at enemies farther down the dock so as not to hit any of her own by accident. She was too excited, making her first shot go wild. She felt Dore grasp her shoulders from behind to help steady her, just as she had done during the battle for the junk. Pam gripped the revolver in both hands, firm, but not too tightly, just as her uncles had taught her, and took a deep breath. She took aim at the chest of a lumbering brute holding a scimitar in each hand, as he shouted bloody murder in his incomprehensible tongue, while running headlong at her friends. Breathing out, she pulled the trigger. There was a red explosion in the center of the brute's chest and he went down like a sack of rocks. The man behind him tripped and fell onto his back. As he started to get up, he received Pam's next bullet through his left eye. It continued right out the back of his head, as brains spurted out like watermelon flesh at target practice.

"Never bring a sword to a gunfight, assholes!" Pam exclaimed, smiling grimly at her handiwork.

Pam took a moment to get her bearingsas there were no clear shots now that the enemy and her men were locked in combat. Gerbald was dancing through the slavers with his short sword, thrust-and-slice-and-step-and-kill. Pam was astounded once more by the old soldier's almost dainty grace in combat, perfected over many years of practice on the bloody battlefields of Europe. Having cut himself clear of the fray for a moment, he reloaded the *Snake-Charmer*, looking all the world as if he were taking a breather from nothing more than a healthy morning walk. Just as he snapped the weapon closed, a wild-eyed slaver ran straight at him, scimitar held in both hands over his head, ready to chop Gerbald in two. Gerbald destroyed his assailant's face with one barrel, stepping aside as the dying man's momentum carried him past, off the dock, and into the water. Pam couldn't help but laugh aloud, as Gerbald wiped the man's sprayed blood from his face with a billowing silk sleeve, smearing the makeup on his forehead. She stopped laughing as she took aim at another enraged slaver headed directly for Gerbald. She shot the attacker squarely in his side, above the ribs, puncturing a lung. Gerbald frowned at her, raising the remaining barrel of his shotgun to as if to say, *"I had him!"*

The French soldiers had been watching and couldn't abide to stay out of the action any longer. Despite their captain's imploring shouts to stand down, five of them decided to enter the fray and began running down the dock toward the action. Perhaps they thought the invaders were distracted by the slaver attack enough they could win their captain back. Perhaps they simply decided they didn't care if their leader lived or died, and wanted to make sure their lucrative little kingdom continued, with or without him. These were desperate men, men who didn't intend to, or perhaps couldn't, return to their homeland.

Pam knew she only had two shots left before she needed to reload. She drew a bead on the first in line, but he saw her, and tried to dodge. Her bullet hit his sword arm and he fell, gasping in pain. Next in line was a rangy fellow with a really bad mustache. He tried to duck, but she was ready for that, so she aimed low, catching him in the center of his forehead, an instant death.

"I'm out!" she cried, feeling both horror and elation at her kills. *Four out of six, not too bad! That brings the count of men dead by my hand to eight, yo-ho-ho!*

Gerbald took down the next soldier with the *Snake Charmer's* second barrel. The remaining two, deciding the odds were against them, came to a skidding halt as Gerbald advanced with his *katzbalger*, its steel stained scarlet. One of them turned and fled back to his ranks, while the other simply dove into the water, taking his chances with the sea, rather than face the awesome might of the Great Khan Gerbald.

Pam reloaded, taking deep breaths to stay calm. By the time she was ready for action again, the attack had drawn to a close. A Swedish sailor, nimble Åke, lay gasping, horribly wounded, and all the slavers were dead or dying. *Not bad, really,* she thought to herself with the cold, cold part of her mind that was Captain Pam doing her bloody work. *We got more of them than they got of us.*

She turned to Dore. "It's time!" she said. "They will have heard all the gunfire by now, so if they haven't started their revolution already, they should do it now!"

They nodded to each other and in unison let out a ringing shout as they raised Dore's colonial flag.

"SAVE THE DODO!!!"

Dore gave the ship's gong a powerful thump with its heavy mallet for good measure. When its deep metal tone faded, they could hear shouts coming from the town and the fields on the gentle slopes above. Shouts of "Save the dodo!" echoed across the harbor as the enslaved Swedish colonists and the fighting men of *Second Chance Bird* took up the battle cry. Up on the fortress walls, Pam saw two Swedish farmers throw a slaver off the gangway running along its top, to fall to his death. One by one, men were shedding their chains and taking up the scimitars of dead and dying slavers, who they now outnumbered.

Gerbald walked to where the captain his fellow officers lay bound and in a row like railroad ties. Gerbald turned him over with his boot as he reloaded his shotgun pistol again. The Swedes reloaded as they reformed their defensive circle. Seeing what the orange-painted invaders were capable of, the remaining enemy soldiers decided to lay down their arms, then shuffle back with their hands raised, while keeping a wary eye on the fearsome deck gun of the *Second Chance Bird*.

Capitaine Leonce Toulon began to beg for his life.

"Please, know my well-being has a rich value in gold. There will be rewards for my safety!" the would-be pirate king pleaded, quivering with fear.

Gerbald gave him a sharkish grin.

"Your riches are meaningless to us! As long as you continue to do as we say, you will continue to live! Now, send one sailor each, into the warships. I want Swedish prisoners freed and sent out first, unbound! Then, the rest of your crew must exit the ships, unarmed, with their hands on their heads. If they don't, I will take great pleasure in killing you. I may yet. It's best to do as I say. Understand? Now tell them!" Gerbald lifted the man roughly to his feet. The captain gave the orders as instructed, his voice at a high, nervous pitch, a fine example of the true coward hiding within a cruel bully, just waiting to be exposed. Two of his men obeyed, jogging up the gangplanks to disappear into the *Muskijl* and *Effrayant's* lower decks.

Dore turned to Pam. "Now that the fighting has stopped, may I go down onto the dock to help the injured?"

Pam allowed herself a smile. "Of course, Dore. Please see to the *Löjtnant* first, his leg is in bad shape." They gripped each other's hands, then Dore ran for her first aid kit.

Pam turned to see a line of dirty, gaunt, smiling men come down the gangplank from the *Muskijl*. The liberated Swedish prisoners carried weapons taken from their former captors, who followed meekly behind, heads bowed and afraid. The captured enemy were directed to lie down in a line to be bound hand and foot beside their officers.

The elated, newly freed Swedes gathered near the *Second Chance Bird*. At first, they stood a little way off, blinking and muttering among themselves, wondering at the identity of their strange looking rescuers, until Pam's crew realized how odd they must appear, and began to laugh and joke in Swedish.

"Do you not know us? We are your brother Swedes! We have disguised ourselves as heathen Easterners to fool these scoundrels!" The freed crewmen started laughing too, and a few happy minutes of embracing and backslapping followed.

The *Löjtnant*, who had come to his senses, despite the terrible injury to his leg, ordered his men to help him stand, despite Dore's insistence he stay down lest the bandages come loose. For once, her orders were ignored. The man was too proud perhaps for his own good, but Pam understood his feelings. She caught Dore's eye, and motioned for her to let him do as he wished. The formidable German scowled but kept still.

Lundkvist saluted *Kapten* Lagerhjelm of the *Muskijl*, a tired fellow with a scruffy blond beard, who barely resembled the proud officer Pam remembered meeting in Bremerhaven so long ago and far away. Lundkvist told a brief version of their adventures, and introduced him to the leader of their rescue, Captain Pam Miller.

Lagerhjelm looked up at Pam where she stood on the junk's castle deck. He looked surprised, then smiled and saluted her.

"Madame Captain, you have my deepest thanks. Considering the excellent work you have done here today, please consider my men yours to command until this crisis is resolved. I'm afraid we are half-starved and too weak to do much good, but we shall try."

Pam saluted him back. "Thank you, *Kapten* Lagerhjelm, your confidence is very much appreciated! It is so good to see you all safe!" Pam felt a sense of growing elation. They had lost good men, but they were winning the day so the sacrifices would not be in vain.

The *Löjtnant* turned to Gerbald.

"*Herr* Gerbald, I am hereby giving you an honorary command in the Royal Swedish Marines, as a sergeant-major, the rank you once held when you fought for our king in the Germanies. If you choose to remain with us after all this is over, I will make it official. Since I am out of action, the Chessmen are yours."

The orange-skinned Swedes all clapped their well-loved German comrade heartily on the back in celebration. Gerbald gave Pam a pleased grin. Pam couldn't stop herself from emitting a rather un-captain-like squeal of glee. *Yes, we are winning, but it's not over yet you fool, save it for later!* she chided herself.

With the dock in order, *Sergeant-major* Gerbald set the next part of their plan into motion. He assigned *Kapten* Lagerhjelm and six of his newly freed Swedish sailors to guard the captured officers and sailors, holding the enemy's own pistols and muskets to their heads. The cowed would-be pirate kings were not going to offer any resistance. They had seen the power of the *Second Chance Bird's* men and guns, and rightfully feared for their lives. Gerbald led his shipmates, and those freed men who were strong enough to fight, through the carnage littering the dock and on to the shore.

Upon reaching the open gate of the unfinished fortress, they split into two groups, one entering the town, the other going around the walls and up the gentle slope to the fields. They were angry men who moved like tigers on the hunt, men on their way to undo terrible wrongs, men with blood on their minds. Pam swelled with pride to see them, her fears for their safety evaporating in the glory of the moment.

Pam turned to Lagerhjelm. "Are all your men all accounted for?"

"Yes, but a few who are quite ill still remain on the *Muskijl*, they need the attention of a physician. There is one we know is being kept out on the *Ide*, who you—" Lagerhjelm was interrupted by an imploring call in English from near his feet.

One of the French prisoners, a man who looked to be in his late forties, wearing neither the garb of a sailor or an officer, turned a pale, mustachioed face up to her.

"*Mademoiselle Capitaine*, please, may I have a word? It is most important you hear me!" His English had a thick French accent, but sounded quite fluent.

Pam looked at the man like a circling hawk would mark a mouse in a field.

"Yes, sir, you may. I'm a-listenin'!" she answered back in a danger-tinged, but still cordial drawl, her West Virginia Hillbilly accent in full twang as sometimes happened when she was keyed up.

"Please, allow me to introduce myself. I am Doctor Arnaud Henri Durand of Normandy. I am a physician, lately finding myself trapped against my will in the service of these wayward men. Please, I can help your wounded, I swear to you on the holy cross! Allow me to assistso lives can be saved."

The man motioned toward Lundkvist with his chin. The *Löjtnant* was lying on his back again, his face a mask of pain as Dore wiped his brow and worried over him.

"Your fine young officer there. His injury is most terrible, he may lose his leg today. Please, if you don't let me apply my skills, he will certainly lose his life before the sun sets! Let me help him!"

Pam gave the man a long, considering study. Sincere, sad brown eyes met hers with a steady gaze, imploring her to see reason. Her gut said he was legit, and so she believed him.

"All righty then. If you make yourself useful, *Doctor*, you will live. Try anything funny though, and I'll shoot yer head clean off myself and make you number nine."

Pam raised her revolver in front of her chest for dramatic effect. She switched back to Swedish.

" Men, go ahead and untie this doctor here, and let him do his work, but keep a close eye on him."

The *Muskijl's* sailors cut the man loose and helped him to his feet.

Once free, the French physician bowed deeply.

"Thank you, *Mademoiselle Capitaine*. It is best we don't try to move the gentleman yet, please allow me to get my surgeon's tools from the *Effrayant*."

Pam sent him on his way with two guards. Durand fell into line in front of the watchful Swedes, walking as quickly as he could without running, which might alarm his escort.

Kapten Lagerhjelm turned to Pam again.

"I can vouch for that man, Captain. He was captured by these creatures and forced into duty. He tried to help us when he could whenever this son-of-a-whore Toulon allowed it, or behind his thrice-damned back."

The *kapten* gave the bound captain a sharp kick in the side for emphasis, making him howl. Pam didn't stop him. She figured the deposed tyrant deserved whatever he got, and concepts like the Geneva Convention were a long stretch of space-time away from the Indian Ocean of the seventeenth century.

"We had to beg them to let the doctor help when they found—" He was about to say more when their attention was drawn away to a commotion on the shore.

Pam and her borrowed crew had been watching what they could of the land battle, occasionally able to see Swedes and the cruel slavemasters locked in combat. Pam prayed none of her people would lose their lives, but knew some would. The battles they had been through today were too big, the foes too numerous. The slavers fought fiercely, with the tenacity of cornered animals, struggling for their very lives. To Pam's great joy, shouts of triumph in Swedish could be heard, the whoops and hollers of free people released from months of sadistic captivity. A band of some thirty of the slavers, the fight taken out of them, were fleeing down the muddy track to the dock, calling to each other in voices filled with fear. They were in a panic, running pell-mell as they headed for their swift, lateen-rigged craft.

Sergeant Sten called out to her, a slight grin on his usually stone-like face. "Captain Pam, the carronade is now ready for firing!"

She turned to see him and his gun crew waiting for her command, their faces expectant and eager for the chance to give their beloved and lethal toy another go. Pam looked at the would-be escapees untying lines and readying their sails. They were utterly terrified, looking over their shoulders at their pursuers with wide, frightened eyes. She hesitated. Should she just let them go, let them carry word back Mauritius was free, and the Swedish colonists were strong? So much blood had been shed already today, should she be merciful to these men despite what they had done? Yes, she had learned to kill, but she still didn't think of herself as a killer. She was a soldier in wartime now, doing what she must.

A contingent of Swedes were hurrying down the slopes, still a few minutes away— they would arrive too late to catch the fleeing slavers. The mix of sailors and colonists were berserk from wreaking bloody revenge on their former tormentors and thirsting for more. Their bellowing shouts rang with hatred, the very sound sent a cold shiver up Pam's spine. *This is what happens when you push these calm, congenial folk of the North too far. The giants have awakened, and they are filled with wrath.*

Following the men, came a group of women, wailing and cursing as they carried their wounded on makeshift stretchers, lifting the injured to the heavens as if to say *"See? This is what has been done to us! We must be avenged!"* Pam saw one young woman born aloft by her kinfolk, splattered in blood from head to toe. Pam raised her binoculars for a closer look. It was Bengta! The woman was suffering from awful wounds, her face pale and distorted by agony, but her eyes were bright, burning with the flames of vengeance. Pam was aghast. The harm inflicted on Bengta was enough for her to make up her mind. This was war, and war is hell.

"You men down there, everybody get down! Sergeant Sten!" Pam's voice cut through the smoky afternoon air with a cold steel edge. "Target those boats trying to get away and *fire at will!*"

The Black Chessmen were locked on and ready. His shouted reply of "Yes, ma'am!" was drowned out by the nearly immediate blast of the deck gun, its lethal projectiles mowing down the would-be escapees by the dozen. Before the smoke could even clear, they were reloading.

Pam called to the Black Chessmen gun crew waiting below decks with the Chinese cannons. "Gun crew! Fire Number One and sink the boat that's getting away." She heard only half of a "Yes, ma'am!" as a *boom* sounded, heralding the exit of a heavy Chinese cannon ball. The projectile plowed through the bow of the fleeing light craft in a shower of splinters. "Number two! *Fire!*" Pam bawled. Another blast tore into the enemy ships still lined up along the dock, breaking apart the boats as if they were cheap toys. Lost *Redbird's* fearsome carronade sounded again, shredding the slavers into a gory mess of bone and blood. The boats were sinking beneath the harbor's calm waters in a widening stain of blood and grease. The Swedes on shore had stopped their charge to watch the destruction happen, cheering the *Second Chance Bird's* gunners on from a safe distance. Dore climbed up to rejoin Pam. She looked at the scene dispassionately, sweat running down her strong, proud face.

"Good God, we tore them all to shreds! I've never seen anything like it." Pam said in a small voice, stunned by the deadly force she had directed this day.

"I have." Dore's voice carried the chill as the winter wind. "Better like that, than with the swords, Pam. Better those devils die quickly, than our people be hurt or killed in more fighting. Our foes chose to do evil in this world, and now they have paid for it."

Pam nodded in agreement. She winced at the awful carnage, but also felt a burning pride. *Fear us, fear the people of the dodo!* The epithet made her smile She might just use it some time. The truth was, the *Fury of the Norsemen* was running hot in her, too. She had caught it from them, and found she liked its burning taste. She rejoiced to see their enemy obliterated, humiliated, defeated. *Blown to smithereens!* she thought with inculpable satisfaction. Whatever demons these days of blood and conquest had loosed in her, she would wrestle with later. Today, she was a fighting woman, an avenging Valkyrie out of the ancient tales. Today, she was Captain Pam Miller, victorious in war.

Garrett W. Vance

CHAPTER 42: VICTORY LAP

"Let's go ashore. Arne, you have the con, Bosun, you are with me. Gun crews, stay on watch. Come Dore, let's go ashore." Giving orders was coming naturally to her, and while it still made her a bit uneasy at times, she played the role she had been given as properly as she could.

Pam had shed her white robes, revealing her sky-blue, gold-embroidered Chinese jacket, the Swedish colors which she wore with pride. They had adopted her, and she had accepted their kinship; she was one of them now. She pushed wisps of her unruly, dishwater blond hair behind her ears and stood up straight. Dore grinned, carrying the colonial flag she had made, fastened to an eight-foot bamboo pole. Pam clapped her friend on the back just the way the men always did to each other, then led her and the Bosun down onto the dock.

The doctor had returned, and seemed satisfied with his work on the *Löjtnant*, who was visibly more at ease, his leg smothered in bandages.

"How is he, Doctor Durand?" Pam asked, having decided the man was indeed who, and what, he said he was.

The doctor's sad, brown eyes were full of relief she had accepted him.

"There is a chance I have saved the leg, we will know better tomorrow. Even so, he will never run again, and will need to use a cane to walk. I'm afraid his days as a fighting man are over."

"Perhaps. I have a job in mind for him where that won't pose too much of a problem. As is my right as victor, I'm claiming the *Effrayant* for the crown of Sweden, to be permanently assigned as guardian of this colony and the surrounding seas. She will need a captain." Pam looked down at the *Löjtnant*, whose hazel eyes brightened at her words.

"She is yours to command, if you will have her, my friend. I can't think of a better man, a courageous hero of the people." Pam told him, her voice trembling with pride just to be a friend of this brave man before her, a man who would have sacrificed his life for their cause, and almost had.

Lundkvist looked up, giving her an exhausted, but proud smile.

"It will be my honor. Thank you, Captain Pam. Your deeds today will never be forgotten. You are the real hero, I merely followed your orders. And fine orders they were!

Lundkvist's praise made Pam's eyes mist up, but she fought back the joyful tears. She smiled at her newly minted captain, then turned away, putting a stern face on. There was another person she needed to speak to, before any celebrating could take place. She motioned to the doctor to join her.

"Come with me please, Doctor Durand. There is a woman on shore who needs you right away, she looks to be in bad shape. Then, once you do what you can for those most badly injured, I want you to see to a young boy on my ship. He fell from the rigging yesterday, and I fear for him. He is dear to me. If you make him well, you can consider me to be your new best friend."

The doctor bowed to her with courtly grace and fell in behind her.

They walked past the rows of captives. Pam came to a stop over the corrupt French captain, the architect of all their suffering. His reckoning day was near. He was the helpless captive now, a tyrant deposed. He eyed her from his trussed-up position, cold, frightened sweat beading on his face.

"Hey, fuck-head!" Her voice seared the air with a heat she hadn't known was within her, a voice that could burn an evil man like this with its very sound. His eyes were bleary, swimming with dread. Pam found she relished his fear, it was delicious. She pressed the pointy tip of the odd, patent-leather Chinese shoe she wore into the captain's large nose, making him grimace.

"I'm going to see to it you pay for what you have done here, Toulon, do you hear me? *Pay*! Your worthless, scumbag life now depends on how many ways you find to make yourself useful to me. We'll start with a full account of just *who* you and those slavemaster fuckers doing your dirty work are, or, in their case, *were*. If you don't tell me everything I want to know, I'll throw you to those people you have been torturing for all these months and laugh while they tear your arms and legs off. I'll make sure they do it nice and slow, too. So, *capitaine*, we'll talk later, at my convenience. Asshole."

The thoroughly humiliated villain didn't even try to speak, just nodded his assent as best he could with Pam's shoe smashing his considerable nose. Pam sneered at him, then walked on, her steel gray eyes glinting with wrath and exultation, chin held high, hardly believing these things were happening, and it was she herself who was making them happen. *Who are you and whatever did you do with meek and mild birdwatcher Pam Miller of Grantville, West Virginia?* a voice in her head mused. *Oh, she's still around, but right now it's a bad-ass warrior-queen of the Norsemen we need, so shush up, it's time for the victory lap!*

They stepped onto the shore before the rescued Swedish colonists. Pam took a deep breath as she took stock. Pam's fighting men, their orange skin smeared with blood, grinned like fools. They had done well, very well indeed. She winced as she counted them, yes, some were missing. There would be time for mourning. Her heart swelled as they came, led by Gerbald, to stand beside her.

The Swedish colonists stared at Pam, whispering among themselves "Who is she? She must be one of our rescuers!" Although they had seen Pam plenty of times, it was plain they didn't recognize her. This made her feel strangely proud. She grinned widely at them, trying not to preen, well, not to preen too much. Then she saw Bengta among the crowd, watching from her stretcher, her startling sea-green eyes shining with triumph, despite her terrible pain. All the pride and thrill of the battle drained out of Pam as she ran to the stricken young woman, towing the doctor along behind her by his coat sleeve. She took Bengta's hand while he went to work.

"Oh, Bengta, I am so sorry. What have they done to you? It's all my fault!"

Bengta smiled, gripping Pam's hand with what was left of her strength. Pam tried not to look at the woman's awful wounds, the doctor was already muttering what sounded like prayers and curses under his breath as he did what he could.

"No, Pam, *you* have *saved* us." Bengta's voice was heartbreakingly weak, Pam had to lean in close to hear her. "If you hadn't come, who knows how long we would have suffered? You gave us hope, made us brave."

Pam tried to reply, but her own voice failed her. She found herself at a loss for words as tears began to stream down her face. All she could do was try to smile while squeezing her heroic friend's hand, praying the doctor could save her.

The women attending the grievously wounded Bengta turned their tear streaked faces to Pam. "Please, ma'am, pray tell us, who are you?" they asked in humble tones, as if they sensed she was important, someone with power.

"Why, don't you *know* her?" Despite the pain of the effort, Bengta spoke up in a loud voice so all could hear, "She is our own Pam Miller, the Bird Lady of Grantville, who led our expedition from the start! She has revealed to us she has the heart of an eagle, the courage of a lion! She is our hero, the liberator of our people, here on this lonely isle so far around the world from old Sweden, this beautiful paradise which we will make our new home!"

Pam saw looks of recognition and adulation forming on their haggard faces. She found her voice and spoke up.

"Thank you, my friend, but it is *you* who are the true hero! It was brave Bengta who led her people to fight for their freedom! All hail Bengta!" she cheered at the top of her lungs, so it rang all around the harbor. The crowd took up her cry and then added "All hail Pam Miller! All hail the Bird Lady!" to the chant.

All of this made Pam blush, and smile, a rakish, fearless smile, one she was quite sure she had never felt before. She found it quite to her liking though and wore it as she was enfolded into the joyous embrace of her people.

CHAPTER 43: THERE'S GOT TO BE A MORNING AFTER

Bengta died during the night. Doctor Durand did all he could, but she had lost too much blood. Pam sat beside her to the end. She passed quietly, with a soft smile on her lovely face. Pam wept, held by Dore. Gerbald and the Bosun stood nearby, while Durand closed her pretty sea green eyes. A tear rolled down the French doctor's tired face, devastated to have lost one so young and brave. Pam decided she would indeed be his new best friend, even if he couldn't help Pers.

The butcher's bill had been counted. They had been fortunate, she knew, but even one casualty was just too damn many. Of the colonists, they had lost twenty-three total. Twelve, mostly older folk, had succumbed to the long months of captivity under cruel conditions. The rest had been killed fighting for their freedom, eight men and three women, including Bengta.

The details of Bengta's torture, when the slavers discovered she had started the revolt, made Pam draw blood from her palms as her nails bit into her clenched fist. By the time the colony's men could rush to Bengta's aid, it was too late. In their rage, they had torn Bengta's torturers apart limb from limb, confirming Pam's earlier suggestion that they were quite capable of doing so. She looked forward to mentioning it to the deposed captain in their next meeting. Pam decided despite her initial misgivings, being blown up had been too good for the slavers who had tried to escape. They were despicable, heartless men who sold their own brothers and cousins into slavery back in Africa, chosen by the renegades for duty here because of their ruthless cruelty. Pam vowed vengeance on their evil tribe.

Of the crew of the *Muskijl,* only fourteen had survived. Pam had lost five of the *Second Chance Bird's* men, two sailors and three marines. Their names and faces paraded through her mind, her friends, and protectors, smiling and full of life. That's how she wanted to remember them. She would never forget their sacrifice for her cause. *Löjtnant* Lundkvist had lost his leg after all, no fault of the doctor, who was a fine physician for his time. The proud young captain would have to walk on a pegleg for the rest of his life. And, finally, there was Pers, who she had brought into her heart as a true son, laying in a deep, silent sleep with no signs of awakening, somewhere between life and death. Doctor Durand told her there was hope, but she hardly allowed herself to feel it.

Pam stood high on the town's wall, looking across the harbor. Beside her, Dore's flag flapped in the early dawn breeze, proof of their triumph. Pam had gone out alone for a walk, needing quiet time to absorb all they had gone through. The torches and lanterns of the fleet of ships glowed warmly in the brightening, purple light, casting long, orange reflections across the bay's clear waters. The *Annalise* and *Ide* had been brought into the dock. The colonists slept there, back in the relative comfort of their bunks after months sleeping on the ground. The prisoners now occupied the former slave quarters, under guard by grim-faced colonists. Pam ordered the prisoners be given food and water, but it must be exactly the same as what the enslaved Swedes had received, not very damn much, or very damn often.

There were a few exceptions among the French. Five parolees were released into Durand's command, men who had been shanghaied into service, just as he had. Pam trusted the man and his judgment, but a couple of White Chessmen kept a close eye on them.

As for *Capitaine* Leonce Toulon, that heartless bastard was now in solitary confinement, locked in an outhouse. Pam had told her men to "Put this shit somewhere small and dark," and they had taken her literally. Actually, she thought it was too good for him, and hoped he was enjoying the stench. They would interrogate him the following night, when he ought to be plenty cooperative.

Pam shook her head in disbelief. How had she come to think such dark thoughts as these? How had she come to be a calm, cold, killer of men? Hard times made one harder, if you lived through them. They had been lucky, so lucky, to have pulled their crazy operation off without even more loss of life and limb. Pam wasn't much of a Methodist anymore, but she did say a brief prayer of thanks to a God that usually seemed distant and uncaring. All told, she thought, maybe He had been on her side for once. She prayed He would take their fallen into His arms up in Heaven. They had more than earned their places in Paradise. The thought comforted her, despite her modern doubts. She would take all the solace she could get.

The sun came up over the ocean as if in answer to her prayer, a golden beauty of a dawn, complete with radiant beams and towering lavender clouds. Pam couldn't help but smile. She had lost much, but she had won more. This island was *hers*, the dodo would be saved, and maybe, there was even hope for a rangy old crow like Pam Miller. Maybe she could make a new and better life for herself now that she had been through all this. *Redemption, la, hallelujah!* She clambered down the bamboo ladder to the trampled path below and set about looking for her friends.

Walking onto the dock, she was greeted by the Bosun who was bustling his way toward the shore. It was plain to see, he hadn't slept much, but his eyes were bright and lively. "Captain Pam! Good morning! I was just coming to fetch you!"

"Good morning! What's happening?"

"You have to come see for yourself, please, follow me!" The Bosun, quite uncharacteristically, took Pam by the hand, and practically dragged her behind him down the dock. Pam had to laugh aloud at such behavior from her usually stolid, and somewhat shy around the ladies, friend.

"What is it? What do you want to show me?" she asked, falling into a near jog to keep up with him.

He turned to her with glee on his red-cheeked face.

"It's a miracle, that's what it is!" and he would say no more. They passed by *Second Chance Bird* to board the *Effrayant*. One of her still slightly orange-skinned marines, broad-shouldered Ulf, stood guard. His face was split in a silly grin to match the Bosun's. Just what on Earth was going on?

Pam was led onto the deck and told to stand looking out at the water. She heard the Bosun whisper, then there were footsteps. She turned to see *Kapten* Lagerhjelm and beside him stood . . .

Pam's jaw dropped. She was seeing a ghost. It couldn't be! There, his long, red-and-silver hair a-glow in the morning sunlight like a halo, stood Torbjörn Nilsson, lost captain of the *Redbird*. Not a ghost, but an angel! He was thinner, and there was more silver in his hair than before, but he was still tall, with a warm smile spreading across his undeniably handsome face, and his icy blue eyes were shining. Against all hope, he was alive. *Alive!* Pam's heart skipped like a stone across a pond, her palms grew sweaty, and her knees wobbled.

Torbjörn chuckled, that warm, rumbling sound Pam had thought she would never hear again.

"Pam! It is so lovely to see you!" She just stared at him, her mind spinning around on a merry-go-round, unable to find a way off. He nodded, understanding her startled surprise.

"My apologies, Pam, I'm sure it's something of a shock, you must think me a ghost! I am so sorry for that. The fates cast me off to the north, while you went south. I suppose I must call you *Captain* Pam now. You have become quite the hero! I always thought there was more to you than meets the eye! It seems I shall have to find a new job. Perhaps you could use an able first mate?" He gazed at Pam, admiration on his face, and something more. Something Pam found perfectly wonderful.

Pam lunged forward, launching herself into an embrace that would have knocked him over if he hadn't been such a large man. She hugged him tightly, unable to form words yet. He hesitated in a gentlemanly way, then hugged her back with equal strength and affection.

"I am so glad to see you, Pam," he told her, "I was so afraid it was *you* who might have left this world. I thought about you every day and prayed that—" Torbjörn was unable to finish his sentence because Pam was kissing him on the lips with a fierce urgency she hadn't felt since she was seventeen. Torbjörn's eyes widened, but the good captain had the presence of mind to kiss her back, and there was no mistaking he was glad to be doing so.

The kiss ended, its initial passion consumed, and resolved into a lingering sweetness as their lips broke contact. Pam blinked at Torbjörn's smiling eyes. She was trembling, excited, ecstatic, and half-frightened out of her wits. *Did I do it right? It's been so long!* Her mind raced, feeling an echo of youthful panic. He held her a moment longer to give her a reassuring squeeze, an unspoken *"Yes, that was good. I wanted it, too."* Pam started a garbled apology for being so forward, but Torbjörn shushed her.

"Don't fret, lovely Pam, don't question this moment. We have much to talk about, and there will be time. For now, I know we all have a great deal of work to do, much of it sad. Go lead your people, they need you. I will be here with the Bosun when you are ready." He looked at her, checking to see if she was really going to be all right.

"That reminds me, I have something of yours!" Pam said, remembering what she carried with her. She disengaged from their embrace and reached into her pocket to pull out the up-time canary-yellow plastic whistle that belonged to Torbjörn, which she had found washed up on the shore after the wreck of the *Redbird*. She handed it to him, and he laughed, delighted, and surprised.

"I never thought I would see *that* again!" he exclaimed.

"I never thought I'd see *you* again." Pam told him, a relieved look on her face.

"Tell you what, you keep it for me, and if you ever should need me, just give a little whistle." he put it back in her hands and closed her fingers around it.

"You'll be hearing from me soon." she said, and they laughed.

Pam favored him with a big smile, a stunner she saved only for special occasions. He returned it in kind.

"I shall be counting the minutes." he replied with a bow and a grin.

Then the tall Swedish captain of lost *Redbird*, recently resurrected from the roll call of the deceased, strode to the far side of the warship to join the Bosun, who, once the kissing had started, had found some critical flaw in the warship's rigging that needed his utmost attention.

Pam grinned as she watched them, then walked back down the gangplank to the dock, feeling lighter than air. She would have skipped, if she hadn't been afraid it would lead to a nasty fall. There were still bloodstains on the rough planks and she was reminded of the mayhem they had created just the day before. It already seemed as if a century had passed, as if it had happened to someone else, a long time ago, or maybe she had just read it in a book. It wasn't the first time Pam had felt this way, and she doubted it would be the last. Was that really Pamela Grace Miller, divorced housewife, obsessive birdwatcher, and dorky scientist, now out sailing around the Indian Ocean, saving the dodo, kissing Swedish sea captains, ordering cannons fired, and sending men and women to their deaths?

She closed her eyes and opened them again. Apparently, it was, as she stared at the convincing bulk of the formerly French warship, *Effrayant* looming beside her, the powerful enemy vessel she had, she felt quite cleverly, and successfully, planned to capture. If not for her madcap plans, there would have been a much greater loss of life, and that comforted her somewhat. Still, too many friends had died. Another part of it was just dumb luck. She had since learned that the *Effrayant* had not been carrying a full complement of soldiers and she intended to find out why.

She took a long look at the vessel, admiring its majestic size and predatory grace. It was a killing machine, one of the deadliest this century had. It was by no means the largest type of warship extant in the day, but the light frigate was well-armed, fast, and deadly, more than a match for merchants, capable of giving the average enemy warship a good drubbing. Pam had since learned that the name *Effrayant* meant 'fearsome', which certainly did fit the beast. It had had beat poor *Muskijl* nearly to a pulp without breaking a sweat. She thought the appellation 'Fearsome' probably applied to her now, too. It fit her well, in fact.

"All in a bloody day's work for Captain 'Fearsome' Pam Miller, she-devil of the southern seas!" she exclaimed in her best pirate accent, shaking her head in wonder at what strange fortunes had brought her to be at the center of events such as these.

"Time travel," she muttered. "Not recommended. Check your expectations at the portal and hang on to your sanity."

Pam stalked down the dock toward the flag ship of her growing fleet, the gaily painted Chinese junk they called *Second Chance Bird*, in search of that sure-fire slice of sanity only a cup of coffee and a good breakfast could provide.

The decks of her ship were quiet, the men still sleeping off their hurts, both physical and mental. Still, there were signs of activity. As could be expected, she found Dore in her galley. Her tireless friend was pulling out all the stops as she prepared a mighty breakfast that could satisfy a hungry band of heroes who had more than earned that pleasure.

She smiled as Pam came in, handing her a cup of coffee. Pam nodded her thanks and sat in an out of the way corner, on an ornately-carved Chinese kitchen stool, painted in crimson lacquer.

Pam took a few sips of the hot, bitter brew, pleased she herself had harvested the wild, purple-and-yellow beans from the slopes of the mountain in the island's south. It was good coffee, with a rich, bitter flavor that would give any Columbia grown variety a run for its money. She inhaled its dark aroma, oxygen to a Himalayan climber. As she finished the cup, Dore arrived with a refill, her timing impeccable as always. Reality began to come back into focus as Dore's familiar movements, and the delicious cooking smoke of the galley worked with the caffeine to clear her head.

"That sure smells good!" she told Dore, now that she had paused from her fix long enough to have gotten a whiff of the delights breakfast was destined to hold.

"The French ship had bacon, eggs and bread! Real bread, baked only yesterday! Please ask your French doctor to identify their cook. I can make use of his talents, if he will behave properly and work for me. I have more mouths to feed now so he would be useful."

"I'll make that happen."

Pam marveled along her bizarre and convoluted way, she had become someone who could say that, and mean it. Neither of them mentioned Dore's last assistant cook, good-natured Mård, who had tragiclly been killed in the battle. It would be a day of funerals, but for now, the two friends needed to simply exist in the comfort and warmth of a civilized kitchen, forgetting they were on the bottom side of the world, and that it was spinning faster than they might have preferred. If Pam closed her eyes, she could picture her little red-and-white tiled kitchen, in her little pink house, in Grantville, back home in Germany. She laughed aloud at that last thought. *Germany is home now?* Dore looked over to see what was so funny, but Pam just waved her mug and asked for more coffee.

Garrett W. Vance

CHAPTER 44: A PRIVATE CONSULTATION

E arlier that morning, the remains of the slavers had been gathered up to be burned on the beach, as far down the shore from the settlement as they could get. Pam looked on, insisting on coming. Despite everything that had happened, one of the Lutheran pastors prayed for their heathen souls. Pam couldn't help but wonder, with no small amount of bitterness, if the slavers would have afforded her dead the same decency. Around nine in the morning, when the tide was right, the French fallen were taken to the open waters beyond the bay aboard the *Annalise*, to be given a Christian burial at sea. Those proceedings were allowed to take place in proper French naval custom, overseen by Doctor Durand and his small group of French parolees, under the respectful, but careful, watch of Swedish sailors and marines. The ceremony made Pam inexpressibly sad. Some of the French soldiers were boys in their teens, no older than her own adopted son, Pers.

Pam had faced war head-on, without hesitation, and had triumphed, but now it was time for the piper to be paid, and his price was dear. She sat in silence all the way back to the docks and no one interrupted her thoughts. Just as they were putting in, Pam turned to the doctor.

"Doctor Durand, I'd like to have a word with you in private, if you please."

"With pleasure, *Capitaine* Pam," he replied with a polite bow.

"Let's go up to my quarters. It's cooler there." She turned to the four Swedish marines from the *Muskijl*, assigned to accompany the small contingent of parolees. She would have to learn all their names at some point, but for now she smiled as she gestured to them for their attention, which they provided with military snap. Choosing the fellow she was pretty sure ranked highest, she gave her orders.

"*Korpral*, is it?"

"Yes, *Kapten* Pam." The man was still thin from his captivity, but well armed, and eager to please. Pam was glad to see confidence returning to the freed captives.

"Good man, *Korpral*. Now I woud like you to go down to the galley and ask *Frau* Dore to please provide your men and the Frenchmen in your charge with lunch. Once you have eaten, give our French guests the liberty of the *Second Chance Bird's* main deck. I shall be in my cabin conferring with Doctor Durand."

The *korpral* nodded, but looked concerned.

"Would you like one of us to accompany you?"

"Thank you, but that won't be necessary. Doctor Durand has proven himself a gentleman so far. If he should prove otherwise, I will shoot his brains out."

She pointed her chin toward the now notorious Smith and Wesson .38 revolver holstered on her belt. Everyone was well aware she had killed eight men with it and were suitably impressed. The doctor looked a bit pale, but maintained his composure.

"So, don't worry," Pam assured him, "I'll be fine. Have a good lunch and get some rest."

"Yes, ma'am!"

The *korpral* and his men saluted her, then led the way to the galley.

"Right this way, Doctor."

Pam motioned toward the ladder to the castle decks. He seemed to hesitate, being a gentleman through and through, but his situation was still tenuous, and perhaps thinking of Pam's revolver, he went first, not making any sudden moves.

The doctor seemed quite impressed by the Eastern opulence of Pam's quarters.

"I see the wealth of the Orient is not exaggerated. You say this ship likely belonged to a merchant, but this suite is worthy of a prince!"

"It's pretty swanky, yes."

She wasn't sure he knew what "swanky" meant, but the doctor nodded in polite agreement anyway.

"Here, have a seat, you must be as tired as I am."

They settled into comfortably stuffed chairs at the broad mahogany table she used as her desk. The doctor was visibly pleased as he settled into the satin cushions.

"*Ahh*, such luxury. Thank you for your kind hospitality, *Capitaine* Pam."

"It is I who owe you thanks, Doctor Durand. Without your help, more of my people would have died last night. You will be remembered as a hero by this colony, not as an enemy."

"That is good to hear. I hope they will not judge all Frenchmen by the gross injustices perpetrated by Leonce Toulon and his bandits. I was as much a slave as your colonists were, although I didn't suffer as they did. Still, I am glad to have my freedom again, or what freedom you grant until I earn your trust, *Capitaine*."

He smiled then, a sincere smile, full of understanding and patience.

Pam couldn't help but like the man, and had to admit he was kind of sexy. If hunky Torbjörn hadn't made his miraculous appearance when he did, this guy might have been in trouble. . . . The thought made her blush, so she laughed to cover it.

"I trust you, Doctor, but I have to give the Swedes more time before I let you and your trustees loose. You understand, I hope?"

" Please, do as you must. We are quite happy with our treatment."

" One of the things I'd like to ask is if you would join my personal staff. We could use a doctor in the colony, as we neglected to bring one! If you want to leave, you will be free to do so. If you leave, would you take the position until then?"

"I would be delighted ! The truth is, I am in no hurry to return to France. I find the weather here suits my tastes, and it would be good to be needed by so many people. How would it be if I promise you at least a year, then make more permanent arrangements if it should work out?"

"You got it, Doc! Welcome to our misfit band! Let's seal it with a toast,if it's not too early for you?"

Pam reached for the bottle of what she thought was saké kept on her desk, along with a set of beautiful red-and-gray glazed porcelain cups.

"By no means too early for a Frenchman, but just a little, please. We still have this evening's proceedings ahead of us."

Pam poured them each a full cup of the nearly clear liquid, then raised her cup to make a toast.

"To new comrades!"

"May we enjoy peace and prosperity!" he answered.

They drank their cups dry, the doctor seeming to like the taste.

Pam poured them each another cupful, which they savored slowly.

"It's a rice wine, I think. I tried it at a Japanese restaurant in my former century. Presumably, the Chinese make something similar. It grows on you." Pam told him, showing him the pale blue ceramic bottle with its gracefully brushed characters. She pointed at the painted label.

"I'm pretty sure these two characters combine to mean 'alcohol', but that's all I know about it."

"Truly, the Chinese are a civilized folk. This is very smooth."

Pam put her elbows on the table and gave her companion a measured look. The doctor met her gaze.

"All right. Now that we are working together in an atmosphere of mutual trust, I do have some questions about your former employers."

"Captors. Yes, I will tell you anything you want to know, that is, if it is something I myself know. Please understand, I was not in that bastard Leonce Toulon's privy counsel, but I saw and heard much."

"Good, that's good. First, how did they find my expedition? Was it an accident, or did they know we were coming?"

"I believe it was the latter. It was whispered the *capitaine* had been contracted by Cardinal Richelieu. A rumor, you understand, but I do believe someone learned of your Emperor Gustav's intention to put a colony on this island, thus beating we French to a territory that one day would have been ours according to the books of Grantville. As you must surely know, and forgive me for speaking frankly, the arrival of you up-timers has given the ruling heads of Europe fits. They are all studying your future history for ways to get ahead of their rivals, for any advantages such foreknowledge might afford."

"Yeah, I know It's gotten to the point where I take my bodyguard, Gerbald, to the library with me. It's full of creepy dudes who are obviously foreign spies, or worse. I'm sure that most of them are up to no good, but official policy is to share the knowledge. . . well, most of it, anyway."

"For myself, I am most grateful for that sharing. I have studied medical texts from your up-time collections. They are utterly brilliant and have been a great help to me in my practice. As for France, I can say little good has come of it. I fear for the future of my country and find it best to stay away for now. And so, after the failure of the League of Ostend, France has been seeking ways to increase its power across the globe. Your native North America is by now dotted with French colonies and there will be no Louisiana Purchase in this world's future history."

Pam was impressed with Durand's knowledge and insights. This guy had done a lot of reading, more than most, and he had his finger firmly on the pulse of current events to boot. *Probably best to keep a close eye on my good doctor, no matter how much I like him*, she thought.

The doctor continued, "And it's not just going to be the Atlantic. Some of our leaders see far, they will have their hearts set on controlling as much of the world as they can, including this Indian Ocean, and no doubt the Pacific beyond it. And so, they send minions to do their filthy works. I am almost certain all of

Leonce Toulon's violence here, and elsewhere, has the secret blessing of someone high up."

"Someone like Richelieu"

The doctor gave a very Gallic shrug.

"Perhaps. There is another thing I saw for myself The *capitaine* was quite taken with stories about bold pirates of the eighteenth century and fancies himself to be one. Are you familiar with the subject?"

"I thought that might be the case! Familiar, yes, I read up on maritime history to prepare myself for what I might face on this voyage. The violence and danger of life on the seven seas was not exaggerated! The whole pirate thing didn't really get into swing until the eighteenth century up-time, but I can see that won't be the case in this world."

"Indeed, I'm afraid *Capitaine* Toulon is the first of many, already he is not alone He was flying the flag of France at his capture, but I believe he had personal plans far beyond serving the crown's interests in these distant southern latitudes. When we sailed past the Cape of Good Hope, we rendezvoused with a small but well-armed galleon. That scoundrel Toulon loaned them half of *Effrayant*'s soldiers. I overheard much of what was said. Several captains are setting up a base on a small island off the coast of Madagascar, called Isle St Marie, which in the up-time history would become a famed pirate haven. The soldiers were needed to subdue a rebellious native population. The island has a strategic location, which is probably how it came to be used for that purpose in the future you come from. From there, they intend to prey upon *all* foreign shipping in the Indian Ocean. I believe the term is 'against all flags'. You have made a great victory here, but more such evil men will come to avenge the capture of *Effrayant* and its *capitaine*, so you must be ready!"

"Indeed. The age of the pirate has come early. Another question, who were those African slavemasters Toulon had working for him? Where did they come from?"

Before the doctor could answer, a worried Dore came rushing in.

"Pam, *Herr* Doctor, Pers is talking in his sleep! I think you had better come!" she announced loudly before ducking back out again.

They both stood, put their drinks on the table, and hurried after her.

"I'm afraid we shall have to finish our conversation another time, Doctor Durand." Pam told him as they climbed down the ship's ladder.

"Of course! I am completely at your disposal, *Capitaine*. Now it is vital that I attend to the boy immediately!"

"Thank you, Doctor!"

CHAPTER 45: THERAPY SESSION

The three of them hurried to Pers' sickroom to find the Bosun standing over the poor boy's bed.

"He was talking, but I don't think he knew I was here. It sounded like he might be back in his childhood, speaking to his mother. He was asking about dinner." The Bosun said in a voice full of hope and worry.

Pam put her hand on Pers' forehead. His skin felt cool, and she thought she could see a bit more color on his cheeks than the day before, but his expression was still slack, the face of one deep in a dream.

The doctor took Pers by the wrist to feel his pulse. He allowed a small smile to curl between his fancily mustachioed lip and pointy brown beard. Streaks of gray could be seen in both, as well as in his long sideburns. Pam found him handsome in a weird sort of way.

"A little better, perhaps, *Capitaine* Pam. You can see his color is returning, and his pulse is a bit stronger. He moved his legs earlier today, also a good sign. We must simply wait and see."

The French doctor kept his expression positive, but Pam could still see the doubt in the man's gentle, perpetually dark-circled brown eyes.

"I've heard it helps to talk to a patient in a coma, to tell them to wake up, and come back to us." Pam said. The doctor only raised his eyebrows, but the Bosun, whose face was amazingly long for one so round and ruddy, brightened

"Here, let me try," the Bosun said, his voice trembling He y feared for the boy, injured while following orders he himself had issued, a boy he doted on even as he frog-marched him around the deck from one duty to the next.

"Pers! Pers, it's Bosun. I'm sorry you're not feeling good, but you need to wake up now."

There was no sign from Pers' slack face he had heard. The Bosun looked over to Pam

Pam had an idea.

" Talk to him like you would when he's awake. You know, order him around a bit! Give him a good shout!"

The Bosun looked taken aback at the surprising suggestion, but then smiled at what he considered must be his captain's great wisdom. Shouting was one of his strong suits. Doctor Durand had an alarmed look on his face. He was about to say something when the Bosun charged ahead with the new plan.

"Right!" he said and flashed them an eager grin. He bent down over the unconscious youth's dreaming face and let loose in a voice like thunder: "You! Boy! Get your lazy ass out of the sack, Pers, and get to work! We haven't got all day, so move it! I want you on deck NOW!"

The resounding shout in the cabin's close quarters made everybody jump, and Pam detected a jerk in Per's lanky frame, a sign that he had sensed the Bosun's voice on some level.

"Good!" Pam clapped the Bosun on the back, "I saw him twitch!"

"As he should, I run a clean deck, and everyone does their share!" He looked at Pers with hope in his eyes. "I hope he heard me, I really hope he did. Wake up, my boy, wake up!" he shouted again.

Doctor Durand stared at them as if they were both utterly mad.

"Excellent!" he proclaimed "What an amazing new therapy! We must write a treatise on its wondrous effects for all the physicians of Europe to share! Now, if you will both, *please leave*, I will attend to my patient in restful silence!"

The good doctor's deep voice rang with that special commanding tone that only the best doctors, teachers, and chefs seemed able to produce, a tone that made even the Bosun jump quickly

"Out!" he added, just to be sure he had been understood, but no further urging was necessary.

Pam couldn't help but laugh as she and the Bosun got stuck trying to squeeze out the narrow cabin door at the same time, in their effort to remove themselves as quickly as possible. Once sorted out, Pam closed the door on what she was sure was a stream of muttered French curses emanating from the good doctor. They fled to the upper deck, still worried about their young friend, but feeling more hopeful for his recovery than ever before.

CHAPTER 46: TWILIGHT AND EVENING BELL

At five o'clock, Pam led the funeral procession from the docks, past the half-finished buildings of the town, and through the gently sloping fields to a pretty knoll that overlooked the bay. This was the site the people had chosen for their Hero's Cemetery, and Pam thought it a good one. The graves had been dug, with temporary wooden markers at their heads, to be replaced with stone later. Bengta was given pride of place in the cemetery's center. Beside her would lie Asmund, who had been her fiancé, also killed in the revolt. Pam mourned the loss of such young souls, their lives snatched away as they were beginning a new future She began to cry and made no effort to stop.

To heroic Bengta's left, were the final resting places of her fellow colonists. Some had died during their enslavement, their remains moved here from temporary graves, along with others who had given their lives in the battle to free the colony. To her right were the graves of the sailors and marines who had guided them here and who died while liberating the settlemen .With its high position and sweeping view of the town and harbor, Pam felt the location itself was a fitting monument to people so brave as these.

Pam continued to let her tears flow as they wished, their release was almost soothing, a gentle balm to the anguish she felt. She stood between Torbjörn and the Bosun, grateful for the comfort of their combined presence. Nearby, Gerbald and Dore looked on. The two were holding hands and just the sight of them made Pam feel better. Her men looked sad and brave, all lined up in their best Chinese finery. She was immensely proud of them all.

The eldest of Lutheran pastors began the ceremony. Pastor Petrus was a serious, but kindly looking fellow in his mid sixties. His voice was clear, deep, and full of what Pam thought of as 'Godly conviction'. Pam's Swedish was now good enough she could understand everything except for some obscure words in the older hymns.

As she expected, Pam would be called upon to say a few words, as would the Bosun and the newly minted Captain Lundkvist. Although he had to be carried to the grave site by his men, Lundkvist stood firmly against his crutch, bearing the pain of his lost leg with grim pride. Pam went last, after stirring speeches from her friends. Being, however unfortunately, an old hand at funerals, she ignored her usual butterflies and stepped forward.

She kept her speech short, filled with emotion, praise for the courage and selflessness of the fallen and gratitude for the survivors of these trials for their stalwart support, and continuing dedication to the cause. She ended by reciting Tennyson's *Crossing the Bar,* feeling she had spoken those beautifully appropriate words too often of late. Pam returned to her place of safety between Torbjörn and the Bosun and found herself taking Torbjörn's hand. He smiled warmly and gave it a gentle squeeze. Her mind was awhirl with emotion, but at least some of it was good.

Pam cried as each shrouded body was lowered into the ground, shedding as many tears for the young colonists as for her beloved lost comrades from the *Redbird* crew. That afternoon, she had found a healthy patch of flowers along the forest's edge she thought were hibiscus, wide yellow petals with a blushing pink center and stamen. They weren't roses, but they would do. She placed one on each grave, whispering farewell to each soul.

She was among the last to leave the cemetery, as the evening shadows grew long, and dusk approached.

Torbjörn waited for her. She was pleased he wanted to be her escort. Other thoughts about the handsome captain clamored for attention, but she pushed them back. She was just too tired for that, maybe tomorrow! They walked down the hill in amiable silence, glad for each other's company. As they walked through town at sunset, bells began to ring, on the ships as well as a proper church bell the colonists had brought with them. Pam couldn't help but chuckle as the long, low tones of *Second Chance Bird*'s Chinese gong joined the medley. They paused until the last bell stopped, a final salute to lost friends.

When they reached the dock, Pam turned and gave a tired, but appreciative smile.

"Torbjörn, thank you for staying with me during the funeral. You were a great comfort to me."

"The pleasure was mine, Pam." His baritone voice was full of sincerity. "Is there anything more I can do for you? I am at your service."

Pam thought there probably was quite a bit more he could do for her, and her body began to tingle in a very pleasant way, but she ignored it. *Not now you ninny,* she chided herself in her mind. *You would fall asleep about the time things got interesting. There's time!*

"That's very kind, Torbjörn, and I will take you up on that soon, but today I'm done. I haven't had any sleep, and I'm about ready to fall down in my tracks." She paused, but made herself press on, "How about you join me for dinner tomorrow night? Dore has amazing recipes in her new Chinese galley. I'll wager it's the best food on this side of the world."

"Absolutely! I have very much missed *Frau* Dore's most excellent cuisine"

He paused a moment before he said, "But not as much as I have missed you, Captain Pam."

Pam felt her heart whiz around a few bumpy corners on its roller coaster ride. She took his hands and stretched up on her tippy-toes to plant a kiss on his lips, accepted with obvious relish. Brief, but as sweet as honey.

"I missed you, too, Captain Torbjörn. A lot."

She started to tear up again, unable to stop.

"I thought you were gone, you know, but I didn't really believe it, not in my heart."

She threw herself into his arms and they spent a few long minutes in a tight embrace, Torbjörn stroking her hair to comfort her.

"I'm here, I'm here with you now. Don't cry, it's all right now, my brave Pam," he whispered softly in her ear, which made her feel like melting butter.

When she stopped shaking he let her go. As they parted, she ran her palm across his chest as if to make sure he was real.

"See you tomorrow," she said, then slipped away to her ship's main deck. Pam couldn't stop a satisfied little smile come to her lips. *Score!* she thought and giggled as she climbed the ladder to her cabin.

Pam fell onto her soft, pillow-strewn bed like a load of lead ingots. She was so excited about her upcoming dinner with the captain, she was sure she wouldn't be able to sleep. Fifteen seconds later, she was out cold.

CHAPTER 47: A MYSTERIOUS FIGURE

Pam awoke early the next morning. She had slept soundly and felt completely rested. She lay in her bed for a few minutes while mulling over the chaotic events of the past few days and felt a bit, despite the terrible losses. She had taken a longshot and it had led to victory. It wasn't often she got to indulge in pride, but now was one of those times. *Good job, Pammie!* she thought, *you really kicked ass!* Not only that, but she had a date tonight with a man direct from the young Kris Kristofferson school of hunkiness! The thought of Torbjörn made her feel like she was falling, but in a pleasant way.

She got out of bed and opened the window. The sun hadn't risen, but she had no doubt Dore would be in the galley and there would be coffee! She slipped on a canary yellow silk robe and slid her feet into a pair of slippers woven from sturdy grass. She had adapted quite well to her Asian wardrobe. The unusual garments were beginning to feel as natural as a pair of jeans.

Down on the main deck, she paused at the rail to gaze at the purple-lit sea beyond the harbor. It would be another glorious sunrise. As she turned to head for the ladder leading below-decks, she jumped A ghost was standing at the rail near the prow, white sheets flapping in the morning breeze. Squinting her eyes for a better look, she saw the apparition was busy polishing the deck rail with a corner of one of the sheets.

"Holy shit." Pam hurried to the prow and paused a few feet from the mysterious figure. She had an idea and hoped she was right.

"Pers?" she asked

Her 'ghost' turned and she saw it was Pers, his torso wrapped in one bedsheet, another sheet over his head, and loosely tied at his chest. His face was pale, but he looked alive enough.

"Hey, Pam!" he answered, as if waking from a coma and polishing the rail while dressed as a phantom was normal "It sure is cold this morning! Do you know where my clothes are?"

He was still about half out of it, but it was a huge improvement over comatose! She grinned, her heart bursting with relief and joy.

"I'm not sure, Pers, but we will find them." Her voice shook but she stayed calm. "So, what are you doing?"

"Oh, the Bosun was yelling at me to get to work, so I thought I better get to it. Say, where did he go?"

Pers looked around the deck, his eyes still a bit glazed, but his awareness was growing.

"What time is it anyway?" The young man's face grew perplexed as he began to realize that maybe his situation was just a bit odd.

Pam felt happy tears roll down her cheeks, warm drops in the cool ocean breeze.

"It's morning and you were sleep-walking. Now you are awake!"

She hugged him tightly then, taking care not to dislodge the sheet he had somehow managed to wrap securely around his tall, lanky frame.

"Oh! Good morning!" he said, embarrassed as he fumbled at the sheets to make sure certain private areas remained fully covered.

"Yes, it is indeed a good morning, Pers! Now come on, let's go get you into some proper clothes before you scare the wits out of someone else!"
***

Doctor Durand was pleased and relieved as he examined a now dressed Pers while Pam, the Bosun, and Dore paced around outside the door, nervous, but hopeful. After determining his patient was out of danger, he callled them in, causing a brief jam-up as they all tried to push their way through the door at once. Durand just rolled his eyes at their graceless Germanic ways. While they sorted themselves out, he *ahemed* loudly to get their attention and spoke.

"My friends, I am pleased to announce that young Pers here is making a strong recovery. His pupils are still a bit dilated, but they are returning to normal, his pulse is strong and steady," he told the delighted onlookers. "Pers, how do you feel?" he asked in English, having been informed Pers could speak the language, thanks to Pam and Gerbald's tutelage.

The young patient looked perplexed, but was coming around.

"I feel pretty good, still a little light-headed maybe. Umm, excuse me for my rudeness, but who are you?"

Everyone laughed. The doctor had spent much of the last few days at Per's bedside.

"I am Doctor Durand, and you are a lucky young man. You have been unconscious for several days. Tell me, what's the last thing you remember?"

Pers' light-blond brows furrowed as he reached for memories damaged by the fall.

"Well, I was climbing up in the rigging and I slipped. I think I fell, and I was very frightened, but then the memory stops."

"You did fall, and you injured your head quite badly."

Pers began to reach up to explore his injury, but the doctor stopped him.

"The injury is bruised and needs more time to heal, so please don't touch it for now. Do you feel any pain there?"

"Just a little, like I would if I bumped my head on a beam belowdecks."

"Well, that's good. Do you remember anything after your fall, and before you woke up ?"

"Why, yes. I could hear the Bosun shouting at me to get to work. I wanted to, but I couldn't seem to get up!"

Pam let out a whoop and clapped the Bosun on the back. The Bosun laughed and they both chanted, "It worked, it worked!" while dancing a happy little jig together.

Doctor Durand once again rolled his eyes.

"Yes, it seems 'shout therapy' might have a place in the care of coma victims, after all. Your friends were trying to reach you, to help you wake up, and apparently their efforts succeeded."

Pers nodded, as he watched Pam and the Bosun's celebration with wide-eyed fascination.

Once they settled down, the doctor turned to them.

"Now, the boy is better, but he is still on the mend. I believe some exercise, both physical and mental, would do him some good, but not too much and not in the heat of the day. Can you find him some light duties, *Monsieur* Bosun?"

"I can indeed, *Herr* Doctor. I'll take good care of him, don't you worry!"

Dore moved over to the bedside to take Pers' hand in hers.

"It is good to have you back with us, young Pers. Now, are you hungry?"

Pers eyes lit up as brightly as they ever had at that question.

"Yes! I could eat an elephant!"

Dore patted his hand, proud that she knew what their patient needed.

"I thought as much. Very good then, come with me."

She and the doctor helped him to his feet. Pam thought he seemed much steadier than he had during his pre-dawn haunting of the deck.

Before they exited, Pam took her adopted son in a careful embrace. "You scared the hell out of me, Pers. I am so glad you're OK now!" She told him, then placed a gentle motherly kiss on his cheek.

"Thanks, Momma Pam. I'm OK now I think. I'm just glad to be back!"

Doctor Durand turned to Dore.

"Madame Dore, I know he must be starving, but please, you mustn't feed him too much, too quickly. I advise you start with a warm broth and barley, or easy to digest food. Once we are sure he can keep that down, you can give him something more, but nothing too heavy, at least for a day or two."

"It shall be as you say, *Herr* Doctor, and thank you for your kind care of our young man."

Dore favored Durand with one of her all too rare radiant smiles, making the cool and collected gentleman blush.

"Yes, good job, Doc, we really appreciate all your work!" Pam stuck out her hand to shake, which he stared at as if it were a hot poker. After a moment's confusion, he extended his own hand in return and let her pump it.

"Thank you for your kind words my friends, but really, I was just doing my duties as a physician It is my honor to serve."

In a celebratory mood, they followed Dore to the galley. Happiness had made everyone hungry.

CHAPTER 48: A BIT OF EXERCISE

Pam had on her hiking clothes and was carrying her grandmother's walking stick when she arrived at the galley for lunch. A slightly less orange-colored Gerbald was finishing a sandwich. It looked like the makeup was finally wearing off.

"Hey! Where are you off to?" he asked, starting to get up.

"Sit down, I'm just going to walk along the forest's edge in those upper fields. I want to check out what kind of trees are growing in these hills and start thinking about intelligent logging. I hate to cut trees, but the reality is, we need to finish the town walls. At least this way, I can control the damage."

"I'll come with you." Gerbald said, before hurrying to finish his sandwich.

"No need today, my friend, take the day off. I'll be fine."

Pam smiled at him. The truth was, she wanted to be alone, and even Gerbald's quiet-when-she-wanted-him-to-be presence was more than she could bear at the moment. Dore handed her a sandwich and a piece of fruit wrapped up in a parcel made of a banana leaf. Pam shoved it into her rucksack, nodding her thanks.

"Be careful, please, Pam." Dore said, concerned for her safety, as usual.

Gerbald and Dore both looked unhappy at Pam going off by herself, but kept quiet, aware of how stubborn their friend could be. The three of them had become very tightknit over the years. Her older 'brother and sister' couldn't help being over-protective of 'their Pam'. She flashed them a grin and laughed.

"Knock it off, you two. What a couple of worry warts! I'm outta here!"

Pam headed up the dock to shore at a jaunty pace, pausing only to say hello to sailors and citizens along the way. Several of them, concerned for her safety, asked her if she wanted company on her walk, but she declined all offers.

"I'm just going to follow the edge of the upper field around. I won't go into the forest."

The Swedes nodded She had learned they valued solitude and could understand Pam needed time to herself.

Leaving the growing town behind, Pam was drawing near the cemetery on its knoll off to her left. Beyond it she could see the compound where the French prisoners were being held *I still need to have my interview with Captain Dickhead, but not today, let's not think about that stuff just now.* With a physical shake of her head that sent her unruly dishwater blond locks flying, Pam cleared all thoughts of death and destruction out of her mind. *I need to get ready for the next phase. I need to look to the future.* Managing to hang onto positive thoughts, Pam hurried, veering to the right to avoid the entire area.

Pam reached the bottom of the upper field and stayed to the right. It was a broad rectangle of twelve acres stretching uphill from the harbor. Stumps could be seen here and there, but parts had been natural meadow before the French decided to have it all clear cut. That made her scowl, but what was done, was done. A small herd of the cows the colonists had brought, watched her with mild brown eyes, while chewing native grass. So far, the cows, a flock of sheep with their well-trained shepherd dogs, chickens and geese, and horses were the only domestic animals allowed on the island. Pigs, goats, and cats were banned due to their penchant for escaping to become destructive feral pests, exactly what this fragile ecosystem did not need.

Pam feared the day a ship would bring rats, monkeys, or worse—it was inevitable. She stopped to look out at the harbor and decided extending the dock would be a priority. In fact, she would order a customs house built right out over the water, creating a buffer between ship and shore. It would at least stem the tide of unwanted animal immigrants. That made her smile. She whistled an aimless tune as she continued hiking.

When she reached the tree line, she paused to look back at the town and harbor, a picturesque scene. The houses and buildings that had been completed were now being painted a rich, brownish red. Pam had learned this was called *falun* red and was a Swedish tradition. The trim was done in white and Pam thought it all looked pretty great.

"A little bit of the old country," Pam said to herself, "Traditions are good, in moderation."

She knew there was going to be a difficult time ahead as the colony put the modern farming methods Pam had taught them into practice.

"We'll make some new traditions here, too."

Working her way along the field's edge, Pam admired the lush, tropical vegetation. Behind a border of light-loving flowering shrubs, tall trees loomed, some of them giants. Pam saw ebony, tambalacoque, and bois dentelle trees among others. They could get rich just on the lumber Sensible logging, forest renewal, and habitat preservation were among Pam's top priorities. There would be no more clear cutting. In her reading, she had learned too many places had foolishly used all their timber within the first fifty-years of colonization, which had resulted in poverty, lacking that valuable resource. That would not happen here.

Pam had spent long hours finding every scrap of information she could on the island's flora and fauna, from both up-time and down-time sources. Still, there were many species she couldn't identify. Eventually, they would have to be documented and named. It would be a daunting task.

"I should have brought along help for that," she grumbled

Turning her eyes upward, she jokingly said "Dear Lord, please send me a boat load of eager graduate students!" Maybe someday. Meanwhile she was on her own, the lone scientist.

Pushing thoughts of the huge amount of work and enormous responsibilities that were hers, she tried to concentrate on the walk. She wanted to get a feel for the land, figure out how to use it best, with the needs of the colony and the environment both in mind.

About halfway up, Pam decided to cut across to the forest on the far side. Walking through the grass and meadow flowers was easy going. She surprised a flock of birds with bright orange heads and throats on an olive-green body. They were startlingly beautiful, and Pam gasped in delight. *A nice reminder of why I am here. It's not just the dodos. This entire island is a treasure trove of wildlife.* The flock disappeared into the trees, a cloud of flaming color dissolving into the cool green.

Reaching the tree line, she cast about in the underbrush at the forest's edge, looking for one particular place. After a few minutes she found it. Pam was standing in the exact spot she had first met Bengta. She sat down in a patch of soft grass. A wave of emotion came over her, sadness and loss, but also pride. Pam began to speak to her lost ally.

"Oh, Bengta, you were too young to die saving the damn dodos. I know you came here for more than that, for a new life, and I blame myself for what happened to you. I'm responsible. You are the real hero. You sacrificed everything to free this colony, to make my dream possible. I will never forget you, and I promise you, I will do everything I must to make this a success! You are my inspiration. Please, lend me your strength, I need it now more than ever. God bless you, Bengta."

Pam smiled through her tears, at the lovely surroundings, thinking maybe, just maybe she could sense the spirit of the heroic young woman, urging her on. Real or not, the feeling was a comfort. Sighing, Pam wiped her face on her sleeve, then pulled herself to her feet with the aid of her grandmother's trusty oak walking stick.

She spent a few more minutes taking in the scene, marking its location with a small cairn of stones

"I will make this place a park in your honor, Bengta."

Suddenly, she laughed aloud, a bright sound among the hushed chirp and twitter of forest birds. It occurred to her there would be a historical marker here, the bulky, stone kind found in old battlefields and around national monuments. Her own name would be inscribed on a copper plate along with Bengta's and the thought of it made her laugh even harder.

"A hillbilly ex-housewife like me, going down in history! I'm going to be part of a future tourist attraction! Holy moly, who'd-a-thunk it?" Still chuckling at the absurdity of it all, she continued up the tree line.

Reaching the top of the vast field, Pam looked down its length. She was a good mile from the town now so all the buildings and boats seemed like toys. She laughed at *Second Chance Bird*, the gaudiest of them all, looking for all the world like a curio picked up at a seaside gift shop. It was three o'clock, according to her trusty watch, and the slow moving air held a golden haze, making the world an idyllic dream.

"Home. This is my home now." Pam decided it for certain, then and there.

She hadn't had much time to think about what would happen after the colonists were rescued and things were put back in order. She knew damned well what the document the princess had written for her meant to her future. She had drafted it herself, even though she had been afraid of the weight of it then. It was an insurance policy, a card to play, if she had no other choice. She didn't have to follow its letter, if she decided she didn't want to. Now it felt like her destiny. She was ready for the responsibility. She would call a town meeting in a day or two, and everybody would hear the princess' wishes. It wouldn't be much of surprise, at least not to the Swedes.

Dore and Gerbald on the other hand . . . Well, they would probably do whatever they felt was best for 'their Pam' and she felt guilty for crazy kind of loyalty, but they had followed her this far, and it had been their choice. Now they would have to make another In any case, it was time to start the long process of making this colony a viable economic and self-sufficient entity, without wrecking the island's ecology. She had signed up for this, and she would see it through.

Her kin back in Grantville came to mind, her elderly parents, and her son's new family. Damn, she wished she could be there for Crystal and the new baby, but wasn't any other way. She go back to Grantville to personally deliver Princess Kristina's dodos as promised, but it wouldn't be until she was sure things here were where she needed them to be She would have to break it to her family that her return was just a visit, not forever. This was where her true calling was.

Heading back into town, an idea came to her, and although she tried to resist, she felt herself drawn to the pier. It didn't take long to find Torbjörn, shirtless and sweating, as he worked under the late afternoon sun. Grinning, she pulled out his little yellow whistle and gave it a merry toot.

His gaze turned and a bright smile appeared.

"Hey you!" she called, "Got time to go for a bit of a walk?"

"Lead the way!"

They strolled hand in hand down the beach, away from town. They didn't talk much, content to enjoy the afternoon and each other. Passing a wooded point, they came to a small river and turned to follow it upstream, walking through soft meadow grass along its low banks. The water was crystal clear and cool. They paused to take a drink, feeling it would be safe in such a pristine environment. Pam turned to the tall Swede, and before she could think much about it, she spoke to him in a soft voice.

"So, Torbjörn... Do you know how to swim?"

"But, of course. Do you?"

"Yeah. What do you say we jump in the river and cool off?"

"An excellent idea." Hand in hand, they strolled farther upstream to a sandy beach, at a bow in the river where the water was slow and inviting, sunlight dappling its smooth surface.

Pam gazed dreamily at Torbjörn, who already had his shirt off. He was one hell of a handsome man, a grown-up version of the long-haired 1970s poster boys that posed on her bedroom walls in her teens. The truth was, she herself looked better than she had in years, more like Pam Miller in her twenties than forties. She was physically fit, and possibly too thin for a change! She had allowed her hair to grow long, down past her shoulders, the silvery streaks of premature gray arcing through it were natural highlights! She untied her ponytail and shook it so that it expanded into a feline mane. She felt Torbjörn's eyes upon her and sensed his approval on some kind of deep, instinctual level.

Oh, what the hell, she thought, whatever was left of her self-consciousness evaporating along with the sweat on her arms in the cool riverside air. *Time to go for it.* She pulled off her clothes and felt comfortable doing so in front of this man. She paused to give Torbjörn a good, long look, then waded in, where she made a graceful, shallow dive. She surfaced and looked to see Torbjörn had now lost his trousers and smiled to see she had, indeed, made an impression on him. He was a glorious nude. Years of hard work had made him into a muscular

Norse god, his long, curly hair a red-gold crown in the sweet, late afternoon light. He charged in after her with a great splash, making her squeal with delight.

They didn't touch for a time, content to swim side by side against the slow current, letting the river wash away the aches and pains of their trials. Eventually, they paused beneath the grassy bank, under a curtain of meadow flowers hanging over its edge. They kissed, softly, barely touching at first, standing with feet lightly anchored in the sandy bottom, their bodies weightless in the gentle press of the river's flow. They drew closer, their kisses grew hungrier, their embrace more powerful.

After a timeless time, Torbjörn pulled himself back from their steamy kisses to look into Pam's stormy gray eyes, a sight which always captivated him, mesmerized him with their power. Pam was a strong and graceful tigress, wild and fearless! He had never met anyone else like her, a warrior goddess from the old stories, confident, courageous! He wanted her, knowing she wanted him, too. He smiled, a question. Pam smiled back, an answer. They embraced, moving together slowly, then more swiftly, their soft cries a chorus for the river's liquid music. Eternity passed by in ecstasy, and then passed by again.

* * *

Pam awoke in a grassy nest, deep in the meadow, naked, a warm, masculine arm draped over her shoulder. She blinked for a moment or two, trying to remember just how she had ended up here, then laughed as the memory of the tumultuous last few days came, with all its terrors and thrills. It was still early evening so her friends wouldn't be worried yet. She closed her eyes for a few more minutes, soaking in the heat emanating from her Swedish sea captain, a comfort in the cool sea breeze. After a cozy little idle, the shadows deepened, and it was time to get back. She removed the delightful arm, sat up, and began to wonder where her clothes were! She found them soon enough, blushing at the thought of the entire town turning out to look for her, and finding her bare as a newborn and not alone!

She awakened Torbjörn with a kiss. They had been through hell, but right now, at this moment, she realized she was about the happiest she had ever been.

"Time to go. Dore will have supper on soon."

Torbjörn's bright smile glowed in the evening shade.

Hooray for me! she thought to herself, as she helped her still drowsy man find his clothes. As they walked back to town hand in hand, Pam smiled, knowing that neither of them would get much sleep in the coming night.

CHAPTER 49: LOOKING GLASS

"You know, we still don't have a name for the colony." Pers said to Pam as they enjoyed the sunrise on the junk's high castle deck.

Torbjörn was asleep in her quarters, she had managed to tire the poor fellow out, a memory she would treasure. Gerbald had not yet emerged, but Dore was up of course, and the delightful smell of brewing coffee came wafting up from the galley. Pam didn't know why she was up so early. By all accounts, she should have slept the entire day away, but instead, she felt more invigorated than she had in ages. *Nothing like a good old roll in the hay to melt the years away!* She tried to stop thinking about her wonderful night and couldn't.

"Hello? Pam?" Pers' young, earnest face looked at her, bemused by her distraction.

"Oh, I'm sorry, Pers. Just spacing out. A name for our new town, yeah, it's time for that, isn't it? Do you have any ideas?"

"Not really. I think it should be up to you and I bet the rest would agree."

Pam moaned, realizing the yoke of responsibility would be settling on her now that the perils has passed. There was a lot of work to do, a whole lot, and she would have to do her part She bit her upper lip in thought as she gazed down at the dawn-lit waters. The sea was perfectly still, not a puff of breeze or errant wave to disturb its crystalline perfection. She smiled at her reflection below, eyes were tired from lack of sleep, but she was looking good, in the best shape of her life. She reached up to adjust her hair, the sea a virtual mirror. A mirror . . .

"Pers, I've got it! I have a name! Look down there, what do you see?"

"I see our reflections. The water is very calm today."

"Right! It's often like this around sunrise and sunset. It's just like a mirror! Do you remember the name of that Lewis Carroll book I showed you?"

"The one that inspired the princess to send us to save the dodo? It was *Through the Looking Glass*, wasn't it?"

Pam marveled at how clear her adopted teen's English had become. He certainly had a knack for languages, a real chip off her block.

"Exactly. What's another word for 'looking glass' in English?"

Pers' bright blue eyes looked upward for a moment as he rummaged through his mind. A moment later, he smiled and said "A mirror!"

"Exactly! Let's call this place Port Looking Glass, in honor of Lewis Carroll. Kristina will love that!"

Pers was always impressed when reminded his new mom was on a first-name basis with the princess.

"That sure sounds nice, and fitting, too." Pers nodded his approval. A hearty voice emanated from below-decks, the call for coffee, and they hurried down the steep ladders to the galley, as fast as they dared.

CHAPTER 50: THE ONES THAT GOT AWAY

Port Looking Glass, Captain Pam's quarters on Second Chance Bird, December 15th, 1635

"They *what?*" Pam shouted, her voice like sharp metal.

Ulf, the Swedish marine who had brought her the bad news flinched, hoping the American saying about 'shooting the messenger' really was just a saying.

"They escaped, Captain Pam, in the night. They all got away, including the officers and their loyal sailors." Ulf's voice was heavy with professional embarrassment. Even though the strapping young soldier had a full foot and a hundred pounds on her, he shrank back as Pam began pacing around her cabin in the grip of a rage.

"How?"

Pam tried not to shriek at the poor fellow, fighting to keep her voice even. Gerbald, Doctor Durand, and Lundkvist, looked on, all staying sensibly near the door.

"One of the French trustees did it. We haven't been watching them closely since the doctor vouched for them."

This made the good doctor wince, his hand moving to his brow in a gesture of pain. Ulf gave him an apologetic shrug before continuing.

"It turns out this one was still loyal to that Toulon bastard. He snuck up to the prison and cut a hole in the back wall. The civilians on guard duty were all asleep." At least he had managed to get that particular buck passed. *Incompetent farmers trying to do a soldier's work and failing completely.*

Pam scowled. *Hot, stinking DAMN!* Their real military guys were stretched thin right now, with a harbor full of ships and a town to attend to, so it wasn't that big a surprise. Even seasoned soldiers were known to fall asleep on guard duty and it wasn't exactly an Alcatraz they had been running. Two more days, and that evil bastard would have been hanging high. She had intended to pull the lever herself!

Doctor Durand looked miserable, his long mustache drooping

"Captain Pam, I am most embarrassed. I hold myself responsible. It was I who thought we could trust the man who did this. He appeared to be an honest young sailor to my eyes, pressed into service against his will as I was."

"It isn't your fault, Doc. You're not a mind reader. That snake Toulon must have bribed the kid with an offer he couldn't refuse." She looked at everyone gathered, her expression becoming sad.

"I want to make it clear, this is all *my* fault. I should have dealt with Toulon right away, but I got so busy with personal stuff, I blew it off for later. Now he's gone. I have only myself to blame. Here I am, leading you when I don't have a friggin' idea what I'm doing. I must be out of my mind, and depth."

"Let me say I disagree with the last statement." Lundkvist spoke up. "Your madcap ideas are what brought us to victory. You are a natural leader and we have faith in you. Do you think a bunch of hardened sea dogs like us would follow you if we didn't?"

This was followed by a murmur of agreement from all gathered. Pam managed a grateful   smile.

"Well, you guys must all be nuts, too, but so be it. Seriously though, if you think I'm screwing up along the way, I need you to tell me, I value your experience, there's no way I could have managed any of this without you."

She turned back to the sweating Marine, who looked somewhat relieved his captain had grown calmer.

"What happened next, Ulf?" she asked him, in what she hoped was a comforting manner. He let out a nervous breath and continued.

"They made their way down to the beach where the traitor had a pinnace waiting, one of *Ide*'s tenders. It could hold them all and is seaworthy enough for the season. We figure they're heading to Isle Saint Marie, that's where they say Toulon has his pirate base. They can make it, if this good weather holds."

Kapten Lundkvist stepped forward, his new, polished-wooden peg leg giving him a maritime air.

"The *Effrayant* can be ready to pursue within the hour. We can still catch them!"

Pam shook her head no.

"I appreciate your gumption, but it would be searching for a needle in a haystack. We need *Effrayant* to stay close to protect the colony. If Toulon is foolish enough to come back, we'll finish him One day, when Swedish power has grown strong enough here, I intend to go burn their little pirate paradise to the ground. You and your ship will be leading the charge, I promise! All I ask is that you save *Capitaine* Leonce Toulon for me. I intend to kill that motherfucker with my own hands, for Bengta and all the others. His ass is *mine*."

Pam glared so fiercely into the distance Gerbald was sure the escaped pirate would feel a tingling at the nape of his neck, wherever he was.

After a long, glowering silence, Pam shrugged, shaking off her frustration and anger.

"Well, that's that, business for another day. Now, we need to get ready for the town meeting, and before noon or not, I need a drink. Any takers?"

All the men breathed a collective sigh of relief to see the storm had passed. They gathered around the big, red-lacquered table while Pam uncorked a jug of rice wine, pouring it into the small ceramic cups the Chinese used for such occasions.

"Looks like you have your own Captain Hook now, eh *Peter Pam*?" Gerbald teased his friend, who wrinkled her nose at him.

"Yeah, the princess has her heart set on calling these islands 'Wonderland', but maybe we better go with 'Never Never Land', instead. All right, 'lost boys', let's have a toast!"

Pam raised her cup high, as did the rest.

"To our enemies! May they lose sleep wondering *when, not if,* we will come for them."

CHAPTER 51: WELCOME TO WONDERLAND

The meeting hall wasn't finished yet, so that balmy afternoon the entire colony gathered in the meadows above town. A podium had been erected, where Pam and other luminaries of the colony stood, smiling at the people, who smiled back. Pam she felt confident. These were her friends and they had been through much together.

"People of Port Looking Glass, thank you for coming today!" She spoke in Swedish. Her voice came out clear and was aided in its course over the crowd by a light breeze off the Indian Ocean.

She opened the small plastic container she had guarded through shipwreck and battle, pulling out the rolled-up paper within.

"I have here, a proclamation written in Princess Kristina's own hand, and signed by her father, King Gustav Adolph the Second. It reads: 'I, Princess Kristina Augusta, do hereby, and with my father's blessings, claim the islands known up-time as the Mascarenes for the crown of Sweden. They shall henceforth be called the Wonderland Isles. Mauritius, Rodriguez, and Réunion, are renamed, respectively, Dodo, Jabberwocky, and Bandersnatch, in honor of the works of Lewis Carroll, from whose works the inspiration for this colony came.'"

Pam paused, having expected the confused blinks from the crowd.

"Folks, I know the names sound strange, but they are from one of the princess' favorite storybooks. As brilliant as she is, she is still a child, so let's humor her, all right?"

Good-natured laughter emanated from the crowd along with murmurs of doting approval. Pam shared a smile with them and continued

"I hope this next part won't be too shocking for you! The princess goes on to say, 'I also hereby proclaim expedition leader Pamela Grace Miller of Grantville as Royal Governor of the Wonderland Isles for a period of two years, after which you may hold elections in the American style and choose your own leaders.'"

Pam paused, giving the crowd a long, serious look.

"My friends, I will not hold you to this, but if you will have me, I will serve." she told them.

The crowd sent up a cheer, hailing their new governor with unmistakable enthusiasm. Pam nodded her thanks, then continued once the hubbub settled down.

"There is a bit more, and it's important: 'Please be good to the wildlife of these islands, especially the dodo. As a Wonderland citizen, it is your duty to preserve and protect nature, including all native plants and creatures. By living in harmony with the good, green Earth, I believe you shall become the healthiest, and hopefully, the wealthiest of all people. Good luck to you all, and God bless you. I pray you are successful in this great endeavor and wish you all my best.'"

Pam looked at the crowd, who applauded with vigor. She spoke again, moving on to the brief speech she had prepared.

"My fellow Wonderlanders!"

The crowd clapped and more cheers went up.

"My first act as governor, is to ask you to select a deputy governor to join me."

This was met with more applause.

"You have suffered much and weathered great hardship! You are the bravest of the brave! The scoundrels who held us hostage have forced us to change our plans but we are adapting. We have sugarcane and potatoes in abundance and that is just the beginning! By this time next year, we will be the 'Spice Basket of Europe', which will make us all rich indeed! We are a free people, we work for ourselves, and each other! Together, we will build the most prosperous colony the world has ever seen! Thank you all!"

Pam bowed, smiled, and waved at the exuberant crowd in what she hoped was proper public official style, hoping their pleasure would last when it came time to enforce certain laws protecting the island's unique natural heritage. Hopefully, her plans for relatively non-invasive agriculture and forest management would be as lucrative as she thought She sighed t, *We will just have to cross that bridge when we come to it.*

CHAPTER 52: THE SHIPS COME IN

Port Looking Glass, One Year Later, December 1636

Pam came out of her office/laboratory, a functional, peaked-roofed, rectangular building on the edge of the forest, painted the same deep *falun* red as nearly everything else in Port Looking Glass. Gerbald had soon dubbed it 'Pam's Bird Barn'. The moniker had stuck to the point where she had given in and neatly painted it over the door.

Pam was on her way to check on the new rice paddies, part of the agricultural bounty they had traded for with a group of Japanese refugees on their way to Grantville. The unexpected visitors had stopped for supplies four months before, fleeing an unfriendly situation in Cambodia. The captains of the two Dutch ships that carried them were good fellows, and shrewd businessmen, eager to make trade arrangements with the Swedes, a win-win prospect for all. She shook her head in amazement at the memory. This really was a Wonderland. There she had been, pow-wowing with real live samurai straight out of Clavell! The visit was quite a story, but one for another day. There was no time to reminisce, she was too damn busy. She wished there were two of her, one to play the governor, the other to be the scientist.

The rice paddies were terraced along a stream that ran into the placid waters of Looking Glass Bay. A few of the Japanese families had elected to stay and join the colony at Pam's invitation. She had been concerned about whether the Lutheran Swedes would accept a group of largely Catholic Asians, but it hadn't been a problem. They understood the newcomers had unique skills to would help their colony's further success. Besides, Pam had seen to it that just as in the USE, religious freedom was law in Wonderland.

In addition to the Japanese, shortly after their victory over the rogue French the year before, they rescued a group of shipwrecked Dutch colonists bound for Ambon, in the Molucca Isles. The Dutch vessel was too damaged to go on, but the gracious Swedes invited them to join their colony and remain in Port Looking Glass, a generous offer the beleaguered refugees accepted

Pam was pleased Dodo Island was becoming truly multicultural. The 'American Way' Grantville had brought back through the centuries was alive and well here in the Indian Ocean, of all places. Pam was damn proud, as her plans were literally bearing fruit, far more than she had hoped for.

As she walked, a soft-spoken, middle-aged Japanese gentleman named Hironaka, their chief rice expert, hailed her with a wave from the low, earthen wall that held the paddy's water Pam waved back, then realized he was pointing, motioning for her to look to the harbor. The town alarm bells sounded. Pam turned to see *Effrayant* leaving her moorage, to meet the fleet of unknown sailing vessels heading their way. *Muskijl* and *Second Chance Bird* followed, in a defensive formation with *Effrayant*, implementing their oft-practiced plan for a sea invasion. Pam gave Hironaka a quick bow. It was impossible not to pick up the habit from her Japanese friends. She hurried toward the pier in a full run.

There were at least nine ships, the lead, a warship large enough to give even fearsome *Effrayant* trouble. Pam paused to catch her breath, breaking out the small birding scope, kept on a leather thong around her neck. Forcing herself to breathe, she focused on the big ship. Yes, banks of guns, but no sign of firing crews making ready. She caught a glimpse of gold and blue. Biting her lip, she scanned the rigging.

There! Pam laughed with delight. The ship was flying the Swedish colors! She began running, buzzing with excitement. Dodo Island was a convenient way station on the voyage from Europe to Asia and back. They had been visited by merchant ships from several nations, but this was the first time a ship from home had come!

The waterfront was filling up with colonists. They made way for her and as she hurried out onto the pier, Pers ran to meet her.

"Pam! They are from Sweden!" Pers shouted, a gleeful expression on his almost-nineteen-year-old face.

The "all's well" bell rang on *Effrayant*, confirming the newcomer's friendly nature.

"Not all of them. Recognize that flag?" Pam pointed at one of the five ships making way into the harbor under escort from their defenders. It was different from the rest, medium-sized, sporting sleek lines that spoke of speed and it was well-armed. Pam recognized the brassy shine of a carronade on its foredeck and grinned. This was a fighting ship of undoubtedly up-time design.

Pers studied the unusual ship with sharp eyes.

"She is flying a naval ensign, red with a black saltire cross bearing gold stars. . . . That's a ship from the United States of Europe!"

"Right you are! Well, howdy-doody, I wondered when someone from my new old country might come to check on us." She took Pers by the arm and said, "Shall we go say hello?"

"Yes, ma'am, t'would be a right pleasure!" Pers answered in his best West Virginia drawl. He was almost as good as Gerbald, who surpassed even most hillbillies in his mastery of the accent.

The commander of the port shore guard, Järv, now promoted to *Löjtnant* and in charge of all Swedish Marines in the colony, including the White and Black Chessmen, as well as the squad from the *Muskijl*, was waiting at the end of the pier with ten of his men. They took up a protective position around Pam, forming an honor guard. She was embarrassed at the fuss, but thanked them She put on her 'governor's hat', wondering for the thousandth time just how the hell *that* had happened.

The USE fighting ship came to the dock first. The sailors in their snazzy USE navy uniforms threw lines to the waiting Swedish marines. The vessel was named *Sandpiper*, much to the approval of 'The Bird Lady of Grantville'.

When the junk that served as their home headed out to meet the newcomers, under the command of Captain Torbjörn, Gerbald had remained aboard with a contingent of the Black Chessmen, but Dore stayed ashore. She joined Pam, her eyes accustomed to the dimness of the junk's galley, now squinting in the tropical sunlight, and most aggrieved she had been temporarily ejected from the realm she ruled with an iron fist.

"All this fuss! I was about to bake potato flour biscuits!" Dore was always certain to be put out at being separated from her work, which she treated with a profound sense of duty and dignity, as if it were a holy calling.

"Visitors from the old country." Pam told her, much of her initial enthusiasm having drained away. Now that the excitement had worn off, she dreaded the official hooplah to come. It would be a shame, having to deal with a bunch of nosy officials on such a nice day. She was behind in organizing her field notes on the dodos, their island's unique eco-system, and found she resented an unannounced distraction. Even so, she put on her best official smile and waved to the ships tying to the pier.

Another ship flying the USE colors was pulling in, a sturdy refitted caravel similar to *Redbird*, which bore the name *Linnaeus*. A crowd of eager teens gathered at the rail, their faces bright and excited. A pert young woman with a magnificent head of curly brown hair and an air of confidence, organized them into a line. Once the vessel was secured, they marched down the gangway to stand before Pam and her guard. Pam noticed Pers was staring at the leader as if she were Helena of Troy come to life before his very eyes. *Oh, brother, I know that look, and they call it puppy love!*

"Welcome to Port Looking Glass and the Wonderland Colony." Pam said in English to the young lady, most certainly a down-timer, but wearing up-time style clothes. She might be as old as twenty and was obviously the one in charge of this gang. "I'm Governor Pam Miller."

The young woman's large, hazel eyes widened as if she were meeting a movie star.

"*The Bird Lady of Grantville*! I've been so looking forward to meeting you. You are our inspiration!" The girl's English was lightly accented, but otherwise perfect.

"That's me, I guess." Pam rolled her eyes at that damned 'bird lady' moniker as she always did. She wasn't ever going to be able to shake it, no matter what her current title and station.

The young woman, a bit embarrassed at her initial starstruck reaction, straightened and stuck her hand out in the American style.. The kid had a good, strong grip. Pam felt herself beginning to like her, despite longing they would haul anchor and go back to where they had come from.

"I am very honored to meet you, Governor Pam! I am Dorothea Weise, a graduate student from the Katharina von Bora College in Quedlinburg. My companions come from higher learning institutions around Europe. We represent a variety of subjects that might be useful to your efforts—botany, geology, animal husbandry, agricultural science, biology, chemistry, just to name a few! We have come to assist you in your work !"

It was Pam's turn to look goggle-eyed. *Assistants? Someone to help with the mountain of scientific work? They're all so young!* It was too good to be true. *Be careful what you wish for . . .*

"Pardon me for saying so, but don't you have a teacher or someone older with you?"

"Oh, of course! We are led by Professor Horst Altmann of the University of Jena."

"Well, where is he?"

"Unfortunately, the sea voyage did not agree with him. He is quite ill, and abed in his cabin. We are very worried about him."

"I'll send our doctor to check on him right away."

SAVING THE DODO

Pam felt a bit flummoxed by this unexpected development. *A helpful boon? A potential huge pain in the ass?* Taking a deep breath, she regained her composure, and managed to ask, "Who sent you?"

"Princess Kristina! She is our sponsor!"

Pam looked northwest, in roughly the direction the USE might lie, and muttered under her breath "Thanks, Princess! Just what I need, a bunch of kids to look after!"

The students, none a day over twenty-one, blinked at her like a pack of confused puppies, unsure, but eager to please. She regarded them for a moment, but then her stern expression softened to a smile.

"You may just prove to be useful. Ms. Weise, you and your group are now the Wonderland Colonial Natural Resource and Wildlife Service."

She handed the stack of field notes she had been carrying, to the erstwhile brunette.

"You are a natural leader, so I'm making you the assistant director of said service. You shall report directly to me."

The young woman looked stunned, then embarrassed.

"Shouldn't such a high office go to Professor Altman? That would surely be the proper thing."

"On this island, I'm the one who decides what's proper. First, I have to see if I like him or not. Don't worry, I'll give him a fancy title too, and hope he proves useful. But, since he's sick, and you are standing in front of me all bright-eyed and bushy-tailed, I'll start with you. Your offices and laboratories are up there, in 'Pam's Bird Barn'." She pointed to her labs on the hillside behind town, the whimsically named, but very sensible building backed by tall, graceful native trees.

"We will have to build some expansions. We can get going on that tomorrow. Read those notes, it's a good place to start." The students and their newly-designated assistant director nodded, murmuring their thanks.

Pam realized Pers was still standing beside her with eyes only for the fetching Dorothea Weise. She gave him a quick elbow to snap him out of it before he started drooling. A wonderful idea occurred to her then.

"*Assistant Director* Weise, this is my adopted son and personal assistant, Second Mate Pers of the Royal Swedish Navy, serving on my ship *Second Chance Bird* in Wonderland's defensive squadron."

Pers turned to her, stunned at his own sudden promotion. Pam gave him a quick grin and whispered in Swedish "You earned it, sweetie."

Turning to her new helpers, she continued in English, "I am assigning Pers to be my liaison to your department. To start with, he can escort you to temporary quarters. If you don't speak Swedish, you will need to learn it. Pers will see to your instruction. He is nearly fluent in English and Thuringian-style German, as well as speaking some French, Dutch, and Japanese. He has a knack for languages."

Dorothea was visibly impressed. Pers looked as if he might faint. He stood frozen in place, until Pam gave him a gentle shove. Blushing, he stepped forward and bowed to the pretty new assistant director. The young woman shook his hand while favoring him with a sunny smile, which made him turn an even brighter shade of scarlet. The smitten lad managed to find his voice, saying in English, "Follow me, please." before marching up the pier toward shore at a considerable speed.

Despite her natural confidence, Dorothea was starting to look a bit overwhelmed. She paused to thank Pam for her kind welcome, before leading her group in pursuit of Pers' lengthy stride. Pam watched them, grinning like a fool. *Well, this may turn out to be a good thing after all.*

Löjtnant Järv and his men were chuckling among themselves, making bets on how long it would take the new second mate to raise his flag on that piece of lovely German territory. Pam couldn't help but chuckle, then saw *Kapten* Lundkvist leading a group from the Swedish and USE warships toward her.

"Straighten up, you degenerates," she growled at her guard, "Here comes the official delegation. Pretend you still have some proper military discipline."

"Yes, ma'am!"

Pam laughed as they all stood up ramrod straight and saluted her in the snappy American naval style they had adopted.

"Governor Pam!" *Kapten* Lundkvist called out, his voice full of excitement, his peg leg tapping a jaunty beat as he rushed ahead of the rest "These people have come from Sweden with supplies and more!"

Pam nodded and raised her arms wide in a gesture of welcome to the newcomers as Lundkvist saluted and fell into place at her side opposite *Löjtnant* Järv.

"It is wonderful to have you here!" she greeted them in her now fluent Swedish, then repeated it in English for the *Sandpiper's* captain, a down-timer in his thirties.

"Captain Fritz Erhard, USE Navy, at your service ma'am. We were sent as an escort representing Emperor Gustav, at the request of Princess Kristina, who is quite worried about you! Also, I can speak Swedish, part of why I was chosen for the job." he told her switching to that language, before giving her a gentlemanly bow.

"Lovely to meet you Captain! Now, let's get out of this sun before we make the rest of our introductions. It will melt you like wax if you let it! Right this way!"

She turned and marched for shore, head held high in what she hoped was suitable gubernatorial bearing.

"To the town meeting hall, Governor Pam?" Lundkvist asked her.

She was excited now, her doubts receding as her mind raced with thoughts of how to make the best of these new developments. She wanted to hurry, but was careful to match the top speed her chief military officer could manage on his prosthesis.

"No, I have a better idea, gentlemen." she replied with a wide grin.

Reaching shore, she turned left, leading them down the freshly constructed boardwalk toward the *Dodo's Nest.* This was a spacious seaside saloon that had sprung up like a volunteer potato in a backyard garden, an inevitable feature of any town's waterfront. It was time for a mug of cool beer and a shot of the lovely herb-flavored Swedish *akvavit* her people were producing, most likely followed by a few more rounds of the same.

"Official business is thirsty work, gentlemen. Here, we do things the Wonderland way."

Her guard shared a conspiratorial grin, knowing full well good old Captain Pam could hold her liquor with the best of them. These muckity-mucks from home wouldn't stand a chance.

* * *

The leader of the fleet from home was the esteemed *Flotilj-amiral* Gunvald Engstrom, an accomplished and highly-decorated career military man in his late fifties. As a 'flotilla admiral', he was currently the highest-ranking Swedish officer in the Indian Ocean. Engstrom had initially been as frosty as a Scandinavian winter wind until Pam got some of her private reserve of Chinese rice wine into him. After several rounds, and much friendly banter, he was just 'Gun', and was laughing at her jokes as if he were a favorite uncle doting over a clever niece. Torbjörn, Järv, Lundkvist, Gerbald, Nils the Bosun, and the rest of her men were biting back their laughter as they watched Pam work the stern old sea salt, playing him like a hooked salmon, ready to jump right into the net.

One of *Dear Gun's* orders was to determine if the colony was being adequately governed by 'That American woman', and it was the first concern to be crossed off the list. He and Pam were already thick as thieves. He clapped and cheered as the men who had followed her through various dangers regaled him with tales of her courage and prowess in battle.

"Pam, you are like a warrior-woman from the old times, you have a heart of steel!" he proclaimed, as she handed him another cup of rice wine, his ninth or tenth. "I can see Wonderland is in good hands!"

Pam put on a modest look and patted her new best friend on the back of his wind-burned hand.

"Oh, Gun, you flatterer! I just do what I have to do for our people and for the glory of the crown. Remember, as a citizen of the United States of Europe, your king is my emperor, *The Lion of Europe*! Here's to Gustavus Adolphus, may he live forever! *skål!*" she raised her glass in toast. Mugs and cups clacked around the room. "Now, Gun, tell me more about what you have brought us!"

As it turned out, it was more than she had expected. The emperor had taken her ideas regarding Sweden missing out on becoming an Asian power in the up-time world to heart. Engstrom's fleet included six fluyts full of colonists and their necessities, three for each of the remaining Wonderland Islands. Looking Glass Bay currently resembled a crowded parking lot. It had been decided if they meant to make their claims to the Mascarenes stick, they had better have boots on the ground, possession being nine tenths of the law.

Pam was assured that she would be governor-in-chief to all the Wonderland Isles, just as the princess had requested and the new colonies would follow the same eco-friendly farming methods as Port Looking Glass, which made her breathe a big sigh of relief. Three more fluyts carried supplies for the new colonies and Port Looking Glass, including ammunition (*Praise the Lord!*), radios (*Sweet jumping Jesus!*) new varieties of tropical seeds and starts gathered from the Americas, donated by several interested botanical societies, additional scientific apparatus, and a small library of useful books. Pam was beside herself with joy at all the new toys.

The flotilla admiral's personal vessel was a refurbished warship, the *Vaksamhet,* or 'Vigilance', employing a variety of up-time inspired improvements. It was big, fast and deadly. *Vaksamhet* and *Sandpiper* would patrol the seas around the colonies along with *Effrayant* and *Muskijl.* The Wonderland Isles would be well protected. All the ships and towns would be provided with new radios, giving them a huge advantage over any would-be threat to their safety. Pam grinned like the Cheshire Cat. It was almost Christmas, and for once, she was getting everything she wanted. Pam was on top of the world until Gun said something that let all the air out of her elation.

"Pam, our dear sponsor, Princess Kristina, has personally requested I ask you when you intend to bring dodos to Europe? She knows you have a great deal of work to do here, but she is hoping perhaps next year? We will help you accomplish this in any way we canas she stressed it's very important to her. She is having a special dodo enclosure made of glass, constructed near the

University of Jena, I'm sure Professor Altman and his students can give you the details. "

Pam smiled and nodded The truth was, she hadn't intended to go back to Europe soon, although she wanted to see her family, which now included a new grandson.

"Yes, Gun, another year at best. It will take that long to start the new colonies and to make ready for the voyage." Pam hid her frown by emptying her *saké* cup and motioned to the barman for another. *Back to Grantville. Bah humbug!*

Garrett W. Vance

CHAPTER 53: TIME FLIES

Port Looking Glass, Wonderland Isles, October 1637

It wouldn't be quite a full year before Pam would make the dreaded journey back to Europe. It was decided, they should leave before the end of October for the best weather. *Second Chance Bird*, *Annalise* and three of the second wave's fluyts, laden with goods grown on the islands, would convoy along the coast of Africa, hoping to arrive in the north's spring or summer. Pam's junk was well-armed and all the fluyts were fitted with guns so there wasn't need of a warship escort. *Effrayant*, *Muskijl*, *Vaksamhet*, and *Sandpiper* had tangled with pirates of various ilk over the last year. The area was thick with them so they needed to watch over the young colonies. Pam assured Engstrom her ship and crew could handle just about anything, and if they couldn't, they still had the benefit of speed.

The good-byes were the hardest part. Gerbald and Dore would go with her, of course, as would Torbjörn, Nils the Bosun, and most of the original crew. Not too surprisingly, Pers had elected to stay. As it turned out, the lovely and energetic Dorothea was as interested in the tall young Swede as he was in her. Wedding bells would likely ring at some point. She hoped she would be back in time for their special day.

The arrival of the students had been a great boon after all. Professor Altman, upon recovering from the voyage, turned out to be a nice old guy, not too stuffy for a down-timer scholar. He was a horticulturist, so Pam put him in charge of their experimental agriculture projects. The colonies were now growing around fifty percent of the spices and fruits she had planned, with more to come.

They were still figuring out how to get the vanilla pollinated without bees. It had been done in the 1800s up-time, in that world's version of the Wonderland Islands as it happened. At some point, they would solve the mystery. The native coffee now grew in abundance on the mountainsides and cinnamon trees from Ceylon were thriving in the island's gentle climate. Pam was especially proud of the cofffee she herself had discovered, that was sure to be a hot item back in the U.S.E. Her generosity to the Dutch merchants carrying the Japanese Ayutthaya refugees to Europe had ensured Wonderland a place on all the latest trade maps. Now it wasn't a rarity to see more than one junk in Port Looking Glass's harbor.

Their understanding of the island's unique ecology grew daily. Pam now had a variety of medicinal plants to bring back to the Grantville Research Center's associated laboratories. She also had half of an encyclopedia's worth of information on the climate, ecologies, and cultures of the Indian Ocean. Without feeling quite like Charles Darwin, she was proud of her scientific achievements. They made her feel better about the center continuing to pay her a salary while she was gone. She had earned her keep, after all. Money would not be a problem in her future, even without her share of the junk's treasure. Pam had now joined the Grantville rich. And so, resigned to the fact she must make the trip, she went about putting her life in Wonderland on hold, vowing to all she would be back as soon as she could manage it.

Inevitably, the day to leave came. The entire town turned out, lining the shore. Soldiers had to keep them off the pier for fear it would collapse beneath their weight. Pam made a point of walking slowly down the boardwalk, shaking every hand offered. Swedish, Dutch, German, French, Japanese—they had come from many lands, but now they were all Wonderlanders, just like her. Pam was having a hard time maintaining her composure, the flow of love from her people was overwhelming, like too much of a fine wine. She was dizzy with it. At last, she stepped onto the pier and was escorted by the town guard, out to *Second Chance Bird*. Pers and Dorothea waited for her there, Pam hugged them and gave them her blessings. They were as much her children as those she had left in Grantville.

"Come back soon, Momma Pam, okay?" Pers implored, embracing her in his strong arms without his former shyness.

"I will, Pers, I promise. I love you, son, and I will think of you every day. I expect you and Dorothea to take good care of things for me while I'm gone, right?"

"You got it." Pers wanted to say more, but the words tangled in his throat. Pam shushed him, pulled him down to a level where she could kiss him on the cheek, then pushed him back into the waiting arms of his love.

Doctor Durand stepped up, his face as long as a bloodhound's, fancy mustachio at half-mast.

"So, have you decided, Doctor? Are you staying or coming with me back to Europe?"

"Yes, Pam. I intend to stay. These people need me."

"I'm glad. I'll feel a lot better knowing you are here with them. I really do consider you one of my best friends, you know."

"And I you, dear Pam." the doctor bowed, perhaps hoping to hide his tears behind the wide brim of his fancy French hat. Pam grabbed him by the arms and hugged him, an embrace which he returned, patting her on the back.

Next came the sailors and marines who had been under her command, but intended to remain on duty in Wonderland, all lined up at attention. Pam thanked them one by one, by name, shaking their hands, and telling them how lucky she was to have had such brave men at her side. For tough seamen, there was quite a bit of moisture around the eyes. At the end of the line, she came to Captain Lundkvist and Flotilla Admiral Engstrom. They both saluted, their faces stony as they tried to hide their feelings behind military pride.

"You know, you guys don't have to salute me. I'm not governor anymore, just crazy old Captain Pam." she told them.

"It doesn't matter," Lundkvist said. "I would follow you to the ends of the Earth if you asked it."

"I know you would, my dear, dear friend. If I were truly going to the ends of the Earth, I wouldn't go without you."

She took his hands, holding them tightly, for a long moment, not wanting to embarrass him with a hug.

"As would I," Admiral Engstrom chimed in, his voice freighted with emotion. "You have done great things here, Pam Miller, great things. The crown owes you more than it can ever repay."

"You saying so is payment enough, Gun." she said, taking his hands next. They were strong, and rough, yet trembled slightly. "I am so proud to have served with you, with you all. It has been the greatest experience of my life. I thank you."

She saluted them both and turned to the gangway before her own tears let loose, making it hard to see where she was going. Gerbald and Dore waited for her at the rail, each taking an arm as they helped guide her up to the castle deck where the Bosun and Torbjörn waited.

"Ready to go, Captain?" Torbjörn asked her, taking her hand in loving support.

"Aye aye, Co-Captain, let's blow this town." She wiped her eyes on the sleeve of her favorite blue-and-gold Chinese coat and turned to her waiting crew. In her best captain's voice, she bawled out, "Make sail, men, time's-a-wasting! Get the lead out!"

The Bosun gave her a wide, yellow-toothed grin, and began barking orders, while the men of the *Second Chance Bird* bent to their tasks, happy to be at sea again. Pam turned and waved at the crowd as they followed *Muskijl* out of the harbor. She would escort them as far as the southern tip of the island, then *Sandpiper* would see her all the way back to Europe. The sound of cheering faded into the distance as Pam took one last look at Port Looking Glass, reflected perfectly in the mirror bright waters of her harbor.

"I'll be back again my friends, count on me." she whispered, then turned her face into the stiff ocean breeze that blew beyond the bay, inhaling the salt air deeply, as if it were the scent of roses on the bloom.

CHAPTER 54: PRECIOUS CARGO

Castaway Cove, Dodo Island, Wonderland Isles

P am and her crew grew somber as they sailed around the rocky headland where the *Redbird* had gone down. They all doffed their hats, standing in a moment of silence for First Mate Janvik, who been lost that terrible day. Pam had brought along a bouquet of beautiful native blooms. She threw it into the aquamarine sea when she thought they might be over the final resting place of her sunken ship while the men saluted their fallen comrade.

Pam didn't know whether to cry or whoop with joy as they pulled into the cove that had been their castaway home for so many months. They would stop to take on the last of their cargo, the most important export of all— the dodos.

Their convoy would wait at anchor while Pam went ashore with her sailors and marines. The Bosun remained on board with a skeleton crew to mind the ship. Dore stayed behind, too, having no interest in revisiting their former refuge.

"I have seen enough of that God-forsaken beach to last a lifetime!" she told them, arms crossed in disgust at the very sight of it.

"We will bring you back some coconuts, my dear!" Gerbald promised, which made Pam let out a very un-ladylike, snorting laugh. None of the formerly marooned would ever relish eating coconut again! Dore just rolled her eyes, with her trademark disdain.

"You two go enjoy your foolishness. Just be careful and come back soon!" She gave them both a quick peck on the cheek before descending to her galley kingdom, head held high with pride.

When the pinnace skidded onto the familiar white sands, Pam was the first to jump ashore. Torbjörn followed and she took his hand.

"You've never been here before, Lover. You missed out on the whole castaway experience. Come on, I have to show you something." As they walked down the strand, Pam picked a few wildflowers along the way.

After a while, they came to the small hill that served as their cemetery. Pam put the flowers on the graves while Torbjörn recited a sailor's prayer in Swedish. They bowed their heads, remembering their missing friends, then Pam led him to have a closer look at one of the wooden grave markers, weathered by the elements, but still readable. She vowed to put up a permanent stone monument as soon as it could be done. With a grin, she pointed at the marker in grand Ghost-of-Christmas-Future-style.

"The reports of your death were greatly exaggerated," she said with a strong drawl. You are a regular Mark Twain."

"I'm not sure who Mark Twain was, but that's *my* name on there! I didn't even know I was sick!" he exclaimed, bending down to marvel at the sight. They shared a short, bittersweet laugh, and embraced.

"You did a nice job, Pam, it's a lovely bit of painting."

"I missed you a lot, you big oaf. I had already fallen for you even back then. I can't tell you how glad I am to have you here, alive and well."

"I can very much say, *me too*! Thank you, my Pam." He pulled her into a passionate kiss.

After a long, blissful while, they parted. Pam cocked her head at him with a sly look

"Want to see my bungalow? We could take a little rest there, if you like."

"Oh, definitely, but I have a feeling we won't be getting much rest."

"No, we'll be busy. Come on." Pam felt giddy, it was like being back at a favorite summer camp, and this time she had a hunky boyfriend to boot!

✳ ✳ ✳

Castaway Cove Camp had weathered its abandonment quite well. The stranded sailors, with nothing else to do, had built to last. Now they were busy sprucing it all up again. Pers and Dorothea intended to make the place a permanent research station and would be coming to stay in the next few weeks. While the sailors worked on that project, Gerbald and Pam went looking for their old friends, the dodos. The trails were overgrown, but Gerbald's *katzbalger* shortsword made a fine machete and soon they were making the climb into the mountainous interior.

Finding the dodos was, of course, key to the mission, and they would take as long as they needed. Pam had been adamant on not capturing any of the birds living near Port Looking Glass. An effort had been made to keep those populations wild, despite their lack of natural fear, but the flock here had grown used to humans, and were accustomed to getting handouts, something Pam was counting on. She carried a hefty sack,full of treats, enough to lure them to the beach and the waiting travel cages. She hated to do it, but had no choice. Besides, it was undoubtedly for the best to not keep all her dodo eggs in one basket. A population in Europe would ensure the species' ongoing survival, even if the Wonderlanders somehow failed in their stewardship.

After an hour, they were rewarded with the sound of deep, throaty coos. Coming into a clearing, they found a small group of the birds, several mothers. and half-grown chicks. The older birds stared at Pam with their disconcerting yellow eyes. Could that be recognition? She was certain she had seen them before. There were small variations in each, and she knew these hens had been among her pets at the beach camp.

"Hey girls, remember me? I got goodies!"

She held out a handful of choice nuts. The dodos let out squawks of pleasure, and rushed to her, nearly knocking her down with their enthusiasm. They were *big* birds! Gerbald rescued her, pushing them back.

"They haven't forgotten their favorite food source!" he said, laughing.

Pam scattered the nuts on the ground and laughed along as the hens gobbled them up, soon joined by their ungainly, but undeniably cute chicks.

They spent the rest of the afternoon playing Pied Piper, moving through the forest until they had a flock of some thirty dodos following them, including enough males to ensure a breeding population.

"Come along, kiddies, it's time to go down to the beach! You get to go on a boat ride!" Pam called out, making Gerbald grin at seeing his friend acting silly for a change. It had been too long. The demands of her office had been great, but now Pam was free to be 'The Bird Lady' again.

Capturing the dodos for transport was ridiculously easy, just a matter of leaving a trail of breadcrumbs up gangways into temporary travel cages made of bamboo, aboard pinnaces and longboats parked on the beach. They would be transferred to the special travel pen Pam designed and the men constructed, situated in the main cargo hold of the junk.

The very last dodo, a rather cantankerous older male, decided that he didn't want to go with the rest, and began making a fuss, clucking his displeasure and trying to back out of the cage. Pam grimaced at him. With as much gentleness as she could, she placed her leather boot in his rump just below his fluffy tail, and shoved him back in. Gerbald closed the door and gave her a wry arching of his brow.

"Thank God, nobody's got a camera," Pam said. "Pam Miller kicking an endangered species in the ass would be just the thing for the front page of the newspaper."

The *Second Chance Bird*'s dodo pen lay directly beneath the large hatch doors of the spacious hold, where the birds, and the many potted trees and plants accompanying them, would have fresh air and sunlight for at least part of the day. By midnight, the dodos were safely tucked away and everyone caught a bit of sleep. They sailed at dawn, Pam keeping vigil on the castle deck, watching the island that had been her home through so much, recede into the distance, until it disappeared over the azure horizon.

"I'll see to it you get back here, if you wish it." Torbjörn told her from his place at the wheel.

"I wish it very much." Pam replied, giving him a kiss on the cheek before going to her cabin to catch up on lost sleep. It would be a long voyage, without much to do.

✳   ✳   ✳

The days passed, one slipping into the next as they headed west, Antarctica to their south, Africa to their north. They would sail as the crow flies, if the winds allowed, taking the most direct route. Their merchant ships were all stuffed with the bounty of the Wonderland Isles, Pam's spice basket plan now come to fruition. Even with such a tempting target as that no one seemed worried about attack from the famed Barbary pirates or potentially hostile European forces. With Sergeant Sten and his Black Chessmen manning their beloved carronade, anyone taking on the *Second Chance Bird* would find themselves regretting it. Besides, it was doubtful they would be molested with the swift and formidable Sandpiper shepherding their small fleet. *Let 'em just try to take us, arrrr!* was Fearsome Pam's opinion on the matter.

Pam often sat on the deck with her feet hanging into the hold so she could watch her charges, listening to the throaty coos and clacking beaks of the dodos, emanating from below. The birds had adjusted well enough to shipboard life and seemed content to eat as many fruits and nuts as she could give them, to the point where they were gaining weight and beginning to resemble the fat and spoiled captive dodo that must have been the model for John Tenniel's illustrations.

The thought of taking these creatures out of their natural habitat and dragging them all the way back to Europe didn't sit all that well with her now that she was actually doing it. But, she had promised the princess, and there was no way around it. It was better she did it herself, than trust the task to anyone else. If something went wrong, it would be on her conscience. So, here she was, making the long trip 'home', when she would much rather be back in Wonderland. Captain Pam chocked it up to fate, and resigned herself to it, instead of fretting the way the old Pam would have done. Her actions mattered to a lot more people than she ever could have imagined. Here was a job only she could do, a need only she could fulfill. Pam smiled into the fading daylight over the South Atlantic as the *Second Chance Bird* and its precious cargo sailed on toward Europe.

CHAPTER 55: MISSION ACCOMPLISHED

Hamburg, United States of Europe, February 1637

It was on a bright, unseasonably warm winter day the *Second Chance Bird* and her fleet came to the end of their long voyage around Africa. There were a great many stares from the shore as the fancifully painted junk headed toward Hamburg harbor, flying a bright, new copy of the dodo flag of the Wonderland Colonies Dore had designed, crewed by tanned Swedes, many sporting blonde hair bleached white by the tropical sun. They had accumulated a large number of local craft following along behind them, curiosity seekers anxious to see what such an odd foreign vessel was doing, plying the frigid waters of the North Sea.

Pam, knowing in advance from the radio there would be an official welcome wagon waiting, put on her favorite Chinese dress, a sexy, side-slitted affair, black silk with a filigree of gold flowers. She knew she looked pretty damn good in the racy little thing. Her necklace of precious 'pirate pearls' went on next, and with a wry smile, she strapped on her revolver's belt, enjoying the feeling of being a bonafide badass. The final touch was letting her long hair free of its pony tail, a wild mane for the lioness of the south. She felt well pleased to make herself part of the spectacle. The shy, retiring Pam of old was long gone.

There was a festive gathering on the dock, including a banner proclaiming 'Welcome Back, Bird Lady!' which made Pam laugh aloud. The moniker didn't rankle her any more. *If you can't beat them join them. The Bird Lady I shall be.*

As they tied up, a USE Naval band started playing. It took her a moment to realize the song was *'Country Road'*. Pam grinned at the choice. At this point, it would be nice to see their little part of West Virginia again. She chuckled to see Princess Kristina jumping up and down, waving crazily, backed by a mob of Grantville students from the old Summer Nature Program—how they had grown! Pam thought the princess looked quite a bit taller and more careworn than before, but she was definitely still a goofy kid. Suddenly, Pam realized who was standing behind her—it was her son Walt and his wife Crystal, and she was holding . . . the baby! Pam really had become a grandma, and while she was thrilled, she had to quell an inner voice that shrieked, *but I'm much too young!*

The next few minutes passed in a blur as she was engulfed in hugs from Crystal, and kissed her new grandson, who pulled her hair and laughed, which made Pam love him all the more.

"Boy oh boy, has your ole' granny got some stories to tell *you,* my lad!" she told him as she looked into his bright eyes. They were the Miller stormy gray, which was good, but thank God, he had his mother's lush red hair!

Walt was quiet, as usual, but they smiled and embraced, their last harsh words to each other put aside, at least for now. His eyes widened when he noticed the revolver she was packing, and Pam gave him a mischeivous grin. *Your ole Momma's been through some stuff, me boyo!* Hopefully, she could make things right with him this time. Eventually, the initial fervor died down, and Kristina approached, a shy smile on her face.

"I'm glad you made it home, Pam. I was worried." Kristina told her in her perfect, yet quaintly accented, English.

Pam smiled and replied in her perfect yet—according to her boyfriend—quaintly accented Swedish.

"It was touch and go for a while. I'll tell you the whole story when we get a chance."

Kristina raised her eyebrows, impressed with Pam's mastery of her own native tongue, and continued in the same, "I should like very much to hear it!'

Pam's face took on a somber cast.

"Some good people died making this happen, and I need you to hear their tales. We owe them a lot."

Kristina bowed her head, her face grown somber.

"I knew that would probably happen, and I'm very sorry to hear it. Even so, I still feel that the cause was worth it. Do you, Pam?"

Pam marveled at how someone so young, could seem like such a wise old adult at times.

"Yes, I do, Kristina, I do. It was all worth it." Pam made her face brighten and took on a cheerier tone. "Sorry for being a downer, there will be time to mourn lost friends later. Today is for celebration, so let's cheer up!"

Kristina brightened as well, but Pam could still see pain in her eyes. Pam had heard the news about the death of Kristina's mother, the queen, and knew Kristina had suffered much in the years since they first met at Cair Paravel back in Grantville. Pam reached into her trusty old rucksack, which a grinning Torbjörn held for her, ecstatic at meeting his beloved princess in person. Pam pulled out a finely carved Chinese box made of teak. With a bow and a flourish, she handed it to the princess.

"Watch out, it's heavy! These are additions to your crown jewels, a gift from the crew of the *Second Chance Bird*. It's *real* pirate treasure, which we captured from *real* pirates!"

Kristina's great brown eyes went even wider, taking on a happy sparkle bright enough to match the jewelry and gems within.

"Real pirate treasure? How grand, Pam, thank you so much! I wish to thank the men myself, as soon as I have the chance." she exclaimed with delight, hugging the box to her chest.

"They would like that, very much. They are all loyal to you, Princess! You are one popular kid!"

"I have something for you, too, Pam." she said, switching into English. She handed the precious box to one of her guards, then raised her hand to get everyone's attention.

"The race to save the dodo is over, and just like the 'caucus race' in Lewis Carroll's wonderful book, everybody wins!" With a grin that nearly split her perpetually pale, thin face, Kristina reached into her pocket to pull out a silver thimble.

"'*We beg your acceptance of this elegant thimble.*'" Kristina quoted the Dodo as she placed it in Pam's hand. It had the Tenniel version of the bird etched on it, along with an inscription in English that read *Dear Pam, thank you for saving us—The Dodos.*

"You did it, Pam, you saved the dodo. Only you could. We are all very proud of you." Kristina gazed at Pam with heartfelt admiration.

Pam laughed, her sharp gray eyes growing misty with emotion.

"Yeah, I guess I really did. And I couldn't have done it without you pushing me out the door. You are the hero, as much as me, kiddo."

Pam felt the weight of all she had been through, all she had worked so hard for, lifting from her shoulders. It seemed like a dream already. Her hand shook as she gazed at the pretty thimble, shining under the northern spring sun, blurring, as her eyes filled with joyful tears.

Kristina saw her friend was feeling overwhelmed, so she stepped forward and embraced her in a hug that would do any bear proud. The young girl was stronger than she looked. Pam hugged her, just as she would her own child, her heart full of pride at their accomplishment. They had changed the world for the better, a small change, perhaps, but one that would reverberate through the centuries ahead, a second chance for a funny-looking bird, no longer doomed to extinction, not in Pam Miller's world, anyway.

"Everybody wins." Pam whispered.

In the hold of the *Second Chance Bird*, a dodo squawked, wondering what was holding up feeding time.

THE END

Made in the USA
Monee, IL
27 July 2022